Essie in Progress

Essie in Progress

A NOVEL

Marjorie Presten

Kregel Publications

Essie in Progress: A Novel

Published by Kregel Publications, a division of Kregel, Inc., P.O. Box 2607, Grand Rapids, MI 49501.

Library of Congress Cataloging-in-Publication Data
Presten, M.
Essie in progress / M. Presten.
p. cm.
I. Title.
PS3616.R479E87 2009 813'.6—dc22 2008054833

ISBN 978-0-8254-3565-2

Printed in the United States of America
09 10 11 12 13 / 5 4 3 2 1

For the two heroes in my life:
Tom, my husband, who always comes to my rescue.
And my dad, who lovingly guided me through this project but passed away shortly before its publication.
Dad, save a seat for me at the banquet in paradise, and we'll celebrate this and so much more.

Acknowledgments

My deepest gratitude goes to:

My mom, Lorraine Hancock, for believing in me. I aim to be the mom to my children that you have been to me.

My sisters, Heather Wright and Jill Miner, for making me laugh so hard, so often, and for so long that I find myself holding my sides, mystified that I haven't developed six-pack abs during our times together.

My sister-in-Christ Beth Lyle for encouragement to follow a dream. Meet you at the gates with sequined slippers on.

My agent, Janet Benrey, for persevering when all signs would have suggested she shouldn't.

Janyre Tromp for a thumbs-up.

Steve Barclift, Miranda Gardner, Dawn Anderson, and all the members of the Kregel team for investing in a first-time author, showing me the rough edges, and teaching me how to polish.

Prologue

1972

In a thirty-second phone call, Hamilton Wells would make a decision that would earn him more money than he could spend in his lifetime. Everything was on the line, but he was not nervous, euphoric, or eager with anticipation. In Hamilton's mind, the matter was not speculative, debatable, or anything less than a sure thing. Hamilton had the gift, and it had never let him down. Yet even before he made the call, he knew money wouldn't cure the unrelenting pain of his grief. He sat at his desk with only a single orange banker's lamp for illumination and cried silently.

Her death had been inevitable, but feelings of helplessness still overwhelmed him. His young son's dependency on him only multiplied his grief and anger. Six-year-old Jack Wells had insisted his father do something to help Mama, but the only thing Hamilton could do was sit at her bedside and try not to cry. Now it was six weeks after her death, and Hamilton knew his son needed him to be strong, to return life to normal. A neighbor had enrolled Jack in the local church baseball league. They played a game every Wednesday afternoon. *It will be good for him*, they'd said. *Life has to go on*.

Hamilton cradled his head in his hands and groaned. The enormity of the risk he was about to take didn't concern him. It was purely mechanical. He would surrender all he owned for just one more blissful afternoon at the lake he and his wife both loved, but now that was impossible. His wife was dead. Nothing he could do would change that.

He remembered the book of Job. *Would a loving and caring God do this to the love of my life? Well, he did,* Hamilton thought bitterly. Earline had lingered for months. The doctors said it was miraculous that she had endured as long as she had. *Be grateful for these last days to say goodbye*, they'd said. But for Hamilton, the prolonged end only added anger to his bottomless sorrow. Standing alongside his son as a helpless witness to her slow deterioration and suffering in the final weeks was more than he could bear. It was the worst time of Hamilton's life. Nothing really mattered anymore, and it seemed he had nothing left to lose.

Under different circumstances, he might have played it safe and put the money away for his son's education, bought a new house, or perhaps invested in a bit of lake property. He could have become like the rest of the players and worn monograms on his starched cuffs so everyone could remember whose hand they were shaking. Instead, he had gone it alone. His brokerage business had few clients. He was the only big player left. Now he planned to risk everything on something happening on the other side of the world.

Ham couldn't remember exactly when he had recognized his innate ability to pick the winner out of a crowd. It had always been there, ever since he was conscious of being alive. The talent had blossomed in the military when the card games occasionally got serious. Now, with every dollar he had to his name, Hamilton approached wheat futures with that same instinct. The Russian harvest had been a disaster, and the United States was coming to the rescue. The price of wheat was going to go through the roof, and then through the floor. He was going to make a fortune on both ends.

He picked up the phone and dialed a number on the Chicago Mercantile exchange. He listened for a few moments as the connection was made. Young Jack tugged at his father's shirtsleeve. "Pop? Can we go now?" Jack held a baseball in his hand and a glove under his arm. Hamilton swiveled his chair, turning his back to his son.

A familiar voice announced his name. "How can I help you?"

"It's Ham," he said. "Short the entire position."

"What? Everything?" the voice asked.

"Everything." No emotion colored his voice.

Young Jack crept gingerly around the chair to face his father. "Pop," he whispered, "come on, the game is about to start." Hamilton shook his head and looked away.

The voice on the phone was still talking. "Most folks are still enjoying the ride, Ham. You could get hurt."

"It's not going a penny higher. Short it all."

"Don't say I didn't warn you."

"Warn me? My wife is dead. What else matters?"

The voice mumbled something about her passing.

"She didn't pass. She's dead. Just do what I ask."

"OK, Ham." The phone disconnected.

Jack was standing there in front of him, shoulders slumped. The ball hung loose at the end of his fingers, and the glove had fallen on the carpet. "Pop, can we go now?"

"Sorry, Son. Not today."

"It's not fair!" Jack erupted. Hot tears sprang up in his eyes. "What am I supposed to do now?"

Ham looked down, silent.

Jack hurled the ball to the floor, wiped his tears angrily, and stormed out of the house.

Ten minutes later on the futures board, wheat ticked down.

It ticked down again.

And so it would continue. Ham would be richer than he'd ever imagined. He'd never experience another financial challenge for the rest of his life. It was not really important, though. Scripture came back to him: "What good will it be for a man if he gains the whole world, yet forfeits his soul?"

He would trade it all to have his love, his life, back again.

But that was not an option.

Out his window, Ham could see young Jack riding his bicycle furiously down the street. He watched with a passive surrender as his son's small frame shrank into the distance.

[chapter 1]

Another Bun in the Oven

The Marina Grill at Lake Lanier teemed with swarming kids and busy parents spreading hot lunches across umbrella-shaded picnic tables. A soft summer breeze swept continuously through the outdoor seating area, carrying with it the waft of grilled sirloin and sautéed onions, the gentle lapping of water on the lakeshore, lyrics of familiar tunes through overhead speakers, and the chime of rigging against the row of masts that sprouted above the peer. The parking lot between the Grill and the Ship's Store and Chandlery buzzed with families loading and unloading children and beach toys.

Jack and Ellison Wells rolled their SUV across the gravel lot and parked alongside the picnic area. Their two young children, Cole and Juliet, squirmed excitedly in the back seat, both anxious to join the festivities. Across the parking lot, Ellison spotted her mother still seated in her Mercedes, evidently preferring to wait in air-conditioned comfort for her daughter's arrival.

Jack lifted five-year-old Cole out of his booster chair, and the child dashed to the sandbox with his pail and shovel. Ellison propped sixteen-month-old Juliet on her hip, hoisted a diaper bag over her shoulder, and hurried over to greet her mother, Pearl. As she swept strands of auburn hair out of her eyes, Ellison's face revealed delicate lines of experience. Her slim figure divulged only the slightest humbling traces of the birth of two children.

"I'm so glad you could join us," Ellison said. With her free hand, she gave her mother a one-armed hug. "Isn't it a gorgeous day?"

"Hello, Essie, dear," Pearl said as she smoothed her collared blouse and donned a wide-brimmed sunhat. She tucked her unnaturally rich red curls behind her ears and slid a billowing shirttail back into creased slacks. "I hope you brought some sunscreen for these children." She leaned over to peck her young granddaughter on the cheek. Juliet opened her mouth wide and kissed back in a sloppy drool.

"I probably have some in the diaper bag. I'll check in a minute." Ellison felt her shoulders tense, but the comforting melody of lakeside music held the tension at bay. "Let's grab a table," she suggested, leading the way.

The women made their way to the Grill and found that Jack, Ellison's husband of sixteen years, had already secured a picnic table near a sandbox where Cole's castle construction was well underway.

"Gami Pearl!" Cole waved excitedly. "Look at what I made!"

Pearl wiggled her fingers at her grandson and blew him a kiss.

"Hi, Pearl." Jack greeted his mother-in-law with a light embrace. Ellison parked the diaper bag on the tabletop and guided Juliet toward the sandbox, while Jack collected the lunch orders and made his way to the Grill counter.

Pearl rifled through the diaper bag and pursed her lips. "Essie, honey, I can't find any sunscreen in here. The children will be burnt in no time."

"Oh, I must've left it at home." Essie dug through the bag and sighed. As usual, her mother wasted no time pointing out her failings. Once again, Essie paused to allow the soothing lyrics of a familiar song to calm her spirit. "Drift Away" by Dobie Gray. Essie had a passion for music, particularly oldies. In difficult circumstances, a favorite tune had a way of restoring her peace. "Well, the kids will only be in the sun for a few minutes until the food is ready. We have an umbrella for shade here at the table."

Pearl shook her head ever so slightly, fidgeted with her shirt collar, and began fanning herself with a laminated menu.

To Ellison's relief, Jack returned with a broad grin and squeezed his long legs over the bench next to Pearl. He raked fingers through brown, windswept hair, but his untamed curls sprang back up defiantly. "Dock-burgers and fries are on the way." He put an arm around his mother-in-law. "While we wait, we have some news to share with you, Pearl."

Pearl brightened and stopped fanning.

"I'm pregnant! Ten weeks." Essie announced.

Jack's face beamed with the proud radiance of an expecting father. He gazed warmly at Essie, and his eyes glistened with flecks of green and gold.

Pearl gasped and clutched the cross pendant that hung elegantly around her neck. "Again! Already? Oh Essie! That is wonderful news!" She stood and embraced her daughter.

"Can you believe it? That's why we insisted you meet us for lunch here today. We wanted to tell you in person," Ellison explained, grinning mischievously.

The burgers came. Ellison excused herself to gather up the children and wash their hands, while Jack cut Juliet's sandwich into small bites.

"Oh Jack, I'm overwhelmed. I had no idea you two were trying for a third baby," Pearl pried.

"We weren't," Jack admitted before he could reel in the words, then added, "but I couldn't be any more thrilled about it!"

Ellison and the kids gathered around the table. As was their custom, Jack bowed his head to pray, and the rest of the family followed.

"Dear heavenly Father, thank you for bringing us together today to celebrate a new addition to our family. We praise you for this gift and all the many blessings you've given us. Thank you for the food we are about to enjoy and for the hands that have prepared it. In Jesus' name we pray." A soft chorus of *amens* rose from the table, and everyone began eating.

Pearl put her sandwich down and clasped her hands. "I am just delighted, dear!" She reached across the table and curled her fingers into Essie's hand. "Three young children! My, you will certainly have your hands full, Ellison." Pearl's expression turned serious. "I suppose you'll have to quit that job of yours, finally."

Ellison stiffened. "Well, actually, we haven't made a decision about that." Essie deflected her attention to Juliet, who had a streak of ketchup across her cheek.

Deep creases formed in Pearl's brow. "What do you mean? I couldn't believe you kept your job with two kids. Certainly, you're not planning to work with three, are you?"

Jack came to his wife's rescue. "We have plenty of time to make that decision. It's still early; the baby isn't due until March. Remember, we just found out about this ourselves and have many lifestyle questions to consider now." Jack smiled reassuringly at both women.

Pearl picked up her menu and began fanning herself again. "I'm sure you'll make the responsible choice." Pearl's cadence had quickened.

Cole had already devoured his fries and made considerable progress on his burger. Still chewing, he asked to be excused, and Jack nodded permission.

With a fry in each fist, Juliet's eyes followed Cole's return to the sandbox. Immediately, she started crying and fidgeting in her seat. Ellison gathered her up in her lap, wiped ketchup off her chin, then sent her toddling toward her brother.

"Please don't worry. Don't you trust us to make the best choices for our family?" Ellison asked with more pleading in her voice than she intended.

"I suppose," Pearl answered flatly. She shifted her gaze toward her grandkids and mustered a thin smile. "Essie, dear, the children are getting sunburnt, and that sandbox does not look clean to me. Besides, don't you think it's time Juliet got her diaper checked?"

Essie shot Jack a knowing glance. Together, husband and wife rose from the table. Essie called to the children, "How about some ice cream?"

Jack offered to stay behind to clear the paper plates, and the women and children headed toward the adjacent Ship's Store and Chandlery, known primarily for its boating gear but popular with the kids for its sweet treats.

When the air-conditioning of the Ship Store hit Pearl's face, she let out an audible sigh of relief. "This is much better. Ellison, honey, I think I'll check to see if they sell sunscreen in here." Pearl headed down an aisle of beach gear. Essie's kids made a beeline for the ice-cream cooler and pointed out their selections.

Essie waved at a clerk slumped in a chair behind the counter. The store was empty except for an elderly man browsing the boat-repair section in the back.

Within a minute, Pearl was at the register with a trio of sunscreens in various sizes. "This will do for now. I found one for the diaper bag, one for the house, and one for, well, emergencies like today."

For a split second, Essie focused on the song pouring through the store speakers in hopes that it might somehow minister a healing salve to her spirit. Finding little comfort, Essie fumbled for her purse to pay for the selections when a familiar drawl behind her declared, "Those are on me."

Essie recognized the unique southern drawl. *Could it be?* She turned to search for the unmistakable face that matched the voice. Behind her stood an elderly man with a small box tucked under one arm. He beamed brightly at her and pulled a crisp, hundred-dollar bill from a tattered jeans pocket.

Essie's chin dropped at the sight of her father-in-law. The last time she'd seen him was from a distance during Juliet's dedication at church more than a year ago. The lines of Hamilton Wells's face mapped a full life of wind and weather, happiness and sorrow. He stood tall, over six feet, with gray hair and eyes that gave a silvery cast to his appearance. He remained slim, although his middle, slightly drooped with age, applied tension to the lower buttons of an otherwise loose-fitting, buttoned-down shirt. Hamilton's eyes moistened at the sight of his daughter-in-law and grandchildren.

Jack rarely spoke to his father anymore. During the few uncomfortable occasions Essie had seen them together, Jack had made no attempt to conceal contempt for his father, his detached and complacent lifestyle, or the related cast of so-called stepmothers. Essie often regretted that her children didn't have a relationship with Jack's father, but the opportunities were rare given Jack's disdain.

Following the death of Hamilton's first wife, Jack's mother, and his impulsively acquired wheat fortune more than thirty-five years ago, Hamilton had made a home out of a rundown sailboat docked in a slip on the other side of Lake Lanier. Given the considerable proceeds from his wheat investment, he never mustered the ambition to pursue further full-time work. It was not altogether clear how he spent his money or his time. He remained a mystery to Essie and the kids.

"Ham!" Essie smiled warmly. "What a surprise to see you! It's been what—over a year now?" Pearl narrowed her eyes at Hamilton's stubbled chin and palm-tree-covered beach shirt that hung slightly out of balance with one shirttail dangling a bit below the other, one button-length askew.

Chimes sounded as Jack opened the door. He stopped in his tracks when he recognized his father.

Ham's face lit up at the sight of his estranged son. He started toward Jack, but then pulled back as though suddenly reconsidering. He tipped an invisible hat to the ladies.

"Must be my lucky day." He kissed Ellison on the cheek and slid his payment across the counter to the clerk. "Good to see you, Son"—he nodded to Jack first and then Pearl—"and good day to you, too, ma'am."

"Good day, Mr. Wells." Pearl nodded politely.

An uncomfortable silence began to build when Pearl added, "Our Essie here has some news."

"I'm pregnant again," Essie explained.

"Another biscuit in your basket? Well, don't that beat the band! Congratulations, darlin', and to you, too, Son. Mighty fine family you have here. Mighty fine," Ham repeated.

Jack simply nodded.

Father and son tempered any show of affection, yet Ham's eyes held a painful yearning that suggested an eagerness forcibly restrained. It seemed too late to display a gush of emotion.

Hamilton knelt down to make eye contact with the kids.

"What flavor you kids got today?" he asked about their frozen treats. Juliet offered a wet grin as Popsicle juice rolled down her chin.

"Strawberry and chocolate," Cole answered brightly for both his sister and himself. Young Cole, having only seen his grandfather a few times in his short life, stared slack jawed at the old man. Hamilton bore a scar that twisted from the right side of his mouth and down the length of his jaw. The pink, ropy mark lent an air of mystery to his expression and his past.

"Strawberry and chocolate!" Ham feigned a look of shock. "Do you want to know what I like best? Frozen bug juice. Icy-fish cones are tasty, too. You ought to try one of those next time," Hamilton teased.

Cole's eyes widened in alarm at this suggestion.

"Hello, Pop," Jack said coolly. "It's a surprise to see you here on a busy family day. Not your style. I'd expect you to be hanging around that old diner, the one with the service you like so much." Jack stared expressionless at his father. "What brings you around on a Saturday?"

Hamilton winced, picking up the reference to his negligent family history and his multiple diner-waitress romances. The wound of Jack's rebuke had clearly stung him, but he smiled and nodded nonetheless.

When his lips curved up, the scar along Ham's face whitened. It was difficult to determine whether it was a mark of hard-edged strength or a mask of confidence and contentment.

"With beautiful women like this in the Ship Store, how can I resist?" Hamilton gestured toward Essie and Pearl. "But while I'm here, I thought I might pick up a couple of parts to repair my boat." He held up the box that had been tucked under his arm. "The starter gives me trouble on occasion. I remember you being awfully handy with such fixes. Sure could use your help. Think you could stop by for a visit?" The lilt in Ham's voice betrayed vulnerability. His eyes began to glisten as the question hung in the air unanswered.

Jack ran a hand through his wind-tossed hair. "Not today, Pop. Some other time, maybe. We really have to be going."

"I understand. Some other time then." Hamilton smiled and grazed his knuckles across his scarred jaw as the family walked out of the store and waved their goodbyes.

[chapter 2]

I'll Have the Usual

Hamilton Wells walked into The Lazy I like he owned the place, which he did not. It was easy to draw the wrong conclusion. So easy, in fact, that many, including Hamilton himself, were reluctant and, in some cases, outright unwilling to be persuaded otherwise by mere facts.

In truth, The Lazy I, originally named The Chicken Chest, was owned by Inman Forbes, a man in his late fifties who flaunted his lack of any legitimate work history as a positive trend. The son of a commercial real estate investor, Inman assumed proprietorship over The Lazy I from his father, whose attentions were dominated by more profitable investments on the West Coast. After a decision to relocate to California, Inman's father, presumably eager to unburden himself from further familial obligations, unloaded The Chicken Chest as a form of early inheritance, quite possibly concluding his son's overall work ethic and unsettling physical characteristics to be a hindrance toward any other career pursuits. Inman had one eye that tended to move independently from the other. According to Inman, the ability to look in two directions at the same time offered special advantages.

Despite his unearned proprietorship, Inman remained preoccupied with games of chance and exploring new uses of his special talent. When he showed up at the restaurant, it was never to work. He spent his time at the breakfast bar, circling picks from the sports section and scrawling cryptic reminders on beverage napkins. After a few months, The Chicken Chest gave way to The Lazy I. Folks debated whether the origin of the new name was derived from Inman's questionable work ethic or his amblyopic expression. Either way, Ham could tell Inman liked the new name. He now considered himself a businessman. Inman clearly took pride in having a business named in his honor, but he did not seem to enjoy the day-to-day responsibilities of running a restaurant. Inman's general attitude suggested a man of his unique talents and wealthy relations must draw the line at any kind of commitment to full-time employment. So Inman was fortunate to have Hamilton around.

When suggestions came in for menu changes, Inman deferred all decisions to Hamilton. "Go ask someone who cares." Inman would look up with one eye while the other studied a dog-racing program. When a position opened up for a cook or waitress, Inman left the choice to Hamilton. "Can't you see I'm busy?" he'd say as he weighed odds and calculated potential proceeds. He lolled one eye in Hamilton's direction. "Go talk to the crazy old man at the end of the bar. He's here more than anyone else."

At sixty-six, Hamilton assumed a natural, grandfatherly authority over the place and its patrons. On Saturday mornings, the diner hummed with the sounds of clattering plates, brewing coffee, flapping newspapers, and the easy murmur of a familiar breakfast crowd. Hamilton entered the diner with a purposeful stride. As was his custom, he stopped at each café table to greet familiar faces. He shook hands with the men and tipped an invisible hat to the ladies, calling each by name and inquiring about children and family members not present. Everyone not addressed by name was *darlin'*, *shuga*, or *hon*.

"Good to see you back, Noodle. Missed you last week. That old boat giving you trouble?" Hamilton asked Silas Getty, a regular diner patron.

Noodle nodded with his mouth full. Noodle was the nickname given to Silas Getty. In the years they had known one another, Silas Getty first became Sy Getty which sounded a lot like Spaghetti. Spaghetti was too long for a useful nickname so Silas had evolved into Noodle.

"I'm too old to do these repairs myself. Tough on the old back." Noodle pressed a palm against the base of his spine and winced.

Hamilton motioned to the waitress. His eyes smiled in the shape of twin crescent moons. It was easier to interpret the smile in his eyes than the one on his scarred face, which, while not unpleasant, was difficult to read.

"Lilly's hotcakes will fix you right up, Noodle. She's got more cure in her little pinky than any doctor in this town." He raised a crooked finger in the direction of the customer's empty coffee cup. "It's the gospel truth. Ain't that so, Lilly?"

The waitress curved her lips into a one-sided smile and refilled the cup. Lilly's recipe for griddle cakes, made from a sweetened mix of pancake and cream-of-wheat batter, had been credited for the remedy of a host of ailments among The Lazy I patronage. Her huevos rancheros were claimed to hold unique medical properties to treat depression, constipation, or a broken heart.

"Load 'em up with another biscuit, darlin'. On me." Hamilton loved to watch Lilly work almost as much as he loved her cooking.

She blew a long black strand of hair from her face as she collected a stack of empty breakfast plates and balanced them on her arm. "Comin' right up, Ham." Lilly shrugged in a need-another-set-of-hands sort of way and gave Hamilton a wink. The simple gesture shot a hole right through Hamilton's chest. The way she moved reminded Hamilton of his second wife, Bonita, who had also worked at The Lazy I years ago when it was still The Chicken Chest. Bonita had the same shiny black hair, which she kept tied back in a silver clasp. All four of Hamilton's marriages had been to diner waitresses. Though he knew his son disapproved, it was a weakness he was powerless to resist.

Lilly slid a buttered biscuit in front of Noodle. Hamilton watched Lilly deliver another half-dozen breakfast entrees with the fluid, efficient movement of a Las Vegas dealer peeling cards off a deck. This also echoed of Bonita, and his mind drifted back to a distant memory. He took a seat at the end of the counter and grazed his knuckles along the scar that twisted across his jaw. It had happened more than twenty-five years ago.

Hamilton had walked into The Chicken Chest just before closing. He took a booth in a dimly lit corner. Bonita was busily wrapping silverware in paper napkins. It was almost midnight, but Hamilton had a craving for pecan pie that could not be ignored. Preoccupied with closing duties, Bonita had forgotten to lock the door as she tallied the count in the register drawer. From Hamilton's view, all he saw of the perpetrator was the back of a skinny kid with a silver chain dangling from the pocket of his black jeans. He was gesturing wildly, jabbing a switchblade in the air in front of Bonita's face. Bonita, mouth gaped open, stood frozen behind the open register drawer. She curled her fingers around the simple cross that hung from a chain on her neck. *"¡Ayúdeme, Dios!"* Her lips trembled with fear as the kid thrust the blade at her and lunged across the counter toward the register.

Without hesitation or thought, Hamilton approached the skinny kid with his usual, even stride. When the startled boy spun around, Hamilton's eyes flashed a strange smile, twin crescent moons. He moved toward the boy with a steady, unwavering pace. Hamilton's face wore the same expression you might expect to see upon stumbling into an old friend. The bewildered boy jerked the knife in Hamilton's direction.

"What do you think you're doing? Get outta here!" the kid shouted.

Hamilton walked right up to him and extended his hand. The boy sliced at the air in front of Hamilton's face, slashing his cheek and ripping it open. The jagged wound ran from his mouth all the way to the tip of his ear, and blood gushed down his neck and chest. Hamilton reached for the knife. He caught the next arc of the switchblade firmly in the palm of his hand, bringing its motion to a full stop.

"No, sir," Ham stated simply.

The boy released the knife handle with the blade planted deeply in Hamilton's steady grip. The expression on the kid's face changed from adolescent bravado to a combination of shock and fear.

"We're closed, son. Take your trouble somewhere else." Despite the gash across his cheek, Hamilton's voice remained steady, his eyes still smiling. The blood from his sliced palm trickled down his arm and fell to the floor in thick drops.

The kid's face had turned ashen. "Lunatic! Freak!" The perpetrator made a dash for the door, stumbled over a diner table, and left a couple of fallen chairs in his wake.

Looking back, Hamilton felt sure he must've feared for his own life. He was certain he must've experienced extreme pain. But when he thought about that night, he couldn't remember any fear or pain. All he remembered was the warmth of Bonita's hands on his face. She was kneeling over him, crying *"¡Mi héroe! ¡Mi héroe!"* Hamilton, who had not felt a woman's touch since the loss of his first wife eleven years earlier, fell in love with her immediately.

She cared for him all through his recovery. Bonita brought meals to his home, which was a forty-five-foot sailboat on Lake Lanier. Hamilton's son, Jack, then seventeen, withdrew brusquely to the cabin below as Hamilton and his new girlfriend sat together on the bow, eating huevos rancheros and pecan pie. Bonita called Hamilton "Mr. Ham" and playfully called Jack "Bacon Bit." Ham recalled the scowl this evoked from Jack, who resented any reference to similarity with his father or any attempted affection from a replacement mother.

"*¿Te gusta,* Mr. Ham?" she would ask about the meal. To Hamilton, the sound of her voice was more lyrical than the tinkle of wind chimes. Even the way she pronounced his name: Meester Hom.

"Just Ham," he would say. "Jos Hom," she'd repeat.

The boat rocked gently in its slip. The sound of rigging clinked against the mast.

"Djur face scar for me," she apologized, her hand lightly touching his cheek. *"Lo siento."*

"Nah, weren't nothin'. Needed some pecan pie is all." He reached for her hand. "Wasn't my good side anyway."

Within three months, they were married. But as any of Hamilton's following wives could attest, life on a sailboat is not for everybody. Yes, Hamilton may have saved her life, but his impulsive marriage proposal shortly thereafter promised another sort of salvation he could not deliver. Hamilton had fanned flickering hopes of a new family of three, but it wasn't long before Bonita's presence at their sailboat home became scarce. The cramped space on the boat and Jack's cold reception to his stepmother's presence created a constant, unspoken reminder that three was a crowd. She began to spend more nights with relatives, visiting Ham only during her brief hours between work and sleep. Eighteen months later, the marriage was over, and Bonita moved back to Mexico to live with her sister.

Snapping out of the past and returning to the present, Hamilton turned his gaze toward a row of windowed booths.

"Afternoon, friends." Hamilton greeted a man and his wife, another pair of familiar faces.

The man gave Ham a nod. "Howdy there, partner."

Hamilton nodded to the wife. "Why I say, darlin', you look as bright as the mornin'."

The lady tucked her chin down and blushed behind a thankful grin. "Good afternoon, Ham. Awful nice of you to say."

Swiveling in his barstool, Hamilton turned to make the acquaintance of a few unfamiliar faces. In front of his chair, a brass nameplate was fastened on the counter surface which read, "Reserved for Hamilton Wells."

A cup of hot coffee steamed next to his name plate. Within a minute and without conversation, Lilly pushed a plate of bacon, two eggs over easy, and a short stack of warm flour tortillas in front of him. Hamilton had enjoyed the same lunch every day as long as anyone at the diner could remember. It had been more than two decades since he had verbalized his order.

"Tabasco?" he looked up.

"To your right, behind the shuga," Lilly said, pointing with her elbow to the adjacent seat.

"I love you," he said.

"You only love me for my tapas," Lilly replied.

"To be sure, darlin'." Hamilton cleared his throat, a little startled by her candor. His crescent moons winked twin smiles at the fit of her aproned uniform. "Those, naturally. And don't forget your cookin', either."

"Crazy old man!" Lilly laughed. "Can I get you anything else? How 'bout some pecan pie?"

Hamilton swabbed a strip of tortilla in egg yolk. His gray eyes twinkled silver as he chewed. "Will you marry me?"

Lilly put a hand on her hip, leaned over the counter, and batted her eyes playfully. "We could head over to the courthouse today. I get off work at three."

His bluff had been called. Though the prospect was nearly impossible to resist, the possibility of another failed marriage was unbearable. How many times would he bet his heart on love and lose? Charm and playful banter seemed to be the best he could offer now. "How I wish I could, darlin'," Hamilton backpedaled, grinning between bites. "Can't make it today, though. How 'bout tomorrow?"

Lilly kicked her hip out to the side and pouted. "I just don't know, Ham. You'll have to ask me again tomorrow."

Hamilton wiped his mouth with a paper napkin. "You can count on that."

He pushed his empty plate to the side. Other than his sailboat, there was no place like The Lazy I where he felt so at home. Between the warmhearted company and the home-style food, it was hard to say which felt most like family.

[chapter 3]

sapling's shadow

"I wouldn't do that, dear. They'll never respect you if you give in. Children need discipline, Ellison." Mother Pearl disapproved of surrendering to the children's pleas to replay the same CD track for the third time—"Loves Me Like a Rock" by Paul Simon. Essie's stomach tightened. She had already pressed play and momentarily allowed her thoughts to drift into the lyrics.

"Lord knows it's not easy. Your father worked two jobs while I raised you and your sister by myself. Of course, I made many sacrifices like leaving real estate, but I made sure you never went without."

There she went again. It had been eight weeks since Essie had announced the big news about baby number three, and her mother had not let up on the pressure to quit work.

"I could've been a top agent, but I chose to stay home with you, instead. That is a mother's duty. I don't understand why you insist on working, dear. You can get by on Jack's salary at Life Cola. Honestly, there's no good reason for you to work there, too."

The song ended, and they drove along in silence for a moment before pulling into Pearl's driveway. Essie gathered her purse and diaper bag and stepped out into the rain.

How many times had Ellison Wells heard the martyrdom-wrought-by-your-birth speech? Essie's father had endured this tale of woe countless times, and lest it be forgotten, her sister and she were reminded at least once a year. Everyone in the family had been a source of disappointment to Mother. Dad was never supportive or successful enough; her daughters were too undisciplined, unrefined. Essie believed her mother had imagined a different life for herself. The story went that Pearl, as a young girl, would pretend to be a Realtor to the Disney cast of princesses, selling Cinderella's castle to Snow White for 7 percent commission, then back to Cinderella again for a small markup but waiving closing costs. Offers they couldn't refuse. Perhaps it was this secret identity that led to her preference to be called *Pearl* instead of *Mom*. She claimed no regrets but wore the burden of her life like a purple heart. Essie felt deep down that her mother longed for a dream she lost and those she loved now carried a measure of shame for having stolen it from her.

Ever since Essie could remember, she, too, had wanted to be something more, someone better, someone great. Even as a little girl, this longing had grown within her like seeds of destiny. All the grand stories of a little girl's youth, fairy tales of beauty and romance, only stirred her heart all the more in anticipation of a happily-ever-after. As a child, Essie believed a potential for greatness existed in the heart of every person, waiting for its season to bud. When her season came, she imagined, her life would sprout forth beauty and virtue. She would grow up, marry her handsome prince, and join him in the adventurous pursuit of some noble calling.

As it turned out, her girlish dreams of greatness had not blossomed into a full-feature Disney film, either. Now, thirty-eight years old with two young children and a third baby on the way, Essie stood in her mother's driveway on a drizzly October evening, losing an argument with her five-year-old. He stiffened his arms and legs, fighting her efforts to help him out of a booster seat.

Red-faced, tears streaming down his cheeks, Cole screamed, "No! I want a Buzz Lightyear."

After an exhausting Friday afternoon at the Mall of Georgia with Cole and eighteen-month-old Juliet, Essie was unloading boxes and bags from her mother's car.

Neat and composed in her button-up, collared shirt and belted skirt, Pearl stood inside the shelter of the garage, smoothing a strand of deep red hair back into place. She had fulfilled the doting grandmother role for the day by treating both children to several gifts from the mall stores: Hot Wheels and action figures for Cole, sparkly bangle bracelets and a pink purse for Juliet.

Although entertaining the children was one of the day's shopping objectives, the primary mission had been to refresh Cole's kindergarten wardrobe, which required jeans without exposed knees, and to get a jumpstart on Christmas shopping. During Essie's failed attempt to sweep all the purchases into her car, Cole had spotted the Buzz Lightyear Space Ranger toy his grandmother had bought and stuffed in the bottom of a shopping bag. Like a hawk recognizing scurrying prey from an unthinkable distance, the boy lunged after the hidden gift.

Calmly, Essie explained, "Gami Pearl has already given you lots of toys today. Remember your Hot Wheels? Remember your Spider-Man? Gami has to save some toys for another day." As if reason might prevail.

"I want my Buzz Lightyear! It's mine!" he wailed.

Essie lifted him forcibly to the ground and aimed him in the direction of her SUV. Standing in the rain, hair matted to her face, patience thin, Ellison resorted to an ultimatum. "Cole, you have until the count of three to get in this car. If you ask for one more toy, I will spank you."

Out of nowhere, a scene from *The Sound of Music* flashed through her head: a lady twirling and singing through a field with happy, harmonizing children following in synchronized choreography. These and similar images from her girlish ideals of parenthood passed through her mind in sharp contrast to the reality of a rainy car ride with screaming kids. Where was her ride into the sunset? Where was her glorious ending?

"One, two . . ." She began the spanking countdown.

"*I want Buzz!*" he shrieked, collapsing on the pavement.

Essie spanked his thigh sharply and heaved him into his booster seat in the back of the Pathfinder. "*I want my Bu-uzz!*" The shriek became a moan.

Meanwhile, Pearl helped Juliet from her car to Essie's so she, too, could climb into her car seat. Juliet was proudly featuring sparkly silver shoes, just purchased to go with her Christmas dress. She accentuated each delicate step across the wet driveway, stopping to marvel at her feet a dozen times.

"Shoes," Juliet observed, beaming. Her eyes were still transfixed downward as Essie strapped her into her car seat and placed the new pink purse in her lap. She swung her short chubby legs, flashing her new silver shoes.

"*My Buzz!*" Cole yowled.

Essie reached across the seats and spanked him again on the thigh. "I told you, Cole, do not ask me again. Do not ask for another thing! You've gotten too many presents today already. I have a good mind to take them all back to the store."

With a palm pressed over her lips and chin, Pearl evaluated the scene. She shook her head ever so slightly as Cole moaned and Essie transferred the rest of her packages into the back of the Pathfinder. Leaving the car door open, Essie sighed and trekked back to the garage to say goodbye to her mother.

"I'll see you at the garage sale tomorrow," Essie said. While mother and daughter embraced, barely touching, fingertips lightly cupping each other's shoulders, Cole belted out again, "*Give me Buzzz!*"

Essie raced to her car and delivered a series of sharp spanks to the thigh.

"*Buzzz!*"

Mother Pearl remained poised and unaffected, a model of control. They waved their goodbyes as Essie maneuvered her slightly swollen belly behind the wheel and backed out of the driveway. Her clothing had already begun to bind around the waistline.

What does greatness look like for a mom of three kids? *"A wife of noble character who can find?"* Essie thought back to the role model of Proverbs 31, a description of the perfect woman. *What would she do in this situation?* she wondered. Essie tried reason again. "Cole, I'm sorry I had to spank you, honey. Gami Pearl and I love you and Juliet so much. We enjoy taking you places and giving you toys. But we have to save some toys to give you at Christmas, OK? Be thankful for the toys you have, honey. It is bad manners for you to ask for more when Gami Pearl has already given you so much. You should call her on the phone and tell her you're sorry for pitching a fit, OK?"

Essie glanced in the rearview mirror to see if any of this was sinking in. Instead of nods of comprehension, she saw Juliet reach over and pinch Cole on the arm. She stuck her tongue out at him, blew spittle, and, satisfied with a job well done, returned her attention to her shoes. Cole wailed all the more, "Mom, Juliet pinched me. She spit on me! *Buzz*!"

Somehow, motherhood didn't resemble the life of beauty and virtue Essie had imagined. A Disney-like memory flickered through her mind where Truly Scrumptious drove the beloved Chitty Chitty Bang Bang while two children, faces beaming, sang her praises from the back seat. So much for the children's choir.

"That's it!" Essie screamed. "You two are impossible! I'm taking all your new toys back to the store. I'm returning every one of your Hot Wheels and your Spider-Man, Cole. And I'm taking Juliet's stuff back, too. All of it!" *Oh no,* she thought, *I sound just like my mother.*

The scarcity of white knights, heroic rescues, and magical car rides combined with the harried prospect of mothering three kids under six years old had led to some adjustments on her views about greatness. Still, the longing to fulfill some grand purpose, to live a life of significance, remained very much alive. Now, she thought of greatness as less a byproduct of a fairy godmother and more a transformation by a heavenly Father. In this case, she figured, it would have to be. It was her only hope. It was a hope that stirred within her most powerfully when her reality, or her mother, reminded her of the many ways in which she fell short, or on those extraordinary occasions when she came face to face with a display of true greatness and understood just how far she had to go.

Essie looked in the rearview mirror. Juliet, oblivious, was turning her tiny ankles to watch the light twinkle and bounce off her sparkly shoes. Cole's lip was trembling, face downcast. Several minutes passed as they drove on in silence. Then she heard her son's small voice from the back seat say, "Mommy, can I call Gami and tell her I'm sorry?"

Her heart welled up in her chest. "Yes, of course, baby."

"Mommy, please don't take Juliet's shoes back to the store."

"Why not, Cole?" She angled the rearview mirror to see him better.

With his five-year-old brow furrowed, he watched his little sister enjoying herself, swinging her sparkly feet. "Because I forgive her."

Ellison saw the mercy on his concerned face. Sitting at a stop light, windshield wipers slapping at the raindrops, she twisted toward the back seat and looked at his small frame strapped in the booster seat. His narrow chest harnessed under those wide belts hardly evoked the image of an oak of righteousness. Yet he did not seem like the same child who moments earlier had thrown a tantrum for more toys.

She dialed the number on her cell phone.

"Hi, Pearl. Cole has something to say to you." She passed the phone back to her son.

"Gami Pearl? I'm sorry. Thank you for my toys. I don't need anything else now. OK? I will wait until Halloween and ask again. OK? Bye." He chucked the phone in Essie's lap without waiting for a response.

No, not perfect, but Ellison recognized those seeds of greatness stirring. And she understood all too well their origin was not from her. Her son wasn't exactly an oak of righteousness, but all the same, she was struck speechless by the beauty of the grand shadow cast from its sapling form.

[chapter 4]

The House Always Wins

Lake Sidney Lanier was man-made, an Army Corps of Engineers project back in the early '50s. It was twenty-six miles long and about one-and-a-half miles across at its widest point. It was a recreational paradise besides being Atlanta's principal water supply. Aqualand was the world's largest inland marina and was also home to Hamilton Wells.

With the auxiliary outboard motor idling, Ham tossed the stern and spring lines to the pier, kicked away, and guided the sailboat toward the "big water" in the center of the lake. In the time-honored tradition of sailors, Ham waved to no one in particular but mostly toward Noodle, another live-aboard and inveterate tinkerer like himself.

"My boat's taking on some water," Noodle hollered at Ham over the wind. "Bad valve again, I reckon."

"I'll come take a look when I get back. I guess we could both use some repairs. My inboard starter's getting temperamental," Hamilton shouted.

It was a perfect day for sailing. Ham loved the purity of just the wind and water, and he figured the steady southwestern breeze would hold for a couple of hours. He quickly hoisted the main and genoa, the boom kicked over, and the boat responded by gently healing to starboard. The knot meter registered 4.5. "Perfect," he commented to himself.

"Who has gathered up the wind in the hollow of his hands? Who has wrapped up the waters in his cloak?" Hamilton recalled a Sunday school

lesson from his boyhood. He remembered trying to imagine the enormity of a God who could harness the wind in cupped hands, scoop up the oceans in his garment. These old Scriptures seemed to float to the surface of his memory whenever he took the helm. He gazed out at the lake, enjoying the way the sunlight glinted off the dappled water. Days like this were rare. It was early Saturday morning, and Jet Skis and power boats were still nestled in their slips. He had the lake to himself.

Normally, you could count on the fickle, variable lake winds to demand close watch, but not today. Steady and regular as pig tracks. Ham heaved a sigh of immense sadness for all the semi-desperate people, idling or otherwise, out on the gaggle of interstate highways just a few miles from where his sailboat glided silently along on a blanket of shimmering diamonds.

Hamilton liked to let his mind wander whenever he sailed the waters of Lake Lanier. Lake Sidney Lanier was large for a man-made lake but hardly comparable to the oceans of the earth. If God carried the world's seas in his cloak, Lake Lanier was probably nothing more than a drop of rainwater on his sleeve. Still, it was plenty big enough for Hamilton.

For Hamilton, sailing was one of life's great pleasures. The women who'd stolen his heart over the years brought the only joy that ever came close to competing. The problem with women, Hamilton decided, was that they took control of his brain. He couldn't think straight around them.

On his sailboat, Hamilton could see more clearly, sort things out. He did his best thinking when he captained his boat alone. Sitting comfortably portside, wheel in hand, Hamilton was his own captain. He was born for this. He commanded his vessel, and it obeyed. The destination was irrelevant. Everything was in the journey. Steering just to starboard of the sun, climbing higher above the horizon, Ham close-hauled the sheets and felt the boat respond instantly. *Darn near six knots*, he thought. Not nearly fast enough to meet his son's standards, but the perfect speed for Hamilton. He couldn't understand his son's need for speed. *No car could ever evoke this feeling.*

Sailing was one of the few arenas in life where Hamilton felt he really was in control. This is why the thought of God holding the wind in his palm and the water in his cloak sat uncomfortably in his mind. As a boy, the enormity of God had filled Hamilton with wonder. As a young man, it gave him comfort. Now at sixty-six, in the twilight of his life, it scared him. There was a time in his youth when Hamilton reveled in the sovereign power of God. Earline's photo resurfaced in his memory. The wife of his youth, his first wife, his true love, the mother of his only son. Hamilton remembered his first proposal of marriage, the tears of joy, the future stretched out before them. God was on his side, and anything seemed possible.

But that was only the beginning of the story. He had loved all four of his wives: Earline, Bonita, Torah, Lauless. Each one so different and so beautiful in her own way. The faces of each of his past wives flipped as though in a mental Rolodex. There they were as he liked to remember them: each a princess disguised in a waitress uniform. Even after so many losses in marriage, Hamilton still searched for true love. But it was hard to recognize among so many counterfeits. It always felt like true love to Hamilton.

The Rolodex flipped to Bonita's picture. Her rescue at the diner had been one of Hamilton's crowning moments. At first, he'd worn the scars on his face and hand as a badge of honor. Before he could replay the memory, another one took its place. The one when he discovered Bonita's note. The English was broken, but the message was clear enough. She'd left him. The memory of one failure triggered others.

Earline, his first wife, whom he had lost to cancer. Jack, his own son, who had needed him desperately after her death. Jesse, his best friend during the war.

He wondered what people would say about him when he was gone from this life. He longed to be found strong, even brave, but the evidence condemned him. Looking back on a full life, the trail seemed marked with more heartbreak and failure than moments of victory.

God, holding all these events in his hands, had not prevented Hamilton's failures. Either he allowed it, or he wasn't paying attention. The comfort Hamilton used to feel concerning God's sovereignty seemed naive now that he was an old man. Hamilton was no longer sure of God's intentions toward him.

Out on the water by himself, floating in a raindrop on God's shirtsleeve, Hamilton's mind churned. Was his life a matter of consequence to God at all? Might God open his palm just enough to let Hamilton and his sailboat slip right through into oblivion? Would he notice if he did? The wind stiffened, and Ham eased the main. He knew the wind's intensification would not last and unconsciously scanned the trees and waves for signs of the next shift in the wind.

For Hamilton, death didn't seem so bad. It wasn't death that bothered him. Hamilton was scared he might soon meet God and discover he had missed the point of his life entirely.

The scars Hamilton once wore as memorials to his bravery now felt more like a disguise. The scar on his face offered a convenient image of strength he could hide behind. His poker face. God, too, Hamilton figured, was a master of games. The House Dealer snapping random cards to each player around the table.

The boat leaned heavily as it made a turn toward a cluster of tiny islands. The boom swung across as the vessel came about. The wind filled the sails once again, and Hamilton pointed the bow between two small islands, each nothing more than a patch of trees. A series of warning buoys bobbed between the island banks. Do not enter. Shallow waters.

Hamilton pondered what card God would deal him next. Were there any aces left in the deck? He thought of Jack. He wished they were closer. He thought of Lilly, her beauty and her wit. He may be a four-time loser in marriage, but Hamilton believed it was never too late for *true* love. He was sure of that. He'd bet on it. He looked at the narrowing waters between the islands.

Hamilton masked his expression, revealing nothing of fear, and placed his bet. Was romance in the cards? Was Lilly the one? Should he attempt reconciliation with his son? Was it too late? He looked to the sky for an answer and steadied his course between the islands. Did his future hold any significance? Was his even a life worth saving? He committed his vessel deliberately into the shallow water. He felt his conscience pricked even as he did it. The first red buoy passed on the starboard side, then another to port. He braced himself for impact. A full minute passed. Nothing happened. He looked behind him to be sure he'd cleared the danger zone. The wake of the boat had sent gentle waves lapping onto the opposite shores. He had sailed straight through unharmed. God had allowed him to pass.

What did it mean? Was it an exercise of God's sovereign protection? Maybe God still had something important for Hamilton to do with his life. Perhaps he still had a crucial role to play. An all-in, Texas-Hold'em–style finale.

Ultimately, the house always wins. Hamilton didn't doubt that God would have the final say in his life. When it was time, God would end the game. Until then, Hamilton would continue to place his bets, keeping the odds in his favor as best he could. He'd stumbled upon Jack, his son, whom he hadn't seen regularly in years. After several awkward phone calls, his son had grudgingly agreed to look at the electric starter on the boat. Hamilton would see where that led and hope to learn more of his grandson, Cole. He'd go to the diner tomorrow, propose to Lilly again. Who knew? Maybe marriage would work out for him this time. He might find true love yet.

Hamilton glanced at his watch. He had lost himself to his reverie. Two hours. Time for a nap back at the dock before Jack arrived. Ham could easily afford to use the repair people up at the lake, but all of them were unreliable and charged more than they were worth. At least, that's the story he'd stuck to since first asking for Jack's help weeks earlier.

He prayed that time had numbed old wounds; particularly since he wasn't too sure how much time he had left. It was a long shot, but one Ham was willing to take. Besides, he'd learned another grandchild was on the way, and a genuine celebration was in order. He came about and sliced toward the marina. He was anxious about the meeting with his son. He wanted to strike a measured balance between wise old man and doddering grandfather. At this time in his life, Ham needed a reconciliation. More than that, he needed a friend who shared his DNA.

[chapter 5]

Lessons in Etiquette and Ethics

Most of the time, Essie's responsibilities as wife, mother, daughter, neighbor, and businessperson competed with each other in subtle, insidious ways. Other times, however, they weren't so discreet, smacking right into one another on the neighbor's front lawn for the amusement of the crowd, like five clowns.

Rayette and Buddy Lee were hosting the annual neighborhood garage sale. Every fall, Rayette planned a multifamily garage sale, invited all the neighbors to participate, and collected 10 percent off the top. She effectively lured participants by promising them the benefits of her robust advertising efforts, including ads in the local papers and a multitude of neon posters planted throughout a five-mile radius. She also offered the best location: a corner lot that attracted even more attention with its labeled aisles of shelving and its decorative display tables, creating a full retail effect.

Last year, Rayette had hosted her most successful garage sale yet. More than fifteen hundred dollars sold! Used baby clothes were the bestsellers. Rayette, however, hadn't called them *used*; she called them *pre-owned*. Her husband, Buddy, wouldn't be at the sale today because the weekends were the busiest time for his business. He worked at the Ford dealership in town. Rayette was confident she could manage just fine without him, explaining that he had already taught her everything there was to know about sales.

Using a few old dolls as models and a bench press as a makeshift clothes rack, she turned a trash bag full of wadded baby clothes into a genuine display that would rival any Baby Gap. Last year's success only mounted the anticipation of this year's yield. For Essie's part, she had widened the offer to participate to her extended family.

Ms. Ada Tuttle had dropped by the neighborhood garage sale to ask if anyone had seen Apostle Paul. Apostle Paul, AP for short, was a short-coated Chihuahua that had escaped from behind its fence two days ago. Ms. Tuttle had tacked posters throughout the neighborhood, offering a hundred-dollar reward for him. All the kids in the neighborhood had been on the lookout. The hundred-dollar bounty had channeled all their youthful energy. There had been several sightings and a couple of capture attempts.

For a while, it was a neck 'n' neck race between Mickey Weatherstone, the eight-year-old boy who lived next door, and Cole. The competition had turned ugly the previous night when Cole and Essie had walked down their driveway to get the mail. In response to a rustling of leaves behind the shrubbery, Cole called for Apostle Paul, but Mickey sprang out from the bushes with his flashlight. Mickey claimed he'd left a bologna sandwich and a blanket out there as bait for the dog and now the provisions had all gone missing. He narrowed his eyes at Cole and said, "Someone must've taken it."

"Not me," Cole insisted. Both boys turned their heads in unison toward Essie and eyed her suspiciously.

Essie assured them, "I may not be much of a cook, but I'd never steal a bologna sandwich from a dog."

The boys looked at each other with mounting determination. A new plan would have to be devised.

As soon as the garage sale opened for business, Rayette persuaded Mickey Weatherstone to purchase an armload of dog-trapping paraphernalia. No one had the heart to tell Mickey or Ms. Tuttle that Apostle Paul was lying dead in the median across from the Citgo station. Poor AP had been hit by a car earlier that morning.

Unaware of the tragedy, Mickey and his cohorts teamed up to buy an old Slip 'N Slide, a Fisher Price Pop-Up Playhouse, and a plastic hot dog all for $4.50. Before investing, they tested the trap in the woods across the street. They arranged the Slip 'N Slide at a sloping angle so creek water trickled down it. Taking turns, they each placed the plastic hot dog between their teeth and slid down into the tent-style playhouse, which collapsed on impact. Judging the trap effective, Mickey had placed the bait at the top of the Slip 'N Slide and then collected $4.50 from the boys. Enormously impressed with their own cunning, they returned to the sale with a bag full of coins and disclosed their plan. Rayette told the boys she'd take fifty cents off since she lost the toy fries that went with the hot dog. Essie suspected she did it because she felt guilty about selling a trap to catch a dead dog.

While Essie set up her own sale items, her father, known as Big Jim, brought over a few boxes of stuff to sell for Pearl. Essie knew Pearl leveraged the garage sale as an opportunity to make her husband clean out the basement. It was a dirty job her father would have to perform alone; Pearl did not participate in such chores. Sorting through a basement was a known sweat hazard.

Big Jim set out an old lawn mower, a bicycle with a broken chain, a singing bass mounted to a wooden plaque, and an original oil painting of a pack of tigers by Cousin Curtis. Curtis had generously passed along his artwork to Essie's mother. Sadly, it had not complemented her otherwise traditional home decor. Pearl had the prices of each item marked on the bottom with masking tape, but Essie and her father failed to notice that detail. So while Rayette sold a Weed Eater to the mailman and Big Jim hauled the lawn mower next door to get a second opinion on pricing, Essie sold the tiger painting to a Latino family for three dollars.

About that time, Pearl, with freshly polished nails and toes, drove up in her Mercedes. Soon after, Essie's sister, Emily, and her husband, Greg, pulled up in a rented U-Haul and unloaded a kitchen table and chairs, a couch, two accent chairs, and a dining-room table, basically the entirety of their downstairs furniture. They saw the garage sale as an opportunity to refresh their furnishings with updated decor for a new house, on which they'd just made an offer. Emily planned to stick around to see what sold and then head straight to Haverty's on her way home while she still had the U-Haul.

"Hey, everyone! I'm glad you could all come," Essie greeted her family. "Dad is next door with Jack and the kids. Go ahead and set up your displays. I'll let them know you are here."

Essie hurried across the lawn and found Jack, who, after occupying the kids with cartoons, had found refuge in his garage, where he'd spent the last half hour polishing the lawn mower Big Jim had brought over to sell.

"Take a look at her now." Jack sprayed the mower with a garden hose. When the water beaded and popped off the glistening paint to his satisfaction, he boosted the price marked on the bottom and turned his attention to his own lawn mower and repeated the process.

"Ours needed a shine, too. If we can get a decent price for this one, I'd like to get one of those new models."

"Honey, did you actually wax the lawn mowers?"

"Sure, why not? I treat my mowers the same way I'd treat a car or a motorcycle."

Both mowers sparkled like a pair of fiery gems.

Essie raised a brow. "I'll go check on the kids."

"OK, I'll haul these over to the garage sale."

In the den, Essie found Big Jim, feet propped up, dozing in front of cartoons, flanked on each side by a child.

"Hey, Dad. Thanks for watching the kids while we get organized next door."

"You bet." Jim fluffed a throw pillow behind his neck and reclined into the couch.

Satisfied the kids were under supervision, Essie made her way back to the sale. Upon arrival, she found Pearl stunned motionless in fear. Pearl had been busy showcasing the working condition of a two-dollar hair dryer to Ms. Tuttle. When Pearl plugged it into the wall outlet, the hair dryer caught fire in her hand, and she stood frozen, staring at it like a deer in headlights. Jack sped around the now full display of lawn and garden equipment, yanked the plug from the wall, and flung the smoking dryer from her hand. It let off a few last sparks and then lay there on the garage floor, lifeless.

"My word." Pearl clasped her cross pendant for safety. "It's a good thing you came to the rescue, Jack. If this had happened at home, it would surely have singed my curls."

"Anytime," Jack said. After one final inspection to make sure the beast was dead, he returned home to resume an unfinished motorcycle repair project in the garage.

Ms. Tuttle politely declined the hair dryer, saying she preferred to dry her hair naturally, anyway. She then added that, while the dog hunt continued, she might as well gussy up her contribution to the garage sale, a collection of vintage dolls.

"I have over a thousand dolls at home," she said proudly. "I've collected them for years. Since I lost my dear husband, they have been my family." She arranged the dolls in individual display cases alongside a baby clothing display, lovingly attending each one. "My dolls and my Chihuahuas are my babies. It's hard to part even with these duplicates. There is nothing more important than family, you know."

"Yes, I agree. I just feel like I have more than I can handle sometimes." Essie cupped her hand under her rounding abdomen.

Ms. Tuttle's eyes moistened, and she smiled warmly. "You don't realize how blessed you are, darling. The Lord will never give you more than you can handle. You just wait. That child will complete your heart."

"Thanks," Essie said, somehow feeling lighter. "Speaking of family, I better head back home to tend to mine."

It was approaching noon, so Essie darted home to cobble together a lunch for the kids. While they assembled a stack of peanut butter and jelly sandwiches, Jack and Essie reviewed the family schedule for the rest of the day.

"Don't forget about your promise to help your dad fix his boat."

Jack grimaced. "I remember. I'm just not looking forward to it. It galls me. I don't hear from him for years at a time, and then he calls three times this week. After so much time, why call me for help?"

Essie shrugged. "I don't know. But why don't you take Cole with you? I know how you feel about your dad, but a boy should know his grandfather."

Jack sighed. "Well, maybe that will ease the tension."

"While you're there, why don't you invite him over for dinner sometime?" Essie prodded. "It'd be nice for Juliet to see him, too."

"We'll see how it goes." Jack dodged any commitment on the matter. "Once a year is about all I can handle of the old man."

Once lunch was prepared, Essie collected a few new sale items from the attic and returned to the garage sale. When she arrived, Rayette was mediating a fight between two customers who wanted Big Jim's lawn mower. Pearl watched, visibly appalled, as Rayette settled the mower dispute in what she claimed was the only honorable way: an arm wrestling contest. The winner bought Big Jim's old mower for $150. Rayette passed the money directly to Pearl, who tucked the bills in her purse and, grumbling some comparison of arm-wrestling to humidity, employed a fifty-cent paperback as a fan.

Pearl fanned more vigorously as she watched the winner load his prize into a truck. The arm-wrestling ordeal had clearly flustered her, and Pearl was strongly adverse to perspiration. It was unseasonably warm and sticky for October. She claimed real ladies never perspire, only glisten on occasion.

"I don't mind the heat, but this humidity is simply un-Christian."

She stepped into the shade of the garage and eyed a one-dollar cocktail recipe book on the card table labeled "Literature."

"Whose is this?" She frowned, fanning herself with *Pride and Prejudice* in one hand and pinching the spine of the cocktail recipe book with the other, holding it out at arm's length.

"It's ours, from Jack's bartending days," Essie replied.

Pearl's fan waved furiously. "Why pass this filth on to anyone? I'd throw it away if I were you."

Back when Essie was in college, she and Jack had worked at the same restaurant. He was a bartender, and she was a waitress. Her mother disapproved vehemently of both jobs. Bars were for Philistine pagans, prostitutes, and the weak-minded. Jack pacified her by explaining that working behind a bar was a great place to demonstrate faith in action by befriending his patrons, remaining true to his convictions, and simply by being different. Jack held minor celebrity status as the only bartender in Atlanta who had never had a drink in his life. The restaurant managers chose Jack as head bartender when they recognized how his honesty and temperance guaranteed unparalleled control on bar costs.

Essie remembered Jack puzzling over drink orders behind the bar. With subtle gestures, he'd wave Essie over for help.

"Essie, margarita? Rum, right?"

"No." She'd smile. "Tequila."

He kept the cocktail recipe book behind the bar for reference when she wasn't there. That was sixteen years ago. Today, Jack and Essie both worked for Life Cola. Through a strange twist of events, they once again worked at the same company. He was in Marketing and she worked in Information Technology.

Pearl tossed the cocktail recipe book aside in disgust and fingered through the other books. Noticing the tiger painting missing, Pearl inquired about her proceeds.

"I hope you got a good price for Curtis's painting. It was a shame to let it go. If only he'd have painted hunting dogs or ducks. Unfortunately, feral cats clash with the picnic scenes on my toile drapery."

"They went to a good home," Essie consoled her. When she handed over the three dollars, Pearl's look pierced her with a fierceness the tigers could have only hoped for. Her mother remained forever poised though, and tactfully explained that it was worth at least fifty dollars, probably more, since it was a family heirloom.

Heirloom? Essie thought. That was like calling an okra patch a site on the National Registry of Historic Landmarks.

Her mother's speech remained slow and calm while her mouth stayed pinned in a tight smile and fury rose in her cheeks, blazing with the same red anger that glinted off her hair. Pearl's tone and expression picked the scab from old wounds, triggering the familiar pain of disappointing her. Essie tried to give her some cash out of her pocket, but her mother would not accept it. She clenched her jaw and turned away, saying under her breath that the whole event was as disgraceful as Cousin Curtis's goin'-back-to-jail sale last month.

"Hello, ladies. How is the sale coming along?" Jack, having completed his motorcycle repair, made his way across the worn bed of pine straw between the driveways.

"Evidently, there are some real bargains," Pearl said tersely and turned on a heel. She located Rayette and collected her remaining proceeds. "Someone better check on those children. Your father couldn't change a diaper." On her way next door, she exchanged a few words with Jack in hushed tones.

"What was that about?" Essie asked her husband.

"She'd like you to bring a few covered dishes to her Thanksgiving dinner next month." Jack hesitated, then added, "She said it's proper etiquette."

As the undisputed queen in the kitchen, Pearl had always discouraged anyone from bringing any food to her house on Thanksgiving. Now, she had told Jack it was bad manners for a lady to come to a dinner party without at least a casserole. Essie had never brought a covered dish to one of her mother's gatherings. Pearl knew Essie couldn't cook; her mother never let her set foot in her kitchen. Essie suspected this was her way of exacting revenge over the tiger painting. How was Essie to recognize heirloom quality in painted tigers? Then again, perhaps her mother was right; perhaps Essie had no more sophistication than Cousin Curtis. He would, no doubt, have approved of the exchange himself, considering that three dollars could've covered the cost of the singing bass and the cocktail recipe book. And if ever he was invited, he certainly wouldn't bring a covered dish to Thanksgiving!

Ms. Tuttle, having overheard Pearl's covered-dish request, leaned over to Essie and whispered, "I would be happy to share some easy recipes with you. I make casseroles for the disciples all the time."

"Disciples?" Essie asked.

"Oh, the dogs." She flushed. "My Chihuahuas are named after the disciples and other Bible characters." Then, as if the thought just hit her, she added, "Halloween is coming soon. You and your children must come visit me for trick or treat. Children love my babies. I'll give you some recipes and introduce you all to my dolls and the disciples."

"That sounds like fun," Essie said amused but doubtful. "This will be Juliet's first year to really enjoy trick or treat. We'll be sure to stop by."

Ms. Tuttle stared off beyond the trees. "I sure hope to find Apostle Paul before then. He loves company."

She still hadn't learned of AP's fate. Essie's heart hurt for her.

It was only mid afternoon, but customers had already begun to dwindle. Emily and Greg packed their one unsold chair into the U-Haul and left for Haverty's with big smiles on their faces and six hundred dollars in their pockets, after Rayette's commission.

Ms. Tuttle and Essie began packing away the meager remains from the bare tables into half-empty boxes lining the driveway while Rayette counted and faced the bills in her money tin.

Jack walked down the driveway to take down the poster-board sign as Walt Weatherstone, recent divorcé and part-time father to Mickey and Annabelle Weatherstone, pulled up to the curb in a shiny new Jaguar convertible. The two men walked together back up the driveway wearing passionate expressions, motioning wildly toward the car.

"How'd the sale turn out, folks?" Walt looped the loose arms of a white sweater around his neck and pulled a tennis ball from the pocket of his white shorts.

"Over twenty-five hundred dollars." Rayette beamed.

"Got any barbells for sale?" Walt asked. "A few curls could add some pep to my backhand and possibly my night life." He winked at Jack.

Jack ignored the innuendo but sat in a lawn chair gazing at Walt's Jag for a long moment.

"I think I have some light weights in a storage closet at home," Essie offered. "If I can find them, you're more than welcome to them."

"Sold," he said. "And congratulations to you, Rayette, darlin'. Let me be the first to welcome you to the next tax bracket." Walt tossed the tennis ball at Jack. "Heads up, buddy. Looks like you'll be in the market for a minivan pretty soon, eh?" He laughed smugly and gestured toward Essie's growing belly.

Jack, still admiring the Jag, managed to catch the ball at his chest. "So, Walt, what kind of mileage does she get?"

"Wanna experience a real beauty? Come take a closer look at her. First, though"—he turned back to Rayette, Ms. Tuttle, and Essie—"if you ladies see my son, Mick, please send him home. He's been hunting some mutt all day that I just found scattered all over the road." He raised his eyebrows at Jack and pointed with his chin to the new car. "She corners like a snake in a rat hole. It's breathtaking. C'mon, I'll take you for a spin."

Jack shrugged sheepishly and followed Walt down the driveway. Essie stacked the last of the boxes inside Rayette's garage, trying to think of what to say to Ms. Tuttle. When Essie turned to find her, she was already walking away. With hands covering her face, Ms. Tuttle crossed the lawn, cutting the distance to her house, and disappeared behind the trees.

Wearing a puzzled expression, Walt glanced over his shoulder at Ms. Tuttle's sudden retreat and under his breath said to Jack, "The ole gal's engine don't hit on all eight."

[chapter 6]

No Such Thing as Heroes

After his grandparents left, Cole sat slumped in front of the TV, still in his Spider-Man pajamas. Normally he looked forward to Saturday afternoons. But from the look on his face, it appeared life had taken a sudden and tragic turn.

"It's not fair," he protested to his mother. His shoulders sagged as if burdened with the weight of injustice.

"He's sulking because I told Juliet she could pick the next cartoon," Jack explained, keeping his voice low so Cole wouldn't hear.

Every other day of the week was structured with nonnegotiable routine, especially now that Cole was a kindergartner. Saturday was the only day he was not rushed to school or church and not coerced into a button-down shirt. On Saturdays, Essie often made giant pancake breakfasts and let Cole lounge in pj's till mid afternoon. If the weather was nice, Jack would usually take him on some sort of adventure. For Cole, Saturday meant riding bikes, playing ball, or going to the park. And best of all, Saturdays meant Saturday morning cartoons, his favorite part of the week.

Essie had been in and out of the house earlier that morning, sorting through the attic and dragging out armloads of merchandise for the neighboring yard sale. Instead of pancakes, she'd placed a bowl of instant oatmeal on the table in front of him. There it had remained, untouched, hardening to a beige cement by a sink still cluttered with breakfast dishes and crusts of PB&Js. *Oatmeal is so good for them*, she had reasoned. Then again, who was she kidding?

"I still have some work to do in the garage," Jack said, standing at the counter, sorting unsold garage sale items, which included a box of electronic equipment nested in loose wires.

"Dad, can I help?" Cole stood at the open garage door marveling over the gleam of chrome adorning the motorcycle and vintage Mustang.

"Not right now, Son. Let me sort out this mess. I need you to stay inside with your sister."

Cole cut his eyes at Juliet. "Sometimes having a sister ruins everything," he complained.

On this Saturday, Juliet flaunted even more sparkle than usual. Though it was nearing 2:00 PM, Juliet still featured her Tinker Bell pajamas. On the toes of her soft, green bedroom slippers hung two huge, yellow pom-poms, which bounced left and right when she walked. Essie noticed Cole sneering at his sister, as though Juliet had been out to get him from the start. Juliet carried the *Peter Pan* DVD case around with her. She held it up to Jack, doe-eyed and pleading.

"OK, twinkle toes," Jack said. He set the box of electronics aside and led the parade upstairs to the TV room.

"Aw, man!" Cole objected, but followed anyway. "Not *Peter Pan* again. I'm sick of *Peter Pan*."

Essie brought up the rear, helping Juliet climb the staircase.

"It's Juliet's turn to pick a show," Jack explained and popped in the disc. "You already watched a Superman cartoon this morning. Plus, you picked the movie last night. *Toy Story*. Remember?" Jack and Essie, on principle, had vowed to keep the number of TVs in their house to one. With that decision came the continued responsibility to arbitrate all TV disputes in a quick and judicial fashion.

Essie overheard the debate as she fumbled through the storage closet, searching for the promised weights for Walt. She found two, eight-pound barbells. Such equipment had become superfluous now that she had children to carry around. Lifting kids offered plenty of strength training.

"But Dad, *Peter Pan* is for babies."

"I thought you liked cartoons, Son."

"I do, but Dad—" Cole dropped his voice to a whisper so Juliet couldn't hear. "I don't like baby shows. Peter Pan and Tinker Bell aren't real. I'm five years old now. I like shows about real heroes like Spider-Man or Batman."

"Or Superman?" Jack smiled.

"Yeah! Superman!" Cole stretched his arms wide and flew excitedly in a circle around the family room. "I can fly!"

Essie carried an armload of dusty exercise equipment through the room, pausing as Jack knelt down and laid a hand on his son's shoulder. "Son, those guys aren't real, either. They are make-believe, too."

Cole froze. The DVD menu glowed on the TV screen. The scene was repeating, waiting for someone to press play. Peter Pan, Tinker Bell, Wendy, and the boys flying toward Neverland with outstretched arms. The smiles on their airborne faces and the familiar chorus repeated joyfully, "*I can fly, I can fly, I can fly.*" From the betrayed look on her son's face, Essie understood. He felt mocked.

"I'm sorry, Son." Jack rose and pressed the play button on the remote. "I've got some work to do if we're still going to go to the lake. I'll be back to check on you in a bit." Jack headed down the stairs.

Juliet rose to her tiptoes and held her closed fists over Cole's head. She popped her hands open and closed, and wiggled her little round fanny, dousing her brother with a generous dose of invisible fairy dust.

"Fly, fly, fly," she insisted.

"Stop it!" Cole screamed as he ran out of the room. Juliet watched him retreat down the hall and then flopped on an oversized pillow in front of the TV and stuck a thumb in her mouth.

Essie put down the hand weights and followed her son to his room. Cole sat on his bed, obviously thinking things over.

"You and Dad tricked me," he accused, kicking over a toy basket by the bed. A pile of action figures spilled out: Power Rangers, GI Joes, Luke Skywalker, Mr. Incredible.

"Oh, honey," Essie soothed, kneeling by his bed. "We never meant to trick you."

"None of them are real. They don't have any superpowers at all. There is no such thing as heroes in real life. It's all baby stuff. Just make-believe baby stuff."

"Cole, those shows are just stories, not lies. Make-believe stories aren't bad. They help you learn to use your imagination."

Cole shot upward in his bed, his brow wrinkled with concern. He narrowed his eyes at his mother. "What about the tooth fairy, then?" Cole challenged. "Is she make-believe, too?"

A few weeks ago, Essie and Jack had tucked Cole in after he drifted to sleep. Jack had swept his hand under Cole's pillow, fumbling around for a tiny pewter box Essie had given Cole for his first lost tooth. When he woke up, a crisp dollar bill lay in the box where his tooth had been.

Essie paused. "I'm sorry, Son. Your dad and I just wanted to make it fun and exciting for you." She stroked his sandy hair. "I love you, honey."

Cole's eyes welled up, and his face reddened. "You tricked me!" He covered his face in his hands and then turned, burying himself into his pillow.

"I'm not dumb," he shouted through muffled sobs.

"Cole, honey, of course you're not dumb. No one thinks you're dumb." Essie reached out to comfort him.

Cole shrunk away from her. Then, jumping out of bed, he pulled the Spider-Man pajama top over his head and slipped out of the pants. He chose a pair of jeans and a T-shirt from his dresser. Essie followed as he wadded the Spider-Man pj's under his arm, headed to the kitchen, and tossed them in the trash.

With all the pride he could muster, Cole made his way to the garage to confront his father. Jack was sitting on the floor of the garage, loading all manner of gear into a toolbox. Essie stood at the open door and sent Jack a look of warning.

"Dad, are there any superheroes in real life?" Cole swallowed hard, bracing himself for the truth.

Jack looked up from the toolbox and noted Essie's expression.

"Come on over here, Son." Cole walked over to his dad. Jack wrapped an arm around his son's narrow hips and pulled him into his lap. "Of course there are. Real heroes are everywhere."

Cole cocked his head to one side, taking a posture of distrust.

"They may not be able to fly or leap tall buildings, like Superman. But there are definitely real heroes." He looked his son square in the eyes. "This is the truth, Son. In this world, there is real good and real bad. Anyone who stands up for good in this world is a hero. A hero is someone who does the right thing no matter what it costs."

"You mean someone who uses the force to fight the dark side, like Luke Skywalker and Darth Vader?"

"Yes, something like that. Luke Skywalker and Darth Vader are not real, but Jesus is real. Jesus is the greatest real-life superhero there ever was. He has already defeated the dark side forever. Now we get to watch as his victory unfolds."

"Whoa! Really?" Cole's eyes widened. He redirected the question to his mom, his face a picture of hope.

Essie nodded to him, her heart full.

Cole swung back around to his dad. "You promise?"

"Really! Now, c'mon. Help me get these tools packed up. Then, we gotta head up to the lake to see your grandfather."

Cole sighed with deep relief. "It's pretty cool to know a real superhero, isn't it, Dad?"

"It sure is, Son." Jack squeezed Cole to his chest. "It's incredible."

[chapter 7]

Twisting wrenches

Hamilton woke to the rumble of an approaching engine. Jack's Mustang GT rolled to a stop in the gravel space beside the dock. A medley of gently lapping waves, duck calls, and clattering marine hardware carried through the breeze. Peering through the trees, he could see his grandson watching Jack pop the trunk of the classic car and lift out a toolbox the size of a large suitcase. The sun bounced off the new box; its Craftsman red sparkled like a gemstone. The Mustang, also, glistened with fresh wax and polish. Its black paint gleamed like onyx.

Hamilton recalled that, according to Jack, cleanliness was next to godliness. And in that respect, his cars, motorcycles, lawn mowers, and even his toolbox, were irrefutably sanctified. Surely God held a special place for them in the heavenly realm. For his son's sake, Ham hoped that somewhere in the backdrop of the holy Trinity sprawled an eternal garage, bays of spotless machinery stretching into infinity.

It was scriptural, Jack had once explained to his father. John 14 promised as much. *"In my Father's house are many rooms; if it were not so, I would have told you. I am going there to prepare a place for you."* Ham figured if the Lord were preparing a place especially for Jack, it was sure to have at least a three-car garage. Ham expected his son looked forward to an eternity in the heavenly garage where he and Jesus might one day work side by side, twisting wrenches together. Until then, Jack would no doubt keep his equipment in pristine condition. So when the time came, Hamilton knew Jack, his Mustang, and his toolbox would be ready. Despite what they say about taking no earthly treasures into the afterlife, Jack seemed to have every intention of taking it all with him. There was, after all, an exception to every rule.

Despite his meticulously maintained equipment, Hamilton suspected that Jack still craved something more to show for his life than well-maintained belongings. Something with more lasting value. He had much to be grateful for already: a loving wife, two beautiful kids, a third on the way, and a promising career in marketing. Still, Ham guessed, something was missing. He recalled a dream Jack often spoke about when he was young. He had hoped to own his own motorcycle shop. Hamilton now regretted having laughed at him. Ham never appreciated motorcycles. Quite the opposite, Hamilton preferred sailing, a sport that never went any faster than the wind carried him.

Nevertheless, motorcycles had fascinated Jack since he was a boy. He loved everything about them: the engineering, the unthinkable speed, the artistry of the machine. After Jack's mother died, Hamilton had grown quiet and distant, often retreating to his boat and leaving Jack at home in the garage, tinkering on bicycles. As soon as Jack came of age, he'd taken a full-time job and moved out on his own. One job led to another, and before long he landed in corporate America.

Hamilton had made plenty of mistakes as a father, but he'd always had one unique gift. He knew how to read people. He could read their cards from the look on their faces. Without ever discussing it, he knew his son had traded a dream for the safety and security that corporate marketing seemed to offer. He was sure Jack was good at his job. But in the early mornings, before daybreak, while all was still quiet, Hamilton bet a dollar to a dime that Jack woke up with an uncertain feeling in the pit of his stomach. Ham wondered whether marketing beverages was Jack's true calling. Somehow, peddling pop didn't seem significant enough for Jack in the grand scheme of things. Corporate success, as Ham knew from experience, wasn't as soul-satisfying as it seemed. A father longs to build something permanent. He wants to invest his life in something that will last long after he is gone. Something his children could carry on. Deep down, Ham ached to leave a legacy of his own and suspected his son felt the same way.

Hamilton felt the motion of their weight upon the dock, the planks see-sawing under their feet. He waved them over to his boat, *Mutual Funs*, a forty-five-foot sloop that swayed at the end of the dock. Hamilton Wells sat at the stern, a John Deere cap pulled down over his eyes.

"Hey, Pop," Jack greeted his father.

Hamilton stretched and removed his cap. He blinked and rubbed his knuckles into his eye sockets, wiping away sleep from a recent nap.

"Mornin', Son," Hamilton greeted Jack. "Where'd your boy go?" He squinted his gray eyes in the autumn sun and quickly spotted his grandson, Cole, lagging behind, exploring the shoreline for shells and minnows.

"Morning? It's after 5:00 PM, Pop."

"Yeah, so what's your point?" Hamilton grinned and extended a hand to help Jack with his load. "C'mon aboard."

Jack lugged the tool chest aboard. "The point is that it's afternoon, not morning," he said flatly.

"On the lake, time is a matter of perspective." Hamilton chuckled and shook his head. "Like everything else, why don't we just agree to disagree?"

Jack sighed as he surveyed the boat's various signs of disrepair. He frowned as he regarded the slip mate's vessel, perhaps seeking an acceptable standard but finding none.

"Looks like every boat around here could use some repairs."

The handrails and, for that matter, all the wood trim on Ham's and Noodle's boats needed to be taken down to raw wood and a coat of Celox applied. Outright replacement was not out of the question. Aboard *Mutual Funs,* Jack noticed a portion of the main sail poking out of the sail cover. Sections of the bimini cover were almost rubbed through. A few lazy red wasps lingered about in hope the resident would soon leave and give them a chance at homesteading.

Jack and Hamilton had a difficult time seeing eye to eye. Father and son sat on opposite ends of the spectrum in many ways. If cleanliness was the path to righteousness, Hamilton and his boat were in serious trouble. The deck floor was streaked with lake grime. Soggy towels, old clothes, crumpled newspaper, and bits of tin foil littered the hatch. Mosquitoes swarmed in the damp air above the cabin entrance.

"Flying teeth, that's what they are," Hamilton remarked, swatting half-heartedly at the living cloud.

"How can you live in this place?" Jack asked.

Hamilton turned his palms up. "That's what I ask myself all the time. Hard to believe, ain't it? I surely don't deserve to be this well-off. Paradise on earth," Hamilton responded, intentionally missing the point. "I have to pinch myself every time I wake to make sure all this is real." Ham thought of their impasse as essentially a struggle between form and function.

Jack stooped over the inboard motor. He pressed the button to start the engine. The machinery responded with a couple of halfhearted clicks.

"I've had to rely on the auxiliary outboard anytime I take her out. Think you can fix it, Son?" Hamilton asked.

"C'mon, Pop. I can fix anything." He crouched over the engine block and studied it silently for a long moment. Hamilton watched his son. He could sense a sort of mystical exchange between man and machine.

Suddenly, Jack launched into action. His hands moved with certainty and purpose. He pulled a wrench from his tool box and applied it to an electrical connection at the base of the starter motor.

When it came to electronics, Ham had mastered only the barest minimum required to avoid death or serious injury as a live-aboard. He marveled at Jack's mastery over all that was internally combustible or electrical.

"With your handiwork and my sense of style, we could make quite a pair. Might even turn a few bucks. Ever think of going into the repair business? You used to be interested in that sort of work. All the folks up here already are shiftless and no account. We'd put 'em out of business in no time. I could handle the—what do you call 'em—public relations."

Jack brushed off the idea. "Nah, never as comfortable with boats as I am tending to bikes."

Ham knew, of course, that Jack could do it, but if he ever did such a thing, it would be on dry land and have two wheels. His son returned his attention to the repair at hand. Within minutes, Jack had tracked down and fixed a broken wire in the electric start circuit.

As Hamilton watched the natural way his son worked with the machine, his mind drifted to a distant memory. It was before Jack was born. The Vietnam conflict commanded the country's attention. His friend Jesse was just a kid then, only eighteen years old. He and Hamilton, then twenty-three, were both infantrymen. Jesse had an easy manner with machines, also. He was a skilled marksman and naturally fearless, which meant his eagerness often needed to be restrained. Hamilton, though never quite comfortable with all the military equipment, had a natural way with people and with cards that Jesse admired. Most of all, Jesse admired his magnetic leadership. Jesse claimed that anyone near Hamilton was sure to be on the winning side. So Jesse stuck close to Ham when their troop was deployed to Southeast Asia.

Hamilton remembered the patrol and his troop leader's order: "There is a clearing ahead. Recon. Two men." Hamilton had chosen Jesse. "Look out for snipers," he added.

Crouching together behind the tree line, Hamilton and Jesse studied an apparently abandoned village.

"Go on, Jess. Take point." Hamilton nudged Jesse. "I'll cover you."

Jesse's eyes lit up. He was used to following, not leading. He nodded and moved out into the clearing. Jesse was about twenty yards away when Hamilton heard the shot. From the brush, Ham watched his friend grab his stomach and double over. A shot to the middle might not be fatal if he got medical treatment fast enough. He wanted to run to Jesse, but his feet refused. The sniper was waiting, and Jesse was already too far away. Hamilton shrank back into the jungle.

Hamilton could not forget the look on Jesse's face as he tumbled to the ground, lifting his head only long enough to search the tree line for rescue. Ham stood frozen behind the tree line and watched the hope drain from Jesse's face. It was a look of fear and shock, but also of lonely resignation.

Even now, more than forty years later, Jesse's face jumped out at him on a small sailboat on the opposite side of the world. That look filled Hamilton with a shame so complete that the memory alone threatened to crush him in its clenched fist.

Jack brushed his hands on his jeans. "That ought to do it." He had replaced the cover before testing the repair. Supreme confidence. He switched the starter button. The engine sputtered and rumbled to life. Jack smiled contentedly, as though savoring the sense of accomplishment.

"It's not a bad idea, really. A repair shop." Jack spoke in the direction of the breeze. "Too bad this old tub doesn't have wheels."

Hamilton raised an eyebrow, amused by the nibble of interest.

Cole joined them with a small bucket of treasures he had collected near the shore.

"What you got there, my boy?" Hamilton peered into the bucket. "Pirate's gold?"

"Only some shells," Cole answered, fixing attention back to the shoreline for riches he might have missed.

"You're growing faster than kudzu, boy," Ham noted with approval.

Cole stared at him with a puzzled look that suggested he had no idea what kudzu was.

Ham turned his attention back to Jack. "Well, I wouldn't be much help to you fixing bikes but I do know some folks. Might help get things rolling," he suggested.

Jack polished the wrench with his shirt front, returned it to its slot, and snapped the lid of his toolbox closed. He shook his head as if to clear the fog of a daydream. "Nah, no thanks. What do I know about running a repair shop? That was a kid's dream. I'm forty-two years old now. It's a bit late in life to decide what I want to be when I grow up. Besides, Essie would never go for it. She and the kids need stability right now—especially with another baby on the way."

Hamilton shrugged. "Whatever you say, Son. And congratulations again to you and that bride of yours! You sure got yourself a fine family." He winked in Cole's direction. "But lemme know if you change your mind about the repair shop. I run a diner that doesn't even pay me. I'm sixty-six, single, and more-or-less homeless. What do I have to lose? A career change could do me some good."

Jack chuckled and regarded him for a moment.

"Come here, my boy." Hamilton motioned to Cole. "I almost forgot. I got something for you."

Ham ducked into the cabin and returned with a small wooden boat.

"Whittled it myself. Thought you might like to have it. Floats, too!"

Cole's eyes lit up. "Wow!" The boy held the delicately carved wood reverently in his hands.

Ham crouched and wrapped an arm around Cole but spoke to his son. "Long time ago, I wanted to be a craftsman, but the tides carried me in a different direction. So now I just whittle on occasion. Reckon it's never too late to dream." He stood and faced Jack.

Jack studied his father.

"I suppose. Well, we better get going." Jack helped Cole out of the boat. Cole's young face beamed with delight over his new treasure.

Hamilton watched his son head back down the dock. The purposeful stride, the broad shoulders, the way he shifted the weight of the toolbox from one side to the other. His eyes moistened at the shape shrinking in the distance. A weighty helplessness pinned him against the railing. Hamilton pulled his cap down tight over his watery eyes. It wasn't the first time he'd stood silent as that very shape walked away from him.

Suddenly, Jack turned around and asked, nonchalant, "Why don't you come over to the house sometime? Join us for dinner?"

"Be glad to, Son! What's on the menu?"

"Who knows? Why, got something particular in mind?"

"You know me, Son. I'm easy to please." He paused, then added, "But age has refined my pallet. Ribs come to mind. No napkins allowed 'til you're done. Might as well be sporting about it!"

"I'll see what I can do," Jack said. "Let me check with Essie on a date."

"You let me know, Son. I'll be there." Hamilton nodded. "With my own barbecue sauce."

Jack shook his head and called over his shoulder, "See you then, crazy old man."

Before Jack reached the end of the dock, the air exploded with the crack of snapping wood and crushing fiberglass. Ham turned in horror to see what was happening to his neighborhood.

[chapter 8]

That Sinking Feeling

When Ham turned to confront the groaning noise, he watched in shock as Noodle's boat sank in its slip. The forty-odd-foot Catalina, *Liquid Assets,* did not go gracefully. The mooring lines, not designed to hold the entire weight of a doomed boat, put up a fight but snapped with a loud pop. The orange, shore power line met the same fate and snapped in two. It was secured in a locking receptacle but snapped and thrashed in the water for a second or two before shorting out. Ham instantly calculated the boat was in about thirty-five feet of water since both vessels were near the end of the pier. As the boat settled, three or four feet of mast remained above lake level.

Ham's brain sounded a shrill, red alert at the realization that Noodle could be trapped in the boat. He yelled for help. With some presence of mind, Ham stripped to his skivvies, scampered off the boat, up the pier, and jumped into the water where the aerometer was spinning insanely. Taking a deep breath, Ham grabbed the protruding mast piece and pulled himself under the water. Hand over hand, he pulled himself lower.

Visibility was a problem. Lake Lanier was a far cry from the crystal clear waters favored by divers. He could see about two feet in front of his face. He found the cabin of the boat and determined that the hatch cover lock was open. Ham figured that if it were open, Noodle would have already surfaced had he been on board. Still, he had to be sure.

With his lungs about to burst, Ham surfaced. His wide-eyed son and grandson stood agape on the pier. Without a single word exchanged, Ham sucked in a gulp of air and again descended to the sunken cockpit of *Liquid Assets* and entered the murky cabin. His slip mate wasn't home. Ham could rest easy and let the salvage folks do the rest.

Relieved, Ham paddled back to the surface. The floating dock finger had been permanently torqued at an angle, bowed as if in reverence to the stricken sailboat. Ham scrabbled back to the main section of the dock to report to his family members.

"Thank God, Noodle's not aboard," he wheezed, trying to catch his breath.

"Good heavens, Pop! You could've seriously hurt yourself down there."

"Had to take that chance, Son. Time was critical. Doesn't take but a moment or two to drown."

In the distance, he heard sirens. Jack had evidently called Fire and Rescue.

"Better late than never," Jack observed.

"That was really cool, Granddad. It was sort of like Aquaman." Cole glanced up at his dad. "Only real."

"Doesn't get any realer, Cole."

Ambling down the pier was Noodle, who dropped the small package he was carrying and turned from his normal pink shade to a sickly gray when he noticed his empty slip with only a mast protruding at an odd angle.

The marina was fairly deserted, but those few who were within earshot when *Liquid Assets* sank were hustling to see the aftermath of the disaster.

"Well, I can see you're not aboard now," Ham observed dryly.

"What happened?" Noodle asked, staring at the water where his home had been.

"Must have been that valve we were discussing the other day. When they go, so does the boat. Should have tended to it right away. Now she's salvage. Down in Davy Jones' locker."

"Who's Davy Jones, Pop? Is he a superhero I don't know about?" Cole asked innocently but with a touch of skepticism.

"No," Jack answered. "Davy Jones is not exactly a superhero. He's a name for the keeper of all things that sink."

"Put your stuff on my boat," Ham offered the still relatively mute Noodle. "Might want to call Mo's Salvage. Things are a mess down there, but the longer she stays under, the worse she'll be."

As Noodle stowed his small package aboard *Mutual Funs,* Hamilton considered the state of disrepair he'd let her fall into. He made a mental note: *Must find a better place to stash all that money.*

Fire and Rescue arrived at the head of the pier, and Ham and Noodle met them midway down the dock to assure them everyone was unharmed. The men insisted on giving Hamilton a brief inspection anyway. After issuing Ham a clean bill of health, the men stood back and stared at the old man, still barely dressed and dripping lake water, and the whole crowd shared a hardy belly laugh. Ham waved his goodbye and stepped aboard *Mutual Funs* while Noodle finished up some paperwork on the wreckage with the rescue team. Back aboard Ham's sailboat with his son and grandson, the first to speak was Cole: "My granddad is a hero!"

Hamilton laughed sheepishly. "Don't be too impressed. Noodle owes me for lunch last week. I can't let him off the hook that easy. A hero is someone willing to sacrifice himself to help others," Ham explained, "sort of like those rescue squad people, or soldiers, or policemen."

"But, Dad, you said anyone who does the right thing no matter what it costs is a hero, right? Like Jesus."

Jack tousled his son's hair. "Yeah, well, I'm not sure this quite qualifies for hero status."

Ham winked at Cole. “He’s right, my boy. I didn’t even get to save ole Noodle. I’m not a hero, but I still got a few tricks up my sleeve.”

Cole stood studying his grandfather as though suspecting he could breathe underwater.

“After all this excitement, I believe everyone could use a little refreshment,” Ham suggested.

“Ham, do you have Mo’s mobile number?” Noodle walked over, folding his paperwork unevenly and stuffing it in his back pocket.

“It’s in the Rolodex by the phone in the salon. Listed under *salvage*.”

Noodle stepped aboard and headed below deck to locate the number.

Ham prepared a round of soft drinks while Noodle called Mo’s Salvage.

“You really surprised me, Pop. Can’t recall ever seeing you move that fast,” Jack observed. “Good thing you left your skivvies on when you dived in.” Everyone laughed except Cole. He was still staring suspiciously at his grandfather, as if he were hiding a secret identity.

“Probably wouldn’t have been the first time someone got naked at the lake. Probably different circumstances, though.” Ham’s response triggered another chuckle.

Noodle looked up from the phone. “Matter of fact, just last—”

“They’re minors present, Noodle. Stow it,” Ham cautioned.

“Right, Ham.” Noodle spoke into the receiver, summed up the situation, and then turned to Ham. “Mo wants to know how many feet of water she’s in.”

Ham peered down into the water. “Thirty to forty. Wedged into some trees. She’s upright.”

Noodle relayed Ham’s assessment into the phone and, in lieu of directions, described his dock address as “the one next to Hamilton Wells’s.”

“He says he’ll be right over to survey the job,” Noodle announced after hanging up. “Reckon I better call the insurance company, too.”

Shaking his head despairingly, Noodle stepped off the boat, taking the phone with him, and headed toward the far end of the dock.

"I expected Mo might be available. It does help to know people." Ham glanced at his grandson and stuffed a few fingers in his shirtsleeve. "That's one of the tricks I still have up here."

Cole narrowed his eyes again. "Are you sure you're not a superhero?" he blurted, clearly unconvinced by his grandfather's protest.

Ham laughed. "No, Son. What I did is not that special. It's just friendship. Noodle and I don't keep score; we help each other out all the time. Not too sure what I'd have done if I'd found Noodle down there. You, on the other hand, are family. I'd take a speeding bullet for you without a second thought." Ham turned his gaze to his son, Jack, and allowed the statement to hover in the silence between them.

Cole nodded in understanding, though he still appeared unsettled on the matter.

"Why don't you go feed the ducks, Cole?" Jack suggested. Cole brightened, only too happy to comply. Noodle was still on the phone. There was a palpable silence between Ham and Jack as Cole gathered a few slices of bread and skipped down the dock toward shore. Ham sensed that something significant was going to be discussed.

"That was a pretty special thing you did, Pop. Not so sure I'd have had the presence of mind to jump in if I had been in your shoes. I'm glad Cole got to see that. He's been asking about heroes a lot today, and you're a hero in his eyes now. Takes a little pressure off me, having to leap tall buildings in a single bound. Sometimes being a father is a pressure cooker."

Ham nodded. "You must be doing something right. You got a fine young man there."

"Yeah." Jack swelled with pride. "He takes after his mother." The rigging sung against the mast as they watched young Cole toss a fistful of breadcrumbs to a gathering of ducks at the shore.

Hamilton decided the time was right. "Son, I know we've had our differences; you take more after your mother, too, a more careful steward of the things entrusted in your care. I know I let you down in the past. I reckon I could've used a bit of superhero strength when you were about his age. But one thing's for sure, there is no way to escape being a father figure, whether for good or bad."

"On that we can agree, Pop. I was angry with you when Mom died. I guess I thought you could fix anything, but you didn't fix her. And then you checked out on me, too. Sometimes, I think I'm still not over it."

"Nor I, Son. I did a little commodities trading back then, and well, I used the job to numb my pain. I wasn't there for you like I should have been. I wanted to be strong for you, but the fact is I had no strength myself. It was never that I didn't care for you, Son. I just didn't know what to do." Ham's eyes misted. This was a breakthrough he had feared would never happen.

Jack looked away, lightening the intensity of the moment. "There's probably a lot of truth to that, Pop. Why don't we just agree that from now on you can help share the superhero duties. It's a stressful job."

"Glad to. I'd like to get Cole up here for a sleepover."

Noodle approached from a distance and hollered, "The insurance company will send out an adjustor today." He climbed back aboard *Mutual Funs* to rejoin the men. "Don't know why we need an estimate. She's got to be raised. Corps won't allow her to stay down there. Navigation hazard and all. Apparently couldn't have picked a better day for her to sink. Imagine all these experts being so available on such short notice."

Cole returned, breadless.

"How about a couple of hot dogs on the grill while we wait?" Ham asked. Anticipating the answer, Noodle fired up the propane grill mounted on the stern handrail.

As the four finished their hotdogs and colas, Mo Pirkle, of Mo's Salvage, walked up to the boat, dragging a small cart filled with equipment. He and Noodle chatted for a moment, and Mo started donning his scuba gear. "It'll be a barrel job," Mo explained. "I'll go down and attach plastic drums to the hand rails, fill them with air from one of my tanks, and she'll pop right up. The trick is to find and fix the leak so that when she comes up she can be stabilized." With that, he put on his mask and fins and slipped into the watery grave of *Liquid Assets.*

Cole's eyes were wide in wonder. "Just like Aquaman, Dad! You think maybe they're part of a secret team?" he asked, still suspicious.

"No, Son," Jack replied. "He's just an expert."

Cole dismissed further protest. "I hope Mom hasn't emptied the trash yet!"

[chapter 9]

creamed spinach, chardonnay, and other WMD

Everyone was enormously pleased that the garage-sale junk had brought such a record-breaking haul. With Essie's negotiation skills honed by the weekend's events, it wasn't long before the workweek brought an opportunity to apply her sharpened talent to a messy business of another sort.

Arriving home from work later than usual for a Monday, Essie stepped into the kitchen through the garage door.

Juliet was playing on the den rug, surrounded by noisy toys. She smashed a singing dinosaur against the floor repeatedly and squealed with delight while Jack force-fit the last baby bottle in the top rack of the dishwasher.

"Can't you get home from work any earlier?" he complained.

"Sorry, honey. Cathcart held a late meeting. My new boss has some ideas for radical change."

Jack cast a sharp glare in her direction. "I have a few ideas for radical change myself."

Frowning at the empty bottom rack of the dishwasher, he brushed past Essie and into the adjacent garage. He came back with an armload of hub caps and stacked them upright, side by side in the dish brackets.

Then, he arranged a bouquet of screw drivers, wrenches, and T-handles into the silverware tray, poured in the detergent, closed the washer door, and threw the switch.

"Honey, are you loading tools and car parts in the dishwasher again?"

Essie was accustomed to her husband's eccentricities when it came to his equipment. Jack felt compelled to fill every space in the dishwasher before running a load.

"Yeah, so? Tools should be cleaned, too."

Essie shrugged. Her husband took clean seriously.

The stuffed dinosaur sang Elvis tunes to Juliet while Jack finished wiping down the kitchen counters. On all fours, Juliet rocked her diapered bottom to the music, used a coffee table to pull herself upright, and toddled away from the blanket of toys.

"Les wock." Juliet mimicked her singing toy. The dinosaur was halfway through "Jailhouse Rock" when Juliet reached a tightly knotted sisal rug and threw up her creamed spinach and diced carrots.

For Jack, this was a call to arms. Battle cries sounded from both sides of the kitchen counter: Jack let out a mournful wail, and the baby began to bawl.

Before Essie could react, Jack had pulled out granite polish, dishwashing detergent, stain remover, glass cleaner, stainless steel cleaner, furniture polish, hardwood floor cleaner, and three varieties of carpet cleaner. So stood the first row in Jack's chemical arsenal under the kitchen sink. The cleaning agents, all neatly aligned and front-facing, were battle-ready weapons of dirt destruction.

Carpet cleaner and scrub brush in hand, Jack worked to repair the damage. The dark green slick on the carpet was scrubbed until the spot wore thin and turned a bleached shade of the original color.

"It's a constant battle. And the worst part is no controls or intelligence can fully prepare for or prevent a creamed-spinach attack." Exasperated but not without his sense of humor, Jack drew upon language from a presidential-election campaign.

"This calls for a sustained, comprehensive campaign," he insisted, "and you, dear, are now appointed head of Homeland Security."

"Security commissioner?"

"There's just way too much to do around here. We need to make some changes."

"What kind of changes?"

"Security policies, for starters," Jack began, tidying up the assortment of cleaning supplies and collecting a pile of soiled dishtowels. "I count on you to enforce preventative measures to mitigate the continual threat of mass property destruction. As wife, mother, and Homeland Security Commissioner, isn't it your job to keep the home clean and orderly?"

Jack took order seriously.

Juliet rested her head on Essie's shoulder. Essie carried her up the steps and laid her in her crib.

A moment later, Essie returned to Jack. She flopped down in an oversized armchair and gently rubbed her fingers along her growing belly. "Honey, do you want to talk about what is really bothering you?"

He paused, looked down at her, face stern, uneasy. When his eyes narrowed on her swelling stomach, she felt a sudden wave of anxiety. They both shared fears about sustaining their pace of life with two full-time jobs and soon-to-be three small children. He walked around the kitchen counter and sat with her in the wide chair.

"Ellison," he began. At the sound of her full name, she braced herself. "I think I'm having a midlife crisis." He seemed to pause for her reaction, but she held her breath and silently waited for him to continue. "I'm forty-two years old with two, well, almost three kids. My youth is gone, and the rest of my life is passing me by. The first half is over, and I haven't done many of the things I want to do. I work hard; we both do. Together, we make good money but rarely get to stop and enjoy the fruits of our labor." He looked intently into her eyes as if to make sure she was following all this.

"The thing is: I plan to make some changes about the quality of my life in its second half. And that's where I need your help."

He linked his fingers in hers, and a sly grin spread across his face. She recognized the look, and she was flooded with the realization that he had been hatching this plan for a while. Jack had seemed lost in thought ever since he and Cole had returned from the lake and relayed their adventure with her father-in-law.

She anticipated something big, but his tone was light so she breathed a sigh of relief and proceeded with caution. "What did you have in mind?"

"A Porsche," he answered, with a mischievous curve to his lips.

"Really?" She raised her eyebrows in disbelief. Thus encouraged, he spilled his proposal.

"See, we both work full time, and we both make decent salaries. But every dollar I make goes directly into the family's expense account. After we pay the mortgage and all the bills every month, I have nothing left. You, on the other hand, pour all your paychecks into our nest-egg accounts. All part of our plan, I know, for our future and for the kids, but shouldn't I get to splurge on myself once in a while?"

Essie endured this patiently; she suppressed an angry impulse, thinking of his motorcycle and his souped-up Mustang GT. He continued, "I work hard, Essie. I even enjoy my job, but it's not the bike shop I always dreamed of owning. I love being married to you and being a father, but if I'm totally honest, sometimes I feel a little hemmed in by all the responsibility. It's not that I'm unhappy, honey, but the corporate job, the wife and kids, the whole package shouldn't have to mean giving up on other dreams, should it? I'm not ready to give them up. But I have a solution."

He hesitated for a second and then blurted out, "I can use our savings to buy a Porsche for Christmas." He produced an *Auto Trader* magazine out of nowhere and flipped it open to a dog-eared page featuring an ad for a 1987 Carrera convertible.

In such negotiations, corporate training kicked into gear. The year before, Jack and Essie had held a marital summit that resulted in a businesslike agreement involving one motorcycle trip in exchange for a separate family vacation. They'd each learned their lessons well and perfected their own techniques. One of hers was not to give away her position too soon. So, expressionless, she raised her elbow to the armrest and rested her chin between thumb and forefinger, a position of serious contemplation, evaluation.

"It'd be a loan actually," he explained. "Twenty thousand. I'll replace the money when I get my bonus, but the family savings account has the cash I need now. This car is a cherry, honey. I have to make my move now."

Inside her head, Essie was screaming, *He must be insane! What does a family of five need with a Porsche convertible?!*

"What's in it for me?" she stalled, while trying to think of a delicate way to say that it was the worst idea she'd ever heard and then suggest he seek counseling.

He seemed startled by her less-than-violent response and evidently interpreted it as cause for hope. A flame rose in his eyes. "What do you want, honey?" he asked, looking for any wedge to open a sincere negotiation.

She was taken off guard by his question. "I don't know," she answered honestly.

"C'mon, Essie. I really, really want this car. What are we planning to use our savings for in the next few months, anyway? I'll pay the account back. Owning a car like this is a dream for me. It's part of the life I always wanted."

He raked fingers through his sandy curls and gave her his most persuasive smile. But she sensed a level of emotion and vulnerability in him that she had not perceived at first. She wanted him to have what he wanted. More importantly, she did not want to be the obstacle that prevented him from realizing some lifelong dream. Something just underneath his playful expression told her that this was about something more significant than she had first imagined. It wasn't about the Porsche or the accumulation of more stuff; it was about his sense of freedom.

She wondered if there was any connection between this so-called midlife crisis and the dramatic events with his estranged father over the weekend. She didn't want to be the bad guy here, but she needed a concession. She started to think more seriously about his proposal and what she might ask in exchange. Sixteen years of marriage and corporate training had taught her an important rule: never accept the first offer. She had to come up with a counter.

"I'm at midlife, too, you know." She started thinking out loud. "My life is full of routines and responsibilities as well. I, too, work hard without spending the fruits of my labor on myself. I'd like some lifestyle improvements for the second half of my life." She looked at this man she loved, a man of expensive tastes, obsessive-compulsive tendencies, and strict, sometimes bizarre, rules of household order. A plan began to hatch.

Fueled with this encouragement, Jack suddenly became quite amorous. He wrapped his arms around her. "Anything you want, Essie. Just name it."

"Sex, drugs, and rock 'n' roll," she said, now with a clear vision of the brilliance of this plan.

"Really? How so?" he asked, taking his turn to raise eyebrows in disbelief.

"First, sex," she began. "Actually, it's more romance, I suppose. Pregnancy may be beautiful, but I don't feel so beautiful lately. Not with all this extra weight. But you could help in that department. You could make me feel desirable again. You know, pursued."

"You got it." He leaned back, propped his elbow on the armchair, and rested his chin on his fist, "And . . . ?"

"Rock 'n' roll," she continued. "I really can't take the nonstop kiddie music and the sappy holiday music when we ride with the kids in the car or gather for dinnertime in the house. I need a break from *The Lion King* soundtrack, *Peter Pan* theme songs, and *Winnie the Pooh* sing-alongs. I'm losing my mind over here. I *need* rock 'n' roll. And I don't mean from Elvis-impersonating toys, either." She surprised herself with the passion she suddenly felt for this cause. *Play Julie Andrews again only after I'm dead*, she thought.

Essie loved rock 'n' roll. If King David were around today, she felt sure he'd love it, too. Sometimes when she read the Psalms, she could almost hear the electric guitar in the background.

"OK," he said, but she could see the wheels turning in his head as he shifted nervously in his seat. He was still fully engaged in the negotiation but was obviously worried about what came next. "And drugs?" he asked.

"I know how you feel about beer and wine, Jack. I know how my family feels, too, especially my mom. Throughout our marriage, I've honored your preference by not keeping any beer or wine in the house. By now you should know, though, that I wouldn't abuse it. I enjoy beer and wine. It is one of life's simple pleasures. And I think I should be able to enjoy it in my own home, as well. After the baby comes, of course." Thus concluding her counteroffer, she sat back in the chair, waiting for his response but expecting that last provision to be the deal breaker.

He stood up and walked over to the counter. "This could be a problem." He paced through the kitchen. "It's a problem not only for me but for both of us," he explained. "Do you realize the grief we will get from your mother if she sees that . . . that stuff . . . in our refrigerator?" Pearl was their only reliable babysitter.

"Have you considered the implications to our childcare arrangement? You cannot seriously expect her to babysit in a house with wine in the fridge."

"I'm willing to accept that possibility."

"I don't like alcohol. Never have," he said, opening the *Auto Trader* again.

They sat in silence. Just when she thought the negotiation had failed, he tucked the Carrera ad under his arm and said decisively, "But if that is what it takes, I trust we will work through it somehow." He extended his right hand to her to shake on the agreement in mock formality. She squeezed his hand, and he pulled her close in an embrace.

She whispered in his ear, "If you think that was tough, you may want to rethink my appointment as head of Homeland Security."

"Oh yeah? Why is that?" he said with arms wrapped around her.

"We both want spinach-free carpet, but I will lobby vigorously against any 'security policies' or 'preventative measures' that make it impossible to live and breathe and eat and sleep freely and comfortably in our own home."

"You mean no rationing of spinach? No vinyl runways across the carpet? No plastic covers fitted over furniture?"

"That's right. I will not relent, because this is a fight for freedom in the home for every man, woman, child, and Elvis-impersonating dinosaur."

"Freedom," he repeated, clutching his *Auto Trader* to his chest. "God bless America."

[chapter 10]

A Wife of Noble Character

With another busy workweek behind her, Essie was driving over to her sister's house for a Saturday afternoon visit. She wanted to celebrate the news of her and Jack's lifestyle negotiations, but a weighty feeling held her back. On the one hand, she and Jack had experienced a kind of breakthrough. Their exchange created a moment of complete transparency and vulnerability that filled her with a renewed sense of intimacy toward her husband. On the other hand, she felt apprehensive that her marriage might deteriorate into a series of negotiations. Marriage should be a bond that completely and unconditionally satisfies each partner without either owing a debt, but since they'd had kids, Jack and Essie had been too busy cleaning up creamed spinach to address growing concerns about their changed lifestyle.

So this latest compromise seemed hugely important as Essie weaved through an obstacle course of scooters, bikes, and tricycles. She navigated down a cul-de-sac and pulled into Emily's driveway. She was eager to get her sister's reaction to the recent negotiation. Was this as big of a breakthrough as she hoped? A defining moment for her marriage or just a quick fix? Emily always had a way of looking at things that helped Essie keep matters in perspective.

Emily's five-year-old, Olivia, zoomed on her scooter alongside Essie's Pathfinder, and they both rolled to a stop.

"Hey, Aunt Essie."

Essie gave her niece a squeeze. "Hey, doll. Are you looking forward to your new house?"

Olivia held Essie's hand as they walked past a for-sale sign and up the steps to a front door plastered with a seasonal wreath of miniature pumpkins, maize, and multicolored leaves.

"Mom says it's the best neighborhood in town."

Through the sidelights, Essie saw Emily cradling her five-month-old daughter, Alicia, on the couch. Olivia and Essie knocked lightly and let themselves in.

"Hey, Sis," Essie said.

A wide grin spread across Emily's face, a smattering of freckles barely visible under her makeup. Her short, dark hair fell over one cheek in a spray of shiny black feathers as she placed the baby on a blanket of toys and then held up an index finger. "Be right back. I've waited all week for this," she said and disappeared into the kitchen. Olivia rifled through a pile of CDs, entered several into the player, and hit the shuffle button on the stereo remote. Aretha Franklin boomed through the den speakers. Emily returned a couple of minutes later with a bottle of wine and two glasses.

"Congratulations on your negotiation with Jack. I can only imagine what Pearl would say, but let's celebrate."

Essie laughed. "I can almost see Mother shaking her head and fanning herself. Thank goodness I have a sister I can call for just these occasions."

Emily smiled. "That's what sisters are for." She lifted the soiled burp cloth from her shoulder and dangled it over her forearm like fine linen. She rested the bottle on her arm, tilted the neck back, and turned the label toward Essie to formally present the wine, a bottle of chardonnay from QuikTrip with a bright orange sticker pasted askew on the label: $6.99.

Essie played along, sniffing the cork and swirling the two sips around in the goblet her sister handed her. "Not just yet," she smiled. "But we'll celebrate in style after this baby comes." Essie admired the way Emily so naturally created a celebratory atmosphere in her home. While Essie worried constantly about the future, Emily enjoyed the moment. Essie felt refreshed and energized whenever she was with her.

"About the baby." Emily sat down next to Essie. "Do you have all the baby gear you need? What do you get for the mom having a third baby? With Juliet still in diapers herself, how about a bigger diaper bag?"

"Great idea. One with both a bottle warmer and a chardonnay chiller," Essie said, clinking her glass against her sister's. The chime alone filled Essie with good cheer—it didn't matter that the wine itself remained untouched. The doorbell rang; Olivia raced to the foyer. She and two neighborhood girls scurried upstairs to Olivia's room. The CD player rotated discs, and Billie Holiday sang a slow jazz number.

Baby Alicia spit up a curd of milk and began to cry. "If I find one, I'll get one for myself, too." Emily grinned. She placed her glass on the table, reached down to return the pacifier to the baby's mouth, and skipped off to the kitchen. A moment later, she returned with a spread of veggies and dip.

Masterful, Essie thought to herself. *Married with two small kids, full-time teacher, vacuum lines as far as the eye can see, a front door decorated for the season, and planning a big move to a new neighborhood, how does she manage so well?* Essie set her glass down on a newly purchased side table next to a small, gold-leaf frame of Proverbs 31, the description of the perfect wife, the role model to which they both aspired. The proverb haunted her when she thought about this third baby.

On the outside, things seemed OK, but inside she was scared to death. *How does Emily stay in such a lively mood all the time? Does she stock vegetable trays?* Essie rebuked herself: her kids hadn't eaten a vegetable in weeks. Her seasonal decor was made up of Hot Wheels and action figures. Her marriage was run like a business. What would happen if her performance dipped? Her productivity declined? Her solvency suffered?

"How's the big move coming along?" Essie asked, pushing her anxieties to the side.

"Our Realtor is bringing a couple by this afternoon. They are eager buyers. Job relocation," Emily said, lips to her glass, eyes peering up at her sister with matter-of-fact confidence. "Remember how I was concerned about my longer commute to work after the move? Well, Greg traded in my car for a new Volvo," she squealed and danced in her seat.

New house, new furniture, new car, new baby, and no visible signs of stress or fatigue. It was both inspiring and annoying. Essie had toyed with the prospect of moving after the new baby came, but just the idea was exhausting. Plus, anywhere she might move would undoubtedly come with a mortgage that would keep her up nights. Emily didn't worry about these matters, Essie reminded herself. She trusted her husband to make the right financial decisions for their family. And everything always turned out rosy for her. Essie wondered why she couldn't be more like her sister. What did all her fears buy her, anyway?

"A new car? That's incredible! I thought money was tight. How did you manage it?" Essie had to ask.

"Greg is up for a big promotion. He's a shoo-in," Emily said with a flip of her wrist, flinging away any doubt like some annoying housefly. "We'll just roll everything into the mortgage. That's the beauty of moving. It'll be fine," she explained, fidgeting with an earring.

"Seriously, Sis, what's your secret? You are so together. I manage, but if truth be told, I can barely balance my responsibilities as they are." Essie picked up the little gold frame, held it in her lap, looked down, and slid her fingers along its edge. "I'm really scared of a third child," she admitted.

Emily looked over at the frame in Essie's lap. "Proverbs 31. Do you really think she's all that different from you or me?"

"Yes, absolutely," Essie said, surprised at the question. "Maybe not you, but definitely out of reach for me."

"Oh, I don't know about that. Let's take a look." Emily reached for the frame and read aloud: "'A wife of noble character who can find? She is worth far more than rubies.'

"She's a rare find. She's valuable. Not so different from us," Emily explained, fanning her hands out, palms up. "Oh, here we go," she skipped a couple of verses down.

"You have to contemporize the meaning. See: 'She selects wool and flax and works with eager hands.' That means she works hard and purchases fine things for her family—just like we do. I like to think of it as, 'She shops at Neiman's and Saks and buys her meat at Sam's Club.'"

"I doubt you'll find that interpretation in any Bible commentary, but I appreciate what you're trying to say," Essie admitted, chuckling.

"I'm kidding, of course, Sis. Let me try again."

Emily continued: "'In her hand, she holds the distaff and grasps the spindle with her fingers. She opens her arms to the poor and extends her hands to the needy.' That could simply mean, 'In one hand, she holds a baby and grabs a casserole from the oven with the other. She opens her arms to the visiting missionary and extends her hands to the Parent Teacher Association.'"

Essie raised a brow, amused.

"All I'm saying is I wish you wouldn't take yourself so seriously. Why don't you try it? Pick a verse and modernize it. Here's one: 'She gets up while it is still dark; she provides food for her family and portions for her servant girls.'"

"In my case, I guess you could say: she gets up early, toasts Pop Tarts for the kids, and, oh yeah"—Essie grinned—"provides a Porsche for her husband."

"Actually, it says 'portions,' not Porsches," Emily pointed out.

"What!" Essie exclaimed in mock surprise. "Where were you last week when I needed you?"

"But you get the idea," Emily laughed. "We both want the best for our families. And we both know the Porsche is not really what Jack is looking for. Besides, you are doing fine, and you will do fine with three, too. Anyway, you always have me. When you need some help, I'll be here for you."

They clinked their glasses again and hugged each other, rejoicing over a newfound, if absurd, discovery of noble character.

Emily put the frame in her lap and reclined against the sofa cushions. "Do I need to go on?"

"I know what you're trying to do," Essie sighed. "And I appreciate it. You always know how to encourage me. But somehow I still don't feel worthy of her title. I mean, we both know the verses mean a lot more than that."

"Yes, but God doesn't expect us to be perfect, Sis. I just think you're being too hard on yourself. OK, so I'm not Beth Moore," Emily admitted. "But I do know one thing for sure: God loves you and accepts you just as you are, Essie. And so do I."

"I love you too"—Essie smiled and reached for her sister's hand—"and thanks."

The stereo was playing a praise song from a church CD. The chorus repeated, "Great is our God."

Emily smiled broadly and sang along, "Great is our God, sing with me." Essie joined the chorus; the sisters lifted their voices together in praise. "And all will see how great, how great, is our God."

When the song ended, Emily said, "Worship is a great remedy for worry too, Sis. Praise songs give me such a natural high." Then she pulled Essie close and held her in a curiously tight embrace. "If only my mortgage and car payment weren't so high."

Smiling, Emily jangled the new Volvo keys for emphasis. "Until Greg's promotion comes through, thank the Lord for free financing."

[chapter 11]

A Golden Oldie

Ham sat at his perpetually reserved barstool at the end of the counter. Inman, as always, sat at the opposite end of the counter, hidden behind the sports section of the newspaper. It was a typical Sunday afternoon, same as any other. On this day, however, something was not quite right. Hamilton felt a sense of foreboding.

He couldn't put his finger on it. What could be wrong? The reunion with his son had achieved far more than he'd hoped. And his daughter-in-law, Essie, had called him already to arrange a date for the promised rib dinner.

At the other end of the counter, Inman scribbled into a notepad. Newspaper pages and racing forms spread out in front of him.

"Winston Pup Winner or Quicker'n Likker?" Inman hollered in Hamilton's direction.

Hamilton cast his eyes to the ceiling, calculating invisible figures in the air. "The Quicker pup sounds good to me. I'd go with him."

Inman narrowed one eye on Hamilton as if questioning Ham's judgment. He let the other eye drift back to his papers, rechecking the stats. Then, with a snort, he hunched over his notepad and scribbled.

"Who asked you?" he huffed.

Hamilton shrugged. Such exchanges were all part of the lunchtime chorus line at The Lazy I.

Inman flipped open his cell phone. Every Sunday, Inman phoned in his bets for the afternoon greyhound races. The automated process allowed him to follow the prompts and press the buttons for his afternoon picks. He rocked back and forth on his stool, alternating every few seconds between holding the phone to his ear and jabbing at the keypad in his palm.

Though Hamilton never bet on the dog races, he was always willing to oblige Inman in his quinella and trifecta selections. Hamilton enjoyed these games as opportunities to hone his instincts. He seemed to know things somehow, foresee outcomes, though he couldn't explain just how. For Hamilton, the fun of the bet was calling upon that undefined source of knowledge that welled inside him, testing it, proving it true.

For Inman, it was all about the dollars and cents. More than that, Inman by nature had to oppose any recommendation from Hamilton. Taking opposing sides on a matter was the essence of their relationship. It made no difference whether it was a question of preferred ends of the diner counter or greyhound picks. For Inman, the best choice was the one opposite Hamilton's.

Coffee percolated. Receipt tape sputtered out from the register in a wide curl. The bell on the door frame chimed as customers came and went. Hamilton closed his eyes and listened. These and the faint beeps from Inman's cell phone added to the familiar harmony of the diner.

The Lazy I typically drew a strong crowd for lunch, and today was no exception. The Sunday special, shrimp and grits, was a local favorite. He noticed that the grits were a little runnier than usual. Could've used another pinch of salt. No one complained though. Hamilton, along with the other regulars, cleaned his plate gratefully. Something was off, but it wasn't the food. It was something else.

He sopped up the last of the grits with a crust of biscuit, slid the empty plate forward, and waited for Lilly to retrieve it. His brief exchanges with

Lilly throughout her shift were the highlights of his day. A hearty meal followed by a bit of humor and Lilly's warm smile was sweeter than dessert.

Lilly approached Hamilton's end of the counter, a stack of dishes loaded on one arm. Without stopping, she scooped up Hamilton's empty plate with her free hand. The expression on her face was of concentration and distraction at the same time. "Coffee," she said. It was more of a declaration than an offer. No lilt to it. No flavor.

Hamilton smiled and nodded, as usual. "And a little sugar, ma'am, when you got the time," he requested, hoping for a serving of witty repartee. Hamilton grinned and the scar along his mouth stretched thin and turned a translucent pink. Lilly managed an absent-minded smile and seemed to look right through Hamilton, her eyes far away. Arms full, she blew a strand of dark hair away from her face and turned back toward the kitchen.

Hamilton rested his forearms on the counter and tried to soak in the familiar refrain of the diner: clattering plates and clinking utensils, the murmur of conversation among friends. The sounds of the diner typically carried a comforting kind of rhythm. Like a favorite 45 on vinyl, the pops, hisses, and scratches in the background only adding to the charm. Hamilton tolerated but never understood the transition to digital media. For him, cleansing the melody of all its imperfections took away some of the flavor. Eggs without salt, biscuits without butter.

Only this time, instead of sliding into the diner's rhythm, Hamilton felt a needle skip on an imaginary record. An unexpected silence in the middle of a familiar song. That's what Hamilton noticed was missing. The background noise that usually flavored his shrimp and grits had changed. It was quieter.

A sudden smack of broken glass exploded from the direction of the kitchen followed by a string of expletives. Lilly, flush with perspiration, rushed from the kitchen, shiny threads of black silk matted against her brow.

"Inman, the Hobart is clogged again. The water won't drain and the dishes are backed up."

Without looking up from his phone, Inman waved her away like a gnat at his ear.

"I'm in the middle of important business now, woman. See if the old man can do something for you."

Hamilton was already on his way to the kitchen. It wasn't the first time he'd been called to repair the old-model dishwasher. Within a few minutes, he discovered that the problem was not only with the equipment. Water wasn't draining in the sink either. The diner was connected to a septic system that, evidently, needed to be emptied. When Hamilton explained this to Lilly, tears began to well in her eyes.

"Ain't nothing to it, darlin'," Hamilton reassured her. "I know a guy. Old friend across town. We'll just close the diner for a couple days till we can get her fixed up."

Lilly's shoulders dropped, and she buried her face in her hands. A soft cry gave way to heaving sobs. Hamilton, unsure what else to do, cupped her shoulder with his scarred hand.

"It's my mother," her voice cracked. "She needs an operation that can't wait. Insurance won't cover it. I'm working back-to-back doubles till I get the money together. If that doesn't work, I'll sell my truck when I get to Florida. She needs me."

By this time, Inman had made his way to the kitchen to fetch Lilly. Customers were waiting.

"Septic needs to be emptied," Hamilton told Inman.

Inman sniffed at the dirty water pooled in the sink and the dishwasher. An industrial dishwasher would run him at least five thousand dollars. The grounds would have to be dug up to get to the septic tank. Commercial grade septic service would cost about seven thousand dollars. Bringing the diner up to local code would cost between fifteen thousand and thirty thousand dollars. Under his breath, Inman cursed the local government for not allowing him to dump in the river. He'd do it in a heartbeat if he thought he could get away with it.

The restaurant would have to be shut down while they emptied the tank and repaired the Hobart. His finger zigzagged in the air in front of him as he estimated the cost of repairs. He held his finger still for a moment and then wagged it again furiously, as if tacking on a final estimate for lost revenue to the grand total.

"My mom is on a fixed income. She doesn't have anyone else. Just me. If the diner shuts down, how will I pay?"

Hamilton knew Inman all too well. Inman would look for an angle, a way he might capitalize on the situation. His mind would speed through several possible scenarios. The diner earned him a nice little bankroll, but he didn't need it to stay afloat. And he certainly didn't need the hassle of repairs.

Hamilton tried to comfort Lilly. He patted her back like a child. "I'm so sorry, darlin'. I didn't even know you were caring for your mama. How soon does she need the operation?"

Lilly steadied her voice. "The doctor says the sooner the better. She's in her mid seventies now. Even if it doesn't add years to her life, it will make her more comfortable."

Inman stood next to Hamilton and Lilly, his face a mask of concern. Only Ham could tell he wasn't worried about Lilly's mother; he was thinking of his investment in the diner. How he might turn it for a profit.

Hamilton knew what Inman would do. Inman would make a few cosmetic improvements, make a convincing show that the property value had appreciated. If necessary, he'd refinance it to the gills before he'd put a dime of his own in it. Then, he'd sell it to his dad.

His dad had accumulated all sorts of commercial property in the area and was becoming careless in examining the minutiae of his real estate transactions. Inman could put a Band-Aid on this little problem and turn the whole mess back over to his old man or someone else.

Inman rattled his head, as if bits of Hamilton and Lilly's conversation suddenly registered in his brain. His countenance grew rigid, and his eyes blazed with intensity, like a scorching steam had surged between his ears, a teakettle rising to a shrill whistle.

He turned to Lilly. "How much do you need?" The scowl on Inman's round face mimicked a hardened form of sympathy, presumably sharing the taste of her bitter misfortune.

"Ten grand," Lilly sniffed. "Why do you ask?"

"Does your mother carry life insurance? If you'd be willing to make me the beneficiary, I'll give you the money right now." He reached for the cell phone attached to his hip as though connection to a multitude of financial resources was simply a phone call away.

Lilly's tear-streaked face was an expression of hurt and shock. "You want to bet on my mother's life?"

Inman shrugged. "Think of it as an investment in her life. Helps you out now, helps me out later. Everybody wins. What's wrong with that?"

"What's wrong with that! The fact that you don't know is what's wrong, Inman." Crimson spread up Lilly's neck and across her cheeks.

Hamilton's expression turned hard as stone. "No, sir," he said to Inman. "I won't allow it." The scar along his tightened jaw twisted in a crooked line like a vein running through a block of limestone.

"My mother's life is not a financial opportunity. Her life insurance is not for sale. You can keep your money." Lilly untied her apron, folded it in a neat square, and handed it to Inman. "You keep this as well." Her eyes glistened like hard bits of onyx. "And you know where you can shove 'em both." She ran toward the ladies' room before they could see the fresh, hot tears tumble down her cheeks.

Inman's cell phone chimed. He pressed a button and watched the letters scroll across the tiny display screen. Afternoon race results.

"Winston Pup didn't even show! That good-for-nothin', worthless dog!" he said, and stomped away.

Hamilton waited for Lilly to come out of the restroom, but she had made her way out the back door. He knew he'd probably never see Lilly again at the diner. Today was certainly the last time Lilly would serve him shrimp and grits. He considered stopping by her house.

The Hobart engine groaned. The belt sputtered forward and pushed dishes on top of one another. A stack of plates and coffee cups tumbled to the floor, sending ceramic shards in all directions. The sweet melody of the diner was gone, and Ham felt something had let him see it coming. A new, melancholy song had risen in its place.

Ham pulled his Ford pickup into the gravel lot next to his dock, turned off the engine, and smiled to himself. He had pulled it off without a hitch. But his satisfaction was mixed with regret. A part of him hoped Lilly would catch him in the act . . . and maybe even change her course. Perhaps his plan had worked a bit too well. In any case, he had made sure that Lilly's mother could be taken care of. Lilly would find a note inside her gas cap cover: *Treasure under your feet.* And then, with a little imagination, she would locate the treasure under the floor mat of her Chevy: ten thousand, in cash. The note with it read: *You forgot your tip, darlin'. A dollar a grit!*

[chapter 12]

cows and coats

Essie was ready, once again, to return to the corporate jungle on Monday. Thoroughly invigorated by her weekend visit with Emily, she knew Life Cola could not possibly damage her fortified psyche. Then again, corporate philosophy could feel like a trip to *The Twilight Zone*. TV theme music cued in her head.

Essie's fifth boss this year, Lewis Cathcart, was a new hire from an elite consulting firm in New York. Cathcart's immediate charge was to transform the beverage business with his information technology team, yet his brusque demeanor had not yet endeared him to his Southern colleagues. She had a meeting scheduled with Cathcart this morning to discuss his vision for a new technology project. IT project management had been Essie's responsibility for many years. She was eager to hear what Cathcart had to say but also hoped to share some ideas of her own.

At 8:57, Essie wheeled her Pathfinder into the employee parking garage. She raced across the lot, rushed through the lobby, slipped through closing elevator doors, and rode up to Cathcart's office. He was pressing buttons furiously on a handheld device when she arrived.

"Ellison, have a seat." He motioned to a chair facing his mahogany desk. "First, please extend my gratitude to your husband, Jack. He configured this new device for me. Now I can unlock my car and open my garage door with the same handheld I use for my e-mail and stock trades.

We need more people like him around. He is part of the solution. Innovation, Ellison."

His phone rang, and he picked it up. "Cathcart," he said by way of a greeting. He nodded and held up a finger to Essie: one minute. He swiveled his chair around, holding the receiver to his ear silently for several minutes.

Essie was not surprised to hear that Jack had already made a positive impression on the new boss. He seemed to win favor with people in a most casual and often serendipitous fashion. When did he configure Cathcart's handheld device? How did that come about? Jack was not even in IT; he worked in Marketing. Yet he'd already met Cathcart, seen a need, and filled it.

When Essie joined Life ten years ago, Jack automatically became an extended member of its family, though he still tended bar for the restaurant. Confident of his contentment with minor celebrity status as the local bartender, everyone was shocked to discover he aspired to make a career move. Jack was pursuing a manager position at a motorcycle manufacturer when his interviewer called upon their Life Cola friends for a personal reference. When Life's operations manager learned Jack was in the job market, he immediately scooped him up for himself.

Jack took to the job naturally, successfully resolving any technical challenge sent his way, including complex software repairs and system performance improvements. Amazingly, his impressive knowledge of technology was self-taught—from manuals and heavy Internet research—fueled by a passion for mastering an understanding of how things work.

"It's no different from working on cars or bikes," he had claimed. "The principles of trouble-shooting are the same. It's all cause and effect."

In the course of his workdays, though, Jack was drawn like a magnet into consultations with coworkers on personal automobile or motorcycle purchases or repairs. Within a year, he became Life's unofficial buyers' agent.

Consequently, no one was surprised when, shortly after fixing a Marketing VP's BMW motorcycle in the employee garage, Jack transferred from Operations to Marketing.

Essie often wondered if the unusual twist of events was meant to be a passing of the torch. Had her purpose at Life Cola been fulfilled once Jack landed an amazing, well-compensated, sought-after position at the same firm? At Life Cola, he could provide for them without her income. Was his new job her cue to take a back seat? To shift from breadwinner to a more traditionally feminine role? Housewife? Volunteer? Stay-at-home mom?

Essie enjoyed her work, though. The money was good but had never been her primary motivation. She liked work for work's sake. She believed work was noble and good. Still, she could not help questioning whether there was any real nobility in her role at Life Cola or if she was just a coward, too afraid of letting go. Pearl's bitterness over leaving her career in real estate terrified Essie. She didn't want to become her mother, pushing the weight of lost opportunity onto her kids.

Still, was Jack's new employment a free ticket, a chance to embark on some lifelong ambition without any financial pressure? If so, what else would she do? And wouldn't she feel less accomplished without her own comfortable salary? Indecision became a decision in itself. So she stayed at Life, happily and by choice, but harbored a fear of leaving that she did not fully understand.

"It's a complex sweater to unravel," Cathcart said into the phone, yanking wire frame eyeglasses from his long face and tossing them onto a leather-bound portfolio embossed with his name. His lean torso arced over his desk. His hair was black and coarse with a severe part revealing a full half-inch wide stripe of gleaming white scalp. "Hmm, yes, I see." He picked up his glasses and polished the lenses furiously. His cuffs were starched and monogrammed. He rotated his chair away from her again and lowered his tone.

"Let's just say I've already packed those sweaters away. They are out of season, so to speak." He held the phone to his ear silently for another minute. Then, "Yes, of course I will," and he abruptly hung up.

Finally, he turned back to face her.

"Good morning, Mr. Cathcart."

"Ellison," he began again. "I asked to see you this morning because I have an exciting new direction for Information Technology this year I want to discuss with you."

"Great, some changes would be welcome. I have some ideas as well," Essie replied.

He held a hand up, presumably to hold any distractions at bay. "This organization is suffocating; it's dying. It needs a fresh infusion of energy. A renewed passion."

His words sent a jolt of excitement up her spine. She ached for a strong sense of purpose at Life. "I couldn't agree more, sir."

In the early days, working in the technology area of Life Cola was like being part of an enormous family. Today, the sense of community they once shared was a distant memory. Like many corporations, Life had suffered some tough years of layoffs, restructuring, and outsourcing. Major strategy shifts and innumerable management changes fostered a culture of fear and self-protection. Additionally, IT employees knew the board of directors viewed information technology as little more than a necessary evil. With no appetite for technology advancement or risk, the CFO severely cut back IT projects, leaving IT project managers, like herself, with little to get excited about.

"The information technology team is not effective. I believe I have the answer, Ellison, and I need your help."

"I am glad to help."

"What we have here is a soup sale at a lemonade stand."

"Sir?" Cathcart had a penchant for awkward analogies.

"The environment is all wrong. I see a new setting. An evolution in thinking. I see the launch of a new generation here at Life. A creative generation. One not stifled with old paradigms. Out of the box, Ellison. Think beyond the box."

"What do you have in mind?"

"In the new generation, there will be no more projects. There will only be Chunks of Work. COWs, I like to call them."

"Cows, sir?" She opened her notepad and wrote the date at the top.

"Exactly. Cows and Goats." His eyes were ablaze with intensity. "Projects are part of the old mind-set. Projects are archaic with firm start and end dates, with rigid financial floors and ceilings. Can you picture the box, Ellison? Don't you feel cramped just thinking about our work that way?"

He cringed as if the walls were closing in around them. "Technology initiatives are ongoing, continuous, and interrelated, part of a much bigger machine, the engine that runs the universe. They never really start or stop: think constant motion, think fluid, think of a fish in the ocean. Do fish ever really stop swimming? Projects are not isolated events: think jigsaw puzzle, think of a masterpiece coming into view. Can you see the chunks? The opportunity is huge. Cows, Ellison. Can you see them?"

Her mind was a jumble of images. She was at a loss for words. She looked down at the blank white sheet in her notepad. She thought the word *nut-job* but she wrote the word *COWS* in block capital letters.

"And Goats," Lewis continued his tirade. "I see a radical shift in the approval process. Eliminate the hierarchy, the bureaucracy. All approvals will be handled by GOATs: Groups of Approximately Ten. Each Goat, a representative body of decision makers, will select a Cow. The Goats will then come together and choose only the most attractive Cows for our annual plan. Empower the Goats!"

Without looking down, she wrote *GOATS* in her notepad. "Mr. Cathcart," she stumbled through her thoughts to find an appropriate response. "I'm not sure I understand how these Cows and Goats improve our plans."

"Imagine the simplicity, the elegance of it." He snapped his glasses into place, eyes shooting into her like laser beams. "The whole approach presents a fresh, new expression of IT's value. This type of thinking will become the catalyst to a new era of creativity and innovation. You do want to innovate, don't you?"

"Well, I guess so. I mean, yes, sir. I think I understand, but what role do I play in this new approach?"

"Ellison, I need you to help me activate this vision, and I'm asking you to lead the first Cow. I want you to walk it and talk it." She visualized herself walking a bellowing Holstein back to her cubicle. Work is noble and good, she reminded herself.

"Here's the plan: IT Recycles Across America." He gazed past her into the distance. A dreamy expression washed over him. "You will launch a campaign to collect recycled aluminum for this great company. The aluminum will be distributed back to our can suppliers and reused in our production facilities."

"How is this related to Information Technology?"

"The real question is: How can Information Technology do more to relate to our overall business? Recycling is a core value for this company. It is up to you to find a way for IT to plug in. You do want to contribute, right?"

"Well, sure, but there are many recycling services already in place. What is the problem we are trying to solve with technology? Is there a way an IT solution could save us money on aluminum expenses? Is there a financially grounded business case for a technology component to aluminum recycling? What is the business benefit?"

Lewis frowned, shook his head, disappointed. "I think you're missing the point, Ellison. Some things are more important than saving money. As a world citizen, don't you feel a passion to do *something* to conserve our resources? IT is the ultimate enabler. If you share the company's concern about the environment, as I do, I'm confident you will find the connection."

He stood up and walked over to the door and extended his hand to her. Realizing the meeting was over, she stood as well.

"Imagine what you could do with a magnificent mountain of old tuna fish cans, vegetable cans, soup cans, empty Life cans, even competitors' cans. The possibilities are endless. It will be groundbreaking. Cows and Goats, Ellison. Walk it and talk it. Remember: you're an important part of the solution."

This cannot be happening, she thought. Outside his office, the hallway looked distorted and unfamiliar. *Panic attack*, she self diagnosed. She rushed to the seventh floor to find Jack.

[chapter 13]

Heroes and Heroines

Most floors at Life Cola featured the same maze of cubicles and motionless bodies staring at flickering computer screens. Finance, Legal, HR, Information Technology, all contained drab cube farms with inert occupants. Not true for Marketing. Stepping off the elevator into the Marketing Department was a culture shock for other Life employees.

The same colorless office partitions used elsewhere had been disassembled and stacked against one wall. In their place was a large domed tent in the middle of the room. Outside its entrance flap, a small electric fan whirred on its back, blowing orange and red strips of fabric upward through a pile of twigs. An iron kettle filled with network cables, adapters, and computer mice hung on a wire above the cloth flames.

Along the interior wall, some desks were pulled together, showcasing an entire army of miniature soldiers and horses lined up on the offensive against an aluminum can pyramid of competitive products. A stuffed parrot with a mechanical beak and an electronic voice box sat perched upon the wall clock. Against the windows were foosball, air hockey, and Ping-Pong tables, gaming stations, dartboards, and a putting green.

When Essie arrived, Jack was in the middle of a vigorous Ping-Pong match with another marketing colleague, Haj Tamul. Haj was wearing a fencing face mask and some kind of industrial bodysuit.

He served. "How about *Viva*, a frothy lime concept?"

"Viva? The American Adventure should be in English, not Spanish." Jack swatted the ball back. "How about *Bronco*, a bitter, coffee-like concept?"

"Bronco? Who wants to drink a Bronco? Tastes like hair." Haj lobbed a return.

"I'm a garbage man," Essie blurted.

"OK, if that's what you want to be. I'll be the town sheriff," Jack flicked his wrist and zipped the plastic ball across the table.

Haj flipped the ball back. "I'll be the surly gambler if Fenton will be Tyvek. It's his day, you know," Haj said.

"Who is Tyvek?" she asked.

Jack grabbed the plastic ball to stop the game and explained. "Tyvek is a protective material made from fine, high-density polyethylene fibers. It offers all the best characteristics of paper, film, and fabric in one. Today, Haj is wearing a suit made out of it. We take turns wearing it on a rotating schedule. The person who wears it becomes a living dry erase board. We write ideas on him all day long."

"It used to be just a material. Now he's an icon for creativity. Tyvek is the Superhero of the Idea Generation." Haj turned his back to demonstrate the power of his assumed identity. The words "American Adventure" were written in red block letters across his shoulder blades. "It's hot in here, though. I'd rather be the surly gambler. It's Fenton's turn to be Tyvek, not mine."

"Where is Fenton?" she asked. Fenton Mac—young, overconfident, and inexperienced—was the newest member of the marketing team. A green college recruit, Fenton was hired for his dramatic idealism and lack of convention.

"In the tent. Taking his nap," Haj said.

Jack explained, "We get much better ideas out of him after his morning nap."

"Morning nap. Morning nap." The parrot echoed, opening and closing its beak.

Jack smacked the ball across the net, resuming the Ping-Pong game. Haj swatted back, and the ball nicked a corner and rolled away. Crouching awkwardly in his suit, Haj followed it under a desk.

Essie felt the weight of her potentially doomed career hanging in the balance while her colleagues took naps and chased Ping-Pong balls in invented superhero identities. What was she missing here? Was she the only person who needed her job to matter, to be meaningful? Was there any nobility to be found in the workplace anymore?

"Jack, can I talk to you? Cathcart just gave me a project—I mean a Cow. He told me to walk it. I don't know what to do."

"Cathcart? That new guy? I configured his handheld the other day."

"Yeah, I heard you made quite an impression already."

"The guy locked his keys in his car. I used his handheld to contact AutoStar to unlock it. No big deal, but he acted like I'd just struck gold."

"Struck gold. Struck gold." The parrot cawed.

"Hold on, I got something." Jack addressed the room, raising his hands in the air. "The American Adventure should include the hunt for some kind of treasure, like the Argonauts on their westward gold rush." He grabbed a green marker and began writing on Haj's protruding rear as the rest of him searched for a ball under a desk. Tyvek never even slowed his hunt as Jack wrote the words "treasure hunt" across his super-seat.

"It came to me in my sleep," Fenton Mac announced, emerging from the tent in an Indian headdress and rubbing sleep from his eyes. Once outside the tent door, Fenton planted his feet in a wide stance and folded his hands out in front of him like an Indian chief.

"Gather." He looked straight ahead, stiff-necked, and motioned with his eyes for Jack, Haj, and Essie to join him around the faux campfire.

They sat cross-legged around the fabric flames. "The American Adventure is the life of a cowboy. We must capture his spirit to appeal to today's youth." With a black marker he wrote *cowboy* on Haj's chest.

Cows, Goats, Treasure Hunts, Cowboys. Had everyone here lost their minds? Had the days of meaningful employment come to an end? Maybe this was some final cosmic clue, the push she needed to give up career hopes and pass the torch to Jack. Yet quitting felt like running away. Even when this place made no sense, leaving felt like losing, giving up. Retreat, or stay and fight for satisfying work: those were her choices. If she stayed and accepted Cathcart's Cow project, how would she reconcile such a ridiculous assignment with her personal philosophy that work is noble and good?

Fenton Mac shook off his headdress and dropped his Indian chief persona. "Think about it. The cowboy is an American icon of wild, unbridled freedom, no stranger to extreme conditions or endurance challenges. We can contemporize the cowboy image. Recast yesterday's hero into today's mind-set. The campaign needs the modern equivalent for riding the range, searching for gold, rescuing the occasional damsel in distress."

"Extreme challenges, endurance sports." Jack's face lit up. "Yes. I see it. Our target market identifies with extreme sports, like rock climbing, snow boarding. Intense experience and an element of danger."

"Can someone clue me in on what we're talking about?" Essie asked.

"Our promotional campaign, The Larger Than Life American Adventure Tour. We promote the new product during the peak holiday season and launch the tour right after the new year. It's the prime time to introduce a new beverage targeting American youth. Today, we are working on the creative elements of the tour and the new beverage concept," Haj explained.

"You're in IT, right? Techy goobs don't get marketing." Fenton assumed a Western drawl. "You're in way over your head here, little lady.

Besides, this is a highly confidential creative session. We'll call you later if we need a Web site or something." Jack and Haj chuckled.

"I see the value you place on technology." Essie gestured to the computer mice stew hanging above them. "OK, Fen, guess I'll be on my way or I might find myself roasting on a skewer. Too bad, though, I might have been able to help you guys."

Fenton Mac waved his hands, "Whatever."

Haj resumed the brainstorming. "*Stud*, a ginseng boost with a sour-apple kick?"

Jack shook his head. "Teenage Viagra? Are you kidding me?"

"Right. Something subtler, like *Stallion*?" Haj tried again.

"Or *Spur*?" Fen chimed in.

"Too masculine. Alienates half of our consumers. The American Adventure beverage should appeal to everyone."

"Jack, can I talk to you now? I'm in the middle of a crisis here."

"Sure." To his coworkers: "Continue. I'll be back."

They found an empty office and closed the door. Despite the panicked retelling of her career crisis, the smile lines radiating from the corners of his eyes betrayed Jack's amusement.

"Cathcart hasn't even identified any technology need. He just wants to be involved in the company's recycling push. Instead of building technology solutions where they are needed, I'm forcing my way into the garbage industry. I know you say if you're handed lemons, make lemonade, but I don't think I can be one of those people who make art out of garbage. Life doesn't value me as an IT professional; they're asking me to run some kind of junkyard. A contemporized rendition of Fred Sanford, only with cuter shoes." She attempted levity, but her voice broke.

"You are so much more than you realize!"

"All I know is I'm the new trash man. Forget the cute shoes. Issue me an orange jumpsuit like one of those prison workers who stab trash with a stick on the side of the road."

Her husband's eyes offered compassion. "Look at me, honey. Have I planned or strategized my way into this job? No. I stumbled into it without a fancy degree or an impressive résumé. Why should I be chosen? I don't even have a marketing degree. There had to be people with more relevant experience than bartending. How do you think it happened? Not by the force of my will or because of my brilliant mind. Don't you see? I'm not the one in control. Only God decides how to distribute wealth, power, and honor. God wants me exactly where I am. If he wants more from me, he'll let me know. That frees me to enjoy myself and my job, whatever it brings." He swung his Ping-Pong paddle to emphasize his point. "But I still hope it brings a Porsche." He grinned.

"That's a convenient philosophy if you intend to cast off all worries and play Ping-Pong for a living!" Essie retorted.

He gripped her shoulders matter-of-factly. "Honey, what I'm saying is your job doesn't make you who you are. What you believe is what makes you who you are."

"Are you saying God wants me to be a garbage collector?" She hung her head despairingly.

"That's up to you. You're a daughter of the King whether you take this assignment or not." Jack tipped his head in a mock bow, knelt, and kissed the back of her hand.

He waited for her response, but she remained silent.

"You know that everything happens for a reason. Who knows where this new project could ultimately lead you? But if you accept it, I know you'll be the best cattle-ranging, goat-herding junkman IT has ever seen. You're certainly the best looking one I've seen." He swatted her playfully with his Ping-Pong paddle.

"I may not go so far as a modernized Fred Sanford"—he stroked her auburn hair—"but you could pass for a Red Foxx. I like the sound of it." He shaped his hands into the square edges of a camera lens and pretended to frame her face. He resumed brainstorming mode. "Cunning and mischievous, a cousin to Pocahontas. I can see the marquis now: The Larger Than Life American Adventure Tour welcomes Princess Red Foxx."

A grin crept its way onto Essie's face. "Maybe I've missed my true calling."

They returned to the campfire.

"Sure, *Camel Spit* is raw and edgy. I'll give you that. But I tell you, man, *Cactus Kick* resonates."

Fenton caught them up. "We're getting a bit carried away with the Wild West imagery."

"Reflexes got the better of me, sheriff," Haj confessed, mixing his eastern Indian and surly gambler dialects. With a dry eraser, he wiped away a cactus drawing extending from his crotch to his chest.

"How about *Shot,* a spicy, cinnamon-red-hot-flavored concept?" Essie offered.

"How about Shot. How about Shot," the parrot repeated.

The room was motionless for a split second. Then markers flew. It was a moment of marketing magic. Haj stood at the campfire as a frenzy of words and pictures grew up his arms and legs.

"A sleek metal container shaped like a bullet." Fenton drew a slim can with a cap curved into a point. "Add ingredients with adventure-promising properties. The product itself leaves a slight burning sensation on the lips, not too much but enough to tingle. The consumer feels it working. A small drink, two to four ounces, tops. Charge a heavy premium."

"A Clint Eastwood–style slogan, like 'Go ahead, make my day,'" Haj offered.

"Yeah, or 'Bite the bullet,'" Jack added.

"Hey, that's good. But I can do better. How about 'Kick some butt.'" Fenton scribbled slogans on Haj's chest.

"Very nice, Fen, but can't do it," Jack laughed.

"Why? You think it will offend the delicate sensibilities of American youth?" Fenton asked.

"Nope. I think it will offend their mothers, who, by the way, are America's primary grocery shoppers," Jack explained.

"You have a point," Fenton conceded. "'Kick some can,' then. And we can easily link that to Life's new emphasis on recycling."

"Let's go with it. Fen, you got the lead on the creative. Haj, run the concept through the supply chain." Jack smiled, pleased. "Yippee ki-yay."

"Mythic," Fenton expressed approval.

"Epic," Haj nodded.

"Essie, sorry I thought you were a technology goob," Fenton said.

"I was. I mean, I am. Well, I'm not sure what I am."

[chapter 14]

chicks dig it

Cole had at least a half hour of play before Essie would call him to dinner. She watched him through the kitchen window as she gathered ingredients for spaghetti. Usually Cole preferred to play video games when he got home from the school's aftercare program, but when they pulled up the drive, he noticed his neighbor Annabelle playing in her yard.

Ever since the day at the lake, Cole continued to investigate the question of real superheroes. He had managed to salvage the discarded Spider-Man pj's, but in the week following the dramatic rescue attempt, Spider-Man had become less of a curiosity than his own real-life grandfather. Since witnessing Hamilton's act of valor, Cole had attempted various displays of chivalry and bravery, even toward Juliet, as if he intended to become a hero, too.

A five-year-old's motivations are fairly easy to read. Cole figured if his own grandfather harbored some secret superhero identity or possessed hidden powers—despite Hamilton's and his parents' persistent denial—then some superpowers might have rubbed off on him. It was an exhilarating possibility that any kid would be compelled to explore. Obviously, superhero DNA was not the type of information a parent would disclose to a minor. Quite possibly, parents wouldn't even know themselves. Her son would have to figure it out on his own.

Essie peered out the window as the pasta came to a boil. The blacktop on Treeleaf Drive glistened in the autumn sun and curved into a backdrop of yellow and orange leaves. The afternoon air had begun to cool, but heat from the Georgia pavement still rose in a watery haze in the distance. Cole was squatting at the bottom of his driveway, surveying a homemade plywood ramp he'd constructed. With his small jaw set, Cole stood his bike upright, lifting it from the grass by a handlebar. From the rubber grip, a helmet dangled by its strap. Cole hiked a leg and straddled the bike. He unhooked the helmet and placed it on his head. Essie kept an eye on the scene as she moved back and forth by the kitchen window.

Annabelle Weatherstone sat cross-legged halfway up the neighboring driveway. Her torso was bent over her legs, and her elbows were propped on the pavement in front of her. She held her face in her cupped hands. Her gold ringlets fell forward. Her eyes presumably followed a trail of ants that often marched along a crack in the driveway. She plucked a little bouquet of freshly planted pansies and laid one across the ants' path. She leaned in farther as though observing how her subjects might navigate over the obstacle. Her gold curls reached the cement as she closely examined some sort of procession climbing over the pansy stem.

At the bottom of the driveway, Cole Wells was clearly stalling for time, waiting to regain Annabelle's attention. He tightened his chin strap as if to secure his resolve. The bulk of his helmet exaggerated the size of his head and further dwarfed his sparrow's chest. He shifted his weight onto the bicycle seat and glanced once again up the neighboring driveway.

Annabelle had retrieved the lone pansy from the ants' parade and returned it to her tiny bouquet. She held the flowers close to her face and studied the velvety white blooms. With the back of her hand, Annabelle flipped a loose ringlet of blond hair over her shoulder. She set to work, plucking each blossom one by one and then tossing the handful of petals into the air like so much confetti. Cole watched the small, white petals float weightlessly to the ground like a shower of snowflakes in the sun.

Essie opened the kitchen window to eavesdrop.

"Hey, Annabelle," Cole said. "That's cool, but watch this."

Annabelle looked at him and heaved a sigh. She returned her chin to her cupped hands and watched him.

Cole pushed all his weight against an elevated pedal and thrust the bike forward. He gained speed as he approached her driveway and then, with a sudden jerk, he yanked the front tire about six inches off the ground. Essie tensed. Cole applied the brake, jerked the handlebars right, and let his back tire slide out from underneath. He anchored his foot to the pavement and turned back to Annabelle. "Did you see that?" he asked. "A wheelie."

Essie resisted the urge to intervene. Boys would be boys.

"Yeah," Annabelle tilted her head to one side. A tiny fist pressed into the flesh of her rosy cheek. "I can do that, too," she said, clearly unimpressed. Essie smiled.

Cole did not appear dissuaded. He returned his foot to the pedal and pushed off. He adjusted the handlebars and rode the bicycle up the driveway. Essie wondered how many stunts her son had choreographed for his tests of superhero strength. His frame, like the bike's, was small and angular. His skinny legs pumped the pedals in tight, vigorous circles. He tucked his chin into his chest and leaned into the movement. The spiked vents of his bulbous headgear faced forward to create the effect of a charging ram.

He and the bike cast an elongated shadow in the yard that made the two appear like a single creature, fast and fierce. As he approached Annabelle, at just the right moment, he braced his thin legs against the bike frame and raised both hands fearlessly into the air. He turned a sharp corner around the balled-up girl and repeated the motion en route back down the driveway. "No hands," he shouted as he whizzed past her.

Essie turned the pasta down to simmer and called through the open window, "Be careful, Son."

Annabelle's eyes had widened. She sat up and tossed the naked pansy stems into the grass. "I can do that, too," she lied. She fastened her gaze on Cole and watched for his next move. Cole stomped the brakes and skidded to a stop, leaving a sharp black mark at the bottom of the drive. He ignored her last remark and tossed his bike into the grass.

Cole stooped low and squinted into the distance. He walked the length of the road to the ramp and back, testing the distance in measured paces. The final preparations for another stunt appeared almost complete. Cole narrowed his eyes at the plywood ramp and contemplated the danger set before him. He had never tried a jump before. Revealing no signs of fear, he lifted his bike from the grass, threw a leg over the crossbar, and clenched his tiny fists around the rubber grips. With no-turning-back-now determination, he thrust forward at full speed.

Cole hunkered down and turned the pedals furiously. Gaining momentum as the distance to the ramp closed, Cole shot one final glance at Annabelle before his front tire reached the base of the plywood.

Annabelle bit hard on her bottom lip. Her body was rigid and motionless, the picture of rapt anticipation. On his ascent, Cole lifted his rear off the bike seat and straightened his legs. In an instant, his body, his bike, and Essie's heart shot skyward.

The bike sailed. By the time its back tire touched ground, Cole appeared to have forgotten all the finer points from his careful planning and diligent preparations. The bike frame tumbled sideways, probably knocking all superhero ambitions from his young mind. Cole's descent was more of an awkward thud than a landing, sending boy and bike in two different directions. The crunch of metal and bone against the indifferent pavement smacked him back to reality.

"Cole!" Essie screamed. She bolted out the door and raced down the driveway.

Annabelle beat Essie to the scene. Cole bit back a swell of tears. He sat curled into himself as his face reddened and strained against the pain. Annabelle knelt by his side and extended a hand to help him up.

"That was cool," she said. "I've never done that."

Red seeped through a fresh gash in the knees of his jeans. A scrape on his chin left a patch of raw, pink skin. Cole struggled to his feet and stood hunched by Annabelle's side. His elbow was tucked into his ribs, and the skin along his forearm was imbedded with gravel.

"My arm," Cole managed, pain squeaking in his voice.

"I'll go get your mom," she said.

Annabelle started to turn away, but paused and quickly gave him a kiss as light as air on his cheek. Then she spun around and, startled to discover Essie at her side, raced up the driveway.

"Oh my son! Are you OK?" Essie wrapped her arms around him.

As soon as Annabelle was out of earshot, Cole let the tears come.

[chapter 15]

The stakes Rise

Hamilton started up his inboard, loosened the ropes, and pushed away from the dock. If he hurried, he might be able to catch Noodle for dinner at the Marina Grill.

Hamilton had begun to share more meals with Noodle. It had been three days since Lilly left the diner, and Hamilton was despondent over her loss. He knew it wasn't rational. There had been no promises made, no real romance in the traditional sense. Still, he had a hard time walking into that diner with the same self-assurance.

When Ham drove by the diner the day after Lilly left, he was surprised to find it open for business. Inman had not closed it down for the septic repair it needed, touting the ingenuity of a bypass he'd rigged instead. Ham took his usual seat at the counter. He and Inman exchanged sharp looks and no words. The cook confided to Hamilton that Lilly had called the diner, looking for him. She had been trying to thank him for the money she'd found under the floor mat in her car.

"She said she had a card for you," the cook had said. "She asked for a mailing address, a phone number, any way to reach you, but I was at a loss. You live on a boat; that's all I know."

Out on the water, Hamilton tried to picture Lilly's face as she called to ask for his address. As if a thank-you card could heal this wound. A kind gesture, sure, but that's all. Ham sighed, realizing the fate of any romance they might have shared would likely have been no different than any of his others. Each relationship ended with the shallow, rehearsed sentiment of a verse in a sympathy card.

His third wife, Torah, was a firm believer in sending greeting cards to acknowledge almost any event of life. Congratulations on your new car. So sorry for the loss of your cat. Happy winter. People love to get cards in the mail, she used to say. Proper etiquette demands it. And besides, it shows good breeding, she would add, as if dime store stationery held the secret of life.

The sails went up, and Ham was once again alone with the wind and the water.

Torah had walked into The Lazy I in response to a Help Wanted sign out front. Ham interviewed her, and to shorten a long story, the interview ended in matrimony. Torah was so organized, Ham was dazzled. Everything she did had a purpose, and her efficiency was like poetry to Ham. Ham admired economy of motion in anything. Maybe she could get him motivated. Maybe she was the answer.

She was also thrilled with the idea of living aboard a boat. She had lived a cloistered life, and she thought living at a marina was like an E-ticket ride at Disney World. Her excitement, however, soon faded. Torah had a number of flaws, in Ham's view. She refused to use the head on the boat. Even though it was functional, with a shower and most conveniences of daily life, Torah insisted on going to the marina shower with an assortment of hair and beauty products. She required that Ham post himself outside to discourage encroachment by others. The daily ordeal would often last an hour.

Ham remained optimistic, believing his life would soon take a dramatic turn for the better. But Torah refused to learn the basics of sailing. She could not be persuaded to pilot the craft while he hoisted the sails. She could not, or would not, get the boat ready to cruise or stow gear afterward. She ignored the proper vocabulary of sailing, insisting on calling sheets or halyards *ropes* and naming marine gear *thingees*.

Torah made sailing difficult because Ham not only had to sail without help but had to tend to her comfort, as well. He consoled himself with the fact that she did look good tanning on the bow.

One day, Ham was greasing the winches and panicked when he couldn't locate the winch handle, which was always in the lazarette on the port side. Torah knew of this tool's importance, but it was hopeless to ask where it was because she wouldn't know it from any other piece of marine hardware. He finally found it, after hours of searching, perfectly centered over a doily in the head. Torah explained that she knew it was important but decided, since it was so ugly, to put it in a place where he could always find it. The relationship was doomed from that moment on.

Wind conditions were ideal, and Ham eased back in the cockpit, accompanied only by his reverie.

Lauless, his fourth wife, had been a perky waitress, almost the antithesis of Torah. He'd fallen in love with her during a spontaneous song-and-dance performance of "Why Don't You Do Right?" she'd given at the diner one evening. He was immediately spellbound by that silky, smooth voice. She couldn't be classified as pretty—she didn't have the classic good looks of his other wives. Her eyes were too big for her head, and she had a mop of curly, short brown hair that always looked as though it had never met a comb. She was wildly enthusiastic about everything. With Lauless, there was no end to adventure. There was no other way to describe her. After she accepted his proposal and the prospect of living aboard a boat, she planned and orchestrated a wonderful engagement party.

Her exuberance was contagious. Ham loved the way she laughed and showed endless curiosity about the most trivial things. They flew to Las Vegas to marry. Her questions about the games and odds were endless. For a while, she was the perfect companion. She made him feel smart. She read about sailing voraciously and asked questions about gear, rigging, and technical matters that were beyond Ham. She wanted to sail in any weather. She asked him after sailing in a storm if he was ever going to unhank the head. Ham wasn't sure what she was asking at first, but finally figured out she meant take down the jib.

She insisted that Ham join sailing clubs and learn how to race. The boat could do it, but Ham had to admit that he could not. The activity level was too frenetic, and frankly, Ham hated going to all the club events and listening to everyone act like they were preparing for the next America's Cup. She finally fell in love with another sailing enthusiast who could drone on about keel shapes all night. He had a bigger boat than Ham and promised Lauless that they would move to the coast, dump this lousy lake, and circumnavigate the globe together.

One failed attempt after another. Lilly would have been the same. Hamilton was a betting man by nature and had been known to take some serious risks in his day. But now, advanced in his years, he had grown to understand Proverbs 4:23 the hard way. He should never have gambled with his heart. It was the one treasure no one could afford to lose.

Rather than pulling closer to the wind and increasing his speed, Hamilton let the wind carry him. He didn't want to live out his days alone. Why did he always lose at love? Why was God holding out on him? The familiar clump of small islands caught his eye. God had allowed him to pass once before. Would he again? Lake levels had continued to fall. The surrounding water was littered with more warning buoys than Ham remembered. Ham felt a surge of adrenaline as he adjusted his course and committed the boat into dangerous territory. If it was a game, Ham wanted to see God's cards. He would raise the stakes. Ham directed the boat between the small islands.

With his jaw set firmly, Ham steered recklessly through the shallow waters. He could feel the brush and debris dragging along his keel. He was almost through the pass when a child on a Jet Ski shot out of nowhere. Hamilton instinctively threw the wheel hard to starboard to avoid a collision. The kid zoomed within inches of his bow, not noticing the danger until it had passed. The kid sliced a frothy arc through the water, spinning the Jet Ski ninety degrees, and stopped with his back to Hamilton. He was tan and shirtless. His yellow hair glistened damp against the nape of his neck.

Hamilton called out to him over the water. "Are you OK, son?"

The boy turned around, and Hamilton felt his knees buckle. He took a step back and grabbed the rail for balance. It was Jesse. The face on the boy he almost hit was the same as the face of the friend he'd watched die in the war.

The boy smiled at Hamilton. Then he twisted the throttle and spun the Jet Ski in an arc sending a spray of lake water in a circle around him. Hamilton watched him do his stunts. It was clear the boy had no recognition of the danger he'd been in. As Hamilton watched, the boy seemed to change.

First Jesse, the friend he could not save.

Then Jack, the son he'd neglected.

Faces continued to scroll through Hamilton's mind. Earline, his young wife, whom he could not heal. Bonita, for whom he'd offered a salvation he could not deliver. Torah, who held a standard of etiquette he could not meet. Lauless, whose fickle affections he could not secure.

Hamilton's heart, like his mainsail, fluttered loose in the wind. He sat and covered his face with his hands.

I've been a proud man, he accused himself, *thinking I had any strength to offer them. Who did I think I was trying to save Noodle the other day? I have no strength to save anyone. Not even myself.*

As the boat drifted beyond the island reefs, the breeze picked back up. Hamilton turned to face it directly, filled with sorrow at the chances he'd taken with his life and the lives of others. He raised his face to God. "I'm not strong," he confessed into the breeze. The wind stiffened, blowing his gray hair away from his face.

But I am, it seemed to say.

[chapter 16]

on the Front Lines

Before children, Saturday mornings were part of a different reality. They replayed in Essie's memory like a scene from someone else's diary. She remembered waking to the warmth of sun rays spilling across the bed in late morning hours, the lazy moments of dewy tenderness with her cheek pressed against Jack's bare chest and his arm curled underneath her. Breakfast gladly waited amid the unhurried desire of morning caresses and slow, easy pillow talk of what the day might hold. Now, however, Saturday morning intimacy had surrendered to the brutal forces of sugared cereal and the Cartoon Network.

Around 9 AM on Saturday, Jack announced that he had some errands to run and would be back in a few hours. He drove off in the Pathfinder.

To be left home alone with the kids all day on a Saturday had historically foreshadowed trouble on the home front. She felt abandoned when Jack left her on the front lines, alone in the kitchen serving breakfast to two boisterous children, while he plunged blissfully into the ample bosom of the auto mall—a series of truck dealerships on one hill and a Harley dealership on another, with a strip of auto-part, tire, and lube establishments in the valley between them. He could easily spend the whole afternoon lost in the cleavage alone. She also felt betrayed when Jack abandoned her while he gratified desires between the long slender aisles of Home Depot, delighting in home improvement's secret pleasures. At least the "other woman" was a hardware store.

Now, however, with many battles behind them, both won and lost, they'd learned from their mistakes and they rarely entertained betraying thoughts of going AWOL on a Saturday. They didn't fall so easily into the landmines of parenthood. With a third child on the way, they'd become not just a skilled troop, but seasoned veterans.

"No parent left behind" was the trigger phrase for weekend afternoons. It meant: take your reprieve but don't leave me without ground support for too long. A workday was much less stressful than a Saturday alone with young, energetic kids. Sure, childcare costs would be very expensive for a working mom of three. But then again, childcare is a bargain compared to rehab.

Today, Essie felt confident, in charge, in control. With both children upstairs motionless in front of a Wile E. Coyote and Road Runner chase, she took the opportunity to throw a load of clothes into the washer and straighten up the kitchen. Her sense of control and accomplishment grew stronger with each completed task. She could do this. She could successfully maintain a house, soon-to-be three children, a functioning marriage, and a career. Life was good; the future bright.

With boosted confidence, she toted a basket of folded laundry upstairs to find Cole dragging Juliet's diaper-changing pad into the hallway. Essie squeezed past him to set the basket of laundry in his room. She returned to the hallway, curious at Cole's new toy. The bicycle crash had not slowed him down for long; rather it seemed to have awakened an appetite for adventure. Cole sat poised at the top of the stairs on his new sled—the changing pad—rocking back and forth to build momentum for a high speed launch down the steps. A throng of dolls and stuffed animals had congregated along the banister to support the event. Essie shrieked and blocked the sled's maiden voyage.

Only an isolated event. No casualties. No damage.

She took away the changing pad, but as soon as she breathed a sigh of relief from the averted disaster, Cole began screaming at the top of his lungs, clenching his fists in protest. "No, Mommy! That's my sled!" About that time, little Juliet rounded the corner at top speed with a black permanent marker. Capless, of course. Unfortunately for Essie, Juliet had become quite fleet-footed over the past few weeks. Essie lunged after her while Juliet, happy to oblige in a game of chase, grinned back at her over her shoulder. "Beep, beep," she giggled, just like Road Runner.

The tip of the marker flailed wildly from the end of a chubby little arm as they raced down the long hallway. Seconds later, Essie heard a young voice rise in an early Christmas carol. "Jingle bells!" Cole had replaced the diaper-changing pad with a new sled, a wide, flat Matchbox car carrying case. "Oh what fun it is to ride in a one-horse open sleigh!" Cole pushed off the top step and instantly spilled headlong among countless miniature sport cars and SUVs.

It was a coup! They had staged a coordinated attack. Breathless, marker in hand, sled tucked under her arm, Essie began to doubt once again her abilities to achieve life balance as a mother, not to mention wife and professional. In a matter of seconds, two small children had replaced her short-lived illusion of control with the reality of their reign of chaos. When did happily-ever-after begin? Where was her fairy-tale rescue? There must be more to life, to motherhood, than this. All the trials, the temper tantrums, the disasters must lead to a glorious ending eventually. There simply must be more significance to the routine, the mundane, the hassles of raising children. She ached to find it.

She consoled herself with reminders that preschool was a transient state of being. Though she had a few hard years ahead of her with three small children, motherhood must surely get easier. Other mothers assured her that tiny reigns of toddler terror mysteriously mutated into manageable childhood interests over time. Her mind leapt toward a future where Cole, all-star hitter, was rounding the bases after launching a ball over the centerfield wall. Juliet was bowing humbly on stage after receiving a standing ovation at her first solo piano recital.

At some point, her well-adjusted children would grow into rational, successful adults, like Jack and Essie. She visualized a grown-up Cole looking into a television camera, waving his ball cap, and saying "Hi, Mom! I love you!" Juliet would be composing her very own symphony with an opening dedication on the playbill that read "For my loving parents, especially my mom." In Essie's daydream, she and Jack smiled at one another, proud parents, sharing the triumph in their achievements, knowing they'd influenced their children's success, congratulating themselves for role-modeling responsibility and discipline.

Focusing on the future made her feel better about the present. For lunch, she fixed the meal of the tired and defeated: a hot dog with a side of Goldfish crackers. As they ate, she reminded Cole that heroism wasn't achieved through reckless stunts. With half the food eaten and half on the floor, she declared lunch over and led them upstairs for naptime, carefully avoiding the miniature cars and motorcycles that littered the steps like a minefield. Small dolls and stuffed animals lurked among the spindles lining the staircase, behind every door, under every bed—a platoon of guerilla warriors waiting for the next signal to strike.

After putting up valiant struggles, their small bodies gave in to sleep. The battle was over, but not the war. They were exhausted, and so was Essie.

This time, the kids won, but she would regain control. She was, after all, an authority in this house. She retreated downstairs to take a rest herself when she noticed someone coming up the driveway. It was Jack returning home from his errands, but he was driving a different car. Instead of the Pathfinder, a gleaming, red Porsche Carrera 911 made its way up the drive.

[chapter 17]

Family car

The Targa top was down, and Jack's head appeared to float above the steering wheel. He parked askew under the basketball hoop. The sun glinted off the hood of the Carrera like a fiery ruby. Jack was beaming, a smile stretched ear to ear. He slid out of the driver's seat and danced around the car, his feet barely touching the ground.

"Got your errand done, I see."

His face radiated ecstasy. "It is perfect. Absolutely perfect. 1987 Porsche 911 Carrera. Only fifteen thousand miles on it. Mint condition. Did you see the spoiler? Look at those wheels."

Essie blurted out her first thought. "How much did it cost?"

"Honey, don't worry so much about money. Everything is taken care of. Just as we agreed, Essie. Remember? One Porsche in exchange for a little sex, drugs, and rock 'n' roll." He popped the trunk, pulled out a bottle of champagne, and handed it to her. He kissed her full on the mouth and smiled euphorically. Bouncing away, he crouched alongside the car to admire it up close. He was bursting with the raw, unabashed enthusiasm of a child. The look on her husband's face triggered Essie's memory of Cole's expression when he got his first train set.

The Porsche itself reminded her of one of Cole's Matchbox cars. Watching Jack admire his new toy, she saw the little boy in his face. Perhaps he wasn't so different from a child. The toys were the same, just bigger and more expensive.

Even though they had an agreement, a part of her was angry about the Porsche, the childishness of it. If parents haven't matured beyond their childhood desires, how are they ever going to role-model responsibility and discipline to their children? And what would be next? Would he bring home a fire truck with the sirens blowing? Quit his job to become a cowboy? Yet his exhilaration was contagious; his laugh infectious. This was the happiest she'd seen Jack in a long time. How could she extinguish his excitement? After all, this was all part of the negotiation they agreed to.

"It is a beautiful car," she confessed, loosening the shackles of her own practicality. Essie wanted to share the joy of this moment with him. She got a thrill seeing him so thrilled. Standing there, holding the champagne bottle, it dawned on her that this was the first time Jack had ever offered her champagne. It was a milestone. He really wanted her support in this decision. Willy Wonka's words echoed in her head: "A little nonsense now and then is relished by the wisest men." She'd seen too many kiddie movies not to understand the value of a little folly. *Besides,* she reminded herself, *this really isn't about a sporty new car; for Jack, it's a symbol of freedom.*

"You will look amazing in it." Once she committed herself to be supportive, the anger began to melt. She put her arms around his neck and pecked him on the cheek. He gave her the grand tour of the convertible, pointing out all its features and functions. Essie soaked in his excitement, allowing it to displace her need for pragmatism, her desire to play it safe, her need for financial security, her want for control. "So, where is the Pathfinder?"

"Oh yeah, that," he grinned mischievously. "I traded it in."

"For this?" Essie felt a shock wave to her brain. "You *traded* our family car for a Porsche convertible?"

"No, darling, of course not," he soothed, putting an arm around her. He was stroking her hair, assuring her, comforting her. "The Porsche is not the family car. It's for me. I traded the Pathfinder for a much better family car."

"What about the Mustang? Are you selling it?" Essie asked.

Jack laughed, stunned by this suggestion. "No way, baby! It's a classic! Why would I get rid of it?"

A vehicle pulling into their driveway drew Essie's attention. Her father. In a Hummer H2.

Jack beamed with satisfaction. "But don't worry. I've got another surprise." He gestured widely at the Hummer. "For you!"

"What?"

Big Jim parked the grotesquely oversized vehicle alongside the little red Porsche. Essie felt a sense of déjà vu when she saw her dad float out from behind the driver's seat and beam an elated smile in her direction. First her husband, and now her father.

She was speechless. Her head filled with steam. This could not be happening. Had these men lost their minds? Was this evidence of some genetic defect at work? Some inherited strain of insanity that permitted affected men to rationalize automobile obsessions and unthinkable impulse purchases? How could Jack convince himself that she would choose a Hummer over a Pathfinder? Did he really expect her to transport three kids back and forth to kindergarten and daycare every day in a tank? And what about her commute to work? How would she navigate the narrow lanes of Ponce de Leon Avenue in this monster truck? She bet it couldn't clear the ceiling of the parking garage at work. She would look ridiculous.

Jack's charming childlike enthusiasm now struck her as selfish and unattractive. A wild rage rose up from the pit of her stomach. She prepared herself for battle.

"You cannot be serious, Jack," she said firmly. "I am not driving this ghastly thing!"

"Just hold on a second. Just listen." Jack and Big Jim combined forces and offered dozens of reasons why this was a wise choice for any working mom. Jack rattled on about the safety features, the advanced air-bag controls, the added capacity of three rows of seats, the overhead DVD player for the kids, the six-disc CD changer, the multiple temperature controls. Her father pointed out the jumbo roof rack and crossbars. "Possible sites for machine gun mounts."

"No! This is not the family car! No way!" Essie insisted.

"Think about it," Jack offered. "An H2 is a celebration of all that is great about America. Essie, do you realize smoking is now outlawed in public restaurants?"

"Smoking? You hate smoking. How is that even relevant?"

"It won't be long until a vehicle like this is illegal, too. America is the only country where a Hummer is even sold! Don't you see? Buying it is a celebration of freedom."

Essie could almost see the Stars and Stripes waving behind him. Cue national anthem.

Rayette and Buddy walked up. "Wholesome beauty. Like motherhood and apple pie," Rayette suggested.

"Second only to a Harley and a Mustang," Buddy added, loyal to his employer, Ford.

"And wait till you try the heated seats!" Jack replied.

Her husband and her father stood in the driveway, admiring the two cars. Owner's manuals were pulled out; hoods were opened. They continued to examine the details of both vehicles, relishing the fine features, celebrating the purchases. Neighbors and passersby noticed the commotion. Soon a congregation of men had huddled in the driveway to pay homage to the absurd icon of strength and exaggerated masculinity.

"What a babe magnet. The women at Paddleboat River Club would admire the size." Walt said, referring to his mixed doubles tennis team. "Size does matter." He winked at the other men.

The men took turns shaking Jack's hand, congratulating him with faces lowered in respect. The scene in the driveway was reminiscent of the closing scene in the *Godfather* when authority changed hands, when Al Pacino became the new godfather. A chorus of praises rose from the men like a choir in a worship service. Essie was vastly outnumbered. She refused to make a heretical scene in front of the devoted parishioners. The Hummer had become a tree house with a "no girls allowed" sign out front. She knew when she was defeated.

Heated seats, indeed! She stormed into the house, remembering her daydream about Cole and Juliet carrying on their family tradition of responsibility and discipline. What a joke! She wedged the bottle of champagne, unopened, in the fridge and slammed the door. Sex, drugs, rock 'n' roll, Porsches, and Humvees. Some role models they were of rational adulthood! *We are doomed*, she thought. *If he wasn't a grown man, I'd show him my own idea of a heated seat.*

[chapter 18]

Halloween

Even after a full week, the sharp edge of the double-vehicle whammy still hurt. Temperatures dropped like the leaves on the trees. Halloween had arrived, steeped in heathen tradition, costumes, and sugar buzzes.

Spider-Man flicked a gloved wrist and flung a web of fish netting over a chubby Tinker Bell. Tink, short and round, was an easy target. She tumbled to the floor in a pile of winged green felt, her ample belly bulging between a tightly fitted tank top and skirt.

"Mama!" she called for help.

It was six o'clock, and Essie was preparing the children for a brief round of trick-or-treating in the neighborhood. A five-year-old Spider-Man and a nineteen-month-old Tinker Bell with a pregnant cowgirl for a mother didn't require a long evening out to complete the Halloween experience. This was Juliet's first real trick or treat, and despite the web attacks, she was eager to make her pixie debut. Spider-Man, true to his nature, was bouncing off the walls with excitement. Their mother was, therefore, obligated to ring a few doorbells with them.

Essie pieced together her costume using a pair of maternity jeans, one of Jack's flannel shirts, and an old pair of boots. She donned a red cowgirl hat and borrowed a plastic gold deputy badge from Cole's toy box and headed out with her posse.

First they visited the neighbors on either side: the Lees and the Weatherstones. Cole raced up to the first door and rang the bell. In a hopelessly preppy shirt—white, collared, and logoed—with white slacks and a "Hi, My name is Walt" nametag pasted on his chest, Walt Weatherstone opened the door, his arm hooked around a giant bowl of candy.

"Trick or treat!" Cole activated his web-flinger glove, but the net did not deploy. It seemed superpowers were hard to come by these days.

"Well, look who we have here! Whoa, Spider-Man! You almost got me, buddy." Walt tossed a handful of candies into Cole's pumpkin-shaped basket. Juliet stared up at him, holding her basket, her green felt wings drooping. "And who is this little one supposed to be? A fly of some kind?" He dropped some candies in her basket.

"Happy Halloween, Walt. This is Tinker Bell," Essie said. "So, who are you supposed to be? A tennis pro named Walt?" She pointed to his name tag.

He covered the sticker self-consciously. "Oh, that. Been to a mixer at the Paddleboat River Club. Out there, forty love ain't just a tennis score, hon. Those women have an appreciation for my serve. So, I've been over there looking for my next mixed-doubles partner, if you know what I mean." He gave Essie a knowing wink and added, "It may be true what they say: mixed doubles was invented by a divorce lawyer."

"Sounds sporting, Walt, but let's not discuss this in front of the kids."

"Looks like the new baby will be here soon. Send my condolences to the sheriff. When you gonna get that minivan, deputy?" He laughed heartily at his own wit.

"I already have."

"You mean the H2? That's *your* car?"

Essie smiled and nodded. "It's the family car." She was still outraged about the H2 purchase but would never admit it to Walt. For her, the new H2 was yet another reminder of her complete lack of control over her own life. While she failed to understand the shame in a minivan, it felt good to deflect Walt's continued efforts to stereotype parenthood. In doing so, she felt the empowerment that comes from breaking a person's mold and redefining the typecast. This, she knew, was what her husband must be after. Making her exit, she prompted the kids, "Say 'Thank You' to Mr. Weatherstone."

"Thank you," Cole said and tried again to launch his stuck web. They headed over to the Lees', leaving Walt staring at his name tag.

Rayette stood on her porch in an enormous blond wig, tight jeans, and a tiny plaid western shirt tied above the midriff, cleavage pressed up to her neck. The kids raced toward her, "Trick or treat!"

"Hello, little darlings. Aren't y'all adorable?"

"Lemme guess. Dolly Parton?"

She fluffed her wig, one hand on her hip. "I hadn't really thought about it, to be honest, shuga. I'm just thrilled to finally have an excuse to go big and blond." She unloaded a shower of candies in the kids' baskets. "Buddy has always preferred blonds."

Buddy grinned guiltily in the foyer behind her. "I'm a lucky man," he said, admiring the fit of his wife's jeans. "Speaking of well-built frames, what you gonna do with that aircraft carrier you got parked out front?"

"Sure wasn't my idea," Essie said.

"Well, an H2 is a fine machine, but a Ford is what you need." He shook his head. "C'mon by the dealership anytime. I'll hook you up."

"I'll keep that in mind," Essie replied.

For their last stop, they hiked a few doors down to Ms. Tuttle's. During the recent neighborhood garage sale, Ms. Tuttle had invited them for a visit to meet her family: a collection of dolls and a herd of Chihuahuas named after the disciples.

En route, Essie smiled to herself about Rayette's choice of costumes. It was refreshing to see married couples flirt, to see them show their attraction.

She admired their playfulness with one another. She pondered what kind of costume might appeal to Jack: the girl who lowers the checkered flag at a car race? The girl in leather chaps and vest who rides her own Harley? The soccer mom driving three kids to the ball field in an H2? Sexy, tough, independent but unrealistic, impractical, irritating.

The choices stirred up a deep anger inside of her, but it quickly withered into a sense of resigned defeat. She couldn't see herself in any of those costumes. Her guesses at her husband's dream girl were simply not who she wanted to be. And worse, she didn't feel like she was the free-spirited wife he wanted her to be.

Wardrobe aside, it was a struggle for Essie to visualize herself as well-suited for any of the real roles she played: wife, mother, professional. She did, however, play a convincing damsel in distress and performed admirably on occasion as the contentious wife.

Since when did practicality and sensibility become so unattractive? Such a turnoff? Why did she feel like such a disappointment to Jack? And why did she feel guilty for being mad about the H2? Wouldn't anyone in her boots be mad?

Cole rang the bell on Ms. Tuttle's front porch, and through the side-lights, Essie saw her rush to greet them. Her creased lips tipped upward in a hot pink strip, and her hair was swept up in its usual bluish-white swirl, looking like something a child would buy at the fairgrounds on a stick. Lining the walls behind her were shelves upon shelves of dolls. Thousands of beady eyes looked down on them, while a crowd of miniature dogs gathered around their heels.

The children stared speechless, awe-struck by the volume of lifelike boys and girls and the swarm of tiny animals. Essie imagined they must feel like giants among so many miniatures. She nudged Cole gently, and he snapped out of his spell. "Trick or treat!"

"Tweet," Juliet echoed.

"Yes, treats most definitely, darlings! I've been looking so forward to your coming. It is my treat to have you. Please, come in."

Ms. Tuttle ushered them inside the surreal surroundings. She led them to an electric toy train boarded by a bevy of small dolls dressed as witches, warlocks, ghosts, and pumpkins. Needing no further instruction, Cole and Juliet immediately set to work repositioning and adding train passengers and navigating them around the track. Ms. Tuttle offered them juice and cookies and introduced them to each of the train riders. She wore her affection for each doll on her face as she held out each one, introducing them by name. Her tender expression reminded Essie of their last conversation, when she referred to her collections as family.

"Ms. Tuttle, thank you for inviting us. You have an amazing collection," she said, recalling the older woman's abrupt departure from the garage sale upon learning of the untimely death of AP, her escaped Chihuahua. She felt a wave of remorse crash down on her for not offering condolences sooner, for not showing more compassion for Ms. Tuttle's loss. "I am awfully sorry about Apostle Paul."

"Thank you, Essie. It is a tragedy about poor AP, but he is in a better place now." Sweeping her hands across the room, Ms. Tuttle said, "But I'm pleased for you to meet the rest of my family. There is nothing in this world more important than family."

Cole deployed his web flinger over a trio of Chihuahuas. Finally, a successful demonstration, not to mention a ray of hope in the ongoing quest for superpowers.

"I agree. I only wish I could offer mine a better wife and mother." Essie's response was automatic and absentminded. The words were out of her mouth before she could reel them back in. "Sorry, I've been feeling a little discouraged lately balancing responsibilities. I have this weird, new assignment at work; my husband is having a midlife crisis; I have this new baby coming." She stopped herself. What was she doing, unloading all this on someone she barely knew? She tried to switch gears. "And I should keep a tighter rein on Spider-Man." She gave Cole a stern warning, and he released the trapped dogs.

Ms. Tuttle laughed. "Honey, you are a fine wife and mother. Divine appointments are never easy jobs. Just ask these little prisoners for Christ." She gathered the released pups into her lap, lifting up each one for introduction.

"This is Peter." She held Peter up to her face and adjusted the tiny black skullcap strapped to his head. "This is Silas." She wound the long tendrils of hair below his ears around her finger, reshaping his forelocks into smooth ringlets. "And this is the new Apostle Paul, the latest addition to the family. The Samaritan woman at the well—Sami, I call her—just had a litter." She pointed to a rotund, long-haired, black-and-white Chihuahua relaxing in a circular dog bed. "So, the apostle to the Gentiles is with us again."

She lowered her voice to a whisper. "But I don't think he needs to know about his predecessor. He's still too young to understand that each of us is called to share in Christ's suffering."

"Are your dogs practicing Jews?" Essie asked, eyeing the yarmulke and the ringlets.

"Oh no, honey, it's Halloween," Ms. Tuttle said, bemused.

"Oh yeah, right," Essie laughed. "Well, their costumes are hilarious. You should get them in the movies and make millions."

"You talk to them. Most of them want to be lawyers!" Ms. Tuttle replied.

Both women laughed.

"Seriously, dear. I remember what it's like to be in your stage of life," Ms. Tuttle offered. "And I'll tell you what helped me through those busy years: remember those beliefs that led you to your biggest life-changing decisions. Hold up those beliefs now and examine them," she said holding up Paul by way of example, "and if they are still true, then stand firm and be confident in them." She kissed the new Paul on his little pink nose. "Sometimes, recalling the basics is all you need to cast away doubt."

"Sounds like good advice. I'll try that," Essie said, feeling nervous and exposed, hoping to close the subject.

"Great, let's try it now." She leaned forward, searching Essie's face. "Let's start with, say, career. What was your original belief about work that has led you to where you are?"

"OK, why not?" Essie decided to play along. *What's the harm?* "I have always believed work is good, work is noble. If you are committed to doing your best, working as unto the Lord, then work is an act of worship."

Almost as soon as she said it out loud, Essie saw the truth she had been missing. *Commitment to do my best. To work as unto the Lord.* In the face of an unattractive assignment and a strange, new boss, she had lost sight of that truth.

"When you examine that belief now, do you still think it's true?"

"Yes," Essie said.

"Then work without fear or shame." Like a heavenly host of cherubim, the dolls hovered above them in silent agreement.

While she still didn't feel committed to the garbage-collector assignment, something in Ms. Tuttle's pronouncement liberated Essie.

"What about motherhood? What do you believe about being a mom?"

"It is a blessing. Children are gifts from God."

"Yes, but what led you to have children, to want to raise children?" Half-a-dozen Chihuahuas scampered underneath the coffee table and tumbled over one another into Ms. Tuttle's lap.

This one was harder for Essie to answer. She hesitated and then said, "Love, I suppose. To have someone to love unconditionally."

Ms. Tuttle repositioned herself against a wide cushion to make room for all the pups in her lap. "Then why are you scared about this third one?

Receive his gift with open arms. Do you believe that God is in control and he knows what is best for you?"

"Of course," she said automatically, but the question sat uncomfortably in her mind. Did God really think three small children was what was best for her, the mom who regularly lost control of the two she already had, the mom who routinely served Goldfish crackers as a vegetable?

"So what about being a wife? What is your deeply held belief on marriage?"

Essie thought back to the days when Jack and she worked at the restaurant together, when he proposed marriage. They were dreamily in love and hopelessly optimistic about their future. She remembered feeling a certainty that their marriage was part of God's plan.

"I believe God handcrafted Jack and me specifically for one another. I believe he has a unique purpose for our lives together."

"Has that changed, dear?"

"Well, no. It's just that life isn't what I pictured it would be at thirty-eight. It's harder, busier. I don't feel like I've become the person I should be, the person I am supposed to be. I feel like a disappointment. To myself, to my kids, to Jack, to God."

"As I see it, honey, if what you fundamentally believe about family is true, then I'd call you a wild success. You have much to celebrate, dear."

Ms. Tuttle's gaze wandered above Essie, and a distant look came over her. "I lost my sweet husband of twenty years to cancer, and I'll tell you my secrets to a perfect marriage: first, honor one another above yourselves, and second, dare to love big and boundlessly."

Curious, Essie asked, "Tell me what you mean."

"Honey, we have to be willing to pour out our lives in order to find them. If you characterize your life by what you give rather than what you get, you will discover that extraordinary, image-bearing child of God you were designed to be. A shining reflection of his glory. Remember who you are, child. You were born to shimmer!

"I remember when I learned I could not have children. I couldn't bear to tell my husband. I was sure he longed for a houseful of pitter-pattering feet. I was ashamed. I couldn't bear to break his heart. When I finally gave him the doctor's report, he just held me tight and said he loved me more than ever, that I was all the family he ever needed."

Essie's eyes softened with compassion. As Ms. Tuttle reflected, she gathered Silas into her lap and tied a miniature prayer shawl around his shoulders. She continued her story.

"Over the years, it became clear that it was really I, not him, who longed for more family, who needed more to take care of. So one day, Mr. Tuttle brought me a little Chihuahua puppy as a gift. It was the tiniest dog I'd ever seen. He said that if we couldn't have children, we could still fill our home with the pitter-pat of little feet.

"The odd thing was that Mr. Tuttle never much cared for dogs; they made him sneeze. That's how I knew he did it just for me. My need was so important to him that he was willing to sneeze his days away to meet it. Nothing could have made me feel more loved. That's when I discovered a love so big for him that it filled the little hole in my heart I had saved for children.

"I learned I already had everything I ever wanted. I told him I didn't need children or dogs or anything else to fill my heart. But ever since that day, he brought me a new Chihuahua puppy every year, and when he couldn't find a puppy, he'd bring me a doll, instead.

"In those months near the end, when the cancer had all but taken him from me, I kept up the tradition myself, lifting his spirits by filling up that hospital room with Chihuahua figurines, each one named right out of the Bible, of course.

"Essie, love big and boundlessly. It never fails. It has the power to conquer any hurt or fear you face in your divine appointments. Love is the most powerful force in the universe." Ms. Tuttle stopped, tucked her chin in, and peered up at Essie, suddenly embarrassed. "Now, just listen to me going on and on."

Ms. Tuttle walked to the kitchen and gathered a box of dog treats, a magazine, and a pair of scissors. "I have an easy dish you could make and take to your mother's house for Thanksgiving." She clipped a recipe from the magazine and handed it to Essie. Then she pulled out a dog treat in the shape of a bacon strip and threw it to the puppies.

Peter and Paul lunged for the treat, each taking an end in a tug of war.

"Look at 'em fight, Mama!" Cole squealed.

"Dogs love bacon treats," Essie explained.

"Honey, they aren't fighting over the snack. Peter is trying to stop Paul from eating pork." Ms. Tuttle picked up Peter and cooed, "It's not real bacon, my little ones. It's kosher." She looked up at Essie and winked.

Essie grinned.

Sami stirred from her dog bed and, with all authority, snatched the bacon strip from Paul's mouth and returned to her lair. Watching Sami gnaw blissfully at the dog treat, Ms. Tuttle observed, "The young ones always miss the point, worrying over the little things. The older and more experienced recognize a gift and know when to enjoy it." She returned Peter to the floor, and the two pups started wrestling again.

"Mom, they're still fighting!" Cole pointed out.

Ms. Tuttle's face turned serious. "That's right. They're arguing about whether I will circumcise them on the eighth day." She snipped her scissors in the air, *fttt, fttt*, then threw her cottony-covered head back and laughed.

[chapter 19]

vehicle woman

Spider-Man climbed into his bunk. "Mommy, can we go back to Ms. Tuttle's house again tomorrow? That was more fun than the fair." Thus far in Cole's short life, taking the rides at the county carnival had been his greatest thrill.

"Yes, it certainly was fun, Son. We'll go see her again soon."

Essie's mind was still full of images from Ms. Tuttle, her house, and her stories. It was strange how God chose the most unlikely sources to send his message. Though it was late and she felt physically tired, Essie was somehow strengthened and invigorated. Ms. Tuttle's tale replayed in Essie's head like lyrics from a catchy song, *Love big and boundlessly. Love is the most powerful force in the universe.*

Tink and Spidey, filled with cookies and candies, went to bed without a struggle. After a big Halloween night out, Tinker Bell gladly shed her wings and curled up in her crib. Placing a thumb in her mouth and curling her other hand against her neck, she fell asleep almost immediately.

With the kids in bed, Essie's thoughts returned to Jack, his new Porsche, her new Hummer. The H2 issue seemed trivial to her all of a sudden. Her anger was gone. In its place was a warm sense of contentment and acceptance. Like the Hassidic Chihuahuas fighting over bacon treats, she'd let herself get distracted by the little things.

What would it mean for her to characterize herself by what she gave instead of what she received, as Ms. Tuttle suggested? Her bargaining to win Jack's approval, her negotiations with him to exchange acceptance of each other's differences had left her with only a hollow victory. What of value did she have to give him without expecting anything in return? How could she show unconditional love? With the force behind her anger now defeated, an idea started to form.

She joined Jack downstairs.

"Hey, honey. Did you get many trick-or-treaters while we were gone? I see most of our candy is gone."

"Annabelle next door came as Goldilocks. Mickey and a few other neighborhood boys were disguised as all manner of superheroes. One kid came in an all-white suit with sparkles all over it. I asked if he was an angel. Turns out he was Elvis."

Essie smiled. She told Jack about Ms. Tuttle and her collections as they mechanically changed into their pajamas and moved to the kitchen. They picked through the Halloween candy and confiscated a few choice pieces for themselves. Sitting across from each other at the kitchen table, the conversation thinned, and the night grew quiet.

Silently, Essie entertained a new fantasy inspired by Ms. Tuttle's advice. What would it mean to Jack? Would it communicate unconditional love and acceptance? Was she giving up her position, her preferences too easily? Was she just a pushover? Or was she just looking for the quickest way to remove the tension between them?

Finally, she pushed all doubts aside, swallowed a lump of pride, and said, "You know, I never really received the complete tour of the H2. Now that the kids are asleep, I thought you might show me how those heated seats work."

Stunned by this suggestion, Jack studied her face for sincerity. "Nah, let's not get into that now. It's late, and you're not really interested."

"Really, I am. I've been thinking about it a lot, and I think I reacted too hastily. C'mon; I really want to see it."

Jack was skeptical. "OK, if you insist." Eyeing her suspiciously, he took her by the hand and led her into the garage. The H2 filled the space like a tank, barely clearing the roof of the garage.

"Get in the driver's seat," he said as he climbed into the passenger's side. She struggled to find a way to lift herself, swollen belly and all, into the driver's seat. Finally she just hiked a leg, pressed her bare foot to the base of the door panel, and with a grunt, gracelessly heaved herself into the seat. She'd have to work on this procedure.

"Why don't we do this another time?" Jack sighed, discouraged. "Footboards are on order. Once they're installed, it will be much easier for you to get in and out."

"No time like the present," she said. "Please continue."

Jack gave her a puzzled, sidelong glance as if to say, *I know there is a trap here somewhere.* Finally, he opened the glove compartment and, retrieving the owner's manual, flipped through the pages until he found a diagram of the dash controls. He became increasingly animated as he walked his wife through the features and functions. She listened and asked questions. Jack inserted a Peter Pan video to demonstrate the DVD player.

"Cole and Juliet are going to love this," she said, adjusting the angle of the video screen toward their empty car seats. "What about the CD changer? Show me how that works."

Jack pulled a stack of CDs from the deep storage compartment between their seats and fanned them out in his palm like a deck of playing cards. "It's a six-disc changer. Take your pick." She selected a few favorites and inserted them in the player. Marvin Gaye, U2, Al Green, the Rolling Stones. The music wafted from all directions, filling the bulky vehicle with an unfitting aura, something akin to romance.

"I like it." Essie smiled broadly at him as the music rushed through their veins, breaking down remaining defenses and exposing vulnerabilities just beneath the surface.

"I thought you hated it, Essie. Why the sudden change?"

"I don't hate it. It's just not what I would've chosen."

"And what do you think now?"

"It's still not my first choice," she admitted. "But you are. When I really thought it through, I realized the kind of car I drive is not all that important to me. But it is important to you. And *you* are important to me."

Jack's hopeful expression turned sour. "So you really don't like it. You'll just cope with it for my sake. Is that what you're saying?"

"No, what I'm saying is, I love you. I am completely and totally in love with you. And I want to help you find what you're looking for, even though I don't think your real search is for something with wheels."

"OK, I get it. Another negotiation, right? What are you after, Essie?" he looked at her sideways.

"No negotiation. I want you to know that I love you just the way you are. I don't care if you drive a minivan or a spaceship. Your car doesn't make you a better man; you're already the perfect man for me. And to prove it, I want you to show me how the heated seats work." She tilted her chin low, eyeing him playfully.

He gave her a puzzled look, "Essie, are you OK? You're acting strange." He switched on the control to activate the heated seats. "All you do is turn this switch."

"Do the back seats heat up, too?"

"Actually, yes." He pressed the button for rear seat controls. She climbed into the back seat, tugging his nightshirt, coaxing him to follow. Now they were sitting close to each other, face to face.

"Look," she explained, leaning in to his face, "I understand what these cars mean to you. Freedom. Our freedoms are constrained with three kids and demanding jobs. You feel hemmed in by your responsibilities, right? And you don't want to surrender your identity, your sense of self. I don't want to discourage your freedom; I want to celebrate it with you. If that means driving an H2, it's no sacrifice for me."

He was still looking at her, bewildered. "So, you're not mad at me then?"

"Do these seats lie flat?" she asked.

"Sure." He pulled a tether and folded the seats into a bed.

Essie spread a blanket between them. "I'm more than a mommy and a wife and a checkbook balancer. I'm still the same crazy girl you fell in love with sixteen years ago. So, if you're looking for a wild ride, then let me be your vehicle, baby." She pulled her husband close to her and kissed him passionately on the mouth. They laid back on the blanket and pressed their bodies against each other.

"People can say what they want about Humvees, but you can't beat 'em when it comes to leg room," Essie admitted.

"You are crazy, you know that?" Tenderly, Jack swept away wisps of hair from her face and then rested his hand lightly on her swelling abdomen. "And I sure do love you for it." He returned her kiss, this time with urgency.

Marvin Gaye sang "Let's Get It On" soulfully in the background, as though offering a bit of advice. Essie grinned mischievously and arched a suggestive brow at her husband, as if the music said it all. And it did.

[chapter 20]

Rearview Mirror

Hamilton Wells eased into the driver's seat of an old Ford pickup. He angled the rearview mirror to check his appearance. Life on a sailboat didn't afford much opportunity for extensive grooming. And the pocket mirror on board was too small to reflect the whole package. Hamilton used the mirror in his truck, and sometimes the one in the diner restroom, to tidy up the occasional dab of shaving cream or missed button on his shirtfront.

He dragged a wet comb across his head, forcing the gray mass to lie smooth and silvery across his scalp. He leaned in close to the mirror and smiled broadly to inspect his teeth. The purple scar along his jaw stretched into an arc of shiny, colorless wrinkles. As Hamilton repositioned the rearview, it occurred to him that most of his life could be found there. All that he was, all his memories, everything he'd ever done: it was all there in the rearview. He wondered how much farther the road stretched out ahead of him.

His mind wandered into the images of his past while he shifted the truck into drive. Gravel crunched under his tires as he left the marina and headed east toward Jack and Ellison's Stone Mountain home. It was the first time he'd been invited to a family dinner at his son's home. He wished Earline, Jack's mother, could've been here to join them.

Earline was Hamilton's first love. She'd understood Ham's displays of affection occasionally lacked sophistication. Though she would never have permitted such distance to grow between father and son in the first place, she'd know just what to tell Ham to do to make amends with Jack now.

Back in 1960, Hamilton and Earline had been high school sweethearts. To Ham, it seemed they were made for each other. Earline, however, took some convincing. At school, Hamilton's devotion frequently took the shape of messages burnt into trees with a magnifying glass.

First, the proud oak in the school commons boasted of Hamilton's love. He charred Earline's name, bold and prominent, inside a lopsided heart. The burnt etching loomed large in the courtyard for the entire student body to see. For reasons Hamilton could not understand at the time, Earline found the defacing of school property with her name less romantic than Hamilton imagined. To her, it was more in the category of crude suggestions written on the wall of a public restroom. Thus, Hamilton's declarations of love were not met with the enthusiasm he had hoped for. So Hamilton tried harder.

In time, every tree on school property vowed his never-ending love for Earline. Nevertheless, Earline remained unimpressed. On the contrary, Earline was mortified by the whole business. She, a budding debutante and active member of the Methodist Student Union, described Hamilton's tree-scarring antics sophomoric and undignified.

Though Earline appeared to ignore his advances, Hamilton did not go unnoticed. He took heaps of ridicule from other students.

"Hamilton doesn't just wear his heart on his sleeve; he wears it on his pines, oaks, and maples."

"Honestly, a heart on every tree? Talk about sappy."

Hamilton was not deterred by the abuse. He interpreted the ridicule as a test of perseverance. Having run out of trees, Hamilton decided to express his devotion on the east wall of the school building itself, a sprawling billboard of his affection. At this, Earline was embarrassed beyond measure. Yet standing in front of the vandalized structure with her hands over her face, peeking at her name through the spaces between her fingers, she couldn't help but be a little impressed by such a grand gesture.

Earline, a pragmatic girl by nature, must have recognized when to reassess the situation. Hamilton, after all, was a nice-looking boy, according to many of the other high school girls. Especially those sparkling gray eyes, some said. And there was little chance any other young men would call on Hamilton's beloved in the face of his pervasive and outrageous acts of devotion.

So Earline approached Hamilton with feigned anger, and in a matter-of-fact way declared, "So I suppose you'll want to take me to the fall dance." It was more of a statement than a question. Hamilton, equally bewildered and elated, stammered his enthusiasm for this idea and made arrangements to pick her up at her house.

On their first date, Earline tried to reason with Hamilton. "I'll go out with you if you promise to stop burning my name into every flammable surface on school property." Hamilton readily agreed, and his heart soared over the moon.

The next Sunday, Earline's family gasped in unison as they prepared to leave home for church and found Earline's name scarred into the overgrown oak that filled her front yard. It wasn't until the following week that another token of affection was discovered. A plus sign with Hamilton and Earline's initials had appeared on the post that supported the mailbox. Ham's defense? It wasn't school property.

Despite her father's protest, Ham worked his way into Earline's heart. Over time, Earline managed to curb Hamilton's destructive tendencies. Instead of burning trees and carving posts, Earline helped channel Hamilton's creativity in more constructive ways. He whittled figurines for her. He learned to make wooden jewelry pieces. He built a swing that he and Earline's father hung from her front porch.

Next, he graduated to simple table and chair designs. Little did Hamilton realize that his woodworking pastime would eventually become his first vocation. He had no idea that these hobbies were to be pushed aside for another, more powerful talent.

Hamilton and Earline married soon after graduation and moved into a tiny, two-bedroom house twenty miles north of Atlanta. Earline took a part-time job at the local diner. The thought of her in her uniform still made Ham weak in the knees.

Hamilton had just landed a job working full time with one of Earline's older brothers building furniture. He learned quickly from the men who worked alongside him. They taught him not only the art and science of woodwork but also the art and science of wagering. To the boys in the shop, poker was a way to pass the time when business was slow. For Hamilton, however, learning how to win became a greater art than the woodwork itself.

It was in the workshop that Ham discovered his uncommon proficiency in gaming—cards, checkers, sports, dice, whatever, Ham was a natural. He had an innate ability to read the gaming table and calculate the odds from the expressions on the faces around it. When he didn't have the cards, he could put on a stony face and bluff recklessly. His dexterity with cards would make him a near legend in the military, where Ham could bluff regiments out of their socks and paychecks with his sphinxlike expressions and aw-shucks attitude.

In 1965, four years after he and Earline were married, Hamilton's draft number was called. He was more than reluctant to leave his beloved wife but remained duty-bound to serve his country. Earline stood at the train station, waving goodbye.

In her hand, she clutched a medallion Hamilton had given her. The shellacked wedge of wood was heart-shaped and inscribed with a handcrafted message: *Ham loves Earl 4ever.* Hamilton abbreviated to make space. He strung a thin silver ribbon through pinholes on either side of the medallion and presented the necklace to Earline the day he broke the news of his assignment. She stood sobbing in her aproned uniform. Hamilton gathered her into his arms, tied the necklace at the nape of her neck, and held her close until the tears passed.

Checking his rearview mirror, Hamilton warmed himself with memories of Earline as his truck merged into traffic on Highway 985. He pressed the accelerator until the gauge read 65 mph. He matched the flow of traffic and settled back into his seat. It was a thirty-mile drive to reach his son's house. Hamilton glanced into the rearview and swung into the left lane. In the mirror, he caught a glimpse of a familiar memory: Jesse and the war. Ham would give anything to go back and come to Jesse's aid when more was at stake than a pile of coins in a poker game. He let up on the gas, allowing the scene to linger.

On the day he left to fight for his country, as the train pulled away from the station, Hamilton felt his heart yanked from his body as if ripped out by its roots. Earline and his hometown were all he had ever known, all he ever wanted to know. On the train, he was surrounded by other recruits, many of whom he had known all his life. Yet only thirty minutes out of town, Hamilton felt a loneliness crowd in that frightened him.

The wheels rumbling along the rails felt strange and powerful. They were carrying him away from everything that meant home and taking him to some distant, hostile destination. The air in the railcar smelled foul; the faces of the boys he'd played ball with looked suddenly unfamiliar. With cold indifference, the train thundered rhythmically along its track.

Hamilton dealt with his fear the way he always had. He shoved it into his belly and mustered up his unique brand of southern charm. Hamilton pinned an easy smile on his face and, in short order, found his place among a crowd of young soldiers playing cards.

By the lay of the table, Hamilton recognized the game instantly as Nugget Hold'em. He found an open seat next to a young kid with straight, white-blond hair and a narrow, fair-skinned face. He was eighteen years old, but the way his bangs hung in a straight line across his brow made him appear even younger.

The kid held four cards close to his chest and stared wide-eyed at the flop, the three community cards upturned in the center of the table. The kid shifted his gaze to his two opponents.

Hamilton regarded the fair-haired boy and followed the kid's gaze to take in the trio of players. One was a beefy farmhand with bulging forearms and large callused hands; the other was smaller, but hard and wiry looking, with sleek black hair and dark eyes. The beefy one tossed two quarters into the kitty. The dark one did the same. The blond kid cast his eyes back to the four cards he held in his hand and did his best to blank his own expression. He stuffed his free hand into his pocket and pulled out a fistful of coins. He flipped two quarters alongside the others.

"Good day, gentlemen," Hamilton said. "Room for another player?"

The dark one flipped the turn card over, shrugged, and without looking up from the table said, "Why not?"

The kid's eyes widened at the turn card, then darted into his lap.

"Name is Hamilton Wells. From Atlanta," Hamilton offered. "Where you boys from?"

"I'm Jesse," the fair one said. "From Tybee. Little town near Savannah, Georgia." He shifted his cards awkwardly to his left hand and extended his right to Hamilton. Hamilton pressed his palm firmly into Jesse's and caught an accidental glimpse of the jack and queen of hearts. Jesse smiled and gave Hamilton a quick nod. On the crown of Jesse's head, a cowlick sprouted a tuft of white hair upright like a down feather.

The beefy one grunted, "Cletus, from Alabama," and tossed in two more coins.

"Frankie, South Carolina," the dark one said studying his cards. "I'm on my way to teach the Vietnamese something about Carolina justice." Two more quarters clinked into the kitty.

Jesse met the bet and was left with only two dimes in front of him. "Me and my girl are getting married soon as I get back," Jesse said.

"And now for the river," Frankie said as he flipped over the last community card, the king of hearts. Also face-up on the table were the ten and ace of hearts, the ten of spades, and the four of clubs.

Jesse shifted excitedly in his seat. His young face beamed for a brief instant and then went solemn as he worked a hand into one pocket after another under the table.

Cletus coughed into his fist. "I seen a picture of my cousin's gal over there. Says she's the purtiest thang on two legs." He squared his cards together and placed them facedown on the table. "Bet is yours, Frankie."

Cletus rubbed his palm over the stubble behind his head, as though unaccustomed to the feel of the crew cut. All new recruits would get a GI buzz when the train reached the serviceman camp. Evidently, Cletus intended to be one step ahead, having shaved his head himself. His tool of choice appeared to have been a gardening device of some sort. It wasn't long before Hamilton learned there was the right way, the wrong way, and the army way, and no advance planning would help where they were going.

Frankie tapped a cigarette out of his pack and hung it between his lips. He pulled a Zippo lighter and a folded stack of bills from his pocket. He lit the cigarette, inhaled, and blew a stream of smoke into the air. The end of the cigarette blazed with the same intensity as the fire in his black eyes.

"I say blow 'em all to bits and send the ashes to Pluto," Frankie said. He peeled a one-dollar bill from his stack and tossed it onto the stack of coins.

Cletus rubbed the short bristles on the top of his head and frowned. He cut his eyes at Frankie. Frankie glared back with a look that could fry bacon and twirled his cigarette between his thumb and forefinger.

"My cousin says some of them gals so hot they's got enough 'lectricity could start a Massey Fergerson tractor," Cletus offered. He grazed the stubble on his chin with thick, callused fingers and leaned back in his chair. "I'll see your buck and raise you another."

Jesse looked at his two dimes, and his chest fell. He turned to Hamilton as if searching for an answer to a question yet to be asked. Hamilton gave him a one-sided smile, slid a foot toward Jesse and flicked his eyes toward the floor. Jesse followed the movement and found a five-dollar bill creased lengthwise and cuffed around the leg of his chair.

Jesse reached down. "What a relief," he sighed. "Thought I'd lost this." The kid restrained any show of gratitude toward his benefactor, refolded the bill along its crease and floated it like a paper airplane into the kitty. "Better to lose it intentionally, I guess."

Cletus and Frankie looked at each other, then back to Jesse and Hamilton. After another cigarette, Frankie called, matching the bet. Cletus rubbed his head some more, presumably for luck, and did the same.

Jesse flipped his cards, revealing the royal flush. He gathered the pile of money to himself with both hands, grinning like a cat. His golden cowlick fluttered above his head like the last of the canary.

"With luck like that, the VC don't stand a chance. I reckon I'll stay right behind this fella," Hamilton offered. The other men smirked, then chuckled in spite of themselves.

Hamilton was dealt into the next game. And though Jesse lost most of his winnings to Hamilton in the subsequent hour, they both knew they'd won something more valuable in the process. Jesse's admiration made it easy for Hamilton to swallow his fear and play the part Jesse quickly grew to expect.

The recollection shrank into the distance as Hamilton's truck slowed to a stop and idled at the stoplight. A few more miles, and he'd arrive at Jack and Ellison's house. The red light switched to green. Hamilton flashed a glance at the rearview and swung right on Highway 78. Somewhere in the mirror, swirling in his wake of fallen yellow and orange leaves, he spotted another view from his past: the day he learned he would be a father.

Earline wrote beautiful letters. Her letters were filled with the kind of love that made a man strong, not weak. He fortified himself with her words. He had been gone only eight weeks when he received a letter that sent an electric jolt down his spine.

"Ham, the Lord has seen fit to give us a child. Just imagine, even now he knits him together inside of me."

Hamilton felt both a surge of strength and an icy fear spread in the marrow of his bones. He told Jesse, "I'm going to be a father."

"You'll make a great dad, Ham. The kid is lucky," Jesse had said. "I hope to have a son one day, too. My girl says she wants a big family."

Jack was the first and only son of Hamilton and Earline Wells, born in the winter of 1966, five years after they were married. Earline raised young Jack on her own for two years before Hamilton came back from the war.

Their reunion was joyous. Earline greeted him, wearing the same wooden necklace he'd made for her years ago. Yet Ham wasn't home long before his wife claimed he was quieter than she remembered. Earline said the war had changed him. She said he still held the moon in his eyes, but it seemed farther away.

Though her face was as lovely as Hamilton remembered, Earline had changed, too. Her body moved with more fatigue, something in her smile seemed much older. At first, the doctor said it was normal—what every other soldier's wife went through. Geritol was prescribed.

Hamilton began to suspect it was something more the day he came home from work to find Earline collapsed in the kitchen with young Jack screaming uncontrollably and standing over her crumpled form.

For three agonizing years, Hamilton watched Earline weaken, wince, and buckle in pain as the cancer consumed her. She spent her last months in bed, helpless. Her death dealt a shattering blow to Hamilton and Jack.

After Earline's passing, father and son lived in the house alone for several years. But for Hamilton, everything about the house reminded him of Earline. The chair by the fireplace, the curtains in the kitchen, the smell of pine in the yard, even the trees themselves. Everything echoed of Earline's absence. Worse, it shouted accusations of Hamilton's inability to save her.

In the evenings, after Jack was asleep, Hamilton would sit in the chair by the fireplace, holding the wooden necklace he'd made for Earline. On its inscription, he had promised her a forever. But he had not delivered. He had not saved her. Instead, he had stood by and let her die. Just like Jesse.

He recalled the day he announced to a teenage Jack that he had purchased a sailboat and they'd be moving to the lake. Permanently. Jack, like most teenagers, thought he alone knew what was best and that his father understood nothing. He protested, wanting to stay near his own friends, not wanting to change schools. At Hamilton's insistence, they eventually moved to the boat. They fought constantly. Or rather, Jack fought and Hamilton, out of guilt and shame, acquiesced. Hamilton carried the responsibility for all of Jack's anger, attributing it to his motherless boyhood and his fatherless infancy.

Jack had made his accusations clear. He loathed his father's surrender to failure, surrender to guilt. Jack thought of him as weak. Like his mother. He didn't believe Hamilton had what it took to win in this world. Jack viewed his father's move to the lake as some kind of self-imposed exile, a punishment of isolation. He knew Hamilton had plenty of money. Jack had been told the extent of his father's wheat fortune but considered it a waste on a man who'd lost all motivation to make any good use of it.

Jack vowed never to be like his father. He had a different plan. He would make something of himself. He wouldn't be carried away slowly by any direction of the wind, like his father on his sailboat. He'd be the master of his own destiny. Get a fast bike, make some real money, and eventually open a motorcycle shop.

Hamilton recalled that day he stood silent on the boat, shielding wet lashes behind a pair of shades, as Jack walked down the dock for the last time, lugging a suitcase. Everything Hamilton remembered about Jack's appearance the day he left—the confident stride, the squared shoulders, the way he shifted the weight of his luggage from one hand to the other—cut like a knife.

Old memories kept in the far reaches of Hamilton's mind had been resurrected. They returned to him now in living color, fully restored to their original vibrancy. Hamilton shook his head, struggling to separate the past from the present.

He pulled the pickup into his son's driveway and pushed the transmission into park. He angled the rearview toward himself one last time to make sure he was presentable. He raised his chin to the mirror and stroked the length of his scarred jaw. *I won't let him go this time*, he thought.

[chapter 21]

I'm No Angel

"He's been married four times? Are you serious?" Ms. Ada Tuttle asked.

"His first wife, Jack's mother, died young. And he's lived on his sailboat ever since," Essie said.

The warm air in Ellison's kitchen hung heavy with the aroma of barbecue. The Southern blues sound of the Allman Brothers drifted through the house, carried from room to room through built-in speakers. Without any prodding, Jack had turned on the player, forfeiting his usual musical preferences for hers.

In the living room, Hamilton and Jack reclined in oversized chairs while Ada, the Apostle Paul, and Essie huddled in the kitchen.

"How is he related to you again?" Ada peered around the countertop to the men in the living room.

"He's Jack's father," she explained. "Quite a character, too. Kinda like you."

Ada frowned. Deep creases formed around bright pink lips. "What is that supposed to mean?"

Ada Tuttle had accepted the invitation to join Jack and Essie for a barbecue rib dinner with a "mystery guest." Since their Halloween visit, Essie and Ada had become frequent guests in each other's homes. Ms. Tuttle had insisted that Essie call her Ada.

Essie was grateful to have her there. It was thanks to Ada that her kitchen was put to any use at all. Before Ada demystified the postmodern, state-of-the-art control panel, Essie had used her dual-fuel oven as a storage space for out-of-season sweaters.

Essie pushed a sheet of garlic bread into the oven. The metal tray clattered against the oven rack, startling Apostle Paul, who ducked behind Ada's ankle and shivered. Ada picked him up, cradled him in the crook of her arm, and stroked his plum-sized skull. Apostle Paul's ears slicked back in appreciation.

The voices of the men rose from the den.

"Seriously, what were they thinking? Brass bolts on chrome. And now there's a new scratch on the tank. It's ridiculous." Jack threw his hands up in exasperation. He was complaining about the quality of work performed on a recent motorcycle service.

"I took it back up to the shop. Wound up fixing it myself in their service bay. They discounted the bill, but it still amounts to another free lesson for their mechanics. I don't know why I bother. I basically held a tutorial for the techs there."

"A what?" Ham asked.

"A tutorial, an instruction session," Jack explained.

"It's a shame," Hamilton agreed. "Quality service is hard to come by. Last guy who worked on my boat left town with my wife. Lauless, the fourth one." He paused. "Then again, maybe it wasn't such a bad deal after all."

"That's exactly what I'm talking about," Jack said, ignoring the last remark. "You just can't find good help anymore. If it didn't void the warranty, I'd have done the job myself right here at home."

Overhearing all this from the kitchen, Essie recognized the familiar topic and rolled her eyes for Ada's benefit. Ada offered a reassuring smile and whispered, "We love him for it. All part of his charm." Jack was renowned among their neighbors for his passion for cars and motorcycles and his intensity when it came to their care.

Hamilton shook his head. "A real shame. I keep telling you, Son: you oughta open a shop of your own. We could do it together. I know a winner when I see one. And you're a natural."

Jack ignored the compliment. "Well, if I ever did, I know exactly what I'd do different, Pop. Biker's Eye."

Ham's gray eyebrows hopped north. "You lost me, boy."

Ada and Essie suspended dinner preparations to eavesdrop from the kitchen.

"There are plenty of guys like me out there, Pop. Guys who invest in nice things and want to keep them that way. They don't want just anyone working on their stuff. They want people who care and who take pride in their work. And most importantly, they want to be able to see what's going on."

"So it's really just another tool of customer service, then," Hamilton concluded. "Just more hi-tech."

"With Biker's Eye, customers can watch their repairs in real time if they want. They'd know the time slot of their repair, so they could sign on to a Web site and watch the work through cameras installed in the service area. Even if they didn't care to watch, knowing they could if they wanted to would give them a greater sense of trust in how their equipment would be handled."

Hamilton let the idea sink in for a minute.

Dinner was ready, so Essie called everyone to the table. "Come and get it, folks. Time to eat."

Cole and Juliet scrambled downstairs to join the rest of the gang. As Jack made his way to the kitchen, Essie spied around the corner at Hamilton. He was still reclined in his chair. He scrawled something hurriedly on a note card and slipped it in his breast pocket.

When he passed through the kitchen, Hamilton kissed Essie on the cheek. "Pretty as springtime, gal," he said and nodded a greeting toward Ada.

Essie returned the kiss. "So glad you could come. Hamilton, I'd like to introduce you to my friend Ada Tuttle."

"Howdy, ma'am." Hamilton tipped an invisible hat.

The Apostle Paul, still nestled in the crook of Ada's arm, shivered and buried a nose into her armpit.

"Evening, Mr. Wells," Ada returned AP to the floor. The pup trembled and tucked himself into Ada's pant leg.

"Please, call me Ham. Fresh vittles, eh?" Hamilton gestured toward the dog. "I haven't eaten varmint since the war, but I'm man enough if you are. Here's the spicy barbecue sauce, just like I promised." He pulled a small jar from his pants pocket and placed it on the kitchen counter. "For anyone who wants to kick it up a notch."

AP crouched even lower, his belly almost touching the floor, and shivered.

Hamilton whispered to the ladies, "Looks like he knows what's coming." He bent down and spoke to the dog. "Don't worry, little fella. You won't feel a thing."

Ada tightened her jaw and narrowed her eyes at Hamilton. "Mr. Wells, if you don't mind, I—"

Essie interrupted, "This is Apostle Paul, Ada's pet dog." She gestured to the quaking pup. "He's a Chihuahua," as if that were explanation enough.

The group gathered around the dinner table and each took a seat. Hamilton chose one next to Ada. Jack set the full platter of ribs in the center of the table. Hamilton pretended to wipe perspiration from his brow. "Whew! Well, that's a relief."

To the dog, who trembled underneath Ada's chair, he added, "For both of us, I'd say!" He winked at Ada, who folded her arms across her chest and forced a thin smile.

"Does he always shake like that?" Hamilton regarded the dog suspiciously and forked a full rack of ribs onto his plate. "Reminds me of my fourth wife, Lauless, whenever we went to church. That gal had been around the block a time or two, and well, being in the house of the Lord made her as shaky as a fisherman trying to write a letter."

"AP is a short-coated teacup Chihuahua." Ada's patience had grown thin. "They all shake. For your information, Mr. Wells, AP is bred from a fine championship line." Ada snapped her cloth napkin open forcefully, then recovering composure, spread it daintily in her lap.

"His eyes are bugged out, too. Pardon me for saying so, ma'am, but he looks like he's trying to pass a persimmon seed."

Cole and Juliet contorted themselves to fit their heads under the table for a better look at Apostle Paul. Hamilton spooned out a healthy portion of cinnamon apples and passed the serving bowl to Jack, who did the same.

Ada pursed her pink lips. A crimson tint rose in her cheeks and spread over her ears.

This wasn't playing out the way Essie had hoped. She cleared her throat lightly, and Jack finally noticed the pained expression on her face. "Shall I say grace?" he asked.

Once the food was blessed, everyone plunged in. Hamilton was the first to palm a smothered rib, paint on an extra coat of spicy sauce, and begin gnawing. Ada held the tips of the rib bone delicately, pinkies out, like skewers in a corncob.

"So tell me more about this Biker's Eye idea," Hamilton said, mouth and fingers stained with barbecue sauce.

"It's a way a customer can watch the work being done without actually being there. Cameras feed the video to a Web site, which customers can watch online. I don't know of a single shop that uses the technology. I'm convinced it would give any shop that competitive edge to win. Under different circumstances, I'd try my hand at launching my own business.

But I'm up to my ears at work already. I just don't have the time to get it going. Besides, with the new baby coming, this is no time to take that kind of risk."

"Sounds awfully complicated," Hamilton said, a spoonful of mac 'n' cheese waiting at his lips.

"You'd be surprised, Pop. It's really quite simple."

"If anyone could pull it off, Jack, you could," Ada offered.

"They're right, honey. It is a risk, but if you want to open your own shop, I'd support it," Essie said.

"Well, I know a little something about taking risks. And it may not be as risky as you think. First thing is you gotta know how to pick a winner." Ham looked at Essie and winked. "Looks like you inherited that particular gift from me. So you got a lot going for you, Son. I say, give your idea a try."

Jack picked up on Hamilton's reference to his wife and patted Essie's knee under the table.

"When it comes to winning in love, I'd say I got you beat hands down, Pop," he teased good-naturedly.

"You got me there, Son. But I've learned a thing or two in my day. And if you're not careful, you might learn something from listening to an old man."

Ham turned his attention to Cole. "At the boat the other day, you asked me if I was a hero. You want to be a hero, my boy?"

Cole, eager to be included in the adult conversation, snapped to attention. "Yes, sir."

"You and I are a lot alike, you know that? I always wanted to be a hero, too. You wanna know the secret magic behind superheroes?"

Cole's eyes grew wide, and his mouth gaped open with cinnamon apples, as if the mystery was about to be unraveled. Essie knew Cole suspected there was more to his granddad than met the eye. The look on her son's face said it all. Finally, he would learn the truth he'd been waiting for. He put his fork down, nodded solemnly, and prepared himself for a full disclosure.

"They aren't in it for their own glory. Superpower comes from putting someone else first."

Cole cocked his head to the side. This didn't seem to clear up the matter for him.

"See, Son, listen to the voice of experience, an old man who used to be just like you. I wanted to be a hero, and on occasion, I may have even persuaded a few people that I was. But really," Ham lowered his voice to a whisper but kept it loud enough for all around the table to hear, "all I was doing was trying to convince myself. That's why I never became a true hero. A true hero doesn't make himself a hero. He is made into a hero by making others more important than himself."

"Is that it?" Cole asked. He scrunched up his nose as if stumped by a riddle.

"Yep, that's it," Hamilton said.

Cole shrugged and pushed another cinnamon apple into his mouth. A shadow of disappointment spread across his young face. The boy's expression suggested grown-ups did this sort of thing all the time and he wished they'd just speak plainly.

"Why, Essie, you and Ms. Ada have outdone yourselves." Hamilton wiped his soiled mouth with a napkin. "This is about the best barbecue I've had." He smiled at Ada and gestured to the rib platter. "Ma'am, do you mind passing the ribs this way?"

Ada smiled back. She passed the tray to Hamilton, her eyes softened toward him.

Conversation flowed easily for the rest of the meal. Jack shared the story of Hamilton's attempted rescue of Noodle, with Cole interjecting all the important highlights his Dad omitted.

"I suppose that proves it." Essie smiled, her gaze spanning the three generations of Wells men at her table. "I thought it was a phase, but it looks like you boys don't outgrow it. Every man around here, young or old, wants to be a hero."

"And they like to show off, too. Reminds me of my late husband," Ada added, reaching for the open jar of hot sauce in front of Hamilton and pouring a dab on the lip of her plate. "Even in the hospital after all those treatments, he'd douse his eggs in Tabasco just to show he was still tough."

"And heroes aren't partial to mild tastes or minivans, are they, honey?" Essie grinned at her husband.

Everyone laughed when Essie retold the story about Jack's latest car purchases. Ada and Hamilton talked about their favorite spicy dishes. It turned out, they shared a similar grief and they both liked hot sauce with their eggs. As soon as dinner had degenerated to mere conversation, Juliet quickly lost interest in the entire affair and followed her brother upstairs to resume their game of "damsel in distress."

On her way, Juliet folded her palm open and closed at her grandfather, "Bye-bye, Popi."

Hamilton's eyes twinkled silver as he waved back. "Bye, little princess."

Jack and Hamilton returned to their recliners. Ada and Essie joined them on the couch.

"So, how's that old truck been runnin'?" Jack asked.

Essie wondered how long it would take to get around to that question. It was only a matter of time before the conversation returned to cars or motorcycles.

"Runs like a champ," Hamilton replied.

"What kind of mileage does she get?"

There it was. She knew that particular question would come; it was an eventuality.

"Uses more gas than it should, I 'spect." Hamilton wedged a toothpick between his teeth.

"When's the last time you changed the oil, Pop?"

"Oh, it's been a couple years, I reckon." Hamilton chuckled.

Jack did not see the humor. He sprang out of his seat as though a fire alarm had sounded. To Jack, failure to change the oil according to the manufacturer's recommended schedule was a profane act of negligence. A violation of the eleventh commandment. Or should have been.

"Years!" Jack looked at him, incredulous. "How long in miles, Pop? In miles?"

Hamilton rose as Jack dashed out the garage door to inspect the pickup.

Hamilton turned a corner of his lip up and his eyes shone in Ada's direction, like a pair of crescent moons.

"Well, it sure is a pleasure to meet you, ma'am. I reckon I better see about Jack and the truck." He looked down at Apostle Paul, who had curled up in Ada's lap. The pup had fallen asleep under the security blanket of Ada's hand resting on its back.

"Some dogs get all the luck. Little fella sure picked himself a winner." He tipped his invisible hat toward the women and followed Jack out the door.

Ada grinned, but then rolled her eyes for Essie's benefit.

"You'll learn to love him for it. All part of his charm," Essie said.

In the driveway, Jack's upper body was buried under the hood of Hamilton's pickup. Once he maneuvered the dipstick back into position, he turned to his father and held the soiled shop rag up to Hamilton's face. It was smeared with something that looked like clumpy black tar. Evidence of a grievous malfeasance.

Hamilton ignored the rag. "That Ada gal is a high-spirited thing."

Jack slammed the hood shut. "You'll kill your engine, Pop."

"At my age, Son, I'm delighted to outlive it," Hamilton replied. "Do you think Ada likes to sail?"

Jack shook his head. "Crazy old man!"

Jack followed Hamilton as they walked back through the garage. Hamilton was in good health for his age, but Jack noticed the sunken, shriveled valleys along the nape of his neck. The way the shirt collar hung loose seemed to betray something in his otherwise sturdy appearance.

Jack put an arm around his dad.

"I've been thinking about what you said, Pop. And you're right. It is hard to get good help these days. So, I tell you what. Let me change the oil and flush the lines for you. See if I can buy her a little more time."

"If you like, Son. But you know what I really wish you'd do for me? Fix me up with that Ada gal in there. You do that for me, and I'll dance for you at my next wedding."

[chapter 22]

chasing Her Tail

The committee leader stepped up to the podium to address the consortium of waste management experts, recycling providers, environmental engineers, and industry professionals. "I'd like to introduce you to Lewis Cathcart from Life Cola."

Cathcart positioned his watch upright against the podium and pulled a stack of note cards from his breast pocket.

A prepared speech? Essie thought this was an informal meeting, a friendly discussion. The invitation came only yesterday. How much could he possibly have to say?

The day before, Cathcart's administrative assistant had notified her that a Goat, or Group of Approximately Ten, planned to convene at the November Aluminum Alliance conference. Cathcart had tasked Essie with winning their participation in Life Cola's aluminum recycling ambitions.

In their last discussion, Cathcart had suggested Essie find a technology solution to further the company's recycling efforts. Essie remained alarmingly unclear on the actual problem to solve and even more so concerning the solution she was now charged to provide.

Cathcart had labeled several Aluminum Alliance leaders as a Goat and persuaded them to come alongside the company's own Goat, thereby establishing a governing herd of two Goats. The Goats would define success for and make the ultimate go/no-go decision concerning the newly proposed Chunk of Work, or Cow.

"Two Goats have a better chance of tackling this Cow," Cathcart had explained to Essie. Pleased with himself, he then pointed out that the acronym remained intact because both ten and twenty start with a T. The barnyard imagery was starting to make Essie itch.

At the podium, Cathcart cleared his throat and began: "You can lead a horse to water but you can't make him drink. You can teach an elephant to dance but you can't prevent ants from being crushed in the performance." He paused dramatically, presumably to allow the profundity of his observations to sink in. He lowered his head, peered up at the audience above his wire frames, and continued.

"Many noble ambitions come with a downside. Many good things come with a trade-off, an unavoidable negative, an unintended consequence. One wins if another loses. That, however, is not the case here. I assert that Life's proposal to recycle across America is a victory for all of us. The decision is in your hands. Several of you have been appointed to the Group of Approximately Ten to determine the fate of this Cow.

"I urge you to be a bold Goat. Be the one that, when faced with waste, dives right in. I'm confident this Goat can sniff out the ripe morsel of opportunity to be found here.

"This team from Life Cola is from IT." He gestured to a table of four nearsighted, slump-shouldered programmers. "They are not environmental engineers. They are not experts in this field, but that has not extinguished their fiery passion for such a just cause.

"So I implore you to join us in this visionary approach to grow our businesses while conserving our natural resources. Our world needs to be rescued. Someone must save the planet."

Cathcart gripped the lectern with both hands as if strangling it. His expression was a portrait of immediacy, his eyes small and dark, neck outstretched, the vein at his forehead at pre-stroke rigidity. He set his jaw and crescendoed with righteous zeal. "And I'm sure you will agree it is a crying shame it has to be us."

Essie had no doubt the assembly did, in fact, agree on that point. The room was filled with furrowed brows and an uncomfortable silence. A man in the back coughed. A cell phone rang like the chirping of crickets. It was Essie's. She recognized the number of Juliet's childcare provider.

"Hello," Essie whispered into the phone.

The table of Life programmers were clapping robotically, triggering a weak round of applause amid the clinking of cups and saucers as everyone refilled their coffee.

"Hey, Ellison," the familiar voice said. "Juliet has a little temp of 99.9 degrees. She's asleep now, but she may be coming down with something."

"Oh, no! I'll come get her as soon as I can get out of this conference," Essie cupped her hand around her mouth and the receiver to muffle her reply.

"No hurry. I just wanted to let you know," the voice said.

Juliet needed her. So did Cathcart.

Cathcart rambled on.

Essie was convinced the Alliance thought they were a bunch of morons. And she could find little basis to argue. Beads of perspiration sprouted on her forehead.

She was an hour's ride from the daycare. So she made a quick call to Pearl. Asking her mother for a favor was not an easy thing for Essie. She knew there would be a price to pay. Pearl never could resist the opportunity to criticize her. Essie put her pride aside for Juliet.

"Mother, I'm at a conference, and Juliet is running a fever. Is there any chance you can check on her for me until I can get out of here?"

There was a long pause, then came the bite. "I guess that's no surprise. Children in daycare get every germ that comes around. Do I need to take her to the pediatrician, too?"

"It's only a low-grade fever. I doubt she needs to go to the pediatrician. Would you just pick her up and meet me at my house?"

The cell phone static hissed through a long, painful pause. "I will be glad to," Pearl replied in a slow, chilly cadence. "You do your job, dear. It must be an important conference."

"I'll be there as soon as I can." Before Essie could justify herself further, she heard Cathcart announce her name from the podium.

"With that, I'd like to turn it over to Ellison Wells, who will represent Life in this partnership. Ellison, please take us all through the details."

Details? What details? A wave of heat spread across her neck and behind her ears. The crowd received her with no warmth whatsoever. She felt a hundred eyes focus upon her. They'd given her their full attention, presumably more out of morbid curiosity than professional interest. The group seemed prepared to witness a public flogging. Essie made her way to the podium as if mounting the gallows. A drop of sweat trickled beneath her arm and dampened her blouse. She was in the spotlight and had no idea what to say.

"Hello. I'm Ellison," Essie began, thinking of her daughter. "This will be quick as I don't have much to propose at this time. Here's the challenge for us: Life Cola, in the spirit of corporate citizenship, would like to take a bigger and more active role in aluminum recycling.

"At the same time, Life would like to strengthen its relationship with our aluminum can suppliers and other business partners. Life believes a partnership with the Aluminum Alliance can help us reach these goals and, likewise, help you reach similar goals of your own.

"I don't have the answer on how this will all work. It is up to us to decide if and how to proceed. With that, I'm here to collect ideas. Is there an opportunity for us to work together to meet shared goals for mutual benefit?"

She stood there staring at a sea of blank faces. She looked far right and left, bracing herself for the shepherd's crook that must spring forth at any moment to hook her and yank her off the stage.

A man's voice rose from the back. "I'm not sure what y'all had in mind, but our company is always looking for corporate sponsors to strengthen our recycling programs. Would Life be willing to sponsor our efforts? Help establish new recycling drop-off centers?"

A murmur of shared sentiment waved across the room. "It's certainly possible." Essie scribbled on her notepad. A ray of hope.

A woman raised her hand in the front. "Awareness is a big issue for us. Life has strong connections with young consumers. Perhaps Life can send a stronger message to America's youth about recycling through their product packaging or advertising."

Another woman piped up: "Not just youth. We need greater participation from businesses as well. We need a way to make it easier, more desirable, for companies to recycle aluminum cans from beverages consumed in their offices." The light in the room seemed to brighten a shade.

A Life programmer chimed in: "We could build an online business-to-business trading hub, lend-a-can.net if you will, providing nationwide commerce in recycled aluminum."

Silence.

"Huh?"

"What did he say?"

The programmer continued: "What if Life sponsored an online solution to increase recycling among businesses? A hub approach creates a network for participating businesses to recycle their cans online, donate them toward community or charitable causes, or trade them with other businesses for some kind of value-in-kind."

Essie understood the idea and paraphrased, "An aluminum exchange."

Some blank faces. More wheels turning.

She tried again. "An online trading and bartering place, like eBay, but instead of using dollars as the only currency, you can use empty cans."

A chinless man with a short forehead and pinched expression asked, "But why would anyone deposit their cans in an online can bank?"

The committee leader straightened in his chair. "In theory, it sounds like Life and other participating companies could join forces to donate their cans to nonprofit organizations to, say, build affordable houses for low-income families. If the government recognizes corporate participation, it would mean significant tax credits for donating businesses. Yes, with the right participants, that could be big."

"Still, I'm not so sure. Aluminum currency?" The chairperson scratched his head. "It's a little far-fetched. I'd like to propose another conference after Thanksgiving to discuss feasibility and funding. Let's take the idea back to our companies and reconvene in early December about our respective businesses' willingness to participate. All in favor?"

All hands in the room went up in murmured support.

Essie checked her watch and calculated how quickly she could get home.

As the meeting adjourned, the programmers remained locked in heated debate over technology platforms.

Thank goodness it's over, Essie thought, sending up a silent prayer of gratitude. Picturing Juliet with a cool washcloth on her brow, Essie quickly gathered her briefcase and cell phone and headed toward the door.

Before she could escape, Cathcart pulled her to the side.

"Bravo! Brilliant, Ellison. I couldn't have said it better myself. Have you ever seen a dog chase its tail, Ellison? It's the beautiful picture of an unending circle, continuity, renewal, regeneration, rebirth. Recycling, Ellison. Do you see it? It's the perfect image of what we've accomplished here today, and where this initiative will take us.

"What I saw today convinces me that you are the dog we've been looking for. Congratulations, Ellison. You have what it takes. Keep chasing your tail. You're going someplace, Ellison."

Right, she thought to herself. *Directly to my daughter.* Whether this crazy idea went in circles or straight to the board of directors, she knew exactly where she was headed—home to be with her children.

On the highway, the phone chimed just as Essie reached her exit. "Hello."

"Honey, the doctor agreed to squeeze Juliet in this afternoon. Should I take her in myself or can you meet me there in ten minutes?"

It seemed there were no other options. Pearl had won the "go to the pediatrician" debate. Essie met her outside the physician's center.

Juliet whimpered and reached for her mom.

"You really saved me today. Thank you." Essie pressed a palm to Juliet's forehead. "She's just a little warm. Do you really think she needs to see the doctor?"

"She has a fever, dear. I never took a chance with you when you were a child."

They rode the elevator in silence to the doctor's office on the third floor. Pearl waited in the lobby while Essie took Juliet inside.

The doctor confirmed that Juliet was not sick after all, but simply had another tooth coming in. Relieved, Essie called her mom's cell phone from the examination room to report the diagnosis.

"We're almost finished in here. She's just teething. The doctor says she'll have a full set soon."

"Oh dear, the poor girl must be in pain. I'll wait for you downstairs by the pharmacy."

Despite the good doctor's report, Essie's guilt remained.

Outside the pharmacy, Pearl presented her with two new tubes of teething gel. "I figured you'd be out."

They headed toward the parking lot.

"Don't forget to give her some children's Motrin or Tylenol, too," Pearl offered as Essie strapped Juliet in her car seat.

Pearl pressed a button on her key fob, unlocking the neighboring Mercedes. She slipped behind the wheel and rolled down her window. "You have a chilled teething ring, don't you?"

Essie nodded through the passenger-side window. "Yes, I'll take good care of her, Mother. Don't worry."

Pearl shifted into reverse and waved a goodbye. Then, reminding Essie of their Thanksgiving plans, called through her window, "Don't forget to bring a covered dish, dear."

Essie nodded and waved back. *As if I could forget.*

[chapter 23]

Eternity Made Easy

Thanksgiving arrived. Tension between Essie and Pearl had not improved since the conference and Juliet's fever earlier in the week. Essie welcomed the day off work, but the casserole assignment loomed ominously in the afternoon ahead. With a family of five, Essie figured she'd have to learn to cook something besides ribs and mac 'n' cheese.

Having overheard Pearl's remark about casseroles and proper etiquette, Ada, out of mercy, had started clipping a collection of quick, easy recipes for Essie. The tradition began Halloween night when Ada revealed her recipe for homemade macaroni and cheese, prep time twenty minutes. At the time, Essie accepted her gift with reluctance and trepidation, making it clear that any suggested culinary undertaking must have a prep time of less than thirty minutes to be taken seriously.

Shortly thereafter, she found instructions sprouting from a bloom of pastel gift tissues for Pecan-encrusted Chicken with Dijon Sauce. A handwritten scribble at the top of the recipe card read: prep time twenty-five minutes. The next day, a shiny pink gift bag carried the secrets to Chicken Florentine Rolls, prep time fifteen minutes. Then, Easy Quiche, prep time fifteen minutes.

Ada encouraged her to make one or two simple dishes per week. She suggested building the repertoire until Essie learned enough quick dishes to design a monthly meal plan. That, Ada assured her, would simplify her hectic, carry-out, fast-food dinner routine during the workweek, and may be nutritionally preferable to a diet of french fries and small, fried animal parts.

Taking on a cooking endeavor was a courageous step for Essie, a venture into the unknown. A lifestyle change, in fact. She had the phone numbers memorized to every take-out restaurant in a ten-mile radius. The culinary arts had long evaded her. Or was it Essie who had evaded them? In any case, she was grateful her husband was usually busy washing their cars and not witness to her early attempts.

Today, Ada's recipe sat on Essie's welcome mat, affixed to a beautifully decorated mason jar topped with a small drawstring pouch of cookie cutters, tied together with a heavy red ribbon. A handwritten note attached to the label read "Eternal cookies made easy. Just add water." Inside was a mixture of dry cookie ingredients.

Eternal? Essie doubted it. Cookies never lasted long around her family, especially around holiday time. But making them sounded easier, and a lot more fun, than a dreaded casserole. The recipe label read:

> This Christmas, trim your tree with treats using
> Dough-It-Yourself Eternal Christmas Cookies.
> Or sweeten your holiday decor with a lasting
> Homemade Nativity Scene.
> 2 cups flour (not self-rising)
> 1 cup salt
> 1 cup water
> food color—optional
> Knead, roll, and shape into ¼-inch thick pieces.
> Bake at 350 degrees on foil-covered cookie sheet for
> 30 minutes.

Neither cookies nor casseroles were likely to impress Mother Pearl. As the quintessential family matriarch and unchallenged queen of all things culinary, Pearl always hosted the Thanksgiving Day gathering for her daughters and their families. The Thanksgiving meal remained her territory, a domain she had kept exclusive for years.

Growing up, Pearl made sure the kitchen was locked down tighter than NORAD, safeguarding sovereignty over its secret operations. Essie was never allowed in and therefore never grew familiar with its mystifying functions. The growing stack of Ada's recipes became a nudging reminder of the challenge she faced in the kitchen.

Although Essie claimed to have mastered mac 'n' cheese long ago, the oversized bulk packaged boxes of Kraft lining her pantry revealed the truth. Even real mac 'n' cheese intimidated her until Ada walked her through the process before the barbecue dinner with Hamilton.

It was a little early for Christmas cookies so Essie decided she'd shape the dough into turkeys, copying the idea from Cole's handprint art at school. As she rolled out the dough and began carving out shapes, she recalled the time Cole came home from Mickey Weatherstone's house talking about the thick and creamy homemade mac 'n' cheese he had enjoyed.

"Can you make it like his mom did? Why do we always have those little orange noodles?"

"I'm allergic to the larger tubes," Essie explained.

Recognizing this fear must be faced to be conquered, she grew to accept Ada's help and her recipes as friendly encouragement. So, glancing again at the first clipping that Ada had given her, she smiled proudly at the deep dish of plump elbow noodles smothered in a creamy blend of butter and cheeses. Now *that* was mac 'n' cheese.

Caught in her own web, she would have to give honorable mention to modern medicine for the timely remission of her allergies. And now, with the addition of these homemade, hand-sculpted Christmas cookies, she was sure to be a success at Pearl's Thanksgiving dinner.

Essie looked forward to seeing the children's beaming little faces around Pearl's dinner table when her two kid-friendly dishes were unveiled. Of course, macaroni and cookies were amateur accomplishments. Her contributions would undoubtedly pale in comparison to her mom's gourmet spread. But she hoped to demonstrate that what she lacked in experience, she made up for in creativity and enthusiasm.

Surveying her handiwork, Essie frowned at the attempted turkey cookies, which looked more like mittens or worse. This job obviously required professional-grade tools. She raked through her drawers, but not a single cookie cutter could be found. She was too far along to stop now, so Christmas cookies it would have to be. Sighing, she shaped the remaining dough using the cookie cutters Ada had provided. Slowly, the dough transformed into nativity-scene characters, complete with Mother Mary, Joseph, baby Jesus in the manger, three wise men, and a variety of mystery animals. Using a sharp knife and toothpicks, she attempted to carve a few defining features into the unidentifiable animals, shaping them into recognizable donkeys and lambs. In honor of Ada, she reshaped the mangled turkeys into moderately convincing dogs, adding several little Chihuahuas to the nativity crowd. She slid the trays into the oven.

Cole and Juliet sat on the floor peering through the oven door.

"What are all those people doing in there, Mom?" Cole asked.

"That is the baby Jesus and his family and friends. It's called a nativity scene. They are bringing gifts to honor the baby Jesus."

"Why?"

"It's his birthday. Christmas is the day we celebrate Jesus' birthday. See those men with the little shepherd staffs?" Essie pointed to the wise men on the cookie sheet. "They are bringing their most valuable gifts to give to Jesus." She combined powdered sugar with some lemon juice and a little water to prepare the icing.

"Why?"

"Because Jesus is God's Son. God loves us so much that he sent his Son Jesus to die for our sins so we can be friends with God and live forever."

"He died! Who shot him?"

"No one shot him, honey. He hung on a tree when he died, but now he is alive again. Easter is when we celebrate that."

Looking in the back of the pantry, Essie found several tiny droppers of food coloring and a bottle of sprinkles. She lined them up next to the icing, then knelt down with the kids to gaze at the cookies through the oven door.

"Oh," Cole squinted through the glass door, brows furrowed in deep thought. "But I thought he was the greatest hero of all time."

"Yes, honey, he is. And he died for his friends."

Cole cocked his head to the side, as if considering the possibility that heroism, perhaps, wasn't about the stunts at all.

Then he suggested, "Let's put chocolate sprinkles on him."

Together, they watched as the tops of the cookies whitened and cracked and the edges browned. Essie stared puzzled at what looked like hardening bits of granite.

She turned to rinse the cookie cutters and rolled a scrap of dough onto her finger. She popped it in her mouth and almost gagged. Then, doing a double take, she reread the instructions. That's when she noticed a key ingredient: salt. The play on words finally hit her. *Eternal Cookies. Now I get it!*

A soft tap sounded behind them, and Ada's cottony swirl of hair appeared in the doorway. She stepped inside the kitchen, Apostle Paul tucked under one arm.

"Why, hello, my darlings. I hope I'm not too late." She held up a handful of thin short strips of red ribbon. The children rushed to greet her, wrapping their arms around her legs, rising up on their toes to pet the little dog.

"Hello, Ada. What are those?" Essie asked.

"Ribbons for the decorations, dear." Ada stooped down to peek at the cookies through the oven door. Apostle Paul wriggled in her arms and clawed his way up her shoulder, seeking higher ground out of reach of children.

"Ah, yes. I just solved the cookie mystery myself. A clue like that might've helped me solve the case sooner." Essie laughed at herself.

"Honey, you didn't think you could eat these cookies, did you? They were made with salt, not sugar, see?" She gestured toward the recipe label on the mason jar. "Turns hard as stone. Lasts for eternity."

"Yes, I figured that out a bit late. After sampling the dough!" Essie stuck out her tongue and made a face.

The timer chimed.

Ada grimaced, then chuckled. "Don't worry, dear. No harm done."

Hoping to avoid further humiliation, Essie quickly rinsed out the bowl of icing mix in the sink.

With the wave of an oven mitt, Ada swept away her embarrassment like stray cookie crumbs. "Now comes the fun part. Let's decorate them." Ada pulled the tray from the oven.

They huddled over the tiny clay sculptures. The Apostle lolled out his tongue and his eyes bulged a bit farther than usual. Essie wasn't sure if his enthusiasm was in reverence to the nativity scene or in appreciation for the Chihuahua-shaped decorations, but either way, the ornaments appeared to have won his favor.

"We'll need some Elmer's glue to go with these sprinkles," Ada said. "And some way to make the holes."

Cole and Juliet were so thrilled to play with glue and sprinkles that they forgot to be disappointed about not eating cookies. Feeling like children themselves, Ada and Essie spent the next hour drilling holes and threading ribbon to finish the project. As they completed the final steps, Jack walked in to find them hunkered over the kitchen table, heads down, wearing the children's swim goggles for protection.

"What's going on?" he asked.

The low hum of the hand drill turned into a high pitch whine as Essie bored the last hole. Cookie shrapnel splintered across the table. Leaving behind a dusty outline against the wax paper, Essie lifted one of the finished products for Jack to admire.

"Making Christmas cookies," she replied.

"With a Dremel tool?" He winced at the surrounding debris.

"Eternal ones," Essie said, deciding that was explanation enough.

[chapter 24]

Thanksgiving Dinner

Climbing down from the Hummer's passenger seat with a decorative basket looked unnatural, like Mary Poppins bailing out of a fighter jet with a pink parasol. Essie helped Cole and Juliet make the long drop from the back seat down to the driveway.

Cole's shoulders slumped in shame, and he crossed his arms to cover the source of his disgrace. Both children wore matching holiday outfits, which included wool sweaters featuring a cartoon turkey carrying a sign that read: gobble till you wobble. Cole stared down at the Spider-Man figurine clutched in his fist, presumably in search of sympathy. Juliet seemed apathetic about the sweater but had been grossly offended by the Spartan, black, buckle footwear that accompanied the new outfit. So a compromise had been struck. Unwilling to completely concede her own sense of style, Juliet chose to set off her Thanksgiving ensemble with glittering silver shoes.

The new Thanksgiving outfits were gifts from Pearl. Though dressed for the occasion, the children were not feeling the spirit of Thanksgiving as they adjusted their heavy sweaters, fidgeting and complaining all the way up Gami Pearl's driveway. Essie, however, was obliged to showcase a little appreciation or suffer the consequences.

The two-story Tudor had been prepped for the holiday season. The lawn was so full of decorations the house could be mistaken for a yard sale. It surprised Essie that the hedges had not been trimmed into pilgrim and turkey motifs. The house itself was a product of the sixties and had received more facelifts and makeovers than a Hollywood star of the same vintage.

Jack bravely took point and led the pilgrimage to Pearl's front door. The children flinched at the paper pilgrims and pumpkins. The pumpkins were a little worse for wear, veterans of Halloween.

Dressed in a white blouse, long black skirt, and white linen apron, sharp creases still visible along the fold lines, Pearl greeted them at the front door. She wore a new shade of lipstick and nail polish, presumably to match her new highlights. Her hair had undergone a complete rebuild, framing her face in tight, peach-colored curls. The starched collar and stiff ringlets combined with the pilgrim-like garb created the effect that typically accompanies a black robe and a gavel.

"Come in, Jack darling," Pearl opened her arms to embrace her son-in-law. "Ellison, come in, sweetheart," she kissed the air next to Essie's cheek.

The interior glowed with holiday splendor. Big Jim and Pearl were veteran grandparents and long ago had ceded the family room to toys, which stretched from wall to wall. The dining room, however, sparkled with hand-washed china and sterling silver place settings. If Waterford offered a line of stemware with sippy-cup tops, she would have it.

"Happy Thanksgiving, Mother," Essie said, offering a basket with her two contributions to the meal.

Pearl peeked inside. "My, what a nice surprise! Cookies and macaroni and cheese?" she observed with arched eyebrows. "You really shouldn't have," she added with practiced sincerity. Then, as if working out a math problem out loud to herself, she muttered in undertones, "I hope we have enough vegetables, then. We'll just have to make do."

The children filed in, drawn magnetically to the playroom where they found their cousins, Olivia and Alicia, also decked in turkey attire. The little ones were clearly uncomfortable in the wool sweaters and waited for the slightest sign to shed apparel and play in earnest. The children, Essie was certain, would rather be playing in T-shirts and jeans, but the obligation to lead them to civility and culture was a higher calling.

"Juliet, dear, where are the cute buckle shoes I bought to go with your dress?" Pearl asked.

Juliet clung to Essie's leg. "No, Mama, no!" She wriggled out of her corduroy skirt and tugged at her stockings.

Essie's sister, Emily, and her husband, Greg, were helping Big Jim untangle a knotted string of Christmas lights resembling a festive bird nest. Emily was doing most of the work as Big Jim and Greg were more interested in the football game than in preparing for the post-dessert tree-trimming tradition.

The dining-room table was set up with its extended leaves to create enough seats for everyone, including two high chairs. China place settings and calligraphic name-card tents were set up in front of each chair.

"It's ready. Y'all come eat," Pearl announced. "Jim, honey, do you want to give thanks?"

Big Jim put down the remote, muting the game, and took the seat at the head of the table. His bulking frame fit awkwardly in the delicately carved dining chair. His presence commanded attention. He rested his hands, large and callused with bulging knots at the knuckles, on the corners of the table. "Cole, you're a big boy now. Would you like to say the blessing this year?"

Brow wrinkled, Cole hid his face behind Essie's arm and looked up at her for the answer. The rest of the family gathered around the table, holding hands and forming a large circle.

Offering assurance, Essie squeezed Cole's hand, pressing his Spider-Man between their laced fingers, and said softly to him, "It's OK. Just tell God what you are thankful for, like our family and our food." Hoping to plant a seed, Essie quickly added, "Maybe your new clothes or any other blessings."

Cole bowed his head. His thin blond bangs fell forward. He squinted his eyes tightly. "Dear Jesus, thank you for our food. Thank you for our drinks. Thank you for my new clothes." *Yes!* Essie congratulated herself silently. Cole unlinked his hand from his mother's and slipped Spider-Man into his pocket.

"Thank you for Spider-Man. Thank you for Buzz Lightyear. Even if they are make-believe." Cole paused, evidently giving serious thought to his new Thanksgiving responsibility. His eyes were pinched shut, his little face strained with deep concern. "But Jesus, I don't like new clothes very much. Or vegetables. So please just send more action figures. And candy. In Jesus' name, Amen." He opened his eyes, relaxed, satisfied.

"Well," Pearl's glare hunted Essie down and fired, "wasn't that sweet."

"Yum! Mac 'n' cheese!" Olivia squealed.

"I want some," Cole pleaded.

Essie smiled to herself as she heaped her mac 'n' cheese onto their china plates. The adults began passing serving dishes in unison. Essie imagined the scene from above must look like synchronized swimming.

"Emily, how is the move to Paddleboat River Club coming along? Don't you close on the new house soon?" Pearl asked, passing the leg of lamb.

"Mother, I wish you could see the fabric I chose for the window treatments. It's perfect. Greg's promotion should be coming through any day," Emily replied as she balanced asparagus stalks on a serving fork and lifted them to her plate. "It means he'll be traveling more. But yes, we move to Paddleboat River Club next month." Emily shifted in her seat and cast an anxious glance at her husband.

"How wonderful! I just adore those gated communities. " Turning to Greg, Pearl fished, "The advertising business must be treating you well, then?"

"We're getting by," Greg dodged, stuffing a buttered roll in his mouth.

"So, how is Life treating you?" Pearl turned her attention to Jack and Essie and smirked at her own well-worn pun.

"Jack is working on a promising marketing promotion," Essie said enthusiastically, hoping to divert attention from herself.

"How exciting for you, Jack! And how about that father of yours? I wish he'd settle down in a nice home, too. I just can't imagine how he gets by living on that boat."

"It's a different lifestyle," Jack answered.

"Totally uncivilized." Pearl shook her peach ringlets.

"And our Essie here is saving the world," Jack quipped good-naturedly, successfully diverting the subject from Hamilton. "You should hear about her recycling program."

Pearl rolled her eyes. "Well, I should hope so. It *must* be important to keep those kids in daycare all day long. I don't see how you do it. And to think of your newborn in that . . . that place." She leaned forward, casting her eyes toward Essie's growing abdomen. With a palm spread against her chest and a quaver in her voice, she added, "It just breaks my heart."

"I'm out of tea," Dad announced.

Pearl hopped up to fetch the pitcher.

"Need more ice, too," Dad hollered after her. "Nice job on the macaroni, Essie." Mouth full, Big Jim nodded his head toward Essie's serving dish.

She smiled. "Thanks, Dad."

"It's delicious," Emily agreed. "Big improvement over your grilled cheese." The sisters both laughed at the private joke.

"What happened with grilled cheese?" Jack asked. Emily looked to Essie with eyebrows raised, waiting her permission. She consented with a one-sided grin.

Pearl returned with a fresh pitcher and refilled tea glasses all around.

Emily began, giggling as she spoke. "Mother never let us in the kitchen when we were little so we never mastered the culinary arts. One day, Essie tried to make us grilled cheese sandwiches. She buttered white bread, slapped some cheese in the middle, and microwaved it." She held a hand to her stomach, trying to hold back her laughter. "It was a soggy, steaming, cheesy mess. We couldn't eat it."

Essie laughed out loud in spite of herself. By way of defense, she explained, "It was toast that I microwaved, not plain bread. Toast."

"It was gross," Emily cried.

Pearl shuddered, her peach ringlets quivering.

The serving platters made their second pass around the table. The kids asked to be excused and raced back to the playroom.

Big Jim pushed the last grains of rice onto his fork with a thumb and lifted them to his mouth.

"Ellison, why don't you bring out that interesting dessert you made," Pearl suggested.

"It's not dessert. They are called Eternal Cookies. The dough works kind of like clay, firm enough to let you mold your own shapes—"

A shriek sounded from the playroom. Emily and Essie went rigid and simultaneously pushed back their chairs and started toward the scene.

Big Jim, unaffected, tossed his napkin on his plate, excused himself, and returned to his recliner, the football game, and the mass of Christmas lights. Jack and Greg followed his lead, finding comfortable spots in front of the television.

"Eternal cookies?" Pearl asked. "They don't look like any cookies I've ever seen."

Halfway down the hallway, Essie stopped and turned back to her mother. "For our tree-trimming tradition." Essie planned to let the children thread the ribbons in the ornaments as a fun after-dinner activity.

Pearl shrugged and selected a little Chihuahua among the nativity scene. She twisted it between her fingers, apparently examining her daughter's handiwork.

"Wait just a second and I'll explain." Essie raced on toward the playroom.

"My, my, aren't you creative, Essie." Pearl shouted in the direction of the playroom. "Is this supposed to be a cat?"

Aware of her mother's inquiry and the urgent need to explain that the cookies were decorations, Essie felt a more pressing need to prevent Pearl from witnessing the disaster in the playroom.

"That is a Chihuahua, Mother. Just hold on a minute."

Juliet, having had her fill of food and restrictive clothing, had shed her pilgrim outfit completely, along with her diaper. She was slumped naked on a toile covered children's dining chair, crying hysterically. In her zeal for liberation, she had had an accident. The worst kind. The fabric seat cushion was ruined.

Like paramedics, the sisters moved into coordinated action without discussion. Essie sped Juliet to the bathroom, cleaned her up, and dressed her in a simple knit shirt and pants, the backup clothing always available in the bottom of the diaper bag. Emily used a kitchen knife to remove the soiled seat cover. She located a matching toile tablecloth in the linen closet and performed emergency reupholstering. Juliet's crying muffled the sound of the staple gun.

Emily completed the task with remarkable speed; she'd done this kind of thing before.

"I never heard of Chihuahuas at the birth of Christ, dear. Jim, have you?"

Coming back down the hall, Emily rolled her eyes at the implied criticism. Essie smiled at her sister gratefully.

"Huh?" Jim looked in his wife's direction briefly and then turned his attention back to the football game.

Essie turned into the dining room just as Pearl popped the sugar-sprinkled pup in her mouth.

"Mother, don't!"

Pearl rolled it on her tongue for a second, and grimaced. She spat the dog out indelicately and picked up the recipe card and red ribbon. Her eyes widened in shock. "Salt!" She located the warning label that had flipped over, invisible on the white tablecloth. "For Decoration Only. Do Not Eat!"

"Mom! That's what I was trying to say," Essie gushed. "They are decorations. I was going to explain, but—"

Big Jim lumbered to the scene. He chose one of the wise men, eyeing him suspiciously. He sniffed it, then licked it. "What the . . . ? Tastes like limestone."

Everyone was gathered around the table now.

"That's very clever, dear." Pearl's cheeks flushed with a mix of embarrassment and anger. "Are covered dishes too much to ask? Next time, I'd prefer a green bean casserole."

The children watched from a distance like a crowd of frightened witnesses to a crime. All except for Juliet, who, despite a tear-streaked face, stood triumphantly dressed in pink knit and silver shoes.

[chapter 25]

An Ace up His sleeve

Hamilton strode into The Lazy I with the resolution of a sheriff out to rid his town of the bad guys. He'd spent his Thanksgiving week alone, thinking long and hard, putting the final pieces of his plan into place. It was time to make his move; conditions seemed ripe.

December was typically a busy time for the diner, but the first thing he noticed was a striking reduction in the number of customers. More peculiar was the absence of the regulars. Even Inman was not hunched on his usual roost, which defeated the main purpose of the visit.

Ham found one familiar face that he hadn't seen in days. Noodle motioned for Ham to join him.

"Just a second, Noodle. Need a cup of coffee."

Ham walked to the counter and tried to attract the attention of the only waitress on duty. "Could I get a cup of your best, darlin'?" he asked.

"I'll bring it to your table, gramps; keep your shirt on. I'm the only one here today," she said without looking up.

Ham walked over to Noodle's booth.

"She new?" he asked his friend.

"Yeah," Noodle answered, "and about as pleasant as advanced cancer, if you ask me."

"Does seem a bit gruff," Ham observed.

"And wait until you taste the coffee. Weak as tap water, and Inman has raised the price on it. You'd think it was whiskey. Keeping track of the refills, too. Charge you for every one.

"Things sure have changed since you ran the place, Ham. Everyone that's been through here since I sat down has asked about you. Come to think of it, I haven't seen you much around the dock, either."

"I've been a little busy."

"I didn't think busy was in your nature, Ham. Folks keep asking where the owner is."

The waitress delivered Ham's coffee, sloshing a little on the table. She wheeled around and left. Ham watched her walk off. He dabbed up the spillage with napkins from a neighboring booth. Their own napkin dispenser was empty.

Ham sipped his coffee and made a face. "Barely potable," he declared. "Don't believe she'll last, either."

"She's not cut out for PR work, that's for sure," Noodle said.

"I reckon you could say *busy* is a bit out of character for me. Matter of fact, been working on a business venture. You know Inman is the owner of The Lazy I, not me, don't you, Noodle?"

"I never gave it much thought. I suppose I assumed you were. Or at least part-owner. You did all the hiring, and you were here about every day. Just seemed natural that you owned the place. But it makes sense that you don't, because your stamp of approval sure ain't on the latest hire."

Ham took another sip of the coffee, hoping it had improved. It hadn't, and he pushed it aside. "Sort of scared to order my usual," he said.

"You'd be better off staying hungry, Ham. I like mine soft scrambled, and they came out so overcooked it took a bit of work to get 'em down."

"I'll consider myself warned. Where's Inman?"

"That's just it, Ham. He's doing the cooking."

"Inman can't cook. Everyone knows that."

"And he proves it with every dish that comes out of the kitchen."

Ham chuckled. Noodle eased out of the booth.

"Come back when you can't stay so long," Ham advised as Noodle grinned and walked to the register. The waitress made her way toward the register, fished her order book from her soiled apron, took Noodle's money, and made change.

Noodle came back to the booth and threw a dollar on the table. "Good money after bad," he quipped. "The food has taken a terrible turn. Don't go there," he advised.

"Like warning a sailor of a squall up ahead," Ham said and waved his friend goodbye. "See you back at the marina."

Ham had been there ten minutes and had yet to order. He watched a few other customers go to the register and pay. It was not a happy crowd.

The waitress came over to his booth. "What'll it be?" she asked.

Ham played it safe, ordering only half of his usual dish. "Just one egg, over easy, and a single tortilla. And some Tabasco, if you please."

"OK, big spender," she said, snapping her order pad closed. "Something wrong with the coffee?"

Ham was ever polite. "Just remembered the doctor told me to cut down."

Ham expected things might go south without his presence and cheerfulness toward the customers, but he was shocked at how fast the decline had happened.

His lunch arrived. The egg yolk was hard as Chinese arithmetic. He forked it onto the tortilla anyway, as usual, to build his egg burrito, but when he cupped the flat bread in his palm, it split and crumbled into stale pieces.

He hadn't been to The Lazy I in a while and had not intentionally meant to harm the establishment, but he couldn't help but smile to himself. Another helping hand from the Almighty. For the hundredth time, he turned the plan over in his mind. Things were going to work out perfectly.

Inman popped out of the kitchen and took stock of the lunch crowd. When his wandering eyes found Hamilton, Inman drilled him with a serious glare.

"Would you join me in the back for a minute, Hamilton?" The cordiality was forced.

"Sure, Inman. Let me finish my lunch."

Hamilton ate the last overcooked bite, threw a handful of dollars on the table, and headed toward the kitchen entrance.

"Where have you been?" Inman asked, his anger apparent. "I've given you free reign to diddle the waitresses you hire, and this is the gratitude you show me?"

"I know I didn't hire the one out there now," Ham retorted.

"Oh, Dorita, she takes some getting used to. I'll probably have to fire her. I think she's dipping into the till, but I can't prove it. I've always depended on you to watch that for me."

Ham saw that he and Inman were the only ones present in the kitchen. "Where's all the help?"

"Cook and dishwasher both walked out this morning. Lazy and no account. You need to hire me a new crew."

"Not going to happen, Inman. I'm still hopping mad at you for what you did to Lilly. That was low, Inman, even for you."

"She was just another tramp, Hamilton. Glad she's gone. I did you a favor." Inman squared his shoulders and puffed out his chest as if claiming moral high ground.

Ham had to restrain himself. The scar along his jaw hardened and twisted like a vein across granite. He felt heat prickle the back of his neck.

Inman sensed the anger. "OK. I'll admit she was a pretty good cook, decent waitress, and fast."

"Fast women and slow boats, that's all right with me." Ham needed to defuse the situation. "Listen, Inman, I've got a proposition for you."

Inman looked up suspiciously. "What would that be?"

"I'd like to buy the diner," Ham stated. It had an air of finality to it.

"What do you know about business, Hamilton?" Inman laughed like he'd heard a dirty joke.

"I know enough to know I'd like to buy the place."

"That desperate to find a new wife, Hamilton?" Inman snorted. "Haven't I been generous enough to give you open season on the wait staff?"

"Matrimony has nothing to do with it," Ham replied.

"At your age, why would you take something like this on?"

"Take me seriously, Inman. The way you've run the place down so fast is downright shameful. You don't know how to treat people. That's clear. And you sure can't cook. That's a fact."

"I really have gotten used to it, and everyone knows how fond I am of it," Inman lied, obviously smelling an opportunity. "Besides, it's a great place to relax with a racing form. Once I get the mechanical things fixed in the kitchen and square away the help situation, she'll be a regular cash cow."

"Name a price." Ham had to let Inman know he was serious.

Inman rubbed his chin with his hand as if Ham had asked him an enormous favor.

The game had begun. Ham read the cards in his eyes.

Inman's regard for the diner was no secret. Nothing would suit him better than unloading the whole mess. It was a royal pain, labor intensive, and the equipment kept breaking down at the worst possible moment.

Inman had used it for years to fund his gaming pastime, but it had become less lucrative in that regard. He would have to find another source of cash, and Hamilton could be the answer. A new owner would have to bring the diner up to code, and the estimates on waste water disposal alone had run higher than Inman expected.

He should've felt guilty dumping it on a friend, but he probably didn't. Inman was convinced he'd make a spectacular profit on the deal.

But Hamilton knew how to play his hand well.

"Lot of goodwill tied up in this place," Inman whined. "I've got some new equipment ordered for the kitchen. You have to take that into account."

"Let's get on with it. Give me a figure."

Inman quoted a price.

"What, you got buried treasure under here? That's way too much. Out of the question."

"You asked for a figure. The goodwill, the customer base. That includes the equipment repairs that are in the works. I just had the front redone. It's a fair price."

"You'll have to do a lot better than that." Ham knew the building was leased, and, if Inman ran the place much longer, there wouldn't be a customer base.

"That's what I mean, Hamilton. You don't know a thing about business. You're way over your head here. Let me explain how things are done. This is the point where you counter my offer."

"I understand the diner's been here a while and has potential with some decent help."

Ham low-balled him.

"We're a long way apart, Hamilton." Inman gave Ham his most sincere look.

Ham had seen his game face before and saw right through it. Inman presumed he was dealing with an old, womanizing oaf who would, on most days, have trouble rounding up bus fare. That was Ham's ace, and he kept that card close to his vest.

Hamilton approximated the sum of hidden cash stuffed in the seat cushions on his sailboat. "Why don't we be reasonable?" he suggested. "We'll get the place appraised and use that as a basis for negotiation."

Inman studied his shoes, a dead giveaway. Hamilton recognized the tell and knew he held the better hand. He also anticipated Inman's next play. Appraisers were bribable.

Inman turned one last card.

"What about the goodwill?" he whined.

"Let's get the place properly appraised, and I'll give you one and a half the fair, appraised value."

It was time to close the deal, and both men knew it.

"I sure will miss the place. It's a huge sacrifice, but for you, I'll do it. It breaks my heart, but yes, I can live with that."

Ham extended his hand, and the two shook on it.

"I'll get the papers drawn up." Inman did his best wounded puppy impression.

"Fine," Ham agreed. "Let's get this done as soon as possible."

"I'll get right on it, Hamilton." Inman dashed away like he was about to wet himself. It was the deal of a lifetime.

"I'll try to find an honest appraiser," Inman offered solemnly.

"Any licensed one will do." Ham turned to leave. "Call me when the paperwork is ready."

"Aren't you forgetting something, Hamilton?"

"What?"

"You need to find me a new cook, dishwasher, and a couple of broads to wait tables."

"Later, Inman." Ham walked out of the kitchen.

Out in the diner, Dorita sneered at him. "Hey, Mr. Trump, thanks for the tip." She waved the dollar bill in his face and thrust it in her apron.

[chapter 26]

Man to Man

Ham eased onto the stool at the Marina Grill's bar and only had to wait a few minutes for Noodle to arrive. Heat lamps glowed overhead, warming the crisp December air. Out of habit, he spent a moment studying the new crop of waitresses—a much younger group than at The Lazy I—serving the Grill's patrons. Decidedly too young for him, but wonderfully entertaining to watch all the same.

"How do birds know when they've flown far enough south?" Noodle asked, sidling upon the stool next to Ham and shaking off the chill.

"How does a thermos know whether to keep things hot or cold?" Ham countered and then answered himself, "Custom design."

Noodle nodded gravely. "Ah yes, custom design."

Given their last experience at The Lazy I, Ham suspected they'd be spending more time on the stools at the Marina Grill.

The Marina Grill sat on a patch of imported sand, sand not being indigenous to this part of Georgia. Red clay was the official dirt of Georgia, and it surrounded the Grill every place that wasn't paved and clung to everything it touched.

"Would you like to see a menu, gentlemen?" A young girl handed each man a tri-folded paper menu.

"I'd forgotten there was a choice." Ham opened the leaflet and puzzled over the words as if they were written in Spanish. He returned the menu to the waitress. "I've always been partial to the special, ma'am. Folks around here have grown to count on me for that. If I changed my regular order this late in the game, it just might throw the whole universe out of balance."

Ham gestured toward the cloudless winter sky and grinned at the waitress. "Wouldn't want to risk it on a day like today."

"Make that two specials, please, ma'am. And a couple of cream sodas," Noodle added.

The girl giggled and scribbled on her order pad.

The Grill's specialty was the dock-burger, a half-pound of lean chuck, invariably cooked medium rare with assorted garnishes. The restaurant itself was a ramshackle building with ten or so stools and a dozen or so tables with colorful umbrellas sprouting from the center of each. A stovepipe exhaust crowned the establishment. Like most everything else, it was slightly askew.

Directly across from the Grill was the Ship's Store and Chandlery. Chandlery, meaning "ship stuff" as far as Ham could discern, was clearly pretentious and misleading since it carried far more snack food and soda pop than "ship stuff." Blow-up rafts were decidedly not *chandlery.*

"How's the love life, Ham? Looks like The Lazy I is running low on prospects. That Dorita gal sure don't compare to Lilly. Have you heard from her? You think she might come back?"

"I doubt it, Noodle. I thought she was a keeper, but I let her get away. Lilly's still in Florida tending to her ailing mother. Got a greeting card from her in the mail. Inman ran her off for good. That's part of the reason why I was at the diner yesterday. He offered to lend her money for an operation if she'd sign over the beneficiary rights to her mother's life insurance policy. The man knows no bounds. That Inman is so crooked they'll have to screw him in the ground when he dies to keep him there."

This was as close to an outburst as Noodle had ever heard from his friend.

On the third stool over from them, a stranger to Ham and Noodle looked up sharply. "Inman? Inman Forbes," he asked, facing the two, "of The Lazy I?"

"Yep. Couldn't be more than one," Ham acknowledged. "A scallywag. I'm Hamilton, Ham to most."

"And I'm Noodle Getty. Proud to make your acquaintance." There was a round of hand shaking, and the stranger announced that he was Lionel Smith, a real estate appraiser.

"We recommend the dock-burger." Noodle whispered like he was passing on a state secret.

"It's been recommended to me before. It's the reason I'm here. Such a beautiful day and all. I've already ordered one."

"How do you know Inman?" Ham asked.

"Doing a bit of appraising for him, and I'm afraid the news is not going to be good. The man must think we're all fools, with that fancy facade, and that jury-rigged kitchen of his. . . ."

"Don't say another word, Lionel; it would amount to insider trading," Ham advised.

"Well, it's no secret that the property has got a lot of problems. All the cosmetic changes in the world wouldn't help that place. Just bringing the place up to code for a restaurant will cost maybe twenty to forty thousand dollars, and that's just for the waste-water treatment."

"I know firsthand about that," Ham agreed.

"I've given it a fair and honest appraisal, and it won't break my heart to give him the news either. I probably shouldn't be telling you this," Lionel confided, "but my wife's sister used to work there. She said Inman tried to cheat her out of some insurance money, or something like that. I heard the girl up and quit in disgust. Moved to Florida to be with my mother-in-law."

Ham was quiet. Their burgers came and conversation ceased for several moments.

After they finished eating, Lionel announced he had another appraisal appointment and took his leave.

"He was talking about Lilly, wasn't he, Ham?" Noodle asked.

"I believe he was," Ham noted, scratching his head. "What's on your plate these days, Noodle?"

"Got the check from the insurance company on the boat today. Been meaning to thank you. Jumping in the lake to try to save me. You're a real friend, Ham. I almost wish I had been down there. Mighty gallant for an old man."

"Pure instinct, Noodle. No nobility to it. Marina rats like you are hard to come by. Most of the pirates up here will turn on you like mayonnaise in the Georgia heat. A fellow like you is worth saving."

"Noodle?" Ham wanted his friend's complete attention.

"Yes, Ham?"

"You know any motorcycle folk or people who are pretty handy with them?"

"Why do you ask?"

"I want my son to go into business with me here at the lake, a repair shop, sales maybe, but he's not willing to take the risk. I know he wants to do it. Just needs a little push is all. I'd like to help him get a head start on his own shop, but I want it to be done right, and I don't know much about bikes. And I suppose this is something I want to do for my son to show him how I feel about him."

Ham glanced around furtively. "By the way, whatever you do, don't say a word of this in front of him. I haven't thought the whole thing through yet, and I'd kinda like to make it a surprise."

Noodle rubbed the stubble on his chin. "You know, my cousin's got a small garage out behind his house. He's long been retired, but lets a bunch of biker buddies of his use it. They work on bikes out there. His wife's been on him to shut it down 'cause of all the noise. They're kind of a free-spirited bunch. I can't say how any of 'em would actually like a regular job, but I could call over there, if you like."

"Might be the sort of thing I'm looking for. Are they tattooed up real bad?"

"Some, but it's mostly patriotic and religious stuff, nothing offensive. They're all in some kind of club—not the Hell's Angels or anything like that—but they all have GG on their helmets."

"GG?"

"Some kind of club. Who knows? They play a lot of gospel music over there. Odd looking fellas. Beards and long hair. One has a ponytail all the way down his backside. Dress like a nightmare, too, if you ask me."

"Noodle, you're an answer to prayer. One other thing, do you know anything about Biker's Eye?"

"Sounds contagious, Ham."

"How about webcams?"

"What?" Noodle blinked. "You should give me some warning you're getting ready to change the subject like that."

"Never mind. Reckon I'll have to study up on that on my own."

"Ham, you're doing way too much thinking. It pains me to see you this way. I miss the regular talk about your latest matrimonial prospects at the diner."

"I've got such a dismal track record at The Lazy I, I've decided to give up on it for love. But I'll tell you something, Noodle. I have met another woman, and she's not a waitress. A bit quirky, but she's a real spitfire."

"Ham, you think this one will show a little more patience with marina life?"

"Hard to tell, Noodle. But I 'spect I've gone about romance all wrong. As a fellow who knows what it means to take a risk, I'm ashamed to admit that I've been playing it safe when it comes to love. Some folks go their whole lives sittin' on the fence, but there's no excitement in that. In matters of love and faith, there's only one way to play. Go all in. This time I'm betting it all, Noodle. My whole heart."

Ham and Noodle were both silent for a moment.

"Noodle, how do you spell *Chihuahua*?"

[chapter 27]

Lunch After Church

Between praise hymns, Emily informed Essie that Pearl was considering either cookbooks or cookware for Essie's Christmas gift.

Emily and Essie's families had met for the 11:00 AM church service and, as was their custom, planned on lunch afterward. However, during the service, the pastor called for volunteers to help prepare the sanctuary for upcoming Christmas events. So Jack and Greg chose to stay behind while Essie and Emily took the kids to eat.

Crossing one arm in front of her and the other behind her, Essie and the kids formed a single-file line as they navigated through the maze of SUVs in the church parking lot. It was easy to spot the Hummer in the distance. The roof rack and crossbars jutted out far above the other cars, like a grotesquely buck tooth. With an infant carrier slung over her right forearm and her left hand resting between the shoulder blades of her older daughter, Emily followed her sister to the car. "I'm in the mood for French. Have you tasted the peeky toe crab cakes with apple curry sauce at that new French bistro on Northside Parkway?"

"Are you kidding me?" Essie clicked a button on her key fob, unlocking the doors. Swinging them open as wide as the cramped parking spot allowed, Emily filed the kids in one at a time. The footboards helped, but Essie felt there must be a technique to getting in the vehicle gracefully while pregnant that she lacked. Each time she hoisted herself into the driver's seat, she forced herself to recall the freedom this vehicle represented for Jack. This maneuver, she decided, however awkward it may be, was a true act of love.

"I've been craving the foie gras terrine and apple confit on brioche toast." Emily said this as though it were everyday vernacular. But Essie suspected Emily had practiced the phrase so it could be delivered casually in mixed company to impress and amaze the less cultured.

"You can't be serious. We have a platoon of kids here. I don't think they are quite ready for fine dining." Lunch after church had been a longtime tradition with the sisters, but as their families had grown, the choice of restaurant called for compromises.

"It's always burgers and fries with the guys. But since it's just us today, I thought it'd be a nice change of pace. The baby will sleep, and the other kids will be fine. C'mon, Essie. It'll be fun."

Emily looked at Essie inquisitively. Her face shone with shades of pink and white, a pallet of optimism.

Essie returned her stare, leaning close and cocking her head as if examining some newly discovered species. "Not a chance," Essie said flatly.

"Why not? What's the worst that could happen? Besides, I'll be there with you."

"You were with me at Thanksgiving, too. Look how that turned out." Essie was a mix of admiration, irritation, and jealousy. There seemed to be no end to Emily's reckless good cheer. Sure, Essie would love to enjoy fine French cuisine on a Sunday afternoon, but a single glance at the crushed cracker crumbs on her floor mats snapped her back to reality. "And that was not even in public."

With all the kids buckled up, Emily climbed into the passenger seat, and Essie started the ignition.

"Where do you want to go, then?"

"Someplace easy, kid-friendly." Essie adjusted the angle of the rear-view mirror and flipped the visor down as if the right answer might be tucked somewhere above her.

For Emily, lunch with children didn't necessarily require the sacrifice of elegance or ambiance. Essie, on the other hand, had limited her choices to places where you order meals by number. She knew her sister would be disappointed with any suggestion she made.

"If you don't want burgers, how about Golden Buffet?" Essie suggested with a tentative lilt.

The H2 merged with the four-lane traffic and picked up speed.

"Fine," her sister answered, but her tone was sharp enough to cut. "Do me a favor, though, and stop at the grocery up here. I have to pick up a couple of items." She pointed to the fresh market up ahead on the right.

"You do realize that kids flick their boogers in the food bar at Golden Buffet, right?" Emily added.

Olivia nodded her head gravely. Cole and Juliet giggled and twitched with excitement at this prospect. "Boogers, boogers," they chanted, becoming almost buoyant in their seats. It was like a team sport, the rules known only to them. Toys became airborne. At least the children were tethered.

Essie pulled to the curb and Emily climbed out. "Having kids doesn't mean you can never go out for a nice lunch again, Essie. You always hated those pig trough restaurants, and now you're suggesting them." As her feet reached the pavement, Emily suddenly dwarfed. Only her head and shoulders remained visible as she stood at the open door.

"Your choice of where to go for lunch reveals a lot about your attitude on motherhood. Binding. Restrictive. Covered with boogers." She paused long enough for Essie to wince.

"You can be freer than that, Essie. You always wanted the fairy-tale life. It's available now, but you won't grab it. You choose to sidestep along the buffet line with the defeated and downtrodden. You can make a different choice. You can take the throne. Remember your fairy tales, Essie.

"You've perfected the damsel-in-distress role, but don't forget the rest of the story. Rapunzel, let down your hair. Let yourself be rescued. Be free." She slammed the door and barked through the open window.

"Think about it, Essie." She raised a finger in the air with the authority of a school teacher, firm and instructive.

Though she was poised in a seat high above Emily, Essie immediately shrank to her self-conscious, uncertain, middle-school self. Emily turned on a heel and marched into the market.

Emily was right, Essie decided. Freedom was a choice. She was tempted to say this over and over as if repetition would make it come true, but fear still lurked, shadowy, in her heart. If she could not strike a balance between motherhood and self when she had only two children, how would she ever find it with three? Lost in thought, Essie slid her fingers across her swollen belly.

A few minutes later, Emily returned with a heavily weighted plastic bag dangling from her elbow. She lobbed herself into the passenger seat and rested the bag at her feet. They drove to the Golden Buffet in silence, except for the occasional outburst from the back seat—"Boogers!"—followed by peals of children's laughter.

"I'm sorry," Emily said. "I didn't mean to be harsh, Essie. I've been a little short-tempered since learning just how much travel Greg's promotion will require. That is, if he even gets it. You're right, fine French dining probably isn't the best choice for four kids. Let's just have a nice lunch, OK?" She produced a warm smile, disarming the tension between them.

"No, I'm sorry," Essie said. "You are right. I want the freedom you have. I really do."

They piled out of the Hummer and into the restaurant. It was packed. The all-you-can-eat venue had attracted not only exhausted mothers of rowdy kids but also the seriously obese. The appeal was understandable. This was where the yellow brick road was actually mac 'n' cheese. The decibel level was just slightly less than heavy construction equipment. *Perfect. What could go wrong?*

They each took a brown plastic tray from the stack and a roll of napkin-covered silverware. An old man in a black-and-white uniform, stained tie, and soiled apron led them to their seats. While he showed them the way to a vacant, picnic-table-sized booth in an enclosed party room, the sisters watched with growing dread and nausea as the mass of tired mothers revolved around the salad bar, kids swarming around their feet, little fingers digging equally into noses and serving bowls. From her pained expression, Essie could guess what Emily was thinking, yet she said nothing. She simply took her tray and merged into the food line.

They took turns fetching platefuls of fried chicken, macaroni and cheese, yeast rolls, and gummy bears for the kids. They worked tag-team. One watched while the other got the food. It was a symbiotic ritual they adopted without conversation.

Once they were all engaged with their lunches, Emily made a final pass at the buffet, making plates for both of them. She came back with two handsomely decorated plates of spinach and strawberry salad, each with a small stack of assorted rolls and crackers arranged around the lip.

Setting one in front of Essie and the other in front of herself, she opened the plastic bag from the market and began dispensing its contents. Looking up at Essie with a wickedly mischievous grin, she pulled out a tiny jar of imported caviar. She spooned out portions in a wide circle on the empty plate between them.

Essie's jaw slackened with surprise.

"If you won't go with me to the French bistro, I will bring the French bistro to you." She unwrapped a foiled block of Boursin cheese and positioned it in the middle of the caviar.

An open-mouthed smile tumbled from Essie's face. The mood at the table became instantly celebratory.

"Excellent with the water crackers," Emily gestured toward her sister's salad plate, a sudden tone of sophistication in her voice.

What the children lacked in coordination, they made up for with enthusiasm. Some food appeared to be getting inside of them, but most of it made its way to the industrial-grade carpeting below, which was beginning to resemble a Jackson Pollock painting.

Emily pulled the last item from the sack, a bottle of . . . sparkling apple cider. "Would you do the honor?"

"My pleasure," Essie said with a smile that had now climbed all over her face, reaching her ears, spreading out behind her eyes. "Not exactly chardonnay."

"You can still toast with it, can you not? Don't miss the point: attitude is everything. And nothing refreshes the attitude like a bit of elegance and finery." She waved her hand above the table like a magician. "So let there be ambiance."

Hiding in their secluded booth behind a wall of diaper bags and purses, Essie popped the plastic cork and poured a small amount into two empty coffee cups. Essie raised hers toward Emily, offering a toast.

"To you, a true queen," she said. "You take the throne wherever you go."

"To Rapunzel," Emily countered. "May the fairy tale be your own."

Moments later, Cole flipped a booger at Juliet. Juliet unleashed an ear-splitting scream, announcing that lunch was now over.

[chapter 28]

Granddad Makes His Move

Hamilton docked his boat and headed up to the Marina Grill to meet his new business associates. When he crested the hill, he found the three charter members of the Greasy Goblins milling around the parking lot of the Ship's Store and Chandlery. During their wait, Ace, Sully, and Marion had revolved around the gleaming chrome and metal of their custom-designed motorcycles. Hamilton greeted each one with a warm smile and a firm handshake.

Ace wore a long, mangled ponytail, black T-shirt, and loose, faded jeans, each leg profoundly frayed at the ends. Sully and Marion featured equally unkempt attire. Sully's bald head gleamed white, but his arms were deep blue with full-sized tattoos, his fingers grease stained, and his fingernail beds blackened. Marion, five-foot-six and pushing two hundred pounds of solid muscle, was completely disguised by an explosion of hair. A curly brown mass on top, wide chops, and a full tuft at the chin. The random bursts of facial hair gave the effect of a topiary gone bad.

Ace, spokesman for the Greasy Goblins, stepped forward. "Mr. Wells, your offer is intriguing."

"The paperwork is all here." Hamilton handed him a manila folder. "If you fellas can abide by the terms, I'd be honored to have you aboard."

The Greasy Goblins formed a small huddle. Marion and Sully were grumbling something about expression of personal freedom, gesturing to one another's tattoos, hairstyles, and clothing. Hamilton overheard their concerns.

"First impressions are hard to shake, and we don't want anyone to get the wrong idea. I want you for what you can do, but a clean-cut operation is a key part of our unique selling proposition. Of course, I expect you to be yourself, not somebody else. We need a few unique individuals with your special talent to pull off this concept."

Ace looked Hamilton square in the eyes. "We don't work Sundays."

"I see no problem with that," Hamilton consented. "Matter of fact, you fellas were hand picked for just such principles. Don't enter a partnership with an unbeliever, isn't that what the Good Book says?"

This received a series of ardent nods from the Greasy Goblins. "Second Corinthians 6:14. 'Be ye not unequally yoked together with unbelievers,'" Ace confirmed solemnly. "I guess you have yourself a deal, Mr. Wells."

Sully frowned and shook his gleaming head at Hamilton. "Ace here is such a purist. A true King James man. Personally, I prefer the New American Standard. 'Do not be bound together with unbelievers.'"

"The NIV really says it best if you ask me," Marion offered in a soft tenor that completely contradicted his otherwise feral appearance.

This triggered Sully, who launched into a narrative about a series of biblically inspired tattoos on his arm. Seeing that business was concluded, Marion gave Hamilton a nod, turned, and threw a leg as big around as a tree trunk over his bike.

When the H2 pulled up to the Marina Grill, Hamilton appeared to be sharing a moment with a rough-looking crowd of bikers, admiring their tattoos. Jack, Essie, Ada, and the kids stared out the tank window with morbid fascination as Granddad pointed out the scars along his jaw and his hand as a kind of friendly comparison to the body art of motorcycle gang members.

"What kind of crowd does your father hang out with?" Ada asked.

"Yeah, who are those guys?" Essie asked Jack.

"I have no idea," Jack answered, a tinge of concern in his voice.

Cole pressed his face to the window and watched his grandfather shake hands and pat shoulders with the gristly looking crew. "Cool," he said.

Jack had suggested the family meet his father at the Marina Grill for lunch. "Bring that fiery gal with you," Ham had suggested. So Essie had invited Ada, who quickly tempered her initial enthusiasm as if realizing her instant acceptance proved her to be more eager to come along than she wanted to admit.

Essie noticed that Ada had dolled herself up for the occasion. It was the first time she'd seen her neighbor wear mascara, and her lips shimmered with a new shade of pink. She wore a new outfit as well: a wide-brimmed sun-hat, a white knit sweater, long khaki skirt, and rubber-soled sneakers. On the ride up to the lake, Essie's suspicions grew each time Ada steered the conversation back to Hamilton.

When Jack spoke about the growing momentum of his upcoming marketing promotion at Life Cola, Ada responded, "Very interesting. And what kind of work does your father do?"

"Oh, he doesn't. At least, not in the traditional sense. Years ago, he made a bundle in commodities trading. He may not show it, but he's got a fortune stashed away somewhere," Jack answered casually.

Ada arched a brow. "You'd certainly never guess it."

When Cole asked if he would get to go on the boat, Ada asked, "So you say he lives on a sailboat? Does he allow pets aboard?" The Apostle Paul remained unmoved by Ada's curiosity and slept contentedly in a tight curl in her lap throughout the entire inquisition.

The group piled out of the Hummer just as the bikers fired up their engines in unison and pulled away from the lot. Hamilton waved goodbye to his friends, then greeted his family. Cole and Juliet made a beeline for the nearby sandbox, as expected, and immediately set to work building a sand castle.

"Good to see you again, Son," Hamilton grabbed Jack by the shoulder and pulled him close for a masculine, slap-on-the-back embrace.

"Hey, Pop. Glad you could make it."

"I'm sure pleased to see you here, ma'am," Hamilton nodded to Ada.

"Thank you, Mr. Wells," Ada fidgeted with AP, tucking him under one arm. "I've heard so much about all this," she waved her free hand at the expanse of lakefront activity. "I just had to see it all for myself."

AP twitched his nose at the smell of grilled meat and fish coming from the Marina Grill.

"Well, after lunch, it would be my privilege to give you the nickel tour, ma'am."

"Why, I'd be honored," Ada said.

Essie sliced a look toward Jack to see if he was picking up on this, but he had turned toward the Grill.

Hamilton, Ada, and Essie joined Jack at a picnic table under a large umbrella. Hamilton, Jack, and the kids ordered a round of dock-burgers with fries. Ada and Essie decided on the fried grouper sandwich. They ate and talked and watched the kids play. It felt like a complete family. Essie laughed at the memory of her Sunday lunch with Emily and the kids.

In her own way, Emily had cured her of being intimidated by taking young kids out to nice restaurants. Essie caught herself in the moment and found that, despite her heavy belly and a little sand in her shoes, she was actually comfortable, not to mention enjoying herself. No, the Marina Grill didn't serve them caviar and chardonnay, but it was the finest dining she could've wished for at that moment. She rubbed her fingers over her rounded stomach and wondered if it would still be possible with three.

Hamilton and Ada walked down the pier to take a look at Ham's sailboat. The usual cobwebs connected the handrails along the walkway. Ada flinched when the couple's footfalls on the pier startled one particularly large spider and sent it scurrying across their path. Georgia winters, rarely dipping below freezing, were kind to marina wildlife. Lake critters consequently remained unmotivated to relocate, an attitude Ham admired and adopted for himself.

"I'm not fond of spiders, Mr. Wells. Do you always keep company with so many bugs?" Ada asked.

"I figure it's their home as much as it is mine. Besides, they keep the skeeters down. Generally, I'd say they make better-than-average neighbors."

Ada grimaced.

"So, you're sure you've never been a waitress?" Hamilton's gray eyes twinkled. "You sure have the right disposition for it."

"No, I haven't." Ada gave Ham a look that warned him to be careful. "But I'll take that as a compliment, Mr. Wells." They had arrived at the end of the pier, where Hamilton's boat swayed gently.

"And indeed, you should. You're a lovely lady is all I meant." Hamilton offered Ada his arm for support to help her step aboard.

Ada seemed to blush beneath her bonnet. "Well, Mr. Wells, let me say, you seem to have a proper set of manners, of this I'm convinced, even though, at times, you, um . . ." She hesitated, apparently searching for the right words. "You show a few rough edges."

"I'll take that as high praise, ma'am." Hamilton followed her aboard, quickly located his oddly stuffed seat cushions for the benches in the cockpit, and offered her a seat. "I must say, Ms. Ada, those earrings of yours look just like one of my favorite fishing lures."

Ham gathered from her startled expression that Ada wasn't sure how to take this. Evidently, she had never had her fine jewelry described in such fashion. Nevertheless, she smiled politely, as though choosing to accept his comment as a compliment.

"I'm glad you like them . . . Ham, should I call you Ham?" Her eyes roamed about curiously, and she recoiled at the sight of more cobwebs on the rigging.

"I wish you would. May I call you Ada?" Ham sensed her distress and brushed the webs away with a casual wave of his hand.

"That's fine. But Spiderwoman, I certainly am not!" she laughed, shrinking away from the mangled remains of web. "Though it would, no doubt, be more appealing to young Cole!"

An awkward moment of silence passed. "Ms. Ada, I was wondering if I might call on you for a dinner date. Something spicy, maybe?"

Ada looked alarmed. "Ham, I think you're a very interesting man, but you should know that I am not one of your fly-by-night romance types. Don't mistake me for one of your waitress flings."

"Absolutely not, Ms. Ada," Ham said with conviction. "I wouldn't think of taking advantage of you. I'm beginning to think that waitresses and boats go together like frogs on bicycles." He paused. "You are obviously far too young and delicate in romantic matters." A smile crept up behind his gray eyes.

Clearly, Ada didn't want to be grouped in the same category as any past relationships, but for reasons Hamilton couldn't understand, she balked at his assurances.

"Well, I don't know about frogs or bicycles. And it's not that I'm inexperienced, Mr. Wells. I'm about the same age as you. And I've been married before, you know. Twenty years before my husband passed away."

Hamilton acted shocked. "Twenty years! Ma'am, surely you are mistaken. You couldn't be more than, what, twenty-nine years old now."

Ham was laying it on thick, and Ada couldn't help but crack a smile. "That'd make you only nine years old when you were courting. Like I said, far too delicate."

"Oh, I don't know. You might be surprised, Ham." Ada looked away as if a bit nervous, a bit embarrassed, or both, but playing along. She fingered a bracelet on her wrist. "I was very popular when I was nine."

Ham smiled broadly, enjoying her wit.

"I can see why." He pulled a tiny wooden figurine from his pocket. "Woodworking is a hobby of mine, and I've made a little something, knowing your fondness for these little dogs." He handed her a small whittled likeness of a Chihuahua.

Ada's cheeks flushed again as she examined the gift closely. Something was etched on the bottom. "Barnabas?"

"I seem to recall the original Apostle Paul had a couple buddies he ran around with. So I figured AP might feel more at home on a boat with old Barney along."

"Why, Ham, that's about the most thoughtful gift you could give me." She smiled warmly. "It almost makes me reluctant to insist that our next visit be indoors."

Essie looked down the pier to see what was keeping Hamilton and Ada. Hamilton was helping her off the boat. Ada used his arm as leverage. Essie couldn't be sure, but from a distance, it looked like their fingers lingered together a moment longer than necessary.

[chapter 29]

You Can Find Everything at Wal-Mart

The Stone Mountain Wal-Mart was a hotbed of suburban commerce. Where else could a busy, working mother have photos made, shop for her kids, and maybe even pick up a few groceries—all on a Saturday afternoon, without having to change parking spaces? The parking lot was filled with attendants in Santa hats and orange reflective vests waving batons like a pack of elfish-clad, air-traffic controllers steering the parade of SUVs and minivans to open parking spaces. Essie was making her annual pilgrimage to the portrait studio, where she had a sitting scheduled for Cole and Juliet in fifteen minutes.

It was a fool's errand, preserving the cleanliness of a five-year-old and twenty-month-old child's formal holiday attire through lunch and closing in on nap time, but she was doggedly determined to send Christmas cards featuring two angelic children's faces this year. The picture of a perfect family. The pride of a successful mother. Circling the parking lot for the third time, she was finally motioned into an open parking spot. Essie liberated both kids from the back seat, and with a tiny hand hooked in each of her own, they walked toward the entrance.

Cole and Juliet wore matching Christmas outfits. Cole walked proudly, chin up but stiff-legged, in his white button-up shirt, gray sweater vest, black pants, polished tuxedo shoes, and silver tie. Juliet toddled forward, looking down at herself with a wet grin, admiring her black sweater, round fur collar, full silver skirt, and sparkling silver shoes.

Approaching the automatic doors, Essie bought a little insurance by offering an incentive. "You both look adorable. If you two will smile for the camera, Mama will let you both pick out a prize. OK?" The doors slid open.

Just inside, a man was handing out flyers at a small booth. He waved a wad of forms at her.

"If I could just have a minute of your time, ma'am. I'd like to talk to you about sponsoring our high school athletic hopefuls' holiday program. By joining, you can support local athletes and bring holiday cheer to needy families." He pushed a form in her face and offered her a pen.

With all hands occupied she nodded in the direction of each of her children. "No, thank you. I'm in a bit of a hurry."

"I'll catch you on your way out then. I'll save your signup sheet right here," he tapped the corner of his booth, calling after her as she hurried past.

They filed into the portrait studio just as the photographer was about to give away their time slot to another waiting family.

"Are you Ellison Wells?" she asked, slicking back several errant strands of wiry gray hair escaping the ponytail that shot out straight from the top of her head.

"Yes. Sorry, I'm a couple minutes late."

"OK, let's get started right away. We have a jam-packed schedule today." To the waiting family, she said, "Sorry, she's here now. You can wait if you like."

"Forget it." The waiting mother sighed and herded two boys in matching red suits out of the studio.

Essie frowned apologetically.

The photographer motioned her toward the back room. She pressed a button, and a motor whined, jerking a snowy backdrop into place.

She flung a furry black covering over a wooden platform and gestured toward the kids.

Essie lifted Cole up to the platform and positioned him between a feral reindeer and a vaguely demonic snowman. Next, she reached for Juliet, who backed away from the scene, wide-eyed with alarm.

"Come here, pretty girl. It's OK, baby," Essie soothed, lifting her next to Cole.

The photographer yanked a large black sheet off the camera, a hulking apparatus with a wide black snout for a lens. She pressed more buttons, the lens rotated, and a smaller, alien snout protruded from the first lens in Juliet's direction, as if sniffing out prey for a midday snack.

Immediately, Juliet's face turned red, and she let out a piercing scream. The photographer's head with its sprouting gray ponytail sprung up from behind the beast. Like an evil puppet-master, she rolled the camera closer and squeaked a bulgy-eyed rubber doll in the air.

"Smile," she sang.

Frozen in fear, Cole forced a tight, obedient smile, but Juliet sucked in a deep breath, a prelude to her operatic announcement that the photography session had reached its end.

Click, click, click.

"Well, that does it." The puppet-master stepped out from behind the beast. "Kids," she held up her hands in surrender. "You just can't make them behave. Some won't smile no matter what. Next time, you might try bringing a toy of your own to distract them."

She handed Essie three proofs of panic-stricken children fleeing a frost-covered hell.

Forgoing the portrait package, Essie ushered the kids out of the studio. They made their way to the toy aisles. The promised prizes would definitely be awarded, not for their winning smiles but to simply restore their trust. She was determined her kids not be punished for the actions of the photographer, who was sure to become the subject of Stephen King's next novel.

Cole quickly found the Hot Wheels, and all was forgiven. Juliet was instinctively drawn to the dress-up clothes and discovered a pair of red sequined slippers and a diamond-studded tiara. The smile Essie had hoped to capture on film appeared. She helped clip the tiara to Juliet's thin blond wisps. Juliet removed her silver shoes and put the sequined slippers on by herself. They were much too big for her tiny feet, but seeing the moist grin return to her daughter's tear-streaked face, Essie realized she had no choice but to buy them.

With their finds, they made their way toward the registers. The main aisle was crowded with promotional and sale items. Holding hands, they weaved through stacks of books, piles of electronics, and towers of boxes. Juliet was shuffling along in her sequined shoes, letting the little plastic heels drag on the ground.

A lady in an elf suit was handing out samples of Chex party mix to customers. Cole ran over to her display table and reached for a sample. Releasing Juliet's hand, Essie walked over to keep him from raking the samples off the trays. She scooped a tiny cupful and turned around to find Juliet marveling over a mountain of boxed princess Barbies. With her knees bent and tiara bowed, she pulled with all her might on the arm of a chosen Barbie at the bottom of the stack.

A fellow shopper reached around Essie, snatched three samples, and observed: "Ma'am, you should really get control of your kids." She eyed Essie's pregnant belly. "People who can't control their kids shouldn't have them," she added gratuitously.

"Juliet, nooo!" Essie lunged toward her daughter as the Barbie box wriggled loose. The tower of boxes wobbled and then tumbled into a heavily ornamented Christmas tree. The domino effect sent doll boxes and bouncing plastic Christmas balls in all directions.

Cole was peeking around an aisle cap of toaster ovens. His face was frozen, a pretzel stick dangling from his lips. All the shoppers paused to look. The store was suddenly quiet except for the tinkling sound of rolling Christmas ornaments and the soft croon of "Feliz Navidad" over the PA system.

"I am so sorry," Essie said to everyone in general and no one in particular.

Juliet was holding the extended arm of a dislodged princess Barbie, partially ejected from its box, cardboard sagging to the ground.

"Mama!" Eyes wide with fear, Juliet stumbled toward her mom through the pile of fallen boxes. Sliding in her oversized shoes, she tripped and fell. The tears sprang from her eyes even before the howling began.

Surveying the wreckage for which they were responsible, Essie was reminded of her new refuse management role at work. Maybe the task fit her after all. Suddenly, she was aware that not just Juliet, but all three of them were crying. She grabbed both kids and sought refuge in a booth in the in-store McDonald's. She was rocking them both in her arms. And they were rocking her. Ray Charles's "That Spirit of Christmas" streamed through overhead speakers, as if extending its own unique and personal form of comfort. Their crying subsided, and Essie wiped away remaining tears.

She stood Juliet in front of her and adjusted the diamond tiara on her head. Her sequined slippers had fallen under the booth and lay askew. Juliet crawled under the booth and came out with the slippers in her hands. Noticing the tears on her mother's face, her mouth turned serious, forming the shape of a small pink bow, and her eyes grew round with concern. Juliet crouched in front of her mom with the tip of her tiara almost touching Essie's knees. She reached forward and rested two tiny sequined slippers on her mom's feet, the buttermilk pudge on her arms forming creases at her wrists like rising biscuit dough.

"Mama's shoes," she declared.

Smiling through her tears, Essie looked upon her daughter's crown in wonder: *She does not understand how truly royal her nature, how magnificent her one small act of love, and how deeply this gesture touches a parent's heart.*

In that moment Essie sensed a host of silent witnesses around her and heard a still, small voice in her heart say, *"Nor do you, child."*

With a surge of renewed spirit, she scooped both kids in her arms and kissed their faces with a mother's unrestrained affection. They returned to the toy aisle first and, with heads held high, made their way to the register. Her son toted his new cars as mother and daughter both paraded past in sequined slippers and diamond tiaras.

As they walked out of the store, the man at the exit invited her again to sign up for his athletic hopefuls' holiday program.

"Sorry, no time," she said.

He surveyed the royal procession of diamond crowns and sequined slippers and smiled. "Off to a rehearsal or something?"

She glanced at him over her shoulder as she passed.

"No, what makes you say that?" she asked with a lilt of surprise in her voice, and thought to herself, *Princess attire is fitting for any occasion.*

[chapter 30]

Gifts from the Heart

Essie woke to the rustling of wrapping paper and gift tissue. From the bedroom, she heard Jack and the children bustling around the Christmas tree, their voices rising above the rattle of boxes and bags.

"So, it's a birthday party?"

"Well, yes, I suppose it is."

"Where are the presents?"

"The wise men brought presents. Gold, incense, and myrrh presents."

"What's murp? Why didn't they just get him a bicycle? I thought they were wise men."

"Myrrh. It's a spice or something. I'm not even sure myself."

"It's probably socks. I bet he didn't like it. Doesn't sound like a good birthday present to me. Who wants socks?" Cole made a face.

"Hmm, I see your point."

"What about from Santa? Did Santa bring him any toys?"

"No. Santa wasn't around back then."

"But you said Jesus' birthday was on Christmas."

"That's right. His birthday *is* Christmas."

"He should get a present. Somebody has to give him a good present," Cole declared with authority.

The clamor in the den softened, and Essie heard an excited exchange of whispers and giggles. A plan was set in motion and concluded with footfalls bounding up the stairs and rolling across the ceiling above her in a series of dull thuds, like distant summer thunder.

The day had hardly begun, and she was already tired. A golden shaft of light made its way across the carpet and crept up the bedspread. A sea of glittering flecks floated through the stream, each on its own silent, private voyage. She shielded her sleepy eyes from the sun and stepped into the cool air of the master bath.

With icy water pooled into cupped hands, she doused her face and neck and combed her hair back tightly with wet fingers. Leaning over the sink, nose to the mirror, she examined her bare face, clean, no makeup. Her reflection struck her as unfamiliar, a strange combination of features, somehow incongruous. Her eyes looked both leaden and empty. Fine lines fanning across her temples exposed weariness from a heavier weight than years alone.

Yet looking deeper, she saw embers of bronze burning just behind each iris, emitting a strength and youthfulness from some distant place. She felt that familiar sense that she had not become the person she was meant to be, that she was meant for something more. Silently, she asked in prayer: *Lord, who am I to you? Who should I have become?*

On the rays of morning sun, a thought sailed into her mind. *You are heir to a glorious freedom.*

The concept was troubling. Beyond reach. *God, was that you? Are you speaking to me?* Freedom? On the contrary, most of the time she was bound by obligations and duties. Her life felt like an endless striving to perform, fulfill responsibilities, satisfy the needs and demands of others. At the end of each day, she found herself not so much fulfilled as exhausted from the effort. Where was the freedom in that?

Cartoon music drifted down the stairs. The aroma from the kitchen announced coffee was brewing. She slipped on a robe and shuffled to the kitchen. She poured a mug and watched as the steam rose in white ribbons and evaporated.

What does it mean to be free, anyway? She tried to picture it. *What does freedom look like for a working mom? What does it feel like?* She padded softly through the house, straightening up, pausing at the window long enough for the mug to warm her hands. She watched the cold, slow movement of winter. The trees were bare, their dried leaves fallen in brittle brown patches. Beyond the trees, a narrow river wound slow and silvery, like mercury, under the clear winter sky. Water slinked across flat rocks and fell lazily over fallen branches into silky pools.

With Christmas just around the corner, toys and gifts were piled under the tree. Scraps of gift wrap, ribbons, and bows were strewn across the den. Jack and Essie had exchanged early gifts the night before. She gave him a portable XM radio with a mounting kit for his motorcycle. Upholding his end of the lifestyle bargain, he surprised her with a silk maternity nightie, an Eric Clapton CD, and a set of crystal stemware.

The dough-it-yourself nativity scene was spread out across the end table next to the tree. The once-tight nativity circle had widened, and she spotted a few recent additions to the crowd. A tiny pair of sparkling silver shoes rested next to the wise men. Between the camels and the lambs lay a small Spider-Man action figure. Toys and shoes in the nativity scene. Did holiday clutter have no limits? It was true; a mother's work was never done. Coffee in one hand, Essie collected the toy and shoes with the other. Only then did she notice the gift tags.

On the Spider-Man action figure, she found a note written in crooked, wobbly letters, "To baby Jesus, from Cole." The handwritten letters, however misshapen, revealed the collaborative effort of a father and son. The slanted print overlaying red crayon scribble on the next gift divulged Juliet and Jack's teamwork. The tag on the shoes read: "To baby Jesus, from Juliet." Essie had discovered the cause of their early morning whispers and giggles.

Her children had freely given up their most valuable treasures. Amazed, she clutched the precious gifts to her chest and crouched down next to the scene. What heart these children had!

God had surely placed a divine spark in the hearts of children. What happened to that spark as one grew older, busier, more responsible? What happened to hers? She yearned for that kind of beauty, too. Yet she found herself kneeling at the scene with no gift in hand, nothing to offer. She had no greatness that compared to this. She had no gift fit to give a King.

As she cradled their gifts in her arms, realizing the significance of their sacrifices, tears welled up in her eyes. How precious these gifts were to her; how much more so they must be in God's sight. Not given out of duty or obligation, out of guilt or shame. Offered simply in love. Given freely to honor him, no other motivation. She was amazed by the simple yet complete purity of it.

In humility, she asked, "God, what do you want from me?"

The answer came: *"Your heart. It is my greatest treasure."*

"But Lord, you already have my heart."

"Then come out of hiding, daughter. You have forgotten who you are."

"Who am I?" She remembered her reflection in the mirror, the uncertainty in it.

"My princess."

A flood of memories passed through her mind. Jack's declaration in the face of a mundane assignment, *"Your job doesn't make you who you are. What you believe is what makes you who you are."* Ada's pronouncement about the image-bearing child of God she was designed to be: *"You were born to shimmer!"* Emily's urging, *"Take the throne. Remember your fairy tales, Essie."* Juliet's heartfelt gift of royalty at Wal-Mart, fitting her with princess slippers, *"Mama's shoes."*

With images of beauty and royalty filling her mind, it occurred to her that God had been speaking all along, declaring her identity, over and over again. His princess. Behind each image, he was there, calling to her, declaring his love, wooing her into a sacred romance.

With a flush of sorrow, she realized he had been waiting for her. Her delayed response suddenly shamed her, and his patience overwhelmed her. Her heart swelled inside her chest. Its binding split, and an inner radiance, one that had somehow become obscured by a veil of routine and obligation, burst through the seams. Unshackled from all her self-doubt, Essie found God's hand extended, proud to carry her on his arm.

Cole walked in, bed hair still sprouting in all directions. She opened her arms to him, wanting to hold her child, so warm and tender in the mornings. She collected him in her lap, and he rested his head on her shoulder.

"I'm very proud of you, Son. I saw the gift you gave to the baby Jesus."

He snuggled closer, burying his face in her neck. She felt his warm breath against her skin. "Do you think it would be OK if I still play with it sometimes?"

"Yes," she smiled, "I think he wants you to enjoy your gifts, too."

It must also be true of her, she decided, squeezing Cole's narrow chest against hers, recognizing the abundance of blessings that surrounded her.

Cole grabbed the Spider-Man figure and gave his mother a look of relief and gratitude. He walked back toward his room, swinging the action figure through the air. Guided by Cole's outstretched hand, Spider-Man flew in undulating waves. Essie watched Cole's bare feet glide across the hardwood floors, his movements easy and fluid. Though Spider-Man was airborne, it was Cole who appeared weightless. This, she decided, was what freedom felt like. Her weightless heart now soared with knowledge of a truer identity, one she vowed to celebrate.

She returned to the window, admiring the beauty of the winter scene in her own back yard. Same tree, same dried leaves, same slow river. Only now, she noticed the small cyclone of leaves swirling along the ground in an elaborate dance. The river's current swayed with twists and turns, silver-white beads leapt over rocks and branches in a liquid ballet. How had she missed it before? The celebration was already underway. All of nature was dancing for the King.

She swung her hips, tentatively at first. Then with growing conviction, she rocked her torso and allowed the motion to travel through her whole body, her arms and legs giving way to the rhythm. In joyful prayer, she offered, *Shall I dance for you, too?* But she already had her answer.

Fully joined in the dance, Essie rose up on her toes, reached both hands in the air, and in princess fashion, twirled in a circle. Casting away all formality and inhibition, she cha-chaed up the stairs, thrusting a shoulder forward, wagging it up three steps and throwing it back for one.

When she reached the upstairs den, she found Jack reading a magazine, the children glued to the TV. The princess cha-cha performance had gone unnoticed. So she stepped in front of the television, swept Cole up in her arms, and wrapped his legs above her hips. Grinning playfully into his startled face, she anchored him tightly against her waist and let her feet fly and her shoulders shimmy up and back in salsa style.

By now, Juliet was reaching up for her, begging for her turn. Essie crouched low and grabbed her daughter's little hands in her own. Holding one hand around Juliet's waist, Essie twirled her daughter along her arm until her small body was pressed against her chest. Essie dipped Juliet's head back dramatically, gathered her back into an embrace, squeezed her once more, and then spun her back down her arm.

The children's laughter joined their mother's alongside the distant chorus of rustling leaves and the lazily flowing river. All were sounds of praise from God's creations, each offering a unique song. Joined together, Essie imagined their collective praise forming a glorious soundtrack for a much larger story.

Grinning, Jack watched the song and dance, the magazine resting open in his lap.

"Care to tango?" she asked.

[chapter 31]

Goat Moves Forward

"The Goat moved forward." Zooming along the highway, Essie reported news of the committee's approval to Lewis Cathcart from her mobile phone. She'd come to appreciate characteristics of the H2 not in the owner's manual. For one thing, it parted interstate traffic like Moses did the Red Sea.

Hearing herself speak in these terms, she felt like a secret agent in some low-budget spy movie using coded language to communicate a priority message back to headquarters. She only wished the code was more sophisticated, less barnyard. *The eagle has left the nest. The package has been delivered.* A good cryptic message promised adventure, perhaps danger, and above all, news of critical import. But *The Goat moved forward*? It took the glamour right out of the job. Left the agent feeling embarrassed, second rate.

The Aluminum Alliance had queried corporate members about their interest in an aluminum exchange, an online can bank that offered new incentives for recycling. The response to the lend-a-can.net vision was surprisingly strong. First, a spokesman for Alcoa, the world's leading aluminum producer, blessed the endeavor with high praise from environmental groups. Next, heavyweight beverage makers and a couple of big-name construction, service, and building companies expressed interest. For many corporations, to aid community housing efforts through recycled aluminum offered an attractive public relations incentive, but more important to the builders, participation actually strengthened their candidacy for upcoming housing projects.

Then General Motors agreed to participate on the promise to reap tax benefits. Once GM's point of view became known, Ford signed on as well, and other automakers queued up. With several heavy hitters on board, many smaller companies soon followed. The stampede was on. Essie suspected the alternative to participation was to be labeled insensitive and politically incorrect. A huge public-relations blunder—who wanted to be labeled anti-environment?

While participation came easily, funding to build the technology solution did not. A cross-enterprise fusion of technology and finance required careful planning and deep pockets. Development requirements included a sophisticated, service-oriented architecture; a high-end, financial-transaction engine; and a flawless security design. All this on the back end with an easy-to-use Web front end no more complicated than Cole's kindergarten "homework." In other words, online usage must be as simple as connect-the-dots or paint-by-number. Factor in costs for project management, offshore development, and wide-scale integration testing; add to it a meager contingency multiplier; and they were looking at a seven-figure price tag.

In the world of technology, enormously expensive ideas were both good news and bad news. The good news was that a costly project actually stood a better chance of getting done. Generally, the industry bias was that inexpensive projects simply weren't worth doing. A small price tag implied triviality. A really big price tag suggested a nobility of purpose that could not be ignored. In addition, the most highly prized, highly skilled technology professionals were interested in working on only the highest-profile—and likewise, most costly—projects. So the best resources pushed their way to the front like Southern Baptists at a bake sale.

The bad news was someone had to foot the bill. Recipients of the bad news always responded in predictable ways. They looked for ways to minimize the impact on their own wallets and shift costs to any others that could be seduced, coerced, or otherwise persuaded they were beneficiaries.

In the case of lend-a-can.net, the Aluminum Alliance proposed a shared investment approach. As a nonprofit trade association, the Aluminum Alliance offered to lead the overall initiative and all promotional activities to boost usage while each participating industry contributed a portion of the funding proportional to their projected level of use and benefit. Using Life's cost projection, the Alliance developed a complex cost-distribution algorithm. The cost model divided expense among the beverage, auto, and building industries in such a way that the individual impact to each member company became negligible, a welcome tax write-off opportunity for a charitable cause.

Life Cola's role was then relegated to financial contributor and technical management. The Aluminum Alliance would hold the purse strings, but Life would source and manage all technical aspects of the project.

"Well done, Ellison. Then, the Cow is on the move. Now, you must hold firm and stay the course." Lewis Cathcart's voice boomed over the phone. Essie struggled to find a spy-worthy response, but it was not there.

Inserting an ear bud, she placed her cell phone in a holster Jack had mounted on the H2's dash and gripped the wheel with both hands. "I'm on my way back to the office, hoping we can discuss next steps around recruitment options for the project team. Bids are in from several firms, and I've narrowed the list to the top three."

"Yes, about the project team. I believe I can save you time in that regard, Ellison. There have been some exciting developments."

Often times, it was not until money was involved that real decision makers were revealed. It sounded like someone was moving levers behind the curtain again. Essie wondered who Oz was this time and what he was up to. She ticked the heater gauge down a notch to minimize background noise and rotated an ocular vent to redirect a light stream of warm air toward her.

"What kind of developments?" The grill of the H2 bore down on a sedan full of commuters. Expressions of fear and weary apathy were just visible through the grate of her brush guard.

"This is not about Life anymore, Ellison. Not about profit. Not about you or me. This is about corporate social responsibility. This is about the rise of an era of global citizenship. The welfare of the planet may well be at stake."

Essie looked over her shoulder and swerved into a fast lane as his voice crescendoed through her ear bud.

"The board agrees that requirements from key funding contributors for this groundbreaking work will be best served by assembling the project team in a centralized location."

Essie listened as she drove. The Hummer careened past a metal sea of smaller cars like a T- Rex after bigger game.

"The Cow will be based in New York. We'd like you to relocate as soon as possible. In New York, you will be much better positioned to work with EarthWise, a consulting company I've engaged that specializes in environmental services. EarthWise is headquartered in the city. We will lease office space through them."

"The Cow is in New York?" That would be a first. A prickly heat spread behind her ears.

"The office is in downtown Manhattan."

"Do I understand correctly? You're asking me to move to New York indefinitely?" She flicked the heated seat switch to the off position and let up on the gas. Relocation was not even a remote possibility. Atlanta was her home, her family's home. She couldn't uproot her family right now. She wouldn't. Not for this cause. Or any cause.

"For at least two years, yes."

"Mr. Cathcart, sir, I'm sorry but I cannot accept a transfer right now." Had he considered that she had two small children and a third coming soon? Besides, Jack's job was here, too. Her sister, her parents. Their roots ran deep.

"Naturally, you'll receive an environmental pay adjustment to offset the higher cost of living. And of course, a moving allowance will compensate you for your trouble."

"I'm afraid I'm not negotiable on this, Mr. Cathcart. I am not available to relocate." The hum of traffic filled the silence.

"Ellison, we need you on this. I thought you were committed."

"I am committed, sir, but not to this calling."

A teenage girl accelerated past her with bass thumping so hard her side mirrors were vibrating. She mindlessly cut Ellison off as she chatted into a cell phone held to her ear. Essie jerked the wheel to the right and changed lanes, barely missing the sporty convertible. The driver chattered away and remained blissfully unaware of the metal tonnage that nearly swallowed her through its steel-toothed grill.

"In that case, I'm afraid you'll have the standard thirty days to find another position within the company or be released. Unless, of course, you choose to reconsider."

"I understand." The connection broke. Reassignment was not likely. That meant thirty days till unemployment. She had a sudden and urgent need to get off the expressway and collect her thoughts.

After a close call on the highway and a probable job loss, she'd ordinarily expect the tension to have driven her shoulders north of her ears, but an unexpected calm washed over her as she exited the highway and wheeled the H2 into a convenience station. An old gentleman in a GM truck darted in alongside her.

She unplugged her earpiece, coiled the wire, and placed it in the console alongside a host of other devices: GPS unit, portable XM stereo,

MP3 player, and a tangle of power adapters. All the technology combined with the complex engineering of the H2 created the effect of a mission control center. She stared at the surroundings. Gauges, dash controls, and the electronic accessories stared back. She considered their combined power to control her environment, all the electronic mastery employed to enforce her will. Even with so many instruments at her disposal to manage temperature, speed, noise, and navigation, she was still not the one in control. She chuckled softly at the irony and felt a strange relief. Then she thought of the staggering amount of money she could've saved on gear if only she'd realized sooner.

Essie needed some air. As she opened her door, a voice came from the convenience-store parking place next to hers. "That was some fancy driving, miss. Saw that young lady cut you off. Atlanta drivers. Most of them are crazy, you know. Defensive reflexes, that's the key." The thin, elderly gentleman was neatly, but not importantly dressed. Amusement flitted across his blue eyes as he lifted a cardboard box out of the truck bed.

"I don't think she ever realized the near miss." Essie stepped down from the H2, smoothed the folds of her maternity skirt, and took a full, deep breath.

"Not a clue," he agreed. "Luckily for her, you're a skilled driver."

"I'm still a little shaken. I was on the phone with my boss at the time. I think I just lost my job."

Soft mews rose from his cardboard box as he walked a lap around her truck. He stopped and appeared to concentrate for a full minute on the Life Cola parking tag hanging from the rearview mirror.

"I like your truck there. I'm a GM fan myself." He eyed the company ID badge clipped to her waist.

"Yeah, it's the family car."

A squeaky whimper came from the box, followed by the scratchy sound of shuffling newspaper. The old man sat the box down between their vehicles and scattered a handful of dog treats inside. Four tiny Chihuahuas pounced on the windfall.

"Ain't no good for hunting, but the wife is crazy for 'em. They just got their eight-week shots today, and now they're ready to find new homes."

"For sale, then?" Essie thought of Ada and her fellowship of disciples. Would she accept an addition to her herd? "How much?"

"Well, miss, the wife tells me these here are from fine breeding stock. She aims to get four hundred dollars a piece for 'em. You interested?" He rearranged the box in the truck bed and headed toward the store.

"Yeah, maybe." Inside, Essie made a beeline for the ladies' room. At this stage of pregnancy, it was a bihourly event. On her way out, she purchased a Life Cola and walked back to the cardboard box and took a closer look inside.

The old man returned a minute later. He looked surprised to see her, regarded her soda, and looked at her again—curiously, as if trying to solve a puzzle. He tilted his head at an inquisitive angle as though he were about to ask a question, but all he said was, "It's a good beverage." He pointed to the soda can.

"Yes, it is," she said and took a long swig. "But the sweetest tastes in life are outside the can."

He smiled.

"Will you take a check?"

"Sure, miss." He tugged a wallet from his loose faded jeans and handed her a card. His name, Rollin W. Plat, was inscribed in a squat bold font on heavy card stock. No title, no association, no hint as to who he was.

She scribbled out the check and handed it to him. "Need a female with strong character." Essie lifted each pup out of the box and held it up to her face. "She's likely to be named from the Old Testament." She chose a sleek brown pup cleaning the paw of another with a small pink tongue. "This one'll do. Looks like she'd make a good mother one day."

He folded the check and slid it into his shirt pocket. Essie drank the last of the soda, took a lingering look at the empty can, and tossed it in a recycle bin. As she tucked the pup under her arm, a clean rain of renewal washed through her.

"I wouldn't worry about that job of yours," he said. "I have a feeling things will work out."

Deciding not to make the trek to the office after all, Essie headed toward Ada's house instead. With the gift cupped in her hand and mewing softly against her neck, Essie rang the doorbell.

"Oh my little darling!" Ada greeted both Essie and the pup with the same expression of endearment.

"For you." With cupped hands, Essie offered the Chihuahua to her friend.

"Oh my! Isn't she the most precious thing you ever saw?" Ada gathered the pup in her arms and ushered Essie inside. They took seats side by side on the couch. The little dog curled into a ball on the seat cushion between them. "What on earth is the occasion, dear?"

"Christmas is almost here, but I can't wait when there is so much to celebrate now."

Ada stroked the puppy's ears. "Why wait, indeed!"

A few curious apostles gathered at Ada's feet.

"I think I just lost my job, but the strange thing is, I'm not devastated." Essie relayed the conversation with Cathcart.

Ada listened, her eyes clear and serene as a glassy sea. "Put your seatbelt on, child, and watch closely. An adventure is about to begin."

"Watch for what? What adventure?"

"Isaiah 43:19, dear. God is doing a new thing. 'Now it springs up. Do you not perceive it? I am making a way in the desert and streams in the wasteland.'"

Essie considered this. "Maybe you're right. Still, it's strange how quickly things can change."

Ada lifted the pup to her face and kissed it. The tiny Chihuahua wagged its tail excitedly, and its wet nose glistened like a shiny brown marble. The disciples danced in circles at Ada's feet, and AP jumped up on the seat cushion, eager to meet the new addition.

"Looks like she'll be quite popular here," Essie observed.

"It's easy to see why," Ada responded, rescuing the newcomer from AP's playful pounce. "She's gorgeous! Look at her shiny dark hair and brown eyes. Just like a beauty straight out of the Old Testament. What shall we name her?"

Ada was halfway through the twelve tribes of Israel when Essie's cell phone rang. Essie recognized the number. She pressed a button to accept the call and muffled sobs poured out of the receiver.

[chapter 32]

Behind Closed Doors

Emily was frantic. Through the sounds of cell static and sniffles, Essie made out that there had been some kind of crisis, Greg was out of town, and she was to come quickly.

A short while later, she stood in Emily's home. "I got here as fast as I could."

Emily sat slumped on a packing crate in her den, surrounded by stacks of moving boxes. Wadded tissues littered the carpet around her feet. Her nose was a glossy red, and her cheeks shone wet with tears. She wiped her face with the back of her hands and blew into a fresh tissue.

"The deal fell through." She lifted her head, and a cloud of shame gathered behind her eyes. "It's all my fault."

"Oh, Emily." Essie squeezed a hip onto the crate next to her sister's and folded an arm around Emily's shoulder. "I'm so sorry. What happened?"

"They have plenty of openings over there, you know? And the commute back here would be an hour and a half each way. I didn't think it would be a problem. So, I resigned." She sniffed. "A teacher can get a job anywhere, right?" Essie handed her another tissue. "But when the lender checked my employment status and reran the numbers, he disqualified us for the loan. Greg's firm finally offered him the promotion, but that didn't make any difference to them. They only consider our past annual income.

'Unfavorable debt-to-income ratio,' he called it." Her shoulders trembled, and she turned her head away. "What am I going to tell Greg?"

"Emily, I'm very sorry. I know this move means so much to you."

Emily leaned her head against her sister's shoulder, and Essie let hers rest against it.

"You shouldn't worry about Greg, though. He wanted this move for you, not for himself."

"That's not the point," Emily sobbed, crushing a tissue in her clenched fist.

"Then what is?"

"I'm embarrassed, Essie. I'm an embarrassment. It's not just Greg, it's everyone, you know? What am I going to tell the neighbors?" A panicked expression swept across her face. "And Mother? I forgot. She's going to be here any minute now. She kept the kids this afternoon while I packed. God help me. What am I going to tell Pearl? Moving to Paddleboat River Club is the only decision I've ever made that she's approved." She brushed the wetness from her cheeks and tucked a fallen strand of hair behind her ear.

"Everyone has their thing, their special talent, their own way to shine. Right? For Pearl, it's her expertise in the kitchen. No one dared compete. For Greg, it's sales. He can sell bacon cheeseburgers to vegetarians." She caught a teardrop at the corner of her eye and flung it aside. Her expression hardened with frustration. "Jack, he understands all things mechanical and electrical like they share some unique language the rest of us don't speak. And you, with your corporate job. You balance work and kids with a gymnast's agility. But what about me? What do I have?"

"Are you kidding me, Emily? Do you honestly have to ask? I admire you for so many reasons. First, the way you so thoroughly enjoy motherhood, despite its occasional indignities. And then there's your unshakable optimism. Most impressive, though, is the way you keep your sense of humor and sense of self intact. Besides, what's so wrong with this house? I like having you close to me."

"Don't you get it? The gated community in Paddleboat River Club was my chance to do my thing, create a beautiful environment uniquely my own. Not just another comfortable place to live, Essie. But build an exquisitely designed home, where the warmth of every color, the softness of the lighting, the smells of real wood and natural gardens make every day positively celebratory. I have strived so long and hard for this. My home is who I am, Essie. I want to be more than . . . than ordinary." She grimaced as though the last word tasted of vinegar.

She shifted her weight on the crate and turned toward Essie, their knees touching. Emily sighed and looked into her sister's face with a cautious expectation. In Emily's expression, Essie recognized a strangely familiar combination of features. They were three years apart, but people had often mistaken them for twins. Emily's hair was darker and a couple of inches shorter, but they shared the same narrow face and deep brown eyes. Beneath those eyes rested familiar shadows of self-doubt and fatigue, yet flames of hope and strength flickered just below the surface. Essie knew this feeling. Emily didn't believe she had become the person she was meant to be. She wanted to be something more.

Essie curled her fingers into both of her sister's hands. "Emily, you are so very much more than your home. You have forgotten who you really are."

Essie led her into the kitchen and made them both a cup of coffee. Over the next few minutes, she described her experience after discovering the gifts her children had placed in the nativity scene. She tried to explain what had happened that day that changed her, that revealed her truer identity. They talked about who they were, who they longed to be, and what it might look like to live in their very own fairy tales. They sipped their coffee. They laughed and cried, but mostly, they just loved one another.

"It's ordinary to be the princess when you live in some royal castle, but it's an extraordinary thing to be one hidden away out here among the suburbs, wearing everyday clothes," Essie said.

Emily wrapped her arms around Essie in an extended embrace. Essie felt a fresh tear against her face, but Emily's smile told her it was not of sadness.

The doorbell rang, and Pearl stepped inside with Emily's two daughters. Emily hurried to the bathroom to make herself presentable, while Essie placed sleeping baby Alicia in her crib and situated Olivia among her coloring books. Pearl saw the trail of crumpled tissues among the moving boxes.

"What's happened?" she asked.

Essie's silence affirmed her mother's cause for suspicion. Even with a freshly powdered face and combed hair, Emily couldn't hide the evidence of emotions in her red-rimmed eyes.

"The deal fell through, Mother. We aren't moving to Paddleboat River Club."

Pearl clasped the base of her neck in shock and disbelief. Her outstretched fingers covered a gold choker and dangling pendant.

"What do you mean? Greg didn't get the promotion?"

"No, actually, he did."

A pregnant pause filled the room. An explanation had to come. Emily struggled to hide her embarrassment, masking it somewhere within her wounded expression.

"Yes, we're all disappointed but I'm telling you it is for the best," Essie said. "You can't allow kids to grow up in that kind of environment."

Emily cast a furtive glance in her direction. Pearl snapped her head toward Essie, puzzled creases lining her brow. "Whatever do you mean, Ellison?"

Essie recalled the way her neighbor, Walt, boasted about his escapades with the Paddleboat tennis team, on and off the court. Though his conquests were almost certainly embellished, she knew Pearl would not approve of even an edited-for-TV version. Pearl was offended when her bridge-club members wore shorts with heeled sandals, so the tennis skirts alone would undoubtedly send her fanning.

"Mother, I'm sorry to tell you this. I know how much you admire the homes in Paddleboat River Club. But . . ." Essie lowered her voice to indicate the need for discretion. "I have it on good authority that the neighborhood practices—how can I say—untoward activities."

Pearl's red ringlets bristled to attention. Emily darted her sister a look that said, You wouldn't dare.

Essie continued, "My neighbor plays tennis over there. Well, anyway, let's just say it started as an innocent mixed-doubles league, but it ended up"—she closed her eyes and waved her hands through the air as if to erase the mental image—"unseemly." If she could have swooned on cue, she would have.

"No!" Pearl cupped her palm over her mouth. "Members of my choir live over there."

"And the depravity is growing. The way Walt tells it, I wouldn't be surprised if they opened an adult novelty store in the strip mall just beyond the gates."

Emily dropped her chin and narrowed her eyes at her sister.

"So," Essie flipped her palms upward as if to fling the unpleasantness away, "you can see why Emily had to break the contract."

"Oh my word!" Pearl dropped herself into a corner chair.

"Mother, perhaps this is the right time for you to go back into real estate," Essie suggested.

Pearl eyed her daughter questioningly. "Why would you say that?"

"It's what you've always wanted to do. And this is a critical hour. They need you."

The sisters watched as Pearl considered this, pressing her fingers to her temples. The three of them sat motionless among the stacked boxes.

"Maybe I will," she declared finally. "There are still some decent neighborhoods in the area. I can't just stand by knowing how my fellow choir members must be suffering." She stood. "Emily, dear, don't you worry about it. You are doing the right thing." Pearl marched toward the door with all the conviction of the crusaders behind her. "I can have my Realtor's license renewed within a month."

She kissed each of their cheeks lightly, tossed her purse over her shoulder, and walked out the door. As she started her Mercedes SL and backed out of the driveway, Essie could hear the faint hum of "Onward, Christian Soldiers" in the rumble of her engine.

[chapter 33]

The search is on

"Rollin Plat!" Haj stared at Essie slack jawed over a powdered doughnut. "I just heard the news. How do you know Rollin Plat?"

"Who is Rollin Plat?" Essie asked. The name was familiar, but she did not place it immediately. After a soul-satisfying Christmas break and New Year's holiday, Essie was back at work, and her mind raced to put the pieces together to make sense of the morning's events.

Haj and Essie sat in canvas folding chairs outside the domed tent that had become the landmark for Marketing's out-of-the-cube creativity. Today, a boxed assortment of individually wrapped breakfast pastries roasted above the fabric flames.

"*Who* is Rollin W. Plat! Are you serious? He's a legend," Haj Tamul exclaimed through a mouthful as he tossed a wrapper in the firewood.

Fenton Mac grabbed a glazed doughnut, positioned another folding chair opposite them, and joined the campfire. "A retired GM exec. Sits on the board here at Life. I did a paper on him in college. He's acquired a reputation as a modern-day Howard Hughes. He's still very reclusive—no one has seen him for several years—but believe me, when he talks, the corporate world listens." He squeezed a Life soda into the beverage holder built into his armrest.

Jack walked up with a lockbox tucked under one arm and a wall map of the U.S. in the other. He nodded his head in silent greeting and threw a knowing smile in his wife's direction.

Essie smiled back and wondered how much he already knew about her mysterious reassignment.

"All I know is that I got a call from some VP's secretary saying to report to the team headquarters for the Larger Than Life American Adventure Tour. So, here I am," she explained.

As she said the words out loud, a tingle rushed up her spine. She kept a cool composure, but inside, she was bursting with excitement. Somehow, her job had been saved by a mysterious benefactor. And now she found herself on the Larger Than Life American Adventure—with Jack.

It felt right, almost mythic, like some storybook collision of destinies. The parallels between her professional and private life were not lost on her. The company name, the tour, the marketing vernacular: they all stirred up her girlish, fairy-tale ideals of romance, grandeur, and noble purpose. No, they were not saving lives or rescuing the planet from evildoers, but forces had placed them together once again, at home and at work, to share in the adventurous pursuit of life's ambitions. In some cosmic way, their partnership must be of great significance, something crucial must be at stake, something that depended upon their unity.

"Evidently, you have friends in high places," Haj said. "Word is Mr. Plat called our chief marketing officer and singled you out to lead the technology components of the tour. Said something about the way you drive. And that you were a good judge of character." Powdered sugar circled his mouth. "What's that all about?"

With wide-mouthed surprise, Essie put the pieces together and the name clicked into place. "Oh yeah. The old guy in the truck. I bought a Chihuahua from him. Nice guy."

"A Chihuahua?" Haj replied, incredulous. "You must be kidding. That's priceless."

"Legendary," Jack echoed. "The mystique of Rollin Plat deepens."

Fenton rolled his eyes. "A nice guy with Chihuahuas. Right. Well, don't expect to find any more nice guys around here, OK? So you pulled some bigwig's string to get on our team, fine. Way to throw your weight around." He pushed another glazed doughnut in his mouth and raised an elbow in the direction of her disproportionately large belly. "Just remember, Jack is still our leader. The Adventure Tour rolls just as planned."

"Hot doughnuts, the price for such fierce loyalty." Jack faced his wife. "I just heard the news this morning. The CMO called me in to make sure there was no problem working as a husband and wife team on this campaign. He explained company policy doesn't prohibit us working together as long as we report through different channels. You'll still report through IT, not Marketing like the rest of us. He also said it's a twelve-week assignment only. No promises after that." He offered his outstretched hand to seal the agreement and dropped into a southern drawl. "So, ma'am, if you'd be so kind to oblige us, we'd be honored to have you aboard."

Essie shook her husband's hand. "I'd be delighted, gentlemen." A twelve-week assignment was not a long-term solution to her career uncertainty, but she was too excited to worry about that now. Besides, twelve weeks ran beyond her due date, so there would be plenty of time to think through next steps while on maternity leave. It was a vast relief in any event to be disencumbered from Cows, Goats, and Cathcart.

The mood around the campfire quickly turned serious as they walked through the details of the plan. Jack unrolled the map and stretched it out by the fire.

"The tour launches here." Using a twig from the pile of kindling, he pointed to the state of Georgia. "The first geocache site will be at Stone Mountain, the largest exposed slab of granite in the world." He circled the map with the tip of the stick.

"A southern route out west and a northern route back. Everyone is sworn to secrecy. We'll place one hundred treasure sites in eight weeks."

He opened the lockbox and displayed its contents: a GPS unit, a miniature motorcycle, a sealed envelope, and two coupons for a free can of Shot, the new beverage concept.

"Shot is not an energy drink, it's an Adventure Drink. A whole new category of beverage requires an all-new promotional strategy." Jack reviewed the basic elements of Shot's debut and its Larger Than Life American Adventure promotional tour.

"The custom chopper just arrived," Fenton announced, flipping his cell phone closed. "It's at the receiving dock."

Life contracted with a custom chopper manufacturer to build a Shot theme bike, a uniquely designed motorcycle to promote Life Cola's latest brand. With wide television, radio, and Internet support, the bike would travel across the United States for eight weeks placing buried treasure, also known as geocaches, at secret locations. Consumers would participate in the American Adventure using GPS coordinates to find the treasure. The first to find each treasure would retrieve the special code in its sealed envelope and redeem it online to receive a prize. And those that didn't find the actual treasures would still experience an American Adventure in the thrill of the hunt. The fusion of adventure, youth, high tech, and treasure hunting had the team electrified with anticipation. It would be the ultimate reality show with the entire country participating, not just watching.

"So you'll feed me the GPS coordinates of each cache site along with some hints about its location. I'll update the tour treasure map online." It was the perfect assignment for Essie. Her technical expertise was needed for a plan that carried with it all the magic and fabled fortune of any fairy tale.

"Exactly."

"Let's go see the bike."

They walked together to the receiving dock. When the crate was opened, the men, speechless, stepped back and gazed upon the steel horse.

The motorcycle was a marvel of Wild West nostalgia and modern engineering. The profile of a stallion began at the seat and sloped upward over an elongated gas tank and dropped to a low slung horse's head midway down enormously extended front forks. The front wheel was stretched way out in front. Even at rest, it appeared to be in perpetual motion.

Black and silver, the tank itself was shaped into a twisted steel mane, which extended past the handlebars and arced forward to a sleek steel head hunched down in full gallop. A small, bottle-cap-shaped headlight was fastened above the horse head like a jewel in a crown. Bullet-shaped cans of Shot were tacked onto the front forks like a slanted ammunition rack. An enlarged bullet-shaped exhaust and fiery, blue-flecked paint along its opening gave the effect of violent propulsion. The wheels were fitted with custom spinners—three interlocking arrows—the symbol of recycling. The foot pegs and handlebars were shaped into slim can renditions of Life's signature product.

"Exquisite beauty." Breaking the silent reverie, Fenton threw a leg over the beast. "Check this out." When the brake light was activated, an insignia blazed through etched carvings in the rear fender: *Life . . . to the fullest.*

"Epic." Haj breathed approval in a hushed tone.

"Yippee ki-yay," Jack agreed.

"Wow," Essie said with a smile. "Quite a promotional attraction. Where's the cowboy to ride it?"

All eyes turned to Jack. When he didn't answer right away, Fenton and Haj looked down, finding sudden fascination with their shoes.

"I've been meaning to talk to you about that." Jack stalled. "The company wants me to be the rider. The Marketing VP said I was his first choice since everyone here knows my passion for motorcycles. Don't worry, though, Essie. I already said no." He spread his hands out, palms up. "There's just no way I'm leaving you this close to the delivery."

After he said it, Essie wondered how she hadn't foreseen it. It seemed obvious in retrospect.

Fenton and Haj stooped near the bike to admire the details. Jack and Essie stepped back for a moment of privacy.

"I can't imagine a better choice than you," Essie admitted.

"Any other time, sure, I'd love to do it," Jack admitted. "But eight weeks is a long time to leave you and the kids, especially with the new baby coming so soon. I won't make the same mistake my father once made. My family comes first."

It wasn't shaping up to be the romantic notion of a shared adventure she'd first imagined, but Essie knew what she had to do. "I think you should do it!"

A puzzled expression washed over Jack's face. "What do you mean?"

"This could be great for both of us," Essie explained, pragmatism taking over. "Think about it. This tour is a once-in-a-lifetime opportunity, Jack. A definite career launcher. And the timing couldn't be better, actually, now that I'm only temporarily employed. Soon we'll be a family of five on a single income."

Amazed and confused, Jack searched his wife's face. "But the baby is coming soon."

"You'd be back well before my due date. The tour will be over the first week of March," Essie calculated. "Besides, the other deliveries were both late. Chances are, you'll be back two weeks before the baby comes."

Their eyes locked in heavy silence.

Sure, she'd hoped this partnership meant a side-by-side adventure, but the truth was no one could give this tour the spark it needed like Jack. Essie should have seen this coming sooner but had been self-absorbed with Cathcart and her own project. This was an important career move for Jack. He knew it as well as she did.

Jack's face beamed with renewed enthusiasm. "I'll line up family and neighbors to help you and the kids while I'm gone. I'll call you all the time."

"I know." Essie understood this lust for adventure. She shared it. She just wished his pursuit of it would lead him closer to her, not away from her. Then again, maybe it would somehow bring greater unity in their marriage. God answered prayers in unpredictable ways.

"I realize now that buying the Porsche was a mistake," Jack announced.

"Really? How's that?"

"I thought the Porsche would satisfy this restlessness, this midlife crisis or whatever you want to call it. Somehow complete the picture for me, you know?"

"But it hasn't?" Essie prepared herself to hear a realization of some deeper truth he'd discovered about the meaning of life.

"No, it hasn't. It's just an expensive toy, not a freedom ride. But between this tour bike and the new Mustang, I can honestly say I have it all."

"What new Mustang? What about your old Mustang?"

"We'll keep the old Mustang, of course. It's a classic. But I sold the Porsche to Walt. He says it's just the inspiration he needs to bring new zip to his mixed-doubles game. 'A chick magnet,' he called it. Sure, the Porsche was a classic, too, but it needed repairs, required too much maintenance. So I went to visit Buddy at the Ford dealership. The company let me choose a companion vehicle off Buddy's lot. They'll let me buy it at a deep discount after the tour. It's an incredible machine, Essie, not to mention, a perfect support vehicle for the Adventure Tour."

"Mustang?" Essie repeated with uncertainty like pronouncing a foreign word for the first time. One minute she was in the unemployment line, and the next she was miraculously dropped into the ideal job. She set out on a great adventure and discovered her part was more solitary than she expected. Yesterday a Porsche, today a new Mustang. OK then, another Mustang it would be.

Recognizing how far removed she was from the driver's seat, Essie resigned herself to simply enjoy the ride. Finding enough faith to let go of the wheel was an adventure of its own. And the unexpected peace discovered in the surrender was like finding hidden treasure.

Control, she mused. *It's not what it's cracked up to be.*

[chapter 34]

Larger Than Life American Adventure Tour

The reporter stood shoulder to shoulder with Jack, admiring the Life theme bike. A hefty man in a white windbreaker unloaded a tripod and camera from a Fox News van. A reflective banner spanning the back of his jacket gleamed under the winter sun in bold blue caps: FOX NEWS CREW.

"You're going how far?" the reporter asked Jack as he tucked the wireless microphone in his waistband like a revolver.

"A loop around the country. A southern route west, up the coast, a northern route east, and back down to Georgia. Around eight thousand miles."

"If the weather gets bad, then what?"

"Numerous support vehicles will shadow me during the trip. Members of our extended team will join me at different locations, some following with cameras and road-trip supplies and many others helping with the treasure sites. No one will know which of us will plant the next cache." Jack was coy in mentioning the treasures. They were a secret as well kept as the Life Cola recipe. All Life employees involved in the project had signed a battery of documents guaranteed to bring about their complete ruination should prize knowledge or location escape into the general public. Essie, Fenton, and Haj stood among a half-dozen spectators looking on from a distance.

"You love your job, don't you?" Ray asked.

"I'm living the dream," Jack said. The role of motorcycles in this particular promotion had lit a flame inside him.

The cameraman angled the camera on the tripod. "Ten seconds, Ray." He folded the hood of his windbreaker over his head, leaned forward, and peered down the lens, allowing his bulk to hang heavily over his waistband.

Jack and Ray turned and faced the camera. Ray pulled the microphone out of its holster and swept his hand carefully over his hair. "Three, two—" A red light flicked on, and the cameraman stabbed a finger at the reporter.

"This is Ray Portafino reporting live from Stone Mountain, Georgia. I'm here with Jack Wells, marketing manager and frontiersman for Life Cola. We are here to kick off an exciting new promotional event for the U.S. beverage maker involving a motorcycle adventure tour and buried treasure." Ray turned to face Jack. "Jack, what does Life have in store for us? And what can you tell our viewers about this tour?"

Suited in protective gear, helmet tucked under one arm, untamed hair arranged in rebellious angles, Jack radiated a contagious energy.

"Today marks the launch of the Larger Than Life American Adventure Tour, a road trip across America to plant buried treasure. This adventure celebrates the introduction of Life Cola's newest brand, Shot, now available in stores everywhere. It is the first of a whole new category of adventure beverages. The tour and the new brand are celebrations of Life and all that is America."

"Shot." Ray flashed the warm smile of a long-trusted friend, the smile that won him his job. "I tried one this morning, and the taste is as bold as it sounds, Jack. Just like this theme bike." Ray gestured toward the motorcycle. The cameraman wheeled around for a close-up of the bike and focused on the bullet-shaped exhaust pipe mimicking Shot's innovative package design.

Jack smiled with pride and leaned into the bike. "The chopper is custom designed to display Life's great love for adventure and the American dream and to showcase our products and values."

The camera followed Jack's hand as it made its way from the horse's mane to the product imagery on the handlebars and foot pegs, then to the tri-arrow-designed spinners fitted in the wheel wells showcasing the company's support for recycling.

"The first buried treasure is already placed here at Stone Mountain, and I'll place another ninety-nine in the next eight weeks as I tour cross-country."

The camera panned back to frame Ray and Jack. A growing crowd of onlookers gathered in the background.

"So, tell us. Just how does this treasure hunt work?" Ray asked.

"You'll need a GPS first." Jack raised a global positioning unit into view. "Then, go to LargerThanLife.com. From there, you can follow my progress and get the coordinates for the buried treasure closest to you. The clues and the coordinates are published so that everyone gets the same chance to find the treasure."

"Well, folks, you heard it. Visit LargerThanLife.com to track the adventures of Jack Wells, the new American cowboy, living the dream."

The red light on the camera went black. Hefty snapped a lens cover in place and carried his gear back to the van. "Nice ride. What kind of mileage you get off her?"

"Not enough," Jack answered. "Plan to stop for gas every two hundred miles."

Fenton, Haj, and Essie stayed behind the scenes as Jack thanked the news crew. After they exchanged goodbyes and drove off, Jack huddled with his coworkers and whispered, "The first cache is placed. Essie, here are the coordinates." He slipped a curled strip of paper into her hand like a fortune-cookie message. Future GPS locations would come via encrypted e-mail. Only those with the electronic key could decode the locations.

It was decided that this methodology would be most conducive to secrecy for the sake of the treasure and to build hype for the Shot introduction.

"I know we agreed on Stone Mountain as the first cache site. But where is it, exactly?" Haj asked.

Jack's eyes met Essie's. "Essie, remember where we found the paper sack full of money?"

She flashed a grin of recognition, remembering one of their dates long ago before they were married. They had climbed the mountain together and found a crumpled brown bag with the lip rolled down tightly. Jack had picked it up and, without opening it, claimed it was filled with money. As they hiked across the granite, their conversation had turned to speculations on what they would do with a million dollars if they had it. When they reached the bottom of the mountain, they agreed that a million dollars wasn't what either of them really wanted out of life. They threw the bag in the trash without ever opening it. That was the day she realized she was in love with him.

Had Jack reached back into her past to make the first treasure a memorial to their lives somehow, or was this just a teasing coincidence?

He turned to Haj. "A special place."

"Wish I could go with you guys, but someone has to stay behind and run this place." Fenton puffed out his chest and rested his hands on imaginary lapels.

"The support vehicle is ready." Haj pointed with his head to the new Mustang convertible. "Still can't believe you arranged a new car for the support team. Or that you want me to drive it. Not that I'm complaining."

"Make us proud." Fenton pumped Jack's and Haj's hands in farewell.

Essie embraced them both, letting the moment with Jack linger for a few extra seconds. It was romantic to think that Jack was kicking off a marketing campaign with parallels from their own lives hidden just below the surface. Jack and Haj were bouncing with anticipation. Fenton and Essie stepped back as the two men mounted their steeds.

Within an hour of publishing the Stone Mountain cache coordinates on the Web, the treasure was found. The lucky winner redeemed his coded treasure online for two round-trip tickets to anywhere in the United States. After the first find, the momentum of the campaign skyrocketed. As did the value of the treasures.

The prizes ranged from cars to trips to motorcycles to sports-and-adventure-related products: rock climbing gear, parasailing, flying lessons, adventure cruises, and much more. No two prizes were the same. The country watched with fevered anticipation to find out who, how, and what would be discovered next.

The tour and the finds were widely publicized, but the cult band of followers that ensued garnered more media attention than Life Cola ever could have paid for. Young motorcyclists and adventure lovers of all kinds began to follow the adventure route, some for the prizes and others just for the sheer fun of the hunt. Shot became an overnight rage. "Life to the fullest" became the instant mantra of Shot consumers.

At times, Jack was forced to modify his route to evade the crowd. Occasionally, Jack would zigzag his way through popular areas to lose a treasure hunter who followed too closely. Other times, he and Haj would take separate routes. More often than not, however, they'd call upon local members of the extended team to place the actual geocaches and to keep the followers from learning the location before the treasure was placed. Ever-more-sophisticated maneuvers were used to evade overzealous treasure hunters in an effort to broaden participation and keep the entire thing fair.

Over the next days and weeks, Jack supplied Essie with the closely guarded location coordinates along with clever hints to post to the interactive tour map online. Many locations were near widely known landmarks, while others were more obscure. Because the location of the Stone Mountain treasure held personal significance, Essie couldn't help but look for the hidden significance in other locations.

She was not disappointed. One treasure was hidden in a playground in Cole City, Georgia. Another in a potted plant outside a shoe store in Mount Juliet, Tennessee. Hardly coincidences.

While in Texas, he buried another on the side of the road near Cadillac Ranch. The hint was "the way to a man's heart is through the garage." She thought of Jack's love for cars and laughed at the memory of their intimate evening in the Hummer. As the online map became sprinkled with X's, she began to see the trail of landmarks as a salute commemorating the tapestry of their lives together. Whenever possible, Jack referenced national landmarks or historic locations that lay within line of sight or walking distance to a buried treasure, encouraging participants to see and experience America's beauty and rich history.

Carlsbad Caverns, New Mexico. A place they visited on their honeymoon, the site of her tragic realization of their radically opposed ideals of honeymoon romance.

Jack hid one within view of the Grand Canyon, a place where they vacationed early in their marriage. She remembered standing on the edge of the canyon with Jack, both of them experiencing an awe so beyond the two of them. They recognized the handiwork of God and somehow knew that they shared a small but critical role in a much larger story of his design. The memory alone triggered flutters in her stomach that she couldn't attribute to the active child inside of her.

Jack was using a national platform to weave together and celebrate the events and moments of their lives.

At the O.K. Corral in Arizona, he playfully weaved music and marketing prowess into his clues. The hint came from familiar song lyrics: "I Shot the Sheriff."

On the phone that evening, Jack seemed distracted, lost in deep thought. He spoke of the XM Satellite radio mounted to his bike in the third person, like an old friend, a trusted advisor. He listened to it all day as he traveled.

"It's like the music is speaking to me," he'd said. "Not just about the tour, but something bigger. It leads me to the next treasure location."

He described the way the songs triggered tender memories and nearly forgotten dreams.

The lyrics Jack repeated over the phone struck an emotional chord with Essie, too. Strung together, the songs, like the treasure sites, seemed to tell a story, forming a soundtrack of their lives, leading them to discover its overlooked beauty and unrecognized significance.

The Golden Gate Bridge. Yosemite National Park. Yellowstone. Mount Rushmore. Each place held a memory, a private treasure. Jack was working his way back east now.

The hint for the treasure near the Statue of Liberty said, "The crown of her beauty is in her freedom." Was he referring to the statue or America in general? Or the crowns Juliet and Essie wore leaving Wal-Mart? Or something even closer to his heart?

Treasure marks continued to spread across the map.

Central Park.

The Liberty Bell.

Gettysburg.

Arlington National Cemetery.

Even though the GPS coordinates made the hints or clues almost superfluous, Jack continued to leave messages that resonated with the country and with Essie's heart. Something new and powerful was at work in him. She could hardly wait for the tour to conclude to be next to him again.

[chapter 35]

pandelirium

Jack's voice came hushed and breathless through the receiver. "Essie, it's pandelirium."

Pandelirium: n. a state of disorder between delirium and pandemonium. Indescribable hysteria and panic.

Jack referred to a term they had coined in their earlier years when, with new parental zeal, they invited forty children to Cole's one-year birthday party. Webster's dictionary offered no adequate word to describe the experience. The combined effect of too much sugar, too many new toys, and too many children in one place at one time created a heretofore unknown state of uncontrolled frenzy and mind-numbing overstimulation. All sense of order was irretrievably lost, and the advent of a new expression found its way into their parental vernacular.

"A television crew raided our tent this morning. I woke up with a camera in my face. They've been trailing us all day. The paparazzi are all over us, too. They're trying to predict the next cache site, staking out prominent landmarks. The paparazzi claim unfairness and corporate misconduct behind the tour. 'Treasure Hunt or Corporate Stunt?' they say. Rumor is that the competition offered them serious bucks to prove the prizes are rigged."

"What?" Essie gasped.

"This thing is huge, Essie. Bigger than we ever imagined. No matter what the naysayers claim, the tour has truly captured the spirit of adventure. People love it. A pack of young bikers are following us. It's a motorcycle convoy. Haj and I ran into two guys who actually claimed to be us. Jack and Haj look-alikes. Can you imagine?"

"Unbelievable! What did you do?"

"We called in the local support team. We explained to the followers that we don't place most of the treasures ourselves, but we still couldn't shake the crowd. The bike is just too distinctive and attracts attention wherever it goes. So we resorted to renting a covered trailer to keep the bike under wraps between stops today. Won't be long before the followers figure it out though. This whole experience—the treasures, the motorcycle, the music—it's helped me to realize something, Essie. I've made a decision."

She heard a low rumble of engines grow louder. Through the receiver, it sounded like an approaching swarm of angry bees.

"Oh no! They're here! Gotta go." Click. Jack was gone.

As she prepared to leave the office, her thoughts were filled with concerns about Jack's safety. A dull cramp traveled through her body. She pressed a hand into the small of her back as she walked through the parking lot. At this stage of pregnancy, even short distances were difficult.

Though the cynics were few, she was angered by the paparazzi's attempt to denigrate Life's efforts and cast doubt on the integrity of the promotion. Not only was the Larger Than Life Tour the most successful promotion in the history of Life's marketing endeavors, it had restored a spirit of adventure to the company at large. And a kind of wholesomeness, without guile.

Getting into her car for the commute home was a daunting task in itself. Was it possible that she was this big with the other two children? She climbed up on the Humvee's running board, made a half turn, plopped backward into the driver's seat, and swiveled her legs under the wheel. To an onlooker, it must have appeared to be some elaborate ceremony. The docking of a dirigible. To her, though, the maneuver served as a reminder of the boundless love she had for her husband. How much she missed him. As successful as the tour was, she wished Jack was back home with her now. *Only a few more days*, she consoled herself.

On the way home, she was forced to repeat the entire awkward ceremony as she stopped at a convenience store for milk. Surely there must be a more comfortable way to propagate the species. Thankfully, the whole ordeal would be over in another three or four weeks.

A female clerk of indeterminate nationality made change, eyed Essie's belly, and tersely asked, "Twins?" Essie considered decking her, but she was safely protected in what appeared to be a bulletproof cage. She settled for piercing her with a hard glare.

"One at a time is plenty." Essie grimaced and turned to leave. As she did, she noticed a height scale on the doorjamb, there to assist clerks in expertly noting the height of fleeing robbers. Where, she wondered, was the measure for width to capture both dimensions of the perpetrator? She reasoned it must be unnecessary due to the low incidence of heavily pregnant felons in the area. She repeated the blimp docking procedure and pointed the H2 in the direction of her childcare provider.

Once there, she found Juliet coloring in the toddler room and Cole, who rode the bus there from school each day, making use of a swing in the playground.

"Watch this, Mom!" Cole shouted. He was pumping his legs to build momentum.

Essie stopped to rest in a child-size chair and called to him, "C'mon! Let's go, Son."

Cole seemed to sense her irritation. He launched himself from the swing and raced over to her. He hugged her neck and smoothed his hands over her hair. "Mommy, you are so pretty. You look like Ariel. She has red hair, too."

"You are such a charmer, honey." She kissed his forehead, stifling the urge to recommend he save it for courting.

As they headed home, a chorus of "grilled cheeses" came from the car seats in the rear. With Jack out of town, something that simple suited her fine. They arrived home, disembarked, and entered the kitchen through the garage.

In front of the stove, she assembled the grilled cheese apparatus, then began to stage drinks, eating utensils, and booster seats. She felt another sharp pang in her back. The doorbell rang. She waddled to the front door, peeked through the sidelights, and immediately recognized Ada's billowy cloud of hair floating weightless above her pink lips and cheeks. Her face was a rose blossom on the first day of spring.

"Essie, dear, I thought you might like a little help with dinner." She held out a still-warm dish of homemade chicken 'n' dumplings.

"You are an angel." She took the dish as Ada called a greeting to the children, patiently awaiting their sandwiches.

"Is something burning, dear?"

"Oh, no!" Essie duck-walked back to the kitchen to find a skillet of blackened grilled cheeses. Blackened may work for fish, chicken, and steak, but not cheese sandwiches. She held the frying pan over the trash to dump the whole mess, but Ada stopped her.

"Don't throw those out just yet, child. Let me see 'em." She made a big show of carefully studying the sandwich remains. "These things can be valuable, my dear. I saw one go for forty-five hundred dollars on eBay. The image of the Virgin Mother appeared in the grill marks."

"Really?" Essie looked dubiously into the pan.

"Oh yes. This one has a Renaissance flare to it. Looks like da Vinci's *Last Supper*."

"Ada, don't make me laugh. These pains in my stomach. While you appreciate the art in my burnt sandwiches, I'll go look for the DaVinci Code in the chicken 'n' dumplings."

Any code remained safely hidden as Essie ladled the dumplings into the kids' bowls. She pressed a button on the remote, and Joe Cocker's raspy lament came through the house speakers.

"Not feelin' too good myself," she groused in unison with the lyrics as she rubbed her fingers over her tightening stomach. The song seemed to fit well at this point in her soundtrack.

Ada glanced at her watch as she bustled about the kitchen. While helping Juliet recover a lost dumpling, Ada accidentally nudged the overnight bag Essie had assembled and left by the door to the garage.

"I see you're ready for number three, dear," Ada remarked.

"Been ready since the seventh month," Essie answered and grabbed her sides with a look of pained concentration on her face.

"Child, are you all right?"

"I don't know. Just tired, I think."

Ada looked at her watch again.

"Honey, another reason I stopped by tonight was to share the good news about the girl pup you gave me. Apostle Paul has expressed intentions for her." She bounced her eyebrows at the implication.

"What did you name her?" Essie asked.

"I've haven't yet, child. Waiting for you to name her. A name is important, dear. It should be a reflection of God's workmanship in a life."

"Well, let's see. I chose her from the litter because she seemed to be nurturing the others. Like a good mother would." She ran through a list of biblical names in her mind as Ada rinsed the plates in the sink. Suddenly, the answer was clear. "Let's name her Sarah."

"Sarah is lovely," Ada said.

"Sarah became a mother late in life. And that's how I think of you, too. I remember your story about wanting children of your own. But the thing is, you've been like a mother to me." Another sharp pain ran across Essie's back.

"Oh honey, I love you and your family like my own." Ada's smile was warm and genuine. "What are you going to name your new baby?"

Essie had not made a final decision. She realized she and Jack hadn't given it enough thought yet. Time was running out, she felt, as another pain seized her.

Ada looked at her watch again.

"Ada, do you have someplace to be?"

"No, child. You do. I've been timing your contractions. You're in labor, dear." Her eyes glistened with wisdom. "It's time."

Essie realized she was right.

Ada lifted the small duffle bag. "Do you have all the essentials in here? Nightgown, toiletries, a newborn outfit?"

"Yes," Essie mumbled. *How could I have missed what was so obvious to Ada? Pandelirium.* The working mom consumed with the tyranny of the urgent. The reality of the moment settled in.

As per prior arrangement, Essie called Emily to come stay with the kids.

When Emily arrived, Essie and Ada were still trying to explain why Mommy had to go to the hospital even though she wasn't sick. The anticipation over the apparent early arrival of number three had them all bubbling with excitement.

"Oh, Essie! I cannot wait. The baby is coming!" Emily rose on her tiptoes and squealed. "So much is happening all at once." In a string of run-on sentences, Emily breathlessly delivered news about Greg's decision to decline his promotion.

"It's amazing how clearly God spoke to us, Essie. With the responsibilities of an expensive new house and that new job, Greg would've been traveling every week. When it came down to it, neither of us really wanted that. Losing out on the Paddleboat house was a blessing in disguise. Now we've found a beautiful little cottage where we can live comfortably within our means.

"Pearl actually pointed it out. She really knows the real estate market better than anyone thought. The new house is closer to you, the cousins can spend more time together, it's right near the new school, and—" Emily grabbed the overnight bag out of Essie's hand, tossed it into the back seat, and gave her a hard squeeze around the neck. "I'll tell you all about it later. It's just incredible how everything works out for the best. Get going, Essie."

Ada made a quick phone call to Hamilton, reporting the news over speakerphone. She canceled their plans for a sailing excursion the following morning, explaining that she wanted to stay near Essie and the kids. Since they had already been on a couple of indoor dates, Hamilton had made a persuasive appeal to give the boat another chance. Yet given the circumstances, Hamilton said he understood and suggested he take Cole out sailing instead. In her state of pandelirium, Essie agreed.

As Ada sped Essie toward the hospital, Essie was overcome with emotion. "Ada, I want to tell you how much I appreciate everything you've done for me—your wisdom, your sense of humor, and the gentle ways you've prepared me for this child. You truly have been like a mother to me." Essie smiled at her. "I'm finally ready for this. Not just to deliver, I mean, but to be the mother of three I'm meant to be."

"I knew you'd find your way, child. But as much as I'd love to be your mother, you have a mother already. So if you want an old woman's advice, I have one more thing to pass on to you. Call her, Essie. Your mother should be with you."

Essie ached for Jack to be by her side. A dozen attempts to reach him had failed. He had to be riding. She flipped her cell phone open again, but this time, she called Pearl.

"Mom, it's time. Will you please meet me at the hospital?" There was no telling when she'd be able to reach her husband. "I would appreciate it if you'd stand in for Jack as labor coach."

"Already? Oh my! I'm on my way. As soon as I get my face on. Oh my!"

At the hospital, Ada stayed with Essie until Pearl arrived. Though they'd met only once, over hair-dryer flambé at a garage sale, the two women hugged and exchanged excited greetings.

Pearl was poised in a crisp oxford, ankle-length skirt, and pumps. Her perfect composure was in a sharp contrast to Essie, sweaty, draped in a hospital gown, hooked to an IV and an epidural drip. Alone with her mother in this way, she felt suddenly awkward and vulnerable. She thanked her for coming and apologized for the late hour.

Pearl waved her hand dismissively. "Not at all. Thank you so much for allowing me to be a part of this child's birth, Essie." She dabbed her eye with a handkerchief. "I never imagined you'd pick me for a labor coach." Her lips quivered, and her eyes darted to the floor.

The emotion in her face betrayed her otherwise sophisticated appearance. Essie was surprised by Pearl's show of emotion. Not sure what to say, Essie simply reached over and curled her hand into her mother's and squeezed. Pearl's eyes misted, and her lip began to tremble uncontrollably. She dipped her head and started to cry in earnest.

"Essie, you have no idea how much it means to me to be here with you. How I wanted my mother with me the day I had you, how sad I was that she was no longer with us. Being here with you now reminds me how much I miss her, how much I needed my mother. A daughter needs her mom at a time like this."

Essie listened quietly. The hum of the equipment filled the room.

"It hurts to need someone. I wanted to teach my children to be stronger than I was, to be independent." She held a handkerchief to her nose. "I have always been so proud of you, Essie. You learned well. I just never intended for you to become so independent. You've never really needed me."

"Of course I need you, Mom. I don't understand. How can you say you were always proud of me? You seem to disapprove of everything about me. First, my husband, then my lifestyle, my job, the way I raise my kids—"

"That's not it at all! I don't disapprove of you. I feel redundant in your presence. It's hard for a mother to see her child become so independent a woman that she chooses a life completely different from the one her mother modeled for her. Quitting work, staying home, living in the right neighborhood, serving elegant meals, looking and acting the part. I wanted to be a role model for you, but you chose a very different path. Everything I demonstrated about motherhood, you rejected out-of-hand. You choose to work, you couldn't care less about living in a gated community, and you don't cook. The things I value are not important to you. So I figured I was not important to you either. You rejected me." She sniffled. "But now, you've asked me here. This is the most intimate thing you've ever asked me to do."

The contractions were coming hard now. Essie couldn't bear their pressure and hang onto her anger at the same time. As she breathed through the pain, she silently released her harbored resentment. When the pain subsided, a flood of peace filled the space it left.

"Mom, I never meant to reject you. We're just different, that's all. I've tried so hard to earn your approval. But what I want most is your love. And your friendship."

"You'll always have that, honey. I love you more than you can possibly imagine. You are my baby. My love for you is the biggest part of me." Their eyes locked. In her mother's face, Essie found a softness, a vulnerability that she had not seen before. She felt her own heart soften.

"I love you, too, Mom."

There was a rush of doctors and nurses. Pearl coached as Essie pushed with all her might.

The baby came.

"It's a boy," the doctor announced.

Pearl and Essie shared tears of joy, relief, and exhaustion. A few anxious seconds passed, and then they heard the newborn's first cry. Essie cradled her new son in her arms. His skin was so dewy and pink, his face so small and innocent.

The first rays of the morning sun fell through the hospital-room window. Essie's child squinted his eyes open with his first look at the day. She thanked God for this living, breathing miracle. Her soul was nourished as the flesh of her flesh pressed against her breast, her life nourishing his life.

Essie gazed out the window and saw a new horizon way out ahead of her. Their family of five many years from now. Her adult kids returning home to visit. All so very different from her and Jack. Different choices, different hopes, different dreams. Yet their love for one another drawing them home to spend time with her and Jack in their old age. Friendship with adult children: the banner of success every parent longs for.

How can it be that she was so richly blessed? She was filled with wonder, awed by the unfathomable generosity of God. She looked into her newborn son's face and sang a favorite oldie—"Biggest Part of Me" by Ambrosia—which fit the moment perfectly as both a praise chorus and a lullaby.

[chapter 36]

A Hero when You Need one Most

Ham had been surprised when Ada initially agreed to go sailing with him. Her only stipulation had been that she be permitted to bring Apostle Paul aboard with her. Hamilton had been somewhat taken aback when she asked about the availability of store-bought life preservers to accommodate the pup. Ham had never heard of such a thing, but he earnestly promised to look into it. Wisely, Ham thought better of suggesting to Ada that she stuff AP into a Styrofoam drink koozie. A comment like that was sure to nip any possibility of romance in the bud.

Ada was a one-of-a-kind gal, and Hamilton felt whole when he was with her. But he didn't trust his feelings. Nor could he personally testify that love could last. His ability to love had never proved strong enough to claim ultimate victory over the battleground of the heart. So Hamilton was not surprised when Ada canceled their date.

She seemed earnest about a rain check, though, and she had a legitimate excuse: Essie was in labor and needed help. Hamilton figured the best way to stay close to Ada was to get involved. It was time to put his whole heart on the line, time to go all-in.

The kids would need looking after for a few days while Jack was away on the tour and Essie was in the hospital. With both parents indisposed, Hamilton seized his own opportunity to help out and spend a little one-on-one time with his grandson.

He confirmed the plan with Emily, picked up Cole before dawn, and set out on a sunrise sail with his grandson. The lake was as quiet and serene as a sleeping newborn. Orange and yellow rays of sunlight were just cresting above the tree line.

Sometime during the previous night, Cole had learned of his new baby brother. Cole's response indicated his approval: "Good. I need some help with my bug collection."

According to Cole, a brother was certainly more useful than another sister. No question about it. For Cole, however, a sailing excursion with his grandfather was far more exciting news.

"I'll need some help with the boat," Ham offered. "A captain needs a strong, reliable crew. You look like the best man for the job."

"Really?" Cole brightened. "You really need *my* help?" Apparently, for a hero to ask for help was unheard of.

"First mate is a big job, Son," Hamilton said. "Hard work, too."

Cole stopped bouncing in his seat and nodded seriously, accepting the challenge, then immediately returned to bouncing.

The combined beauty of the gently rippling water, the changing colors of the sky, and the full sail were no match to the beauty Hamilton saw in Cole's dancing eyes, eager smile, and wind-whipped hair. Ham was also eager to see if his gift at picking winners was latent in Cole. Jack had it, but hadn't learned to trust it. Maybe Cole would—maybe Hamilton could show him how.

Earlier that morning, Hamilton had briefly second-guessed the trip. The local newspaper reported dangerously low water levels at Lake Lanier. As he helped Cole tighten the sheets and tend to other hardware, Hamilton experienced his everyday sailing maneuvers as if for the first time. A simple act, one he'd carried out countless times, was suddenly made new through the eyes of his grandson. And to think, the mysteries of nautical knot tying still lay before them! Hamilton could never have let the boy down.

As the boat came about, Hamilton recognized the site where he'd barely averted disaster on his last sailing trip. His heart grieved at his recklessness. On his journeys to prove his strength, how many had been hurt in his wake? How prideful he'd been to attempt to force God's hand to prove that his was a life worth saving, that destiny somehow needed him.

A hope of greatness, a hope for something that required his unique strengths, still remained, but it was no longer seeking a glory of its own. Hamilton no longer felt that a woman's affection, a well placed bet, or the accumulation of wealth were the things that defined a man's strength. He now found himself a full vessel looking for an empty one to pour himself into.

Hamilton steered the boat wide of the red warning buoys, keeping *Mutual Funs* far from the shallow-water markers. The sails fluttered for an instant and refilled.

"How can the boat move without a motor?" Cole asked. "Dad says just about everything needs a motor to go!"

"It works a lot like the birds. They fly without motors. They don't usually go very fast, not fast enough for us humans, that is, but God sees to it that they go fast enough to get where they're going."

Cole cocked his head and squinted at his grandfather. "I should've thought of that. People don't have motors, either; at least I've never seen one with a motor. You could probably get just about anywhere if you didn't mind walking there."

Cole quickly changed the subject: "Think there are any pirates out here, Pop?"

"There are still some pirates out here to be sure, but most of the lake pirates are pretty tame, and I think you and I can handle them, Son."

Cole's face lit up. He bristled to attention and scanned the horizon.

There were no warning buoys, no indicator of danger, but a sudden sense of foreboding came over Hamilton. Somehow he knew. He sensed it before he felt anything.

"Get down in the cabin, Son," he ordered Cole with a voice that expected nothing but obedience.

Cole scooted to the top rung of the ladder just inside the cabin door and poked his head out the hatchway.

The force of the wind was carrying the boat toward shallow water. Evidently, the lake was even lower than the authorities had reported. Hamilton immediately turned the boat into the wind, but the boat's momentum kept her moving. He focused all attention on the depth of the passage ahead. He vaguely registered that an audience had gathered on the near shore.

It happened right as Hamilton reached for a boat hook to measure the depth of the water. The boat had slowed to three knots when the keel hit and the boat jerked to a stop. On the water, from three knots to zero is a jarring crash—like a ten-thousand-pound SUV hitting a concrete wall. The jolt reverberated through the vessel, and everything aboard not tied down plunged forward. Ham turned his head in time to see Cole's small body, arms and legs flailing, airborne. Evidently, the boy had crept out of the cabin. Hamilton heard a startled cry followed by a small splash. Without hesitation, Hamilton leapt overboard feetfirst.

Ham dove down, feeling with his hands through the murky water. He pushed through the brush and clay. No sign of Cole. The lake was so murky, he could barely see his hands in front of his face. He flashed back to his search for Noodle. His lungs screamed for air, but he frantically searched on until his chest was about to explode. His hands plunged through the tree limbs and sludge until the pain in his chest, whether from lack of oxygen or grief at the prospect of losing Cole, was more than he could bear.

He cursed himself for not making Cole wear a life jacket. For not even having one in Cole's size. For this negligence not even occurring to him until now. He rose to the surface and gasped a lungful of air and dove down again. In that instant, his brain registered a siren.

Underneath the surface, all was dark and quiet again. An inexplicable calm overcame him. This time, he widened his search another few feet away from the boat and swam, sweeping his arms in wide arcs, praying and hoping, all the while feeling for Cole's trapped body. He reached through the mud, under a tree limb, and felt something—a boy's shoe. Cole's foot was entangled in a submerged tree branch, his shoe laces snarled around a limb. He wasn't struggling; his body was still. Hamilton pulled Cole's foot out of the shoe, held onto his body, and pushed his way to the surface.

By the time Hamilton reached the surface, a smaller boat had made its way to the scene. Hamilton refilled his lungs with air and screamed, "Jesus." He cried out. "Jesus, help me!"

The approaching boat threw a lifeline over to Hamilton. He heaved Cole's still form onto the ring and let himself be pulled in.

"Jesus, I need you! Please save him!" Hamilton cried, his head bobbing in the water.

The onlookers ashore watched and listened as Hamilton confessed his faith and desperate need for a Savior. The rescue boat pulled them from the lake, raising him out of the water in an act that under different circumstances would look remarkably similar to the one performed over the ages to associate a believer with the saving work of Jesus Christ, a symbol of passing from death to new life.

On board the rescue boat, Hamilton positioned Cole's body and started CPR with the earnestness of a man possessed. He saw Cole's chest rise, fall, and stay fallen. Cole was turning blue. He cried out again to the heavens. *I would give my life for him, but only you have the power to save.* He filled his lungs with more life-giving spirit. Intensifying his efforts, he breathed his air into Cole's lungs and began to pray. *I would gladly give my life for this child.*

He heard the words as plainly and clearly as though they were said aloud.

And that is exactly what I've done for you.

Tears streamed down his face as he heard Cole gurgle and expel a stream of water. The cyanotic color left him, and he coughed and spit up more water.

Another boat approached and asked what the problem was.

"I . . . I almost lost him," Ham stammered. "Throw me a blanket."

He heard Noodle's voice from the other boat. "Good heavens! They're going to pin a ribbon on you for sure now, Ham."

[chapter 37]

Happily Ever After

To Essie's amazement and irritation, Lewis Cathcart was the first to knock on the door of her hospital room.

"Ellison?" his lean, towering frame filled the doorway. In his hand, he carried a long, slender box. "I heard you were here." He walked over to Essie's bedside, oblivious to the sleeping infant, and handed her the box. "I brought you something."

"What a surprise," Essie said. The newborn wriggled in her arm as she opened the box to reveal a pen and pencil set.

"I had another reason for stopping by," Cathcart continued. "I understand your temporary assignment in Marketing is coming to a close soon. I've made a few calls, and you're in luck. There's an opening on the recycling team. We need a forward thinker, Ellison. And this opportunity gives you a chance to reconsider your hasty decision to leave such a critically important project."

"Mr. Cathcart, I want to thank you." The baby winced and stirred uncomfortably. She tucked the loosened receiving blanket around him snugly. "I want you to know that you've really helped me discover what I want to be in life. So, it's with absolute certainty that I can say: I am not the right woman for the job." Essie smiled satisfactorily and returned the lid to the gift box. "But thanks for the desk set just the same."

Cathcart frowned. "A tactical move, Ellison. Short-sighted. I encourage you to think big, Ellison. Be a part of something far bigger than yourself. Think beyond this moment. Think of the possibilities the future holds."

"I am, sir." Essie relaxed and so did the baby, now asleep again in her arms. "For once, I really am."

It wasn't until mid morning that Essie learned about the scare at the lake.

"I beg your forgiveness, Essie. I love that boy more than life itself. I'd do anything to keep him from harm; I'd gladly bleed myself dry for him."

Hamilton continued apologizing profusely with anguish and broken speech. He returned Cole, fully restored and more animated than ever. Their words stumbled over one another as they rushed to retell the heroic story.

"I'm sorry, Mom. Granddad told me to go below deck, but I snuck back up to see what was happening."

"The emergency-room doctor released him a few moments ago. Said he's just fine. Praise God!"

"My granddad rescued me! He's a hero!"

Essie gasped, "Oh, Cole, honey, I'm just so relieved you're OK." She pulled her son close and kissed his forehead.

Her relief to see Cole scampering about unharmed outweighed any angry or hysterical impulse.

"Hamilton, thank you. You saved his life." Essie assured Ham—and then Cole—of her complete forgiveness.

Cole climbed into the hospital bed with her, and together they admired their new family member as Hamilton made a quiet exit.

Soon after, Pearl and Big Jim, Emily, and Juliet arrived. Pearl brought gifts for Cole and Juliet to recognize their new status as big brother and sister. Cole raced toy cars along the hospital-bed frame. Juliet, comfortable in Pearl's lap, admired a new beaded tiara and hot pink sneakers.

"It came so natural for her. Like a duck to water." Emily talked excitedly with her hands. "She barely had time to get her Realtor's license renewed before the sellers were lining up to list their homes with her."

"Oh, honey, really." Pearl blushed with pride. "Any God-fearing woman would've done the same. My conscience simply cannot abide the spread of depravity."

Emily continued: "Essie, there was some truth after all in what you heard. I would not have believed it without hearing it firsthand. The scandal rocked the Paddleboat River Club tennis team. The Home Owners' Association met on the matter and issued a formal definition of permissible 'recreational activities' to set straight liberal interpretations of the clubhouse rules by certain members of the tennis team. Despite the HOA's ruling and subsequent sterilization of the swim and tennis facilities, three houses immediately went on the market For Sale by Owner. Pearl scooped up all three within the week."

"Mom, that is wonderful." Essie beamed a congratulatory smile in Pearl's direction. The news of actual misconduct at the Paddleboat River Club was as much of a surprise to her as anyone else, but she kept her shock to herself.

Pearl dismissed the praise with a wave of her hand. "The Lord's work, dear, not mine."

"So, Essie, now that the baby is here, I guess you'll take some time off. What are you going to do about work? Are you going back?" Emily asked.

"The Larger Than Life Tour was only a short-term assignment. It concludes soon, so I really don't have a job to go back to. Not the right one, anyway."

"Will you go back to work at Life Cola though? Eventually, I mean?"

"All I know is that I'll recognize the right assignment when it comes," she said.

Cole's car accelerated along the bed rail like a stunt driver up a ramp.

"A husband, three kids, and a full-time job. Sounds unrealistic, Essie. Do you really think it's possible to manage all that?"

"No, it isn't the most practical choice. But Jack and I seem to have left certain conventions in the rearview mirror several miles back. Besides, sometimes the common-sense life holds a person back from the supernatural life. Thankfully, I'm not in it alone. I leave plenty of room for divine intervention."

The wide, hospital-room door swung open, and Jack stepped through in full riding gear and dark sunglasses. His windburned face and heavily lined brow carried the weight of anguish and deep concern.

"Essie, I'm sorry. I should have been here. You shouldn't have had to go through this alone," he said.

Essie beamed at the sight of her husband. As soon as he had learned the news, he had driven twelve hours straight through the night to reach her. Haj was left behind, criss-crossing through less traveled roads in the Mustang to continue caching treasures.

"Oh, Jack. It's OK. I wasn't alone. I'm just so glad to have you back! Everything happened just the way it should," she said. She thought of the tender reconciliation with Pearl, the support and wisdom found in Ada.

Jack leaned over to kiss his wife. His troubled expression melted at the first glimpse of the sleeping newborn nestled in her arms. After a frenzy of warm welcomes and congratulations, the family made their excuses and ushered each other out of the room to allow Jack and Essie a moment of privacy with their new child. "We'll take Cole and Juliet with us and meet you all back at the house," Emily announced.

The room emptied and became quiet. Jack leaned over the hospital bed and cupped one hand against his wife's cheek and the other on the sleeping newborn's downy crown.

"Essie, you are more beautiful than ever."

A lump rose in her throat. "I'm not so sure about that," she replied, sweeping back her disheveled hair and adjusting a gaping hospital gown. "But isn't he beautiful?" Essie lifted the swaddled child to him. "Meet your son, honey."

Jack cradled his new son, the smooth newborn head in the crook of his elbow. He marveled at the baby's tiny features, the eyes so like his own. Clearly struck with wonder, Jack searched for something to say. He looked to the ceiling to find the right words. He started to speak but stopped and gazed again upon the child.

Finally he declared: "My heart is so full it is spilling over." He kissed the sleeping child and nestled him back in the crook of Essie's arm. "I love you both so completely.

"Essie, I never got a chance to explain what I meant when I told you I'd made a decision. I found what I've been searching for. God was telling me all along. Through this tour, the treasures, and the music, he was speaking."

Jack handed her a thin plastic sleeve. "I made this for you. All this time, I thought the adventure was somewhere out there, but I was wrong. All the clues are here. It's a birth CD. These songs remind me of you and our family. I collected them while I was on the tour. It's the music you love, and it speaks the language of my heart. Sometimes lyrics say it better than I can."

He squeezed her hand, and their eyes moistened.

The dramatic entrance and heartfelt confession held all the grandeur of any fairy-tale rescue. Essie's heart leaped, and her eyes welled with new tears of joy. Looking into Jack's eyes, she could almost feel his heart beating, strong and steady. He loved her. He'd endure anything for her. He'd have come any distance to reach her.

She slid the birth CD into the bedside player.

Ben E. King's soulful vocals filled the room. *"Your love, your love . . . supernatural thing."*

"You're my prince, Jack."

Jack sighed. "Hardly. But I plan to be from now on. And I'm going to start by taking some time off."

"Sounds great to me! And a fitting end to the tour. Home is where your treasure is."

"But my greatest treasure is right here." With a finger, he made a criss-cross over her heart. "X marks the spot."

She closed her eyes and smiled. In her mind, she tucked this moment away and sealed it in her heart.

"X marks the spot. I like that." She stroked the baby's head.

"What are we going to name him?" he asked.

"We never really decided on a name. A name is important, you know. Ada said it should be a statement of God's activity in our lives, how he's brought us to where we are."

Jack sat on the edge of the hospital bed and laced his fingers with hers.

The music played on with female voices harmonizing in the background. The lyrics seemed to punctuate her emotion. *"Supernatural Thing."*

"X marks the location of the treasure . . . X marks." Essie began a wordplay with the phrase. "X Mark . . . Alex Mark, a living reminder of the greatest treasures we have: each other."

He smiled. "Welcome to the world, Alex Mark."

It seemed as though God was tightening the threads of their lives. There with her husband and child, the distant silhouette of a long-ago dream came into full view, sharp and clear and vastly more beautiful than she had ever imagined. What she hoped to be true had come to pass: the belief that, in due time, love conquers all. And a heart filled with true love cannot help but burst with abundance. Essie wished every life could be rich enough to experience at least one moment when personal theology became reality, a soul-stirring encounter where faith and sight finally met.

Such moments of intense, unconditional love between a husband and wife echoed of another, deeper love that was even harder to fathom. The certainty of her ransomed heart caused her belief that God loved her to collide with an experience of God's love so personal and magnanimous that it made her feel microscopic and infinitely valuable at the same time. Love found itself on the other side of a long, sustained attack and now stood victorious over the battleground of her heart. Its wounds had made love not weak but stronger and wiser, immune to defeat. Bulletproof.

With Jack beside her, she held their new son. She absolutely felt like she belonged in this moment. Now. Here. In this place, at this time, with this man and these children. She was exactly where she was meant to be. What rich treasure to discover that this was where she found herself.

Jack squeezed next to her on the narrow hospital mattress. Their heads rested against each other for a quiet moment. Both sets of eyes remained fixed on their new child, soaking in the wonder of him.

"Essie, I came to another conclusion, too," Jack said. "I want to open my own motorcycle shop. I want a family business that I can grow and leave as a legacy for our kids. Not sure when or how, but I'm going to do it."

"Oh Jack, that's wonderful! It's certain to be a wild success. No one could do it better. So much excitement in one day!"

She told Jack about the close call with Cole on the lake. They recognized it was truly an accident and agreed that Hamilton had acted heroically in saving their son. His overt love and devotion touched them both deeply. Over the next several hours, while admiring the beauty of their new son, the couple excitedly discussed plans for their future and shared all the missed details about the birth and the tour.

Jack was still at her side the following morning when a light knock on the door announced visitors. Haj and Fenton stepped into the room. Haj was road-weary and looked like he hadn't shaved or showered in days. Fenton was dressed in a black, collarless shirt and black pants, business casual chic. Both men looked quite out of place in the postpartum environment.

"Congratulations, you two." Haj nodded to Jack first, then Essie.

"Yeah." Fenton managed an expression of shared sentiment. He rested a small bag at the foot of the bed and shook hands with Jack.

"Thanks, guys. Congratulations to you, too. The tour has been more successful than we ever imagined," Essie said.

"Yeah." Fenton stared in astonishment at the infant cradled in her arms. "Epic," he whispered.

"Sorry to have pulled Jack away so close to the end," she added.

"I'm not." Fenton quickly turned his attention to Jack. "Best thing that could've happened."

"What do you mean?" Jack asked.

"The board held an emergency session last night. It's been decided. The tour won't end here in Georgia as originally planned; it's been extended," Fenton explained.

"I just heard the news myself," Haj confirmed. "The people want more. So the adventure will continue down to Florida and then on to the Caribbean. Your assignment has been extended too, Essie."

"Really?" Essie asked.

"Absolutely. They want you back as soon as you're ready. They also offered you a flexible work schedule, if that helps," Haj clarified.

"Wow, that's a great offer." Essie looked to her husband. "Jack and I will have to talk about it. Working from home would be ideal, but I'll need some time."

"The Caribbean? But, you can't ride the Shot bike across the water," Jack said.

"That's just it." Fenton bounced animatedly toward the falsely presumed gift bag and pulled out its contents. "The bike will rendezvous with her new sister at the handoff site. That's when we launch the Shot Jet Ski."

Removing the object from its protective packing material, Fenton unveiled a model replica of a customized Jet Ski featuring the same Life themes and design elements as the motorcycle. "The tour moves on to the last frontier, the ocean. Next stop, the Caribbean. After that, who knows?"

"Are you insane? You are going to ride a Jet Ski to the Caribbean?" Essie asked.

"Well," Fenton looked to Jack with eagerness written all over him, "somebody is."

"It's not as dangerous as it sounds, really. We've done all the research." Haj pulled a sheet of paper from his back pocket and read from his notes. "It's only a two-and-a-half-hour ride. You'll carry twenty gallons of fuel containers with you—"

"Oh no." Jack grinned and shook his head. "Not me, guys. I'm in the middle of a great adventure right here. Right now, the only place I'm going is home."

"I was kinda hoping you'd say something like that." Fenton beamed. "Can we offer you a ride?"

"Sure," Jack smiled.

Fenton and Haj talked excitedly about their plans for the next leg of the Adventure Tour. Without Jack riding point, the backup plan would be put in motion. Fenton would ride the Shot Jet Ski, and Haj would provide support. The recommissioned cowboys fantasized about the media reaction to the horse that could ride on water. They discussed the treasures they intended to plant at sea and on the islands. Interviews on *Oprah*.

A member of the hospital staff came to the door with a wheelchair to escort Essie and the baby to the car. He stared at Haj, turned a double-take toward Jack, and said, "Hey, aren't y'all the Adventure Tour riders?"

The three of them nodded in assent.

The orderly's eyes widened. "Man, it really is you!" As they wheeled down the hallway, he announced to the passersby, "It's them! It's the Larger Than Life Adventure Tour riders." Automatic doors hissed open, and Essie was rolled outside into the parking lot.

"Y'all are famous around here. You know that?" The orderly parked her by the car and marveled at the Mustang as he helped them load Essie's overnight bag, an assortment of gifts for the newborn, and a bouquet of flowers. "Hey, man, isn't that the Shot bike?" He walked a slow circle around the motorcycle, keeping a respectful distance. "What a beauty! What kind of mileage you get off her?"

Jack glanced at the bike and then turned to Essie before answering. "More than you could imagine." He ran his fingers through his matted curls. His face was ruddy and handsome. He still looked young except for the fine creases around his eyes that suggested wisdom beyond his age. "And the best miles are still ahead of me."

Jack carefully secured Essie and the infant carrier in the Mustang as Haj and Fenton finished loading the gift bags and the flower arrangement. The vehicles moved out slowly like a small parade.

Jack rode point on the Shot bike one last time. A car link behind and to the right, Haj and Fenton drove Essie and the new baby in the Mustang.

In the distance, the afternoon sun melted orange and red like molasses over the southern pines, suggesting that sometimes fairy tales do come true, and if they looked just over the horizon, they could see happily ever after.

[chapter 38]

grace-burgers and Tater-tots

Cole insisted that Hamilton—a real-life hero—make an appearance in his kindergarten class for Career Day.

Jack and Essie, consumed with their new infant, encouraged Ham to participate. Alex Mark, less than a week old, had become the new boss in the Wells household, demanding the full-time attention of both parents. Hamilton had no choice.

The kindergarten class of First Fruits Christian Academy started promptly at eight thirty, with Ms. Judine Peach at the helm. She had a plain, round face with soft jowls that jiggled when she marked on the chalkboard. She wore no makeup except orange lipstick. The most prominent features of her face were her bright orange lips and wire-rimmed bifocals that perched on the end of her nose. She was a sturdy woman, with the bulk of her roundness having drifted south, giving her a pear shape. She dressed around it, wearing a sack dress made of denim.

"Welcome, Mr. Wells." She smiled. "The class has been quite eager to meet you."

Hamilton tipped his invisible hat. "Good day, ma'am. I'm honored to be here, but I fear my grandson has oversold me."

Hamilton took a seat at the back of the class where a handful of other career-minded relatives had already gathered.

Cole had warned Hamilton that his teacher wore a baked potato on her head. Hamilton now understood why. Ms. Peach kept her hair pinned back in a large brown lump at the back of her head. Dozens of bobby pins impaled the brown mass, creating a pocked and lumpy effect. By Hamilton's turn during the Career Day presentations, Ms. Peach's spud had begun to flower. A few sprigs sprouted free from their bobby-pin restraints.

Only the children had the courage and that strange combination of honesty and cruelty to address the fashion directly. "Ms. Peach, your tater's gone bad again," Annabelle Weatherstone offered in all innocence.

Ms. Peach rolled her eyes skyward.

Cole sat at the desk next to Annabelle. He, and the rest of the class, regarded Ms. Peach's bun and nodded solemnly.

"Thank you, Annabelle." With a hand to her head, Ms. Peach felt for the sprigs of brown hair and used a pencil to restore order.

Noting the contrast to Ms. Peach's potato, Ham caught Cole stealing a glance at Annabelle's long, flaxen waves. The infamous Annabelle. An appreciation for beautiful girls was part of the boy's heritage.

Annabelle's hair looked beautiful and mystical, like an octopus. At least, that's the way Cole had described his classmate to Hamilton during the appeal to win his grandfather's participation in Career Day: "I don't know why, but when I told her that her wavy hair looked like yellow tentacles, she punched me in the arm. I promised her you'd come," he had pleaded with his granddad. "She wants to meet a real hero."

Hamilton had inspected the arm. It was the same arm Cole had injured trying to impress Annabelle with a bicycle stunt that, however unsuccessful, won him a kiss. Cole had recovered quickly, and now only a shiny pink scar remained.

"In that case, I suppose I must," Hamilton had finally agreed.

A parent finished a detailed account of a day in the life of an accountant. The children's faces had glazed over with boredom, and it was finally Hamilton's turn.

"Well, Mr. Wells, you are our last speaker for Career Day today," Ms. Peach began, "and I understand you have something to share with the class about being a hero."

"Yes, ma'am." Hoping to please his grandson, Hamilton intended to supply a grand finale. He stood in front of the rows of children, ogling at the scars on his face with a less-than-subtle combination of morbid fascination and envious admiration.

"It's true what Cole has told you about me. I got these scars saving a young lady from a dangerous criminal." Hamilton pointed his chin north to give the wide-eyed children a closer look. "But what I really came here today to tell you is that every one of you can be a hero. It's simple. All you have to do is help a friend in trouble."

Over the next several minutes, Hamilton shared the details of Bonita's rescue and, with Cole's urgent prompting, described his grandson's rescue at the lake.

Ms. Peach nodded appreciatively toward Ham and then turned back to her students. "Class, please thank Mr. Wells for coming today." A round of shouts and enthusiastic applause followed.

"Mr. Wells, you are welcome to stay with us for our Bible study lesson, if you like." She gestured to an open chair under a decorated felt board.

After such an ovation, Ham couldn't resist. He nodded at Ms. Peach and took a seat. Ms. Peach turned toward the chalkboard. She wrote the word *grace* on the board and underlined it.

"Today we will learn about grace. Now, who can tell me what it means?" She turned back to the class, still squirming with excitement over Hamilton's stories.

"Ms. Peach! Ms. Peach!" Annabelle bounced in her seat with her hand stretched high.

"Yes, Annabelle. Please tell the class."

"Ms. Peach, Mama says that one bad tater will spoil the whole bag. You better check your bag." Annabelle, a picture of legitimate concern, referred once again to Ms. Peach's spud and gestured vaguely to her shapeless sack dress.

The prospect of a stockpile of decayed potatoes inside Ms. Peach's clothes aroused the curiosity of the entire class. Children angled their heads in all directions to get a closer look.

Ms. Peach gave the girl a stern look over her spectacles. "That's enough, Annabelle. I don't want to give you a thundercloud." With raised eyebrows, she nodded toward a large flannelgraph board on the classroom wall. The board was covered with gold swaths of star-shaped felt, each bearing a student's name. The threat hung in the air for a few seconds. Ham caught himself holding his breath.

Then Ms. Peach offered Annabelle a forgiving, bright-orange smile and returned to her lesson. "Grace is unmerited favor. That means giving what is not deserved."

Ham let out his breath slowly. Evidently, it took quite a bit to rattle Ms. Judine Peach.

"Think about what Mr. Wells taught you about heroism. A hero rescues a friend in trouble, even when it's not deserved."

Ham nodded his agreement for the benefit of the class.

The threat of the thundercloud treatment persuaded the class to dismiss the bad tater theory for the moment.

Ms. Peach continued, "For example, when Jesus came to earth to live among us, he chose to be among the guilty even though he was innocent. He loved us even when we didn't love him. So let me ask you now. I'll give you a situation, and you tell me what might be a gracious way to respond."

Ms. Peach surveyed the class and noticed a dark-haired boy facilitating a heated battle between two action figures under his desk.

"Garret, what if you had two action figures, but your neighbor had none? What would you do?"

"These are mine," Garret clarified, looking up from his battle. "Joey left them on the lunchroom table yesterday, so now they're mine."

Ms. Peach sighed. "OK. So Joey, sounds like you shared your action figures with Garret at lunch. Is that right? Sharing is gracious."

Joey's jaw dropped at the discovery of his stolen toys, and he locked his eyes on Garret. "Hey, give 'em back, you bath-fart."

Ms. Peach held up a finger to both boys. "Boys, I will not tolerate—"

"I shared a cheeseburger with my brother," a freckled, red-headed girl offered, cutting off Ms. Peach's warning. "It had pickles on it. Pickles are disgusting."

Ms. Peach jabbed at her spud with a pencil. A wiry clump of hair unfurled from the brown lump. Annabelle's eyes grew wide as though a ghastly idea had hatched in her small mind. She shot her hand up again.

Ms. Peach offered another scenario. "Let's try something different. Say there was a little boy or girl who didn't have a friend and needed one. What would you do to show grace?"

"I'd give her my cheeseburger," the red-headed girl suggested. "If it had pickles on it."

Annabelle's hand stretched higher.

"Thank you, Penelope. Annabelle?"

"Mama says some taters grow eyes. Is that true? Are those eyes on the back of your head?" Annabelle blurted out in the single breath she'd been holding.

The class laughed uncertainly. The idea that Ms. Peach could see out of the back of her head and actually observe the questionable activity that went on was clearly unsettling.

Ms. Peach's orange lips formed a tight, thin line. She marched to the flannelgraph and flipped over the felt star with Annabelle's name, revealing a gray thundercloud accented with a jagged, white lightning bolt. The lightning bolt pierced Annabelle's name.

Hamilton shifted uncomfortably in his seat.

"Anyone else care to make a comment?" Ms. Peach asked calmly.

The class grew silent.

Annabelle stared at her name stricken by a lightning bolt. Her dark cloud stood out among a sky of golden stars. Her face flushed with pain and confusion, the crushing weight of the fall of the kindergarten class now mounted on her small shoulders. She slumped in her chair and hung her head in shame.

Ham sat quietly and watched Cole try to get Annabelle's attention. Cole stretched his foot across the aisle, but it didn't quite reach. He made funny faces at her, but she didn't look up. He even flicked a spitball on her desk, a sure way to cheer a classmate. Nothing worked. Annabelle remained despondent. At a loss, he looked to Hamilton for suggestions, but Ham stayed silent.

Ms. Peach kept her composure and tried to preserve the lesson. "Now class, I want you to think about what it means to show grace. Who can give me an example of what that looks like?"

Cole glanced again toward his grandfather. Ham could see the concern in his grandson's face. Cole glanced back at Annabelle, whose bottom lip quivered behind the blond tendrils that veiled her profile. Cole looked up at the flannelgraph, at the lone thundercloud, at Annabelle's name singled out in a storm against an otherwise starlit backdrop. He winced as though he couldn't bear it. It looked so lonely.

Suddenly, Cole rose to his feet and proclaimed, "Tater head."

Ms. Peach's mouth gaped open. Ham imagined she must be accustomed to elementary student harassment, but this was too much for thirty-five thousand a year. Her composure began to crumble. "Cole Wells! I have had enough, young man!"

"Tater-head! Tater-head! Tater-head!" Cole chanted.

"Son!" Hamilton stood up, shocked.

"I'm sorry to have to do this, especially with your grandfather here."

Ms. Peach stomped to the flannelgraph and flipped Cole's star to the thundercloud side.

The class was frozen in fear. Cole's knees buckled, and he fell back in his chair. The color drained from his face, and his mouth gaped open, stunned and afraid, clearly unsure of what he'd just done.

But when Cole looked back at Annabelle, he found his answer. She was smiling. It was only the smallest hint of a smile, but it was there. Ham followed her gaze to find its source. There it was on the flannelgraph. Two clouds, side by side. She was no longer alone. Cole had crossed over willingly from gold to gray just to be with her.

The bell sounded. The lesson on grace was over.

"We are not finished with this topic, class! Cole and Annabelle, the class looks forward to hearing your explanation of grace when we start again tomorrow." Ms. Peach dismissed the students quickly before more harm was done.

Hamilton stayed behind as the class began to file out. Annabelle and Cole stood side by side, lagging behind the swarm for the door. Ham thought he saw Annabelle punch Cole playfully on the arm.

With caution, Cole approached Ms. Peach. Annabelle shadowed right behind him.

"I'm sorry, Ms. Peach. I didn't mean it," Cole said, darting a glance at Hamilton for approval.

"Me too," Annabelle echoed with a small voice.

Ham gazed into their young, tender faces. Behind Cole's clear, green eyes, he saw a flicker of something familiar. Ms. Peach must have noticed it, too. It was something she had surely learned to recognize in the children she taught: comprehension.

"I accept your apology. Thank you." Offering nothing more, Ms. Peach turned around and began to erase the blackboard. With her face hidden from the children's view, Ham saw her smile. Teaching kindergarten had its challenges and its rewards. She had earned her pay today. And then some.

Ham followed the children toward the door. Outside the classroom, Annabelle whispered something in Cole's ear, loud enough for Hamilton to hear. Only two small words, but packed with a magic that made any boy, young or old, feel certain he could fly: *my hero.*

[chapter 39]

Bet Goes Down

Inman's voice on the phone was terse, so Ham expected bad news. "The appraisal has arrived. Come on over, and we'll open it together. Bring a witness."

Inman would now use every trick in the book to try to renegotiate the arrangement. The saving grace was that the agreement was in writing and all the lawyers in New York couldn't undo it.

Noodle had passed along the diner gossip. Inman had worked tirelessly to find a bribable appraiser, but the firm he had counted on was unavailable. Rumor had it, the principal was under indictment for various nefarious acts including fraud, tax evasion, and bribery. So Inman had been forced to rely on one he selected at random, Lionel Smith, to be a malleable novice that he could cajole into an inflated number based on the cosmetic changes he had made to the diner, averting any attention from the underlying structural and waste-water system deficiencies.

What Inman didn't realize was that the stiff, tight-lipped appraiser had noticed the cleverly concealed bypass Inman had made to dump the dishwater, replete with phosphates and other contaminates, into the small tributary in back of the diner. By agreement, the appraisal letter was certified and to be opened by the two of them in the presence of a witness, and Inman was sweating ball bearings.

Ham, on the other hand, was enjoying a peace he had not felt in a long time. He gathered the funds he would need for the transaction, stuffing them inside an old satchel, leaving the boat's seat cushions much less lumpy when properly filled with the original foam.

Ham sipped his second cup of coffee aboard *Mutual Funs* before the meeting with Inman. He wasn't taking any chances on the coffee at The Lazy I. He was also trying to sort through his emotions and set straight in his mind the motivation for his actions. Ham was still chagrined at his own recklessness in letting so many years pass without reconciliation with his son or developing a rapport with his grandson. The circumstances around Cole's rescue remained unsettling because of his own carelessness in not having insisted that Cole wear a life preserver. But the purchase of the diner was not an attempt to buy forgiveness for negligence in the recent or even distant past. Jack and Essie's quick forgiveness and assurance that he was one of the family's true heroes had turned the corner for him. Then Career Day with his grandson yesterday had settled the matter for good. He was the father of a line of heroes. Motivations behind his plan were pure: this would be an act of love.

Memories of past failures rose up to condemn him once more. Jesse, his past wives, his past pain. These and the loss of Earline had left him emotionally crippled for too long. This time, Ham exercised a newly discovered authority to push the condemnation aside. He took the thoughts captive and forced their obedience to Christ. He made a decision: those chapters in his life were closed.

A new chapter would start today.

Purpose and meaning had filled his vessel. Ham had never felt such power in the forgiveness and grace of God in his life. For a fleeting moment, he reasoned the whole thing was simply God giving him the chance to set things right, get all the debits and credits to balance, but that was the false, earn-your-way-into-his-grace theology he had adopted in his youth. Unmerited favor was what he understood now, just as Ms. Peach had proclaimed. The bounty of God awed him. He laughed out loud with complete joy.

It was chilly at the dock, so he grabbed his sweater and stuffed satchel and made his way to the truck and his rendezvous with Inman. Noodle had reported that he had some errands to run but would be at the diner to witness the appraisal-letter opening when Ham arrived.

The first thing Hamilton noticed as he pulled up to the diner was that the cheap, whitewash paint job on The Lazy I's exterior was already starting to chip and fade. The new asphalt in the parking lot was crumbling in a number of spots and was already sporting a major-league pothole near the entrance. Only a blind appraiser could have failed to notice these defects. Ham's spirits were lifted further by remembering the bitterness of the appraiser toward Inman during the impromptu meeting at the Marina Grill.

"God will control all of this, whatever comes," Ham murmured to himself. "For his glory now, not mine."

As he entered The Lazy I, he immediately spotted Noodle in a corner booth and walked over. There were no customers, and Dorita and Inman were nowhere to be seen.

"I wouldn't have believed it could go downhill so far so fast," Noodle remarked solemnly. "It's actually worse than last time."

"Sad, but true."

"So I suppose that Dorita gal will be your employee soon. Reckon you can warm up to her?"

"Unlikely, Noodle." Ham's expression soured. "That would be tougher than putting raw oysters in a parking meter. Where is everybody anyway?"

Dorita emerged from the kitchen with a scowl. "We're out of bread, so no toast. You want a doughnut?" She pointed at the bell jar covering a lonely doughnut of dubious vintage.

"I see the big tipper is back." She gestured toward Ham.

"Think I'll pass, ma'am," Noodle said.

"Please tell Inman I'm here. And I'll pass on the doughnut, too, as long as there is none of that gourmet toast to be had," Ham added, unable to conceal his amusement.

Dorita huffed and returned to the kitchen.

"You sure you want to do this, Ham? This is the sorriest way to start a restaurant career, especially with your commitment to leisure time. All the customers have been run off. It doesn't make sense. What about the repair business with your son?"

"It's just perfect, Noodle. It will suit me to a T. Is Inman's witness here?"

"Don't know he's got one."

Inman walked out of the kitchen with a manila folder under his arm. Dorita followed him. His expression was dour and resigned. "Mr. Wells," he announced, "let's get this over with."

He joined Ham and Noodle in the booth.

"Where's your witness, Inman?" Ham asked.

"Dorita, my best employee, will have to do," he stated flatly.

"And only?" Noodle observed.

"Whatever," Inman whispered.

"Would you do the honors, Inman?" Ham motioned toward the paperwork.

Inman opened the letter from the appraiser and let loose a moan as his eyes quickly darted to the bottom line.

"Sounds like your breakfast didn't agree with you, Inman," Noodle observed. "Might consider a new cook."

"Stow it!" Inman groused, his face a study in disappointment. The appraiser hadn't missed a thing.

"Let me see." Ham reached for the document and examined it.

"What's fair is fair, Inman. Don't forget, you're getting half again the money for the goodwill. Don't suspect there's much of that." Ham motioned around the empty diner.

Ham reached for his satchel. "A deal is a deal, Inman." He snapped open the case and watched Inman, Dorita, and even Noodle go nearly catatonic at the stacks of neatly wrapped hundred-dollar bills.

"I've got the sale documents right here, Inman. I came prepared in case the appraisal was higher, but this should do." Ham counted out the cash. "Sign here."

Inman was mesmerized by the cash, surely recognizing the opportunities for tax evasion, and quickly scrawled his signature on the documents.

"Oh, and Inman, have a day at the track on me," Ham thrust a small stack of hundreds into his hand. "And Dorita, don't forget your tip before you go."

"Where am I going?" Dorita asked, staring at the money.

"Anywhere you want, as long as it's not here." Ham handed a fistful of bills to her. "Here's for your trouble."

A speechless Dorita took the money, turned, and walked away.

"Where in the world did you get all that money, Ham?" Noodle asked, dazzled and perplexed.

"I made a wise investment in wheat."

"Ham, I told you that you knew nothing about the restaurant business," Noodle said. "What do you need wheat for? The wheat comes inside the bread."

"In my case, it's more the other way around," Ham said.

[chapter 40]

Heavenly wheels

Ham hadn't worked this hard in thirty years. Though he'd been at it only three months, he already feared the worst: he was developing a long-latent work ethic. His early self-doubt was replaced by a confidence that he was doing what God wanted him to do.

At first, Ham had barely understood the mechanisms of business. Though he had been a commodities trader many years ago, he had been risky to the point of reckless with most of the customers and had eventually become his only customer. He had been unable to cope with the play-it-safe, conservative investment goals of his clients. His work experience had not prepared him for the rigor of levelheaded entrepreneurship. After Earline's death, he was a poor steward of the things entrusted to his care, indifferent toward his own son, and lousy company to family, friends, or clientele. Now he was forgiven for all this. There was no opportunity to change the past, but the opportunity to give freely was now before him.

God's voice was as subtle as the roar of a bike's custom exhaust pipe. *You are not alone. I am always with you.* Ham realized with utter clarity that his life had purpose and his juvenile testing and retesting of God was, at best, annoying and, at worst, an affront to the Almighty.

It didn't take Ham long to get the business basics in order. The accounting had been easy, and Ada had some experience in the manual traditions; she only required a quick conversion to the computer varieties. Relations with federal, state, and local government agencies, and the myriad fees, licenses, and permissions were not that difficult in themselves, but the stupefying design of the forms, awkward wording of the questions, and endless repetition drove him to the brink. Instinct had kicked in. The knowledge that this operation was certain to be a success kept him going.

The competitive advantage and unique design components of the project were clear. Heavenly Wheels was to be a completely new concept, a fresh and modern version of the traditional shop. The dingy, grease-laced shop with scary mechanics who looked prone to maim or assault an uncooperative client had to be completely redressed. Jack seemed to live by the "Cleanliness is next to godliness" mantra, and Ham had no intention of denying his son's preferences. Appeal to the meticulous was key to the success of the project.

Biker's Eye had been the most difficult part. Ham had difficulty understanding the intricacies of the idea, but once the overall concept was mastered, the application of the technique was relatively mechanical. Ham was, after all, a big-picture kind of guy. Positioning of the cameras was subtle so as not to make the crew self-conscious, but every position had to be covered. The bays were arranged with geometric precision. The clients were going to be completely awed by the operation, and Ham, once again, knew he had picked a winner.

The techs were a challenge as well. The ragtag group of Greasy Goblins with their body art and scraggly hairstyles had been reluctant to change at first, but money talked. The three men had been averse to neat haircuts and spotless uniforms. Ham's natural leadership abilities from deep in his past resurfaced, and he persuaded the group that the package would make history. The crew believed him and soon talked endlessly about their impending notoriety.

The signing bonuses alone were utterly convincing, but it was Ham's style that sealed the deal. His presentation had been so matter-of-fact it had taken the men completely by surprise. He had added the signing bonuses and profit sharing as an "oh, by the way" codicil to the final arrangement.

Timing was everything, and Hamilton knew the time was right.

"Ada, I think we're ready." He threw the comment out more like a statement than a question. Still, he wanted her confirmation.

"I didn't know you had it in you, Ham, but I must admit it's beautiful. Just like you, old man." With her fingertips, she gently brushed the scar along his cheek.

"I wasn't looking for beautiful, Ada, but I'll take it. And don't be calling *me* beautiful. People will think you're feeble-minded."

"Let 'em think whatever they like, Ham," she said, brushing off the comment.

"I must admit I'm as nervous as a politician trying to tell the truth, but I have to trust that my instincts are in tune with the Lord. This project is a labor of his love and mine, but he gave me the inspiration and a gift for picking winners, and it would be a poor to-do if I didn't act. The concept is sound, the finances are solid, the guys are great, and you'll be pretty as springtime behind the counter. Even AP fits in."

AP's ears kicked up at the mention of his name, but he quickly resumed his nap.

"Make the call," Ada directed with a gorgeous smile and dramatic flourish.

Ham made the call.

"I really don't want to go to the diner, Essie," Jack protested.

"We owe this to your father, Jack." Essie had gotten wind of what was going on, as Ada had been unable to keep a secret from her. They were strapping the kids into the Hummer as Jack complained. Essie was giddily excited.

On the ride over, Essie enthused over Ham's selflessness concerning their family's needs, mentioning Cole's rescue at the lake, Ham's star performance on Career Day, and his numerous offers of babysitting services ever since. Whatever his failures as a parent to young Jack, Ham was being a stellar grandparent, an official hero.

"Yeah, OK, I'll admit it: the old man has grown on me. But why does he want us over there, Essie? Has he hooked up with another waitress? My job may be much more behind the scenes now than before, but I've still got a lot of work to do to support the tour. I really can't afford the time off. I don't have the luxury of working on it from home like you do."

After twelve weeks of maternity leave, Essie had returned to work on the extended tour under the condition that she be allowed a flexible work schedule, including work-from-home days.

"Jack, your father has been seeing Ada. I've suspected there was a spark between them since our lunch at the lake, but I think it's getting serious now. I saw some suspicious lunch plates over at Ada's the other afternoon when I stopped by to pick up a recipe. The dirty dishes were on the kitchen table, and I know for a fact that she wasn't serving a buffet to the apostles. Besides, who else eats eggs over easy with flour tortillas and hot sauce for lunch?"

Once Essie had finally came right out and asked her about it, Ada, blushing with embarrassment, had told her everything.

"Ada's quirky," Jack mused. "She'd probably be the perfect woman for him. But still, the diner is a weird place to do this, whatever it is," Jack insisted.

"Let's humor him," Essie suggested as they wheeled into the parking lot.

Jack immediately noted that the parking lot had been paved and the diner's sign had been removed. As if sensing their presence, Ham appeared in the doorway with a huge, tarped object on a dolly. Close behind him stood Ada, with AP nuzzled into her armpit.

Ham greeted his family. "Thanks for coming, gang. Your timing is perfect."

"What's up, Pop?" Jack looked puzzled. Ada and Essie exchanged knowing glances.

"Hey, Pop," chirped Cole. Juliet studied her hot-pink high tops while dismounting the Hummer.

"Got a surprise for you, Son." Ham beamed. "Made a few changes to the diner."

"I can see that. The parking lot looks freshly paved."

"Yeah, had to. Place had more potholes than a DOT worksite. I bought the place from Inman, and the weasel had taken every shortcut in the book."

"You bought a restaurant, Pop? But it doesn't even look like a diner anymore," Jack observed, his interest piqued. "I figured you kept a bankroll hidden somewhere, but I had no idea you still had that kind of money."

"You could say I've been sitting on it a while. Come on in." Ham gave a broad "follow me" gesture and turned to walk back inside.

"You don't mean the boat, do you?" Jack cocked his head in disbelief.

"Think of it more as a treasure trove."

Jack's chin dropped. "You really are a piece of work, Pop!"

They all trundled toward the doorway, with Essie bringing up the rear. She sensed Cole watching her, as though supervising the unloading as she gathered up Alex Mark, their newest treasure. It warmed Essie's heart the way her eldest son was already developing protective tendencies toward his younger brother.

"Jack, you're right. It's no longer a diner," Ham declared. "But before we talk about that, I have something of major importance to announce. Ada, with the approval of the apostles, has agreed to be my bride. The last one."

Ham smiled broadly. Ada blushed. AP looked up from his niche in Ada's armpit as if to confirm the announcement.

Jack looked shocked. "I just found out you were seeing each other a few minutes ago. Isn't this a little hasty?"

"After we overcame the peculiarities we've both acquired over the years, we discovered we have more in common than most," Ham explained. "Ada calls it inner beauty."

Ham gave Ada a brief hug, drawing a squeak out of AP.

There was a flurry of kissing and hugging. Ada proudly displayed her engagement ring. The diamond was impressive.

"Of course, we'll live at Ada's place. Wouldn't want to risk the relationship by living on the boat. Hasn't worked out so well in the past. Ada says I'll get used to the apostles. Hope we make good neighbors."

Jack was speechless, his expression filled with unmasked surprise.

Ham gathered Jack to his side. "There's more," he added mysteriously.

"What's with all this chrome at the old counter?"

"It's a lot more appropriate for what's inside."

Ham led Jack into the back, which had once been the kitchen, cold storage, and office areas. Three neat, professional individuals stood in back, each by his massive tool box. Chrome highlights were everywhere. The urethane floor glistened. Stylized motorcycle art hung on the walls. Safety equipment and waste disposal facilities were present in each bay.

"Meet the Greasy Goblins," Ham said, introducing Ace, Sully, and Marion individually to his family.

"Hello, gentlemen." Jack shook hands with each one. "You look familiar. Aren't you the folks I saw talking with my pop at the Grill a while back?"

The men nodded.

Jack's jaw had gone slack.

"The very same. They agreed to a few changes before coming to work here at Heavenly Wheels."

"Heavenly Wheels?" Jack was now wide-eyed as well as slack jawed.

"That's right, Son. That's the name of the most modern, state-of-the-art motorcycle repair shop on the East Coast. Our shop."

"Our shop? What do you mean?" Jack asked, puzzled.

"Our shop," Ham emphasized. "Although you're going to do all the work."

"I don't believe it." Jack stared in disbelief.

"Did I mention that we have Biker's Eye?"

"Biker's Eye?"

"See, Son, the customers can go to our Web site and find the time slot for their bike repairs and watch their services performed through a webcam without actually interfering with the fixing. You gave me the idea." Ham was understandably proud and showed it.

"Is this what heaven is like?" Cole asked. Evidently unclear on who was the best authority on heaven, the question seemed to be thrown out at large.

"It's at least Heavenly Wheels," Ham replied. "The sign is on the dolly outside if I could get a little help to mount it. Oh, by the way, Jack, our Web site also features performance and specification data on the most popular cycles. Plus, it has tutorials—is that the right word, Ada?"

"Of course you're right, Ham," Ada said.

"Yes," Ham continued. "Customers can sign up for tutorials on bike maintenance and ways to customize their bikes."

"I don't believe it," Jack cried, his eyes literally filling with tears.

"Well, it's all yours now. You play the most crucial role, Son."

"I'd say *you've* played the most crucial role, Pop."

"I suppose at some point along the way everyone gets a moment in the sun sooner or later." Hamilton smiled with pride at his extended family. "In any case, Ada and AP have agreed to help with the business end."

"What about you, Pop? What are you going to do?" Jack blinked and shook his head, his mind clearly reeling with the possibilities.

"I'm going to keep the back porch swept, and as the PR man for this outfit, I'd like to keep my reserved spot at the service counter warm." Hamilton gestured to his brass nameplate preserved on the former diner countertop.

"Pop, this is going to be incredibly successful," Jack said solemnly.

[chapter 41]

career Mom

The dress code at the lake was elegant shabbiness. Pearl was decked out in her new topsiders and nautical outfit. Jack and Big Jim stood on the bow, enjoying the breeze. The gentle sway inside the cabin had lulled Juliet and six-month-old Alex Mark to sleep in the forward berth before the crew ever raised the mainsail. Cole draped a blanket over his siblings and, as a safety precaution, assembled a border of towels and pillows around them.

Once the crew reached the open lake waters and raised the sail, the boat leaned gently to starboard and cruised at a steady clip.

"We're moving right along," Essie observed.

"The wind does all the real work," Ham explained.

How true, Essie thought. *God is so good.* The whole family, a bit larger and a good deal wiser, greeted the wind together and allowed it to carry them toward their next adventure.

Essie took a seat in the stern and propped up her feet. "I hear Heavenly Wheels is drawing quite a crowd now. Jack says he's not missing corporate life at all. He also tells me you're already thinking of expanding."

"Yes, ma'am. But not the shop itself, just the services we offer." Hamilton stood at the helm with one hand on the wheel. "Turns out motorcycling and sailing have more in common than I thought."

"How's that?" Essie asked.

"It's not just a sport; it's a fellowship. Folk don't come to Heavenly Wheels just for the bikes or the skilled technicians; they come for the company. It's the community that makes Heavenly Wheels a magnet for bikers. It's a place to tell stories, make plans, and dream big dreams. That's what got us started on this new idea for organized tours and adventure rides."

Essie raised a brow. "Like the Adventure Tour?" The promotional campaign was over now, but the marketing team was already busily preparing for the next promotion. Essie had been offered a permanent role, but it wasn't the same without Jack.

"Sorta," Ham chuckled, "but a lot less commercial. Ada is up to her elbows in plans and paperwork. Sure could use some tech support to get this thing going. Know anyone who might be interested in that sort of thing?"

Essie offered a one-sided grin and addressed Ham as though sailor to sailor. "I might. I know one gal, hard worker, but she's got three kids and a husband that come first. I have to warn you, she's renowned for showing up late and leaving early. Oh, and long commutes, overtime, and insensitive bosses make her hard to get along with."

Ham flashed a one-sided smile in return. "Sounds like the kind of gal I'm lookin' for."

"I'll mention it to her, then," Essie offered. "Some folks say she's learned the hard way, but she knows a winner when she sees one."

"Runs in the family, darlin'."